Emma Henderson

Emma Henderson's first novel, *Grace Williams Says It Loud* (Sceptre, 2010), won the McKitterick Prize and was shortlisted for the Orange Prize, the Wellcome Book Prize, the Commonwealth Writers' Prize for Best First Book and the Authors' Club First Novel Award, as well as being runner-up for the Mind Book of the Year.

Emma Henderson worked at Penguin as a copywriter for two years, then spent a decade teaching English in comprehensive schools and further education colleges before moving to the French Alps where, for six years, she ran a ski and snowboard lodge. Having studied at Oxford and Yale University, she is now a lecturer in English and Creative Writing at Keele University. She lives in Derbyshire.

'Tackles taboos and extends our sense of humanity . . . *The Valentine House* illuminates too, mortifying us, even, with the idea that neither "ugliness" nor "disability" need preclude beauty.'
Emma Claire Sweeney, *Financial Times*

'A lively, complex novel, and Mathilde is a splendid character'
Anthony Gardner, *Mail on Sunday*

'Henderson's *Grace Williams Says It Loud* was shortlisted for the Orange Prize and this more than matches it.'
Elizabeth Buchan, *Daily Mail*

'Full of mysteries . . . and enjoyable humour . . . a strong read, with excellent characters, an intriguing plot, and a stunning setting.'
Bookbag

'Engrossing. The slow unravelling of the secrets is beautifully done with a clever building up of the tension. I was very impressed with the writing – intriguing plotting and yet there are deeper themes of love, identity and different cultures. Highly recommended.'
newbooks

'I totally loved *Grace Williams Says It Loud. The Valentine House* is another compulsive, original read told with a delicious wit, while remaining harsh and mysteriously life-affirming.'
Helen Lederer

'An intriguing tale of two cultures . . . She also vividly describes the drama and dangers of the Alps, an area the novelist knows well'
France

THE VALENTINE HOUSE

Emma Henderson

First published in Great Britain in 2017 by Sceptre
An Imprint of Hodder & Stoughton
An Hachette UK company

First published in paperback in 2018

1

A CIP catalogue record for this title is available from the British Library

Paperback ISBN 9781 444 70404 4

Typeset in Sabon MT by Hewer Text UK Ltd, Edinburgh
Printed and bound in Great Britain by Clays Ltd, St Ives plc

Hodder & Stoughton policy is to use papers that are natural, renewable and recyclable products and made from wood grown in sustainable forests. The logging and manufacturing processes are expected to conform to the environmental regulations of the country of origin.

Hodder & Stoughton Ltd
Carmelite House
50 Victoria Embankment
London EC4Y 0DZ

www.sceptrebooks.co.uk

For Laura and Cordelia

Part One

Arete

Here they come. Here they are. *Les anglais*, the English, *les rosbifs*.

The first English tourist to arrive in Hext came by horse-drawn carriage. By the time I met him, in 1914, we had trains and cars, and he was a doddery old codger. But I can imagine a young Sir Anthony Oswald Valentine, full of fancy and English vim, coming to summer among the Alps.

One

The valley is a vagina, a frilly French quim . . .

Sir Anthony strikes through the word 'quim', replaces it with 'cunt', tries 'contrapunctum' and 'crinkum crankum', before rewriting, neatly, 'quim'.

. . . French quim, inviting penetration. How I long to lose myself in this moist and perfumed . . .

Sir A half smiles and wrinkles his nose in pleasurable anticipation of the word coming next.

. . . tuzzy-muzzy.

He blots the ink on the page of his diary, dated 27th May 1865, and closes the pocket-sized leather-bound book. With the pad of his thumb, he makes a soft dent on the calfskin of its cover. His movements are slow, measured and careful, but there's a tremor in his eye where the surge of his written words registers.

Summer foliage curling like hair on the fleshy labia of the hillsides, he has written on the previous page. *Feminine folds, animal smells, earthy wetness and the whore's promise of more, always more.*

The church clock in the village square chimes eleven. Sir A lifts the iron spiral of the window latch, pulls inwards. The window opens smoothly, but the wooden shutters, carved with hearts, are stiff, and they moan when Sir A presses on them, concertinaing away from him and unfolding backwards against the cold stone wall.

Fresh air on his face, the smell of woodsmoke, pine and damp soil, the noisy rush of the river, a big gibbous moon, silver clouds in the blue-black sky, the notched outline of mountains with bright skirts of snow on their summits: white ladies of the night.

Write it. Write it down. There's a quickening in his breast, a stirring in his loins. But scholarly, punctilious Anthony Oswald Valentine, classical philologist at University College London, alpinist, diarist, philanthropist, amateur botanist, geologist and glaciologist, exercises the self-control for which he is renowned. He opens the desk drawer, pulls out a thin sheet of pale pink writing paper, shuts the window, moves the candle closer and begins a letter to his wife.

My dearest Charlotte,

I write in some haste, but with much pleasure, to reassure you of my safe arrival at the Auberge Dorée. The landlord and his wife received me with their customary warmth. They send their regards and look forward to seeing you in five weeks' time.

I dined alone, but satisfactorily, on a rich stew of unusually dark meat (horse, I suspect), washed down with passable red wine and followed by a sliver or three of Reblochon, to which I am, as you know, most partial. Plus, a very small glass of green and rather bitter génépi.

The journey from Geneva to the border was swift and smooth, but as soon as we'd crossed into France, things took a turn for the worse. Bad weather, stubborn horses, an irascible driver. We had to change carriages at Bonneville . . .

Et cetera et cetera.

Sir A asks his wife about the garden, the roses, the weather and whether Edmond, their firstborn, has taken his first steps. He reminds her to arrange collection of his watch, which he sent for repair to that new place in Holborn a good two weeks ago. He mentions the delicate matter of her new pregnancy and expresses his hope that the sickness has passed. He promises to write again soon.

After a decent night's sleep and a hearty breakfast, Sir A sets out on the stony track that leads up from the village of Hext, past the cemetery, to the hamlet of Hext-en-Haut and beyond. It's a clear sunny day. The sky above the valley is sapphire blue, the high pastures are peridot green against the darker jades and blacks of the forests, and, close up, each blade of grass has its own dewy hue. Wild flowers – red, gold and purple jewels – glisten by the roadside. And between the sky and the flowers, as if suspended between heaven and earth, the white-capped, rising, rising ridges, cols and peaks.

> *Pillage and rape. Silver necklaces of snow, pearly icicle-earrings, the cheap chipped glass of the glaciers: my desire is to rip them apart, smash and scatter them, thrust myself naked against this unadorned* pute *of a landscape.*

That is what Sir A will write in his diary later. He will stay up beyond midnight, observing the stars, watching and listening for wildlife, writing, recording, exciting himself with language and nature.

But now, jaunty, he slings his satchel over one shoulder and turns off the track onto a narrow path that snakes up through dense, evergreen trees. His satchel contains nothing but a half baguette of bread, a hunk of smoked ham, two flasks of water, binoculars, notebooks and his diary. The porters will follow later with provisions for the summer, plus Sir A's trunk, the ten heavy boxes of books, Charlotte's several painting easels and his own unwieldy tripod, telescope and folding chair, all of which he himself helped wrap in padded canvas, overseeing the strapping and labelling, in Geneva last week.

After striding at a slow but steady pace – up hill and down dale, as he likes to say, or over the hills and far away, as he likes to hum and sometimes sing – until the sun is almost directly overhead, Sir A arrives at the spot where the only dwelling is a large, square, wooden chalet: Arete, his alpine eyrie.

Xavier is on the balcony. Both men raise an arm and wave simultaneously. Xavier hurries down the balcony steps. Sir A shifts the weight of his satchel, ignores his pounding heart and bounds across the last furlong of tufty grass.

The men shake hands, slap shoulders.

'By God, it's been too long,' says Sir A.

Xavier nods and smiles. He glances back up to the balcony, where a small figure now stands.

Two

Tall Paul – I never knew him small – remembered standing on the balcony at Arete.

Sir A, said Paul, was beaming, gleaming, huffing and puffing like a dragon, while Xavier (Paul's papa and the best guide in the valley) spoke to the rich Englishman in the rich Englishman's tongue as if they were equals.

But Tall Paul told tall stories, so that might have been one of them. He was three at the time, he said.

*

My story starts in the soft summer of 1914, when I was fourteen.

Only we uglies went to work at the Valentine house, and I was uglier than most. But did I care? Was I scared? Not a jot. I was curious. Keen, even. Besides, I'd been there before: six times to the bend in the path from where you can see the back door, and once, with Miss Margaret Valentine, inside, to the hall.

Margaret Valentine. 'Spit, spat.' That's what she said. 'That's families for you.' What she meant – angry – was clear; I was there; but then she went and disappeared. Why she went, or where, none of us knew. Everyone wondered, rumours flew. Now, seven years later, rumours were still flying. I wondered if any of the Valentines would or could tell me, if I asked, what had happened to Margaret.

Valentine women are more than at the core of my story – they're its beating bloody *anglais* heart – but I didn't know that then. Valentine women and Valentine men: good things as well as bad have come of my connection with them. But back then, the simple truth was, I had a job for the summer. I couldn't wait.

I had my bag packed by Thursday. I had to unpack and repack it on Friday, because Madame Tissot, who visited our farm to check that I was ready, insisted I take my schoolbooks with me (she said she didn't want her clever clogs forgetting everything over the summer) and some of them were very big. Eventually it was done, but I couldn't sleep on Friday night for thinking about the faraway, high-up house, full, from June to September, of *rosbifs*.

Various Valentines had already arrived: Sir A, with his telescopes, cameras, journals and maps, and Lady C, 'my dearest Charlotte', who was, by all accounts, already in front of her easels and wearing her wispy white dress. I wasn't quite sure who else to expect, but I knew there would be family friends – women in trousers, no less, scrambling up rock faces, what's more, and men in checked skirts (kilts, to be precise) dancing to jiggy music from the flaring horn of a wind-up music box. Not to mention the children, shapes and sizes galore, many of them pale as unrisen bread. These things we'd all heard about. These things awaited me – ugly, clever-clogs, sleepless me. 'Yes, please.' I practised the foreign words in a whisper.

Nearly everyone in the village said English was a dirty language. Our parents forbade us to use it. But our teacher, Madame Tissot, would tilt her head and roll her eyes.

'Nonsense,' she'd sniff. 'Or, "stuff and nonsense", as our English friends would say. English is as fine a language as any.'

It was dawn before I finally dropped off and, before I knew it, the moment to rise, with scarcely time enough to milk the cows, load the milk onto the cart, feed the horse, harness him to the cart and drive the milk down to the village. I had to wait at the train station for the milk to be picked up, collect yesterday's empties, then coax old Slowcoach all the way up the hill again. By the time we got back to the farm, Madame Tissot had arrived. So it was goodbye to my mother and my prettier sisters, and a wave to my father, who was busy mending the mazot which had collapsed last winter under the weight of the snow. Like everyone, we kept our valuables, our Sunday shoes and fête-day finery in the mazot. The collapse meant the wet got in, mould ruined the lot, and, for months, we had to wear our work clothes to church.

Madame Tissot accompanied me, as she had in the past, as far as the turning off the track above Hext-en-Haut. This time, though, instead of retying my cap, patting my apron, kissing me on both cheeks and saying, 'Goodbye, Mathilde. Mind your P's and Q's. I'll be here this evening, at five o'clock,' she retied my cap, patted my apron, kissed me on both cheeks and said, 'Goodbye, Mathilde. Mind your P's and Q's. I'll be here on the thirtieth of September, at five o'clock.'

I followed the path up through the forest, crossing three streams, none of which had much water in them. It had been a dry spring. Papa said our first crop of hay would be early that year. I was sorry I'd miss the haymaking. During the haymaking, we stayed at Sortilège, our haybarn half an hour away, above our farm, and I liked the change: hard, hot-work days, warm, not-work evenings and sticky, tickly nights. We all slept together in the only room there was, next to the hay. The smell was as intoxicating to me as the wine we all drank, watered down, at the end of a good haymaking afternoon.

The higher I climbed towards Arete, the heavier my bag seemed to become, even though I swapped it regularly from one hand to the other. The sun sliced through the tall, spiky trees, chopping the air into oblongs and wedges. Yellows and greys, shadows and haze. Left foot, then right. Bag in my right hand, then in the left. Then, for short spurts, on my back. But that hurt. I could have done with a drink.

Eventually, the path came out onto the Plateau des Bergers. My word, there it was hot! Rocky underfoot, and my clogs rattled and banged. I stopped for a moment to catch my breath. When I turned round, I could still see the village, but it was too far away to distinguish one building from another, apart from the church. Above the village and the slopes on the opposite side, the dark forest of Zizipompom was studded with haybarns, each in its own, bright clearing, and I could see le Nid, which belonged to my friend Benoît's family, right at the very top.

Sweat ran down the back of my neck. I took off my cap and used it to dab the wet away, then I knotted the cap (we were allowed to do this at haymaking, when the heat rose unbearably) like a man's hanky around my neck, to catch the sweat. The only sound, apart from my slowing breathing, was the faint whap-whap of wings high above me in the plateau's craggy overhang.

At the far edge of the plateau, the path forked – south to Chamonix, east to Arete, which meant a sharp zigzag down, across a narrow gully, up again over a small bank and into the high pastures. The cows up there were still thin from the winter, but they looked happy, swaying their heads, munching away, making the heavy bells around their necks jangle and clank. The grass was bright and new, and although the sun still warmed my head, neck and back, the air was much fresher.

Dozens of tracks, human and animal, furrowed the pastures. All the farmers on our side of the valley used this land for grazing. It was permitted. The land belonged to the commune.

The track to Arete, wider than the others, was easy to spot. The hard mud on it was marked from the tramp of dozens of footprints made earlier when half the men in the village had loaded donkeys, mules and horses and portered luggage and provisions up to Arete for *les anglais*. The men, when they returned, said they'd carried no fewer than sixteen crates of tins containing food. Tins, we women wondered? Corned beef, baked beans and sweetened milk, apparently. Four crates for each month – one for each week. This year's convoy also included a new tin bath and a small sailing boat, to go with the rowing boat moored on the tiny pool which Sir A himself had dug, many years ago, and which *les anglais* called the Round Pond. The men also mentioned a phonograph (gramophone, to be precise) and a blue-painted trunk, light but large and which two of the men dropped when crossing the first stream. The trunk broke open, spilling its contents: toys and clothes, but oh, what toys and clothes! Plied with questions from the rest of us, the men did their best to describe what they'd seen – china dolls, silver crowns, satin capes, a black top hat – but words, in my opinion, failed them, for I was left tantalised and frustrated by the meagre snippets of information.

I adjusted my pace as the path wound down to more trees. The trees thinned and I saw Arete, a bit higher up, through them. Two more bends. But as I rounded the second grassy, ferny, high-banked bend, with Arete only a glance away, I all but stumbled across the prone body of a girl. She lay on her stomach, beating the ground with her fists and the tips of her boots which were, I noticed, brown leather boy-boots, new, scarcely a scratch on their soles.

'Good morning, miss,' I said, as correct as could be.

'Daisy,' came the muffled reply.

This limby, lamby, long-legged girl scrambled to her feet and stood facing me with her hands on her hips. Her dark-brown eyes, which matched her hair, were dry, but their whites were dirty red from crying and rubbing.

'Daisy,' she repeated. 'My grandpa's Sir Anthony Valentine. Who are you?'

'Mathilde, miss.'

'Daisy. It's Daisy, once and for all. Not "miss", for heaven's sake. You must be the new—'

I nodded.

'Well, how d'you do?' Daisy put out her right hand. When I didn't take it, she stretched across, picked up my right hand and shook it.

'Excuse me, yes, how d'you do?' I imitated, inwardly kicking myself for not immediately remembering this English way of greeting.

'Not very well, actually.' Daisy unclasped her hand from mine. 'Livid, in fact. Everyone's gone off on paideia. Well, not everyone, but all three of my stupid brothers. Again. Weather permitting, I'm allowed to swim. Otherwise I'm pretty much stuck here, bored stiff. I'm convalescing, you see. Listen to this.'

She coughed.

The sound – a high-pitched squeal, not unlike the bellows of a little-used accordion – reminded me of Louis, who coughed so much in class one day, Madame Tissot sent him home and told him to stay away from school. She said she would go and see him at the end of the week and if he wasn't better by then, she would pay for the doctor to visit. But Louis was dead by the end of the week.

'*Coqueluche*,' said Madame Tissot. 'I thought as much. I should have intervened earlier.'

'Whooping cough.' Daisy patted her chest with both hands. 'Grandpa calls it pertussis and says it will last a hundred days. I'm counting. Twenty-five more to go. And then it's my birthday. I'm fine, though. Fit as a fiddle. Just bloody hot and bloody bothered. You look bloody hot, if you don't mind my saying. Let's get you a drink, shall we? Come. I'll take you in. Give me your bag.'

She grabbed my bag, and before you could say Jack Robinson, or I could ask what she meant by gone off on paideia, Daisy took my left hand in her right and led me the last few steps along the track and across an open grassy spread to the back door of Arete. Out of the corner of my eye I saw the Round Pond – yes, there were two boats bobbing on it, and one of them definitely had a mast.

In we went, first to the kitchen, which was empty and where I drank a good, cold bowlful of water, and Daisy splashed her face. Then along the corridor – 'games room', said Daisy, indicating a door on the left, and 'dining room' on the right – and into Arete's enormous front hall with its huge staircase in the middle.

A woman was sitting on the bench in the hall next to the open front door, through which you could see, like a picture, the 'V' of the valley and the crumpled folds of the slopes surrounding it. The woman had one trousered leg stuck out in front of her and she was lacing her boot.

'Mother,' said Daisy. 'She's arrived.'

'Who, darling?' The woman looked up. 'Oh.'

'Good morning, madam,' I said.

'Well. You'll certainly do on the looks front. How's her English, Daisy?'

'My name is Mathilde,' I said. 'I speak English and read and write it really rather well. Also French a Parisian would be proud of and the rudiments of Latin. So says Madame Tissot.' This speech was rehearsed and I was pleased with its delivery. I smiled, trying not to let the sucking sound escape through my gums.

'Heavens above!' Daisy's mother smiled back, but not in a way I liked. I decided she must be Margaret's sister because she looked similar to the Valentine woman I remembered, though this one was more thickly built – a strong-bodied woman, you could tell, and her face and teeth and horsey smile were strong too, almost too strong. 'An educated cretin. What an odd thing. But it's your domestic skills that matter here.'

I was indignant: I was not a cretin. Ugly, yes. Stupid, no. Ugly as sin, said the boys in the village. (Not Benoît, but the others.) And their sisters – and mine – tittered. Did it hurt? Yes. But so did many things. Papa's stick, for one. Maman's hand-thwack for another. Burns from the fire, blisters from the mangle, cuts from the thresher: they hurt. Maman sighing and saying I'd never marry, she'd never get rid of me or get the extra man-help she needed on the farm: that hurt. And above all, the cold. Oh my! How that hurt! For months on end, it could literally tear your skin off.

So I was ugly. So what? I was sturdy and squat, a bit squashed, with features uneven, I knew. But so were some of my favourite mountains: lumpy, off-kilter, with mismatching planes and pointy bits.

And I was clever. This woman, Daisy's mother, was wrong.

'Madame Tissot—' I began, but the woman cut me off.

'That's enough of Madame Tissot. So long as you know how to clean and cook, you'll manage. Do as you're told. You'll soon learn. Show her where she's to sleep, Daisy,' said the woman and, having finished lacing her boot, she strode like a man out of the front door.

Daisy pulled me by the hand up the stairs. My clogs thumped on the polished wood, even though I trod as lightly as I could. At the top of the stairs, Daisy pointed to a ladder.

'I'll pass your bag up to you and leave you to get settled in.'

I climbed the ladder, took my bag and found myself in a grenier, except that there wasn't a speck of hay in that grenier. It was a space as large as the house itself, floorwise, but with the sloping roof as a ceiling so you could only stand up in the middle.

One end of the grenier, above the back of the house, was a mess of objects and pieces of furniture the likes of which I'd never seen. The front part had eight beds arranged higgledy-piggledy, four by four. Only three of them looked as if they'd been slept in. I sat down on an unmade-up bed next to the small window at the front and looked out: I had the same view as through Arete's front door except wider, because I was up close and could move my eyes, and when I opened the window and looked out, the view was even wider: I could see bits of the path I'd walked up earlier and I could see the high pastures, a few cows outlined on the horizon. In the distance, I could see la Concierge, the small mountain at the entrance to our valley. Benoît said its soft contours reminded him of a woman's curvy body – of the baker's round and pretty wife, to be precise.

Beneath me was the terrace. Daisy and her mother were standing at the far side of it in the shade, next to a tall, thin, elderly woman who wore a wispy white dress, had wispy white hair and was dabbing with a paintbrush at a canvas propped on an easel. Every now and then she raised her eyes and stared intently at the mountains in the distance. Lady Charlotte. And directly below my window I could see the head, or rather the flat-topped, narrow-brimmed hat, of what could only be Sir Anthony. He was sitting on a cane-backed, folding wooden chair. This, I learnt later, he called his star-gazing chair. One leg was crossed over the other, and I could see shiny black leather shoes and matt black socks pulled up over long slim shins. Sir A's elbows rested on the wooden arms of the chair and he was reading and smoking. His pipe-smoke wafted through the air to me and I breathed it in – a lovely smell – which made me cough. Sir A looked up.

'Who's that, Beatrice?' said Sir A, peering over his reading glasses.

Daisy's mother glanced at the window, frowned, and shaded her eyes with her hand.

'What are you doing, Mathilde? What on earth's she doing up there, Daisy? Come down this minute.'

I withdrew my head from the window and lowered myself and my bag back down the ladder. Clop, clop, down the stairs and out through the open front door. Daisy hurried over, followed by Beatrice. Lady C stayed where she was and continued to paint, ignoring the rest of us.

'Sorry, Mother. Grandpa,' said Daisy. 'I forgot. Sorry, Mathilde. What a silly billy I am. The servants used to sleep in the grenier, but the boys are up there this year. I completely forgot. Dizzy Daisy, that's me. There are new quarters for you all now.'

'Welcome, Mathilde,' said Sir A, standing up and extending a hand.

I was quick off the mark this time and extended mine too. Our hands met and I was astonished by the smoothness of Sir A's palm and the pads of his fingers. Like, I imagined, a grand lady's. Even Madame Tissot's – and she was quite grand – were rougher, with callouses I liked to think came from holding her pens for so long, but were probably due to the mopping and swilling and mending she did like the rest of us.

'Take Mathilde to her lodgings, Daisy. And show her the bath house on the way. I've rebuilt it and installed a bigger tub,' said Sir A, letting go of my hand and gesturing with both arms. 'It's this wide. And longer than you, even at a stretch. Stand up straight, child, can you not?'

I could stand up straight, but it was an effort. My back was ever so slightly hunched. Not that you'd notice, if I always stood up straight. But doing so meant forcing my shoulders uncomfortably, and I tended not to bother.

Sir A put his hands on my shoulders, just as I was grimacing and moving them backwards.

'That's better,' he said. 'Keep them like that. Imagine you're riding a horse.'

I'd been riding Slowcoach, with the milk, through summer dawns and winter darks, every morning for as long as I could remember. Those early two or three hours were usually a time of pleasant drowsiness. I'd sit slumped on his back and let my mind wander. When it was very cold, I put my head down on his scraggy old mane and let the heat from his body seep into mine. I'd never sit upright with my shoulders pulled back. What would be the purpose of that?

'Off you go.' Sir A nodded towards the back of the house. 'I hope you settle in well, Mathilde.'

'Thank you, sir,' I said.

'Come.' Daisy turned to go.

As I followed, I heard Sir A's deep, clear and, to my ears, tuneful English voice again.

'And where are you off to, Beatrice, my dear?'

'I thought I'd take a quick turn up the Little Loo, Pa,' was the reply. 'Meet the boys, perhaps, on their way home.'

The petit Luet was the steep rock face that rose like a wall behind Arete and was topped by the narrowest, sharpest of ridges.

If I didn't know better, I'd have thought Arete was named after the ridge of the Luet, *l'arête du Luet*, but, like so many Valentine things, names were deceptive. Sir A, for example, wasn't actually a sir when he first visited our valley. He became a sir later, but back then, strictly speaking, he was Mr Anthony Valentine, and Charlotte, his wife, just Mrs.

It was his guide, Xavier, who introduced them as Sir A and Lady C. Xavier was prone to exaggeration. It ran in the family. From Xavier to Paul to Benoît, the gift of storytelling was passed on proudly from father to son. And since the villagers knew no better, the names stayed.

As to the Valentine house, Madame Tissot said that *arete* was a Greek word meaning virtue and excellence in all things. The Valentines made its rhythm and rhyme chime with charity, she said, but beware – their *anglais* guests might pronounce or stress it in myriads of two- and three-syllable ways.

You could see the petit Luet from the valley floor, and the sun often shone on its high granite ridge, turning the ridge orangey gold. But even on the brightest day in midsummer, the sun didn't warm the Luet's lower damp and stony surfaces. There might be a group of chamois on one of its precipices, a third of the way or even halfway up. No living thing without wings above that. So what Beatrice meant by a quick turn up the Luet, heaven only knew.

'Good for you,' said Sir A. 'Which route will you take?'

I didn't hear the answer because Daisy and I had reached the corner of the chalet, where a small lean-to had been added. The wood was pale and unweathered, and there was a shiny new latch on the door.

'The bath house,' said Daisy, lifting the latch and pushing open the door.

We both went inside. There wasn't anything in there except a rough bench and a tin bathtub, which was indeed large.

'Hot water comes from there.' Daisy pointed to a pipe sticking out from the wall. 'Straight through from the stove in the kitchen. You can turn it off and on.' She demonstrated, twisting the tap above the pipe. Steaming water flowed out and splashed into the tub. I took a step back in awe.

'It's not like at home,' Daisy went on. 'In London, we have a bath and a basin, two taps each, and a water closet with, well, something that makes the, you know, the everything disappear. The boys call this slumming, and it is, in a way. Nevertheless, you've got to admit Grandpa's bloody clever to have designed the place himself all those years ago. No wonder he's pleased with his new bathtub. It's so big, you and I could have a bath in it together. Couldn't we? The boys often share, especially when they get back from paideia, all glistening and full of themselves.'

'Paideia?'

'Some say pie-day. We say pie-dee-uh.'

Daisy had confused me. 'What does it mean?' I took a step back through the doorway.

'It's a special sort of expedition. Meant to educate us. Make us better people,' said Daisy. 'Grandpa invented it. Well, not originally. Knowing him, it's probably Greek. Anyway, you can use the bath house whenever you like. Unless, of course,' she put a hand to her mouth and lowered her voice, 'one of the boys is already in there. Right. To your lodgings, Mathilde.'

We set off from the bath house towards the group of small huts behind Arete on the flattish piece of mossy, grassy land before the rise of the Luet. We passed a privy, an outhouse and the mazot on the way.

'Thunderbox, laundry room and Grandmother's – Lady C's – painting studio,' said Daisy. 'And there are the servants' quarters. Your sleeping huts. Though we use them for overflow too.'

'Overflow?'

'When the house is full up, which it often is. You'll see. The huts were shelters for cow and goatherds, you know, once upon a time. Before Grandpa bought the land and built the house. He fell in love, he said.' Daisy laughed – a squeaky laugh – like pretty Angélique, at school, whenever Benoît's name was mentioned. 'He fell in love with the land.'

Once upon a time, cowherds, goatherds, most of the people in the valley, in fact, were anxious or angry about Sir A asking to buy this land. It was before my time, so I didn't know the ins and outs of it, but people feared for their livelihoods, I knew that much. The land included grazing land owned by the commune and land with trees, which Sir A proposed to cut down. We needed our trees – not just for fuel and to build our houses with, but as a way of slowing down the avalanches which tumbled willy-nilly down the mountains every winter.

There was, in addition, the rumour of gold in the vicinity, and some people suspected that Sir A knew its whereabouts.

Sir A, moreover, was not a catholic. Priests, peasants and the majority of the villagers were reluctant to say yes to the sale of the land to a rich, protestant *rosbif*. There was argy-bargy in the village and loud opposition to the sale.

Afterwards, however, many of these very same people were willing to take Sir A's money in exchange for their labour as builders, porters, servants, guides, messengers, maids, gardeners, dogsbodies. Perhaps they were good at hiding their resentment in the darkness of their hearts, but Sir A, it turned out, was a fair and generous man in employment matters, and, in addition, he donated a considerable sum of money to the commune's general coffers. Not that this stopped the gossip about Sir A and what he and his family, or he and his friends, got up to in the mountains and at their *maison de plaisance*.

More than forty years later, though, people were still benefitting. My family would certainly profit. With the money I would earn, we planned to buy a new horse to replace old Slowcoach. We also hoped to replant our potato field with the best potatoes, bought from a farm on the opposite, more fertile side of the valley. Two years ago, weeks and weeks of autumn rain soaked the fields around our farm. The slopes on our side of the valley weren't steep enough for the water to run away as it usually did, and all our potatoes ended up getting some sort of blight. It seemed like a never-ending winter. We became weak and skinny – even Maman, who was pregnant again.

The baby came early and was, as usual, dead. All Maman's babies came early and were dead. My sisters and I were milk sisters, not blood sisters. There were several women in the valley, like Maman, paid to take in bastards, orphans or foundlings, nurse them with milk from their aching titties and raise them as their own. It was a job, Maman said, like any other.

It was my job to wrap the dead baby in hessian and carry it up to the roof, where it would stay until spring; it couldn't be buried until then because the ground was covered in snow and too hard underneath to be dug. The baby was a boy and perfectly formed, except for being smaller than a marmot. I wondered how long, cocooned in snow, preserved by the cold, the baby would look the same. What colour was frozen skin? It wasn't the sort of question I could put to Maman, whose own skin stayed grey with fatigue for weeks after the birth. My sisters might have known, but none of us talked as we lay in our bed at night, close together for warmth.

My sisters went to sleep with pegs on their noses (to beautify them, they said). Both of them snored. My nose, even as a child, was long and thin, with a prominent bony bit just below my eyes. My sisters said there was no point trying to beautify it. If I crossed my eyes, which came easily to me, I could see all but the tip of my nose where it turned down towards my mouth. I could touch that tip with my tongue. Breathing also came easily to me and I knew I didn't snore. My sisters said I slept with my mouth open, grunted like a pig and kicked like a horse, but no, thank the Lord, they said, at least I didn't snore. I would lie awake, listening to them. The noise of their snores irritated me no end, and sometimes I'd remove the pegs from their noses. They would sigh and sink into a deeper, quieter, more peaceful sleep, and I could hear, then, the night sounds. Creaks and rustles, inside and out. Animals stirring and stomping. The sow grunting. A distant barking. And sometimes, if I listened carefully, the gentle hiss or muted thud of snow falling on snow.

There was a belief in the valley that exactly the same amount of snow fell every winter. In varying quantities, at different times, of course. But if you could count it all up, it would come to exactly the same amount every winter. Like emptying a sack of flour – in flurries and gushes and sprinkles. Like in the legend of the white gold. But what if, one year, there was too much? An avalanche. The equivalent – or the result – of *anglais* overflow.

'Overflow.' I repeated the word, and Daisy laughed again.

'That's right,' she said. 'And here we are. These four are overflow.' She gestured right and left. 'And this one's yours.'

We both stopped walking.

'You'll be sharing, naturally. The other uglies are all probably in there at this hour. Having a rest. I'll leave you to it. I'm going to read to Grandpa. See you at supper, I expect.'

*

I did see Daisy at supper, but not to talk to. I and two other uglies served the dishes and cleared them away, but none of the Valentines appeared to notice us. There weren't as many people as I had imagined. Madame Tissot had warned me numbers changed from week to week, from six to twenty-six or more. But what they lacked in numbers (only ten that night) the Valentines and their visitors – an elderly couple and a large, hand-flapping man – made up for in noise. They clanked their china plates and clinkled the silver cutlery, speaking in loud voices, often at the same time. Only Lady C was silent. When she wanted me to refill the water jug, she indicated using just her pale grey eyes. I could see immediately that she didn't recognise me from the incident with Margaret Valentine seven years ago. Which was no surprise really – I hadn't grown much taller, but I'd filled out and wore women's skirts and blouses now, not the cotton smocks and hemp leggings of childhood.

Daisy's three brothers were the noisiest, all wanting to describe what they'd seen or done that day. Parliament Hill was mentioned, along with a rock-hopping contest and three different types of kestrel spotted diving for prey. The boys were older than Daisy, but behaved younger. They teased her about not being able to go with them and made fun of her cough, whooping with laughter when, just as I was serving the pudding (an *anglais* concoction called jam roly-poly, with milk – 'condeeny' – from one of the tins), a coughing fit began. It was the sound of the madhouse, said Stephen. Daisy was a witch and ought to be burnt.

'Remove her, Mother. Lock her up. She's the devil in disguise.'

But Beatrice didn't intervene until Daisy turned the same colour as the jam in the roly-poly pudding, and then only to tell her to go outside until she felt better.

By the time Daisy came back, supper was almost over and talk had turned to the evening's entertainment: charades or consequences, music or billiards, sitting room or terrace, whisky or brandy? I listened while stacking the pudding bowls, but I lost the thread when Sir A and Lady C began discussing an event in the future called the garden party. It involved sausage rolls, crustless cucumber sandwiches, cricket, a marquee and a drink called Pimm's.

Stephen and Ted, meanwhile, were arguing about the merits of medicine versus law. I'd deduced that earnest, talkative Stephen was Daisy's eldest brother, because of the way he spoke (superior) to Ted, a kind but nervy young man who kept picking at the edge of the tablecloth, tapping his glass and fiddling with the unused cutlery.

The third brother, who looked about fifteen, was puppyish and lively and they called him pretty Johnny. I heard Daisy ask pretty Johnny whether he'd describe her hair as chestnut or chocolate. And pretty Johnny said he'd give the question some serious thought.

I was excused washing-up and sent to bed early that night. I had the hut to myself and I thought I'd fall asleep quickly, but I found myself going back over the day. I wished I could tell Benoît about it all. Together, we'd have managed to make some sort of sense out of the odd *anglais* ways. I tucked the sheet closer and turned on my side. Chestnut or chocolate? I'd have said foxy, if anything. But the Valentine hair was basically brown. Thick and wavy. Rich as shit. Sir A had it. And he'd passed it on to his daughter, Beatrice, and her daughter, Daisy.

When I was very young, I thought my own hair was the cause of the taunts I received. It was short, coarse and colourless. Even as infants, we wore caps or bonnets most of the time, including at night. But we took them off for washing and when it was hot by the fire, or hot from the sun outside. My sisters' hair reached to below their shoulders. Mine didn't seem to want to grow more than a couple of inches. Moreover, it was sparse and brittle, like parched shoots of grass. Maman told my sisters off if they poked fun at me, but even she occasionally called me Little Broomhead. And there was nothing Maman could do about the village children, who pretended to be scared (perhaps they really were) when I was sent, as soon as I could walk, on errands in the valley.

But it wasn't until I went to school that I realised my ugliness was in my face and in my small, stout body too. Madame Tissot had to put a cushion on my seat because I was so short. She told the class, 'Be kind. Mathilde is only five. She's here this young because she reads already.'

'We don't play with the uglies, whether they read already or not,' said Angélique at lunchtime on my first day at school, when I went over to the huddle of girls in the corner, exclaiming as they peeped into each other's apron pockets.

Angélique said I was so ugly that my mother must have been one of the witches of Morzine, which scared me rigid – and I was Mademoiselle Wet-Knickers for the week, because I was indeed born in Morzine, at least that's what Maman said she'd been told.

The uglies were left out of all the girls' games and gangs, and we didn't gang up together either, not even with the redheads. Madame Tissot did her best on the redhead front to dispel the myths, with doses of Poil de Carotte and stories of Cleopatra, the red-headed queen of Egypt who bathed in the milk of seven hundred donkeys. But the myths persisted: ugly, red-headed Henri le cretin had a far worse time than me at school. He cried so much that the lids of his lashless eyes swelled and thickened like a toad's.

Henri le cretin lived in the farmhouse next to ours, which meant I occasionally had to walk some of the way to or from the village with him and – worse – his big brother Cédric. Cédric was the toughest boy in the school, but not the most handsome nor the cleverest. He was slimy-faced and wobble-lipped, with dirty, gappy teeth, and he was always trying to stick his fat tongue in some poor girl's mouth.

The boys were less vicious than the girls with their words, but often, on my way out of school, they would hide, then try to scare me by jumping out. Sometimes they'd circle me, imitating my uneven gait or pulling at their cheeks so they looked even worse than Henri le cretin.

Only black-haired Benoît didn't join in. He was by far the cleverest pupil at school. Not always top of the class, though. Sometimes I beat him. He said he thought that we were equally intelligent, but that I, unlike him, had an imagination to rival La Fontaine's.

Benoît and I often stayed behind at school to help Madame Tissot put the books away and sweep the floor. That's when we learnt the most from our teacher, for she would speak differently – still teacherly and strict, but she would tell us things and explain things, then, that we knew the others would have had trouble understanding. The world, for example: we had no globe, but there was an atlas on Madame Tissot's desk and she let us flip through it sometimes, teaching us which bits of land belonged to which country. Idiomatic English. She showed us the book she'd bought in the Charing Cross Road, London, in 1895, *A Handbook of Common English Idioms*, which she said was invaluable. The poetry in the poems we copied and recopied, day after day. The finer points of handwriting, grammar, spelling, punctuation.

It was the circumflex that brought Benoît and me together. We were still young enough to call it a hat, although Madame Tissot encouraged us to use the correct word.

And it would be correct to say that a hat, my real hat, was actually what started things off.

It was late spring, and I'd only been going to school for a few weeks when I had to stay up most of the night helping Papa with a kid goat who'd been born too quickly, all wrong, and looked like he'd probably die. We did our utmost not to let that happen, but he stopped breathing just before sunrise and this time our rubbing and cajoling didn't revive him. I went to milk the cows as usual, but Papa said no, he'd do my chores that morning, and I was to go and sleep for an hour. But I couldn't sleep, so it was still early when I set off for school. I had time to go the long route across the fields, following any one of a number of paths through the cool, dark, dense mass of trees: oak and ash, elm and beech – I counted twelve of each, plus six budding sycamore trees before, suddenly, I was out and stomping through the thickety, moist undergrowth down to the river, thus avoiding the road into the village and reducing the risk of a ragging.

I loitered when I reached the river. It was flowing very fast, rushing green and foamy-grey over the stones and boulders from all the melting snow. It didn't look like water at all. You couldn't see the bottom. You certainly couldn't cross it, as you would be able to easily later in the summer by stepping or leaping from one stone to the next. The only way to get across now, apart from going back to the village and over the bridge, was to climb onto the trunk of a fallen tree. There were several of these, all still half-rooted, with torn branches and splitting sides. I picked the thickest, safest-looking one I could see. It was slippery and I had to crawl, but I quite liked peeping down from time to time, seeing the swirl of water below me. It looked as thick as simmering soup, but I knew, if I fell, its iciness might kill me.

Branches overhung the fallen tree on the high bank, and, as soon as I could, I pulled myself up with these. My hat – a plain, grey-felt, childish thing – caught in one of them. I stretched an arm to retrieve it, but that made me lose my balance. I wobbled and clutched wildly at the branches, dislodging my hat and sending it tumbling towards the river. Two more steps and I was safely on the other side. I turned and looked at the river, expecting to see my hat whisking away in the soup. But no. It had fallen into a narrow gap where the water had made a trough of mud between the riverbank and the boulders at its edge. There was my hat, several feet below me, safe and sound – it had even landed the right way up – but I knew I couldn't climb down to retrieve it.

At that moment, Benoît appeared on the far side of the river. He was carrying books under one arm and a fishing rod under the other. He saw me, and he saw me looking down at my hat. He put his books on the ground, climbed onto the tree trunk and made his way across it. He didn't crawl. He put one foot in front of the other and held his fishing rod horizontally across his body for balance.

'Take my hand,' he said when he'd nearly reached me. 'This is always the tricky bit. I don't trust those branches.'

I reached out my hand, but Benoît didn't need it. He jumped, nimble as a squirrel, onto the riverbank and then turned and looked down at my hat lying on the mud below us.

'Hmm,' he said. 'Seems to me you've lost your circumflex, Mathilde. Definitely a case of the hat falling into the abyss. *Le chapeau de la cime est tombé dans l'abîme.* Remember?'

I couldn't help smiling. This was one of Madame Tissot's many aides-memoires, to help us spell. We'd spent the best part of the week having the importance of the circumflex drummed into us.

'It makes all the difference,' Madame Tissot said. 'It's as important as any letter in the alphabet. Like its friends – you learnt about some of the accents last week . . . remember the curly cedilla? – it tells you how to pronounce correctly in Parisian French. But it also, sometimes, tells you the history of a word. The circumflex might, for example, indicate a missing "s". Take Benoît,' she continued. 'There's a circumflex on the "i" of your name, isn't there, Benoît? Do you know why?'

Benoît said that he did. He said his father, Tall Paul, gave him a name with a hat on it because he was born with so much black hair on his head that it looked like he was wearing a hat.

'That's not quite what I was expecting.' Madame Tissot smiled and wrote 'Benoist' on the blackboard, then crossed out the 's' and changed the 'i' to 'î'. 'But it reminds me of a couple of useful aides-memoires.' She wrote, '*On met un chapeau sur la tête*' and, underneath, '*Le chapeau de la cime est tombé dans l'abîme*.' We had to copy and learn, copy and learn. All morning. Copy, learn, recite. Copy, learn, recite.

Madame Tissot's teaching was turned against me at lunchtime that day when Angélique flipped the hat from my head.

'Look at Mathilde,' she said. 'Truly an ugly beast. *On met un chapeau sur la tête* to hide what's underneath – *une vraie bête*.'

'I can't go to school without my hat,' I said now to Benoît, the smile dropping from my face. My eyes even prickled with tears at the thought.

'No, you can't,' Benoît agreed. 'Your head,' he added, 'definitely needs its circumflex.'

He was the first person ever to refer to my looks without making me feel ugly through and through.

'I'll get it for you,' he said.

'How? You can't climb down there.'

'With this, of course,' said Benoît. 'We'll fish it up.'

He unwound the string from the fishing rod, pulled a hook from his pocket, tied it to the end of the string and dangled the rod over the side of the river. He stretched as far as he could, but the hook didn't reach my hat.

'I'm going to lie down. You hold onto my feet. Tight, mind. I don't want to die by drowning.'

Benoît lay on his stomach. I grasped his bony ankles with both my hands and he wriggled forwards to the edge of the riverbank. He bent his body so far over it that I couldn't see his head any more, but I could hear him breathing heavily as he reached and stretched.

'Come on,' I heard him mutter. 'Come on, little hat.' He sounded like Papa earlier that morning trying to coax the tiny goat to stay alive.

'Got it. Keep holding on, though, Mathilde, while I kneel up.'

He sat back on his heels, and although I was still holding onto his ankles, I saw, over his shoulders, my headgear dangling in mid-air like a great big trout.

The felt hat was damp and a bit muddy, but I put it on, and Benoît and I walked together the rest of the way to school. Just as we were about to go inside, some girls came over. They pushed Angélique to the front of the group.

'Will you sit next to me today, Benoît? It's Friday,' she said, undoing the bow beneath her chin and loosening her bonnet, so that pretty ringlets of hair fell about her face. Once a week, Madame Tissot let us choose where we sat; otherwise, it was she who decided. 'We can go to Zizipompom later, if you like.'

We didn't know exactly what it meant, but we all knew that, out of season, the empty, unlocked haybarns in the Zizipompom forest were a trysting place for courting couples, and we knew to say, 'Oo,' in silly voices, if an invitation to go there was issued.

'Actually,' said Benoît, 'I was hoping to sit with my friend, Mathilde. I appear to have forgotten my books. We read at the same level and speed, you see.'

I didn't know what to say, I was so surprised. Angélique looked at me and sneered.

'La bête? I didn't know you liked ugly animals so much, Benoît,' she said.

'I like all animals,' said Benoît. 'It's stupid people I've no time for.'

I didn't learn very much at school that day. I was too busy enjoying sitting next to Benoît. At the end of school, Benoît went his way and I went mine – and we never went to Zizipompom – but we sat together regularly from then on, because we were friends.

*

Every September, I went fruit-picking with Benoît. The sweetest apples, the juiciest pears and the most succulent bilberries were to be had in the meadows beyond Alessandro Costanza's house, where the river bends, the land is gentle and the sun's rays warm the earth for most of the day in the summer months. We'd lie on our backs in the shade of one of the trees, eating apples or pears and staring at the sky, oval and tooth-edged from the mountains all around. We'd argue about what the mountains resembled: Mont Blanc was a pig's ear and the Aiguille Verte a circumflex, but there were titties, cocks and arses, the *curé*'s nose, the webbed toes of dimwitted, slitty-eyed Henri le cretin, his big brother Cédric's grey-streaked, uneven teeth, the blacksmith's broken thumb, Madame Tissot's Sunday bonnet, and, on a sunny, sharp September day, clean underwear hanging out to dry.

Sometimes we'd dawdle outside Costanza's workshop, which was also his house. If there was music coming from his windows, we'd sit down on the grass next to the brambles and listen. Costa mended violins, but also sold the wood to make them. He tuned pianos and made glue (from a secret recipe), which he sold too. People were suspicious of Costa because he'd been born on the other side of the mountains, in Italy, and because of the unusual jobs he did. They were jealous because they thought he might be rich. There was even a rumour that the fire in 1907, which destroyed the property and killed Costa's parents, might have been started deliberately. Costa left the valley after the fire, aged only seventeen. He returned three years later and set about repairing the house, rebuilding his father's business, but he kept himself to himself, and people didn't like that. He aroused suspicion and envy. Some people even said he wasn't quite right in the head. Costa never went to church, but he often had a beard, which I thought made him look like Jesus Christ. Plenty of people came to the village and asked directions to Alessandro Costanza's place, but they were clients from towns and cities, not friends.

*

Daisy and I became friends that first summer at Arete. Stephen, Ted and pretty Johnny were polite but distant with me. Daisy, however, wouldn't leave me alone, and, to start with, I was irritated. There was a lot of work in the mornings and again in the evenings. Even when we'd cleared away supper, there was often the waxing of walking boots and the re-coiling of the day's climbing ropes after checking the strands – two hemp-coloured, one red – for wear and tear.

The afternoons weren't so busy. Sir A and Lady C were too old, by 1914, to go on any major outings, although they did still revisit their favourite peaks and picnic spots in the close vicinity of Arete. Most members of the family and their guests, however, were usually off on paideia or some such (scrambles, rambles, excursions, expeditions, walks, constitutionals, paideia, reccies: I didn't realise, for a long time, how carefully the Valentines distinguished between these *anglais* pursuits). A few people took siestas – post-prandial naps – in their bedrooms. Others sat in the sun or under parasols on the terrace; they read books, wrote letters, filled in their journals, stuck things into scrapbooks, drew, painted, played parlour, card and board games. We uglies could rest, if we wanted to. And I would have rested – and perhaps even read some of my big books – if Daisy hadn't pestered me to join her.

We discovered we were the same age.

'I'll be fourteen next month. As old as the century,' said Daisy. 'I hope we both live to be a hundred.'

She was watching me clear the remains of lunch from the dining room. She followed me into the kitchen and got in the way as I dried the cutlery, crockery and cooking utensils.

She picked up the Mrs Beeton cookery book, which Beatrice referred to when overseeing our kitchen activities (which, being a bossy boots, she did quite frequently).

Daisy read out a recipe for soused mackerel.

'Ugh. Sounds horrible.'

She flipped over the pages.

'Mmm, jelly,' she said. 'Look, Mathilde – a picture of jelly, two colours, two tiers. Will you make it for my birthday?'

And when I didn't reply:

'What's this for?' She banged a flat wooden spoon as long as her bare forearm on the edge of the sink.

'We use it to skim the cream from the milk for Sir A,' I said.

Daisy laughed.

'Kippers and cream for Grandpa. Porridge and milk for the rest of us. I'm looking forward to being old. I'll have kippers and cream, cake and summer pud for breakfast then. What's this?'

And this? And this? Her questions were endless. When she picked up one of our carving knives, still wet and dripping from the sink, I frowned and held out my hand, like Madame Tissot demanding contraband from a child. Coin, pebble, crust of bread or scrap of ribbon – all would go in the bottom drawer of Madame Tissot's desk until the end of the day.

'No,' I said. 'That is not a toy. This is a kitchen and that is a kitchen tool. Give it to me, please.'

Daisy handed me the knife, saying, 'Don't be cross, Mathilde. I'm so, so bored. Will you do something with me this afternoon?'

'What would you like me to do?'

'We could go for a swim? Or look for fossils? Start our own Alpine Club, for girls only, like Lizzie Le Blond? Try on some of the new dressing-up clothes? Or how about a boating trip on the pond?'

I didn't know the correct reply. I looked to Sylvie, the cook, for guidance. Sylvie spoke mostly patois and was a woman of few words. She got on with her job, which included managing the rest of us uglies, without enthusiasm, but without complaining. She came from one of the poorest farms in the valley, and was the only woman in a chaotic household of brothers and uncles, and a father who drank. Which is probably why cooking meals and doing *les anglais*' dirty work was as easy as pie compared to keeping house for her good-for-nothing relations. There was a purple streak across Sylvie's face. It covered one eye and seemed to pull her eyebrow down towards the lower lid so that her eye was half-closed. On her cheek it was livid and patchy, and it went down her neck too. We all wore high collars and our caps at work, but at night, in the servants' quarters, when Sylvie removed her cap and apron, unbuttoned her collar and began to get undressed for bed, I saw the purple mark, like a cloudy sunset, spread under her jaw and halfway down her neck. Sometimes she put a hand to her neck, and I wondered if the purple mark itched or hurt.

Without the purple, Sylvie might have been an attractive woman. She had black hair, blue eyes and thin, delicate cheek- and jawbones which gave a pretty shape to her face. But without the purple, Sylvie would not have got the job of cook at Arete and would not have been able to save up some of her money every year, ready for the day she would move to town. This is what she told us she planned to do. It was the only conversation she was happy to have, and we had it more than once, that's for sure. She had to give most of what she earned at Arete to her family. But, she said, she saved a bit each year and hid it in the mazot. One day, she said, she would have enough to move to town. She never said which town. Just that she'd heard there were many hotels in town. She would find work in one of them as a cook. She lived for that day, she said.

She was quite stupid.

So were the other uglies. All four of them. Cretins, almost. They were known to me, of course – farm girls, like myself, all of us as strong as tree trunks. But they were older than me by a good two or three years, and none of them had attended Madame Tissot's school. They kept together and left me alone. Unlike Daisy.

Sylvie nodded, so I said yes to Daisy.

'Dressing-up,' she decided. 'The box is in the attic.'

I climbed behind Daisy up the ladder into that hot and airless space again. Daisy opened the small window at the front, but then walked to the back and stood surveying the piles of objects. I stood next to her. The mess perplexed me. We would never have left a storeroom in such a state. But then we would never have had so many things we didn't use. When Benoît gave me an ibex he'd carved out of wood, Papa had said, 'Not bad,' even though Benoît hadn't managed the horns very well. 'Of no actual use, though.'

Papa was a skilled woodcarver himself and he taught me and my sisters some basic knife-work. By the time I was five and about to start school, I not only knew how to choose a good, young fir-tree branch and turn it into a strong wooden walking baton, but also how to carve simple stars onto it. The pattern I created meant it wouldn't get muddled with my sisters' or my classmates' alpenstocks. In the winter, Papa made all the wooden tools we needed for the farm, as well as wooden plates, bowls, spoons and stirrers for the kitchen. Moreover, he did all this before Christmas, leaving himself plenty of time for the charcuterie: our pigs were fat and meaty, and Papa was famous for his jambons and diot sausages, which he flavoured with nutmeg, pepper and mustard powder. The only decorative things Papa ever carved were outlines: suns, moons, flowers and, occasionally, a heart on the back of a chair.

Maman put my wooden ibex on one of the beams above the fireplace, and it stayed there for ages, becoming grey and ashy and eventually all but invisible against the grey, ashy wood of the beam.

Another thing without a use at the farm was our picture of the car. This was stored away at the back of a drawer. The picture was cut from a newspaper. A Geneva newspaper. Madame Tissot – who was half-Swiss, had friends in Geneva and regularly took the train to visit them – brought it to us. It was only an advertisement for an automobile, but whenever we looked at it, we all burst out laughing.

A month earlier, I'd been sitting next to Papa up on the roof, passing him the hammer, a chisel, nails, a wooden tile, when the sound of an engine – a sound I'd never heard before – made me turn. The sound got louder.

'Papa,' I shouted in terror.

Round the corner in the valley down below came something I'd never seen before – a car, black-bodied and shimmery, with glares and grids of silver.

I promptly slid off the roof and fell to the ground.

The car disappeared with a roar, and I was left with nothing but noisy, black and bendy silver flashes in my head and a very swollen ankle. It wasn't funny at the time.

The car in the picture Madame Tissot brought us was identical to the car that had passed through Hext the previous month. Every time we looked at the picture or retold the story, it became funnier.

As to the mess in Arete's grenier, my fingers itched to sort and rearrange it. Tidying, however, was the last thing on Daisy's mind.

She stepped across to a large, blue-painted trunk, lifted the lid and proceeded to pluck things out of it. Clothes and toys. But oh, what clothes and toys!

'Here. For you. It probably belonged to Mother or my aunt Margaret once.' Daisy passed me a dress made of purple velvet, soft and warm as a pig's underbelly and with a faint, familiar smell of sweat. 'Golly!' she said. 'A clown's costume! I'm having this.' She stepped into the legs of the costume and tugged it up over her skirt. It was far too big for her, but she shoved her arms down the sleeves and waved them around.

'Hextraordinary, 'ilarious, fantabulous,' she said.

I couldn't help laughing. Daisy was a fat ball of colours, stripes and checks. I started pulling the purple dress over my head. Even on top of my clothes, it was too big for me – as heavy as a coat and twice as long – but not enormous. It must have belonged to Daisy's aunt Margaret, I decided, rather than big-boned Beatrice.

'I wonder where the clown's hat is.' Daisy rummaged through the box. 'Ah, here we are.' Daisy put an odd-shaped yellow piece of material on her head. It had two little bells, one at each end, which jingled at the slightest movement. 'You look like a queen,' she said to me. 'Now all you need is a crown.' She plunged her hands back into the trunk. 'Ah. Even better.' She passed me a silvery band decorated with glittering jewels. 'A diamond tiara. Fake but fine. Good enough for any queen. Put it on, Mathilde.'

I hesitated, hung it on my wrist, ran my fingers over the surface.

Daisy snatched it back.

'On your head, dum-dum. It's your crown.' She removed my cap and placed the band on top of my head. 'Yes. That's good. Much better. Royalty aren't known for their looks, anyway. What we need now is a mirror. I bet there's a mirror here somewhere. Aha. Here we are. Help me pull it out.'

The heat was stifling, and we were both dripping by the time we'd manoeuvred the cracked mirror from behind the two trunks stacked on top of each other and leant it against a beam. We stood side by side and stared at our reflections.

'Queen Mathilde,' said Daisy.

'Clown Daisy,' I replied.

*

Daisy bounced into the kitchen again after lunch the next day.

'Would Queen Mathilde like to come swimming with me?' she asked.

We went to the Ladies' Pond, which was what the Valentines called the pool below the Cascade du Nezet.

'Gentlemen by invitation only,' said Daisy. 'Though Ted creeps off there at night sometimes. With friends. With drink. I know. Johnny told me. Ted gets drunk.' Daisy sounded thrilled and shocked.

If Ted had been my brother, or any of the men – young or old – from my valley, he would have been in the Auberge Dorée getting drunk three, four or more times a month. Ted was eighteen. It confused me that Daisy's brothers were still called boys. At fifteen, even carefree pretty Johnny, had he been one of us, would have been working on the farm or, more likely, like Benoît, up in the high pastures, keeping an eye on the cows and the goats, collecting their milk, turning it into butter and cheese.

At the Ladies' Pond, I watched in horror as Daisy stripped off her clothes – every single one of them – and dived into the water. I refused to do anything of the kind. Gradually, though, by cajoling, by making fun of my timidity, by inventing insults – 'You're a nincompoop, Mathilde. Every Tom, Dick and Harry under the sun likes swimming' – but above all by looking so delightful and delighted with herself, Daisy lured me into the water. Not in the buff, not then. Daisy didn't force that on me. I removed my shawl, apron, blouse, skirt and clogs, and made a neat pile of them next to Daisy's dress and scattered undergarments.

Daisy taught me to swim by chasing me from the shallows into the deep. I was stumbling on the underwater stones and laughing so hard that I didn't notice how close to the deep we were. Before I knew it, there were no stones underfoot.

For a second I panicked, like I did the time I nearly fell when Benoît and I climbed up to free two goats stuck on a ledge. We'd just managed to turn them round and slap them into shuffling back down the way they'd come when I slipped on the ledge myself. I spent a nasty few minutes clinging on only by my hands and the strength of my arms until Benoît was able to reach far enough over the ledge to haul me back up.

'Why didn't you use your feet?' he asked later.

'What for?'

I'd looked down, once, from my hanging position, and when I did, I saw my bare feet dangling like hams above an expanse of jagged rock. My clogs had long since gone clattering down. I didn't want to think about my feet, let alone the rest of me, following them.

'There isn't always a foothold, of course,' said Benoît. 'But you have to assume there might be, and there often is. You'd be surprised. Don't trust your eyes. Not by themselves.'

I knew what he meant. You can't be sure of anything just from what it looks like. Avalanches had taught us that. The mood of a mountain can change in minutes.

'You have to feel the mountain against your body, like another body,' said Benoît. 'That's what my papa says. Any body. Man, woman, child. Beast, bird, fish. If your clogs hadn't fallen, you should have kicked them off. You should have used your toes to explore every inch of the rock face. Slowly and carefully.'

'I was too scared,' I said.

'Well then, you should at least have kicked your feet – any old how, any old where – against the rock. You might have found a tiny jut you could have used.'

So that's what I did in the water. I kicked, and it worked. I didn't sink.

'Flap your arms,' said Daisy.

I flapped.

'You're swimming,' she shouted. 'Keep going. I'll join you.'

She slipped into the deep, like a peeled leek into a pan of water. No splash at all.

I made a lot of splash at first, but I soon learnt to move more calmly, and when Daisy turned onto her back and floated – with just her face, the tips of her little titties and a waft of dark hair at the top of her legs above the surface of the water – I did too.

As a result of her success in tempting me to swim, and before the week was out, Daisy had me joining her for a steaming hot bath in the famous bath house. And washing myelf in Sir A's great bathtub soon became something I looked forward to, with or without Daisy, and even when I had to share the tub with Sylvie or another ugly. I wallowed in the warm, deep water and enjoyed the clean, tight feeling on my skin afterwards from washing with a bar of the Valentines' red Sunlight soap.

*

I'd been at Arete for just over a week when Costa came up to the house to tune the piano in the games room. I listened to him while I swept the corridor, the hall and the sitting room, which was separated from the games room only by folding doors. When he'd finished tuning, Costa played a few of the sing-song pieces Benoît and I had heard him play on his fiddle while we sat in the sun outside his workshop. Costa ate lunch with us uglies in the kitchen and he was still there when Daisy danced in, insisting I accompany her on a flower-picking trip. Costa asked Daisy the question I was asking myself: why?

'We're best friends, Mathilde and I,' she replied. 'Aren't we? And it'll be fun, picking flowers. I'm going to put them in Grandpa's flower press afterwards. He said I could.'

We walked as far as the petit Luet, scrambled up and along a few feet, and then through a narrow gap which led to a wet and stony goat track but eventually came out onto a stretch of green, spotted with colour. The flowers from the spring were almost over, but there were summer ones just beginning and Daisy was ecstatic. She'd forgotten to bring anything to put the flowers in, so I removed my apron and folded and knotted it, turning it into a bag. I made the ties into handles.

When we got back to Arete, Daisy said, 'Right. Flower press. In the library, Grandpa said.'

The library was a small room off the hall, opposite the sitting room. Sir A had a kneehole desk in there, two chairs, one for writing and one for reading, a globe, a small table with a carriage clock, a glass, a jug and a decanter on it, and books. There were books everywhere – on the shelves, which lined three of the four walls (the fourth had a window in it, looking out, like the sitting room, to the front), but also on the desk, on the arm of the reading chair and on the floor.

I couldn't have read all those books even if I'd had the time. Most were on subjects and in sentences that were beyond me, written by men with short, stern names: Smith, Hume, Locke, Mill. But I peeped at *The Playground of Europe*, *A Tramp Abroad* and *Scrambles Amongst the Alps,* because I liked the titles. I pondered lines of poetry by Wordsworth, Coleridge and Tennyson because I liked the polysyllabic names of the poets. And I delved delightedly into the definitions, in Sir A's dictionaries and reference books, of English words and phrases, idioms and expressions I was learning by the baker's dozen.

One of the first Arete tasks to become my sole responsibility was cleaning Sir A's library. I enjoyed the work and did it methodically and not fast, because I liked everything about that room – the objects in it, the way the light fell on its woody surfaces, the lingering smell of leather, damp wool and Sir A's pipe smoke.

Sir A was very particular about how his library was cleaned. The main thing was to make sure everything was thoroughly dusted yet leave Sir A's papers in the same order and his books open or markered at the same page. Woe betide anyone who was clumsy enough to pick up a book and let the marker fall out. This could happen very easily, for Sir A didn't always use proper bookmarks. He had a supply of them in a pile on one corner of the desk, but he chose, often, to use a folded sheet of writing paper, a page torn from a notebook or a column clipped from an *anglais* newspaper. Sometimes, not even that – I'd come across a train ticket, a bootlace, a strand of wool, old leaves, bits of bark, even a shred of snakeskin. I decided that it would pay off to flip quickly through all the books that weren't on the shelves and memorise the page numbers where there were markers before starting to clean. Accidents can happen, even to the most careful duster.

The flower press, Daisy said, was in one of the drawers of the desk. Some were locked, but most of them opened smoothly.

It hadn't crossed my mind, while cleaning, to look in these. Having discovered how untidy the *rosbifs* could be, I preferred not to see the evidence, if I could help it. Sir A's desk drawers weren't too bad, but they were very full: pens, inks, spectacles, coins, bills, receipts, blank pieces of writing paper, sealing wax, unused notebooks, Charlotte's lithographs, a few photographs, some legal-looking documents, a monogrammed snuffbox, scissors, pipe cleaners, tobacco. And at the very bottom of the bottom drawer, buried beneath two copies of the *Alpine Journal*, the flower press.

I'd never seen such a thing before and was fascinated as Daisy unscrewed the nuts and bolts, loosening the five hexagonal pieces of wood they held together. Between each piece were several layers of discoloured tissue paper. Daisy peeled these apart to reveal the flattened corpses of a gentian, two edelweiss and several forget-me-nots.

'I wonder who put them here,' she said. 'They're pretty, but very faded. How old would you say they are?'

I had no idea. I couldn't think why anyone would pick flowers and press them like this. I watched as Daisy removed them – 'I'll ask Grandpa,' she said – and placed the new ones between the sheets of tissue paper. She slid the paper back between the pieces of wood and screwed the whole thing tight again.

Daisy produced the old pressed flowers at supper.

I hovered, serving the soup deliberately slowly.

'Let me see.' Sir A put on his reading specs and examined the flowers. 'Not mine.' He placed them on a side plate and passed them to Lady C. 'Yours?'

She looked at them and shook her head.

'Well, they must have been somebody's once, surely?' said Daisy.

Stephen feigned a lack of interest, Ted asked to have a look, but pretty Johnny grabbed the plate first. Opinions were voiced. Loudly, as usual.

I'd already been hovering too long so I turned to go, but as I turned I'm sure I heard Beatrice whisper to Lady C, 'They were Margaret's, weren't they, Marmee?'

Lady C didn't bat an eyelid, merely pointed to the butter dish, and I suddenly realised how rarely I heard Lady C speak at Arete. I remembered the shrieky tone to her voice in the scene I'd overheard seven years ago at Arete, between her and Daisy's aunt Margaret. I asked Daisy later if she knew what had happened to Margaret Valentine.

'No one will talk about her,' Daisy said. '*Persona non grata*. End of story. Yawningly boring. I think she must have gone with Scott to Antarctica.'

*

The weather remained clement, and towards the end of June a calm and easy routine settled upon Arete. I was kept busy, but my chores were neither too onerous nor too tedious, once I'd got used to the customs of Arete and the quirks of *les anglais* therein. Lady C, for example, was frequently incommunicado, which meant she'd retired to her painting studio and we had to tiptoe in with her meals on trays. Sometimes she was incommunicado for two or three days at a stretch.

The Valentines had a plethora of guests, all of whom seemed as enchanted as Sir A by the place. 'What a magnificent view!' If I heard that once, I heard it ten times, spoken by *rosbifs* agog on Arete's terrace. There were arrivals and departures. Parties, picnics, paideia. Dances, cricket matches, croquet and quoits. Daisy's old uncles – darling widowed Edmond and poor, unmarried Harold – settled in for a long stay. They amused themselves with childish pursuits such as trying to dam the stream or playing endless games of backgammon. And there was Daisy, who continued to occupy what little spare time I had, but whose company I couldn't deny I enjoyed.

'We're best friends, Mathilde and I,' she said when Beatrice queried the amount of time we spent together. 'Bosom friends, actually.' She pointed to the title of the book she was reading. 'That's us.'

The book was by Angela Brazil and Daisy had several. They were all stories set in a school, she said. *The Nicest Girl in the School*, *The New Girl at St Chad's*, *The Youngest Girl in the Fifth*. And they were all about girls.

'That's why I like them,' she said.

I tried one called *The Fortunes of Philippa,* but I couldn't picture Philippa, let alone follow her fortunes. Daisy said I probably wasn't ready for the dazzle of Brazil, the daring of darling Angela. She lent me other books by different lady authors – *Little Women*, *What Katy Did* and *Anne of Green Gables* – but we discovered I wasn't ready for them either; Daisy had to explain the stories and the girls. She knew the books more or less by heart, she said. Sometimes she acted out whole scenes, reciting the characters' lines most dramatically. This I enjoyed, even though I still couldn't make much sense of the stories in those storybooks.

Four days before her much-anticipated fourteenth birthday (four days also before the much-anticipated end of her hundred-day whooping cough), on the very day her father was due at Arete, Daisy said she wanted to explore the dressing-up box again. I agreed. It was an easy day for us uglies. Sir A had announced an Open Session at the Ladies' Pond ('ladies and gentlemen to remain appropriately attired at all times, including in the water'), so he and Lady C, with a group of friends, plus Edmond and Harold, were picnicking at the pool and hoping to net butterflies in the meadows nearby. Beatrice and all three of Daisy's brothers had walked down to Hext to greet Beatrice's husband, 'Daddy', due to arrive on the 4.30 *petit train* from Geneva. They'd left straight after elevenses and planned to have a late lunch at the Auberge Dorée. Daisy was thrilled that Daddy would be at Arete in time for her big day. She said he was a very important man, a banker in London, and couldn't take holidays at the drop of a hat. I'd overheard Sir A complaining to Lady C about his son-in-law. 'I simply don't like the cut of his jib. There's nothing wrong with him, but I detect gilt-edged ambition – greed. And he's a dreadful bore, Beatrice's banker husband.'

I didn't mention this to Daisy.

So there we were after lunch, Daisy and I, up in the hot grenier again, trying on costumes, parading up and down in front of each other and the mirror, giggling. There was a slight breeze and, with the window wide open, fresh air was sucked towards the big, square hole in the floorboards where the ladder went down to the landing. This kept the place a blessed bit cooler. Only the nightly drop in mountain temperatures made it possible for anyone to sleep in the grenier. Even with the breeze it was uncomfortably hot up there during the day, and I didn't take much persuading to strip to my underwear.

Daisy wrapped me from top to toe, diagonally, in a length of shimmering turquoise.

'It's a silk sari,' she said.

The smoothness of the material and the movement of the wrapping were like lapping water. While she was wrapping, Daisy told me that when she was a little girl, her mother called her Silky because her hair was so shiny and soft. I told her I used to be called Broomhead.

'No more Broomhead, please, Mathilde' said Daisy. 'You're an Indian temptress, a luscious memsahib now.'

She persuaded me to step out of my clogs and into a pair of ladies' pointy shoes, far too big. She herself wore enormous brown boots, plus fours and a man's white shirt. She tucked her hair into a peaked cap.

'We're lacking a jacket,' she said. 'Those are all wrong.' Gesturing. 'I know. Grandpa's reading jacket. In the library. Perfect.'

We both went downstairs, I (unwound from my sari and back in my work clothes and clogs) to the thunderbox, she to the library. I expected to meet her in the hall on the way back, but she was still in the library. She was standing next to Sir A's desk with his pipe in her mouth, both hands raised, trying to light it. She set the pipe and matches down on the desk when she saw me.

'I've often asked myself what it's like,' she laughed. 'But never mind. Another time.'

Sir A's tweed reading jacket hung on the back of his desk chair. Daisy put it on. She folded back the cuffs of the sleeves, popped the unlit pipe into her mouth and strutted from one end of the library to the other.

'What do you think? Do I pass muster, my dearest?' Daisy put her hands in the pockets of the jacket, imitating Sir A in manner as well as voice. 'Oh! What have we here?' She lifted a small object from the left-hand pocket, held it up.

I stepped into the room and looked at the key between Daisy's fingers. I'd never seen it before.

'I wonder,' said Daisy. 'Is this the key Grandpa used to tell me about?'

I looked more closely at it.

'It might well be,' Daisy went on. 'When I was young enough to find it amusing, Grandpa would let me play with all the keys on his keyring. My favourite was the shiny flat one to the front door of the house in Seymour Street. Grandpa told me it came from America and was made by a man called Linus Yale Junior. Funny name! Ones like it, he said, were used to unlock the doors in New York's new skyscrapers.'

'Skyscrapers?' I asked, but Daisy was too curious about the little key in her hand to stop talking.

'Grandpa said his favourite was the simple old-fashioned key to his desk drawers at Arete. He said he kept it separately, in his reading jacket pocket. So let's see if this is it, shall we?'

The key did indeed unlock the four locked desk drawers.

'Lo and behold!' Daisy exclaimed.

There seemed to be hundreds of handwritten notes, on scraps of paper, in the first drawer we opened, but the scraps were folded between bigger bits of paper, each neatly labelled. The next drawer revealed bundles of letters tied carefully with string or black ribbon. One drawer held dozens of notebooks, stacked in piles of five. In another were Sir A's private diaries.

Daisy took several of these out.

'What a stink,' she said, putting a volume to her nose and passing another to me. 'Old leather – dead skin.'

The handwriting in the diaries flowed and was neat, but it was sometimes difficult to decipher because there were a lot of crossings-out. I tried to concentrate, but Daisy kept pointing to words and oo-ing.

'Rude,' she said. 'Look. Sir A was writing dirty, disgusting things.'

We swapped diaries; I read a few of the dirty, disgusting things Daisy indicated and I wondered if this was what the villagers meant when they said English was a dirty language. The *rosbifs* certainly seemed to have a love of our land so overwhelming that some of them – the writing men – could only express it in language that was base, bestial, lustful and violent. I'd read, if not myriads, a number of *anglais* ways of describing our land in the poems and histories and travelogues in Sir A's library, and, although I knew most of their meaning had passed me by, I'd definitely understood snippets; I'd discovered that Benoît and I weren't the first to compare the alps to living things with fingers and thumbs, titties and bums, feelings, thoughts and magical powers. And I'd noted that a long time ago – long before Sir A's time – the *anglais* rudely designated our mountains 'barren deformities', 'monstrous excrescences'. One of our peaks was 'the devil's arse'. And they called our hillsides and valleys 'nature's pudenda'. I tried to explain some of this to Daisy, but she kept collapsing with laughter and repeating individual words and phrases nonsensically.

'*A fat courtesan in a dirty pleated frock, with ermine trim.* That's how he describes Mont Blanc in the spring melt,' said Daisy. Which, when Daisy explained, made me laugh too. I decided the rude things in Sir A's diaries were Sir A following a well-trod *anglais* way, then letting himself stray, just a little bit. Exploring. That's how I saw it.

Besides, most of the writing wasn't rude. Most of the early entries simply detailed Sir A's days spent discovering the wondrous valley of Hext and its stupendous surrounding hills and mountains. With Xavier. Later entries spoke about introducing the wondrous valley of Hext and its stupendous surrounding hills and mountains to all comers, 'first and foremost, my dearest Charlotte,' Sir A had written. That was in 1862. By 1863, Charlotte was his wife, Arete was under construction and, in 1864, Edmond was born.

Time sped, that afternoon. So much so that when there was a knock on the library door, I understood entirely the English expression 'to jump out of one's skin'. (How much of Sir A's writing either of us entirely understood is another matter.)

Daisy gasped and put a fist in her mouth.

'Oh golly! I shouldn't have.' There was more terror on Daisy's face than on my sisters', when Papa raised his stick. 'What are we going to do, Mathilde?'

Pretending to be braver than I felt, I stood up and walked to the door.

'Who is it?' I said.

No answer. I opened the door an inch.

'Sylvie!'

Only Sylvie. Only Sylvie come to tell me she needed me in the kitchen, it was long past five, we'd supper for eighteen people to prepare and why wasn't I there?

I said I was sorry. I said I'd be along in a few minutes. I shut the door and turned to Daisy.

'What are we going to do, Mathilde?' Daisy repeated. Her cheeks were red, her hair dishevelled. 'Heaven help us if Grandpa catches us.'

'We'll just put everything back and forget all about it,' I said. 'I think that's best.'

'But we haven't time. It's ten to six already. Mother said they wouldn't be later than half past. It'll take ages to put all this back how it was.'

I looked at Sir A's carriage clock, then at the mess of paper and notebooks around us and then at dizzy Daisy, still sitting on the floor.

'I have time,' I said. 'You go. Splash your face with water. Brush your hair and change your clothes. Then read a book, practise the piano. I don't know. Wait for the others to return. I'll tidy up here. No one will be any the wiser. I promise.'

'Are you sure? I could help?'

'No.' Daisy would only slow things down. 'Go on, Daisy. You go. I'll be finished in here in no time.'

When Daisy had gone, I began to put everything back in the drawers as accurately as I could remember – and that would have been quite accurately, knowing me. As I did so, I couldn't help slowing and marvelling at the thousands of words – all, bar the letters, in Sir A's handwriting. The letters were from his friends, fellow alpinists – climbers, walkers, explorers, mountain-lovers all of them.

I was systematic. I retied the letters in bundles. I locked each drawer when I'd filled it.

Before sliding the last of Sir A's old, brown, calfskin-covered diaries into the drawer (and I remembered it as having been on top because it had a big smudge of ink on the front, and what looked like candle wax and grass stains on the back), I put it to my nose and, along with the leather, I could smell Sir A's pipe smoke. I wouldn't have called it a stink.

A shadow flashed across the window. Someone on the terrace. No time to lose. But I dropped the diary and, as I picked it up, a small piece of paper fell out. The letter (for it was a letter) landed on Sir A's desk. Footsteps in the hall. I needed to be quick. Into the drawer went the diary. The sound of the latch being lifted. I locked the drawer and, just as the library door opened, I managed to slip the key and sweep the letter into my apron pocket.

'Mathilde?' said Sir A, 'I wasn't expecting to find you here. Don't you clean the library in the morning, as a rule?'

'I do, sir,' I said, scuttling past Sir A, towards the hall. 'But we were baking all morning today. In preparation for Daisy's birthday.'

I was surprised by how easily this lie came to me. Less surprised when I lied to Sylvie later to explain how a few minutes had become more than half an hour – I told her my monthlies had arrived and I'd had to return to our sleeping quarters for a napkin and clean underwear.

While we were preparing supper, I felt the crackle of the letter in my apron pocket, and when Sylvie went to lay the table in the dining room and the other uglies were fetching the evening milk, I took the letter out and read it. The letter was in English, very old – the date at the top of it July 1872, and the writing wobblier than in Sir A's diaries and notebooks. It seemed to be the rough draft of a love letter from Sir A to Lady C. 'My darling Charlotte,' it began. Then a few sentences, soppy and sentimental. 'My pearl . . . our nest . . . light of my life . . . so many joyful years together.' It finished with a thick, dark cross, which was, I knew, the *anglais* sign for *bisou* – a kiss. Daisy said you could put as many kisses as you liked at the end of a letter, but too many would be vulgar.

I returned the letter to the drawer, to the diary, during supper, but there was no tweed jacket hanging on the back of Sir A's desk chair, so the key went into my apron pocket again.

Daisy cornered me after coffee and liqueurs had been served in the sitting room. I was able to report that all had gone well.

'Except that I still have the key.'

'Give it to me,' she said, anxiety making her frown. 'I'll put it back.'

I passed her the key and said once she'd done that neither of us needed to worry. I told her to forget the whole thing. I certainly intended to.

And I did, I did, for more than sixty years.

I did, until 1976.

Three

1976. The hottest summer on record. The year the tarmac melted, railway lines buckled and the tennis balls at Wimbledon burst. Pubs ran out of beer, there were standpipes in the streets and people sleeping in their gardens, washing-up water in the toilets, forests ablaze, a plague of ladybirds and George's ma and da killed in a head-on collision with a lorry on the A303, half a mile east of the Podimore roundabout in Somerset.

George missed it all: the fatal collision, because he stayed at home to revise for his A levels, and the heatwave because rather than spend the next few months with a retired accountant in Penzance – his father's bachelor uncle and George's only living relative in the country – he accepted Inez's offer. 'Come to Arete, George. Come. For the whole summer.'

Inez was his mother's sister. There had been a falling-out four years ago, and the sisters hadn't spoken since. But Inez turned up at the funeral, all jangly earrings and bracelets, Jesus sandals, red flowing skirt and a creamy, see-through blouse with so many buttons undone that it didn't need to be see-through to see that she was braless. George tried not to stare while Inez banged on about bygones being bygones, burying the hatchet, black sheep and bugger it, family's family at the end of the day. She urged George to book tickets, pack a bag and join them all as soon as possible at Arete: our mountain retreat, darling – it'll do you the world of good.

Arete. It wasn't George's first visit. He'd been there in 1972, at the falling-out.

He also remembered – mostly because of the World Cup – a holiday in 1966 when he was eight. Da had helped rig up the old radiogram and they'd all listened to the match. The thrilling end, which George only half heard because his cousin Jack was running around yelling, 'Twenty seconds, twenty seconds!' Crowds on the pitch afterwards, and the England players going down on the turf, hugging each other. And all the youngsters, including George, dropping to the ground and rolling around together like wrestlers. The hard bristles of Jack's crew-cut hair and the surprising softness of the pine needles. The grown-ups had drunk too much génépi and forgotten about bedtime. George recalled the sudden coming of night as the sun slipped behind la Concierge, the small, pear-shaped mountain at the entrance to the valley, and he and his cousins playing hide-and-seek in the woods behind the house. George had been too frightened to say he was frightened and would have preferred to go indoors.

They were at Arete in 1960 as well, but George was only two then. A photograph taken on 8th July, his grandmother Daisy's sixtieth birthday, showed them all. Great-grandma Beatrice was still alive, and so was one of her brothers, the gaga one. Edmond? George couldn't remember. They were both in the middle of the photo, tucked with tartan rugs into old wooden bath chairs. Daisy stood behind Beatrice. She had one hand on Beatrice's shoulder and was waving a straw sun hat with the other hand at the photographer – who was the photographer? George couldn't remember that either – and grinning like mad. Daisy was always grinning like mad. The rest of the family stood around in clumps, slumped in deckchairs or sitting too upright on stools, dining chairs, the stepladder from the library, the bench from the hall. Ma's older brothers, fat Uncle Rory and Uncle Josh, the artist, plus four young children and a baby, were squeezed together on the sawn-off trunk of a pine tree. In front of them, on the lawn, a young Inez knelt between her husband, Bob, and their four-year-old son, cousin Jack, who was holding an alpenstock and wore nothing but swimming trunks. Children of all ages were milling around, most of them apparently unaware of the camera. But there, super aware, were George's ma and da to the far right, Da slightly behind Ma, both looking as straight-laced in the photograph as they had in life. Da was frowning. George himself stood between them, clutching Da's white flannel trouser leg. If he remembered anything at all of the occasion, it was the feel of that flannel, cool and smooth against his cheek. And cheese. 'Say cheese.' The word repeated and elongated to meaninglessness in silly, sing-song voices. It echoed around the mountains, and the family added, one after the other, 'Tomme, Reblochon, Abondance. Persillé des Aravis. Chèvre, Cheddar, Stilton . . .' Until the words were drowned by laughter.

The framed photograph was in George's suitcase. He planned to give it to Inez. There wasn't anything else from his parents' possessions he thought she'd want. He wasn't even sure she'd want the photograph, but he didn't want it and giving it to Inez, he thought, was the right sort of gesture. He wanted Inez to warm to him because he was planning to ask her about the row with Ma four years ago. Ma had always refused to explain, saying he was too young to understand, and George thought he'd try to get to the bottom of it, if the opportunity arose, over the summer.

George was expecting Inez to pick him up at the station. But no, there was his cousin, Jack, waving at him from a battered old soft-top, light-blue, left-hand-drive 2CV. George waved back and struggled with his suitcase across the station forecourt to the car.

'Fling it in the boot,' said Jack. 'And jump in.'

George lifted the boot lid and wedged his suitcase between a pair of walking boots with socks stuffed into them, several empty wine bottles, a wooden box of strawberries and a basket of brown-speckled eggs with muck and a few feathers still clinging to them. He took off his jacket and placed it on top of the eggs.

It was baking hot and George was grateful for the opened Orangina bottle Jack passed to him as he folded himself into the passenger seat. Jack wore cut-off jeans and a grandad vest and was barefoot. George, damp and dirty, envied his cool cousin: Jack was lazy, brainy, good-looking, athletic, sophisticated; educated at international schools around the world because of his father Bob's high-powered job with the UN, he was now doing American Studies at East Anglia. Da said that this was a non-subject at a second-rate university. But Da, who had taught maths at Reading, had a chip on his shoulder about such matters. Reading wasn't exactly a top university either, was it? And Da had been passed over for promotion more times than George could remember. The chip on Da's shoulder was due to the fact that he came from a small family in the north of England – I'm basically a bit non-U, he used to say – and, for only-child George, this was another reason he, like Da, easily felt like an outsider among the vast sprawl of posher cousins on Ma's side of the family.

'Drink. It'll help,' said Jack, revving the tinny engine and reverse-turning the car with a jolt. 'Sorry about your parents.' Jack sounded awkward.

'Don't mention it,' said George, realising, as he put the bottle to his lips, that he himself had sounded odd – abrupt, peremptory, upset probably.

'And sorry we can't have the roof down.' Jack quickly hid any tension. 'It's bust.'

George took a swig from the bottle and nearly choked.

'Steady on, old chap,' Jack laughed. 'Martini and orange not your cup o' tea?'

'Martini?'

'Sweet, white and yummy,' nodded Jack. 'Vermouth. We found a whole stash of it in the mazot. Must have been left over from last summer. There's water, though, if you prefer.'

'No, this is fine. Great, actually. Thanks.' George sipped more carefully. The fizz had gone out of the Orangina, the shingly glass bottle was warm and sticky, and the vermouth left a dentisty aftertaste. Nevertheless, George continued to drink, as

Jack manoeuvred the car through the narrow streets of the village.

It was market day in Hext. The village square was packed with people. There were cloths spread on the ground, piled high with earthy vegetables, fat tomatoes and glowing strawberries; stalls selling cheap household hardware; tables where farmers had stacked their cheeses, alongside hams, eggs, sausages, herbs and honey.

'Why are we stopping?' asked George, as they double-parked next to the *mairie*.

'We're to pick up old Mathilde.' Jack switched off the engine. 'What do you drive?'

'Nothing,' said George. 'I don't . . . I haven't . . . I was going to start lessons with Da this summer. But—'

'Oh Lord. Sorry.'

'That's okay.' George didn't mind people mentioning his parents' death. Other people's embarrassment seemed greater than his own, and it was definitely embarrassment he felt, not grief, not really, not yet. He'd been given a leaflet by his form teacher that said grief happened in stages, and numbness was one of them. George wondered whether embarrassment counted as numbness.

'Here she comes. As ugly as ever, poor thing.' Jack honked the horn and waved an arm out of the side window. 'And bloody cantankerous these days, too.'

Mathilde was descending, one at a time, the wide stone steps of the *mairie*. Her stubby body looked older than George remembered, the hunch of her back more pronounced. She was hatless, but wrapped in several shawls as if it were the middle of winter.

'What's she been doing in there?'

'Asking questions, registering objections, being a busybody,' said Jack. 'I'm not entirely sure. There's an election here at the end of August. New municipal council, new mayor. You know, big deal in places like this.'

'Is it?'

'Yep,' said Jack. 'It's *une année exceptionelle*. There were mass resignations in the spring, apparently. The mayor and his deputy. Brothers – some sort of land dispute. Very big deal for Mathilde. Luc's standing for election and she won't support him. Her own son. They're not even on speaking terms.'

'Blimey.'

'Yep. That's why we're picking her up. No more lifts in Luc's Land Rover, for any of us, I'm afraid.'

Luc's Land Rover used to belong to Arete. Ma said Inez had driven it all the way from England one summer in the early 1960s, crammed with family and friends.

'Including children,' said Ma. 'Terribly dangerous. Why on earth, I've no idea. Just Inez being Inez, I expect.'

But nobody had ever bothered to drive it back. So it stayed. And Luc, who had a passion for cars, was allowed to drive it and then to keep it and gradually, eventually, effectively, it became his. George had vivid memories of jolting along, squeezed between his cousins, earwigging their World Cup tattle, in the back of the Land Rover: its two long metal seats, facing each other sideways on, always either too hot or too cold on the bare skin of his thighs; the stained, grey-green canvas overhead, smelling of grass and rain; and the view out of the back – no door, no window, just an open view of the road or track, jumping and lurching like one of Da's bad cine films.

As Mathilde drew closer, George saw that her face was older too, the skin thin and soft, with patches of scalp showing beneath tufts and straggles of hair.

'I'll get in the back.' George put his hand on the door handle.

'George!' Mathilde raised her arms in welcome as George stepped out of the car. 'Jack said he was fetching you. But I don't trust that boy. I thought he might be teasing. Now here you are.' She hugged George and kissed him on both cheeks, held him away from her and shook her head. 'Drink, George. I smell it. I'm sorry for your sorrows. I am. I am. But please – don't drown them.' Then she hugged and kissed him again.

George, who was still holding the Orangina bottle in one hand, could see Jack, in the driver's seat, laughing at his discomfort.

On the untarmacked road between Hext and Hext-en-Haut, they didn't talk. They couldn't, because Jack's 2CV made such a noise and Jack, taking the hairpin bends at speed, wasn't fully in control of it, in George's opinion.

'Bloody exhaust, again,' Jack shouted above the clunking. 'Not ideal terrain for my poor, froggy little car.'

At Hext-en-Haut, they all got out. Jack inspected the exhaust.

'I've seen worse,' he said. 'Wonder whether the eggs survived, though.'

He opened the boot and passed George his jacket.

'Pretty idiotic to come with a suitcase, Georgio, if you don't mind my saying so. Why didn't you bring a knapsack? And look at your shoes.'

George looked down at his wrinkled desert boots.

'I know. Idiotic of me. I meant to buy a knapsack in Geneva and switch. And some walking gear. But there wasn't time.' George didn't say that he'd underestimated how long it would take to get from Geneva's main terminus to the small Gare des Eaux Vives in order to catch *le petit train* up the valley. Nor did he say that he'd actually been far too anxious about the whole journey to consider a shopping spree in Geneva. Jack was only two years older than George, but he often made George feel ridiculously young and pathetic.

'Well, we'll lug it,' said Jack. 'But we've got this other clobber as well—'

'I'll help,' Mathilde interrupted. 'However, you must both drink water before the ascent. I think George is not the only one who has had a nip of alcohol, is he?'

'Two beers at the Auberge Dorée while I was waiting for Georgy's train. That's all. Scout's honour.'

'Scout's stuff and nonsense,' said Mathilde. 'But never mind. Now, I saw a large, full bottle of water on the floor in the back of your car, Jack. Fetch it.'

Jack did as he was told, drank from the bottle and passed it to George, who gulped the water with relief, even though it was stale and tepid. Jack put on his socks and walking boots. George tied the arms of his jacket around his waist.

Mathilde, meanwhile, had removed two of her shawls. She knotted them in large loops to the handle of George's suitcase.

'I'll take the eggs – none broken, by the way. And the strawberries – mushy, but fine,' she said. 'You two carry the suitcase between you. Pull the loops taut. Take one each. Keep them taut. You'll see. It'll be easy.'

It wasn't easy, but it worked. Mathilde set the pace, slow and steady, with regular stops. George could see that although one of her legs was clearly giving her trouble, she'd not lost her stamina. He was ashamed at how quickly he himself tired. By the time they reached Arete, he was pouring with sweat and breathing heavily. Jack, on the other hand, was bouncing with energy.

'Lunch,' he said. 'That's what we need.'

'Leave lunch to me,' said Mathilde. 'Take George's case upstairs. Show him his room.'

George had never before slept in the bedroom Jack led him to. The youngsters at Arete usually shared the attic or one of the cabins behind the house. Sometimes, when the place was really full, they erected tents. This bedroom had two single beds in it, but only one of them was made up.

'Just me in here?'

'Yes,' said Jack. 'I'm next door. And the three girls are in the attic. For the time being, it's only my kid sisters, Polly and Tess – the twins, that is – plus our young cousin Isobel.'

'Why not the rest of Uncle Josh's lot?' asked George. He knew that Uncle Rory was a big-shot lawyer in LA these days, so he wasn't expecting him or any of his family to be at Arete, but flaky painter Uncle Josh and co. usually came over from Dublin.

'Dunno. Something about spending the summer with Josh's latest arty-farty boho family on the west coast of Ireland. Isobel didn't want to go, doesn't like her new stepmother, so the poor kid got sent to us.'

'Where are they at the moment, Polly, Tess and Isobel?' asked George.

'The twins wanted to see the reservoir and how empty it already is because of the weather. It's a three-hour walk.'

'Blimey.'

'Yep, quite a hike. Isobel made a fuss at first. But Thomas is around. You know – Mathilde's grandson, the guide.'

George nodded.

'So I got him to take them. That cheered Isobel up. They'll be back this evening.'

'What about Inez?'

'Inez?' Jack looked surprised. 'Didn't you get her telegram? She's had to hop over to Megève again. Another Grandma Daisy crisis.'

'Oh. No, I didn't. Not – ?'

'Yep. 'Fraid so. Pills this time. Inez says Daisy'll find a way sooner or later. She's a sneaky old bird. Been hoarding the pills for weeks, it turns out. Hiding them under the rim of the lav. They found her slumped, half-dead, on the floor of the bathroom two days ago.'

'God. How horrible. When do you think Inez will be back?'

'No idea,' said Jack cheerfully. 'Depends on doolally Daisy, doesn't it? And meanwhile, Georgy-porgy, I'm in charge.'

'And just Mathilde?'

'No other servants, d'you mean? Slaves, maids, skivvies, uglies? Nope. Just Mathilde. And she's not what she was. Bad hip or something. No being waited on hand and foot, this year, I'm afraid.'

After lunch, which Mathilde served out on the terrace, George returned to his bedroom via the external stairs and the balcony and unpacked his suitcase, leaving the photograph for Inez at the bottom, and pushed it under the bed. Then he lay down. He knew he must be exhausted: midday train, yesterday, from Reading to Paddington, boat train from Victoria to Paris, sleeper train from Paris to Geneva, little train from Geneva to Hext, and all the tricky bits in between, not to mention the hot climb to Arete from Hext-en-Haut. Nevertheless, he was surprised to find his eyes somewhat watery and an immense feeling of loneliness threatening to engulf him. Jack's condolences had been so clumsy, he thought. So stupidly English. George put this supersensitivity on his part down to Inez's absence. He supposed he'd been counting on her to welcome him, to swoop him magically into the bosom of the family, into an unproblematic Arete, to make everything somehow all right. He wished she hadn't had to go to Megève.

George knew about Daisy's doolallyness, of course. He'd even witnessed her doolally behaviour when they were at Arete in 1966: the increasingly strange turns any conversation with her took, her tendency to wander off, especially at night, into the woods or up the mountain dressed in an old party frock or just her underwear. The family tolerated what were still termed 'Daisy's eccentricities', despite decades of treatment, until she started to harm herself. It began with knives, apparently, stolen from the kitchen drawer and elsewhere. Then there were several incidents, Ma said, when Daisy tried to, or pretended to, drown herself in the Ladies' Pond. And finally, one day, she threw herself down a ravine. She broke a leg and both arms and was only rescued because a team of army recruits happened to be training nearby. Two of them managed to clamber down with ropes, and she was hauled up. The team carried her all the way to the village. From there, she was driven to a hospital, which saw to her broken limbs, but nothing, it seemed, could be done for her mind. That's when she went to the private clinic in Megève, and stayed there. It wasn't too bad, Ma said. She'd visited a few times, first with Inez, later with Rory and Josh. It used to be a sanatorium for people with TB. Quite luxurious, really. George tried and failed to imagine the loony bin in the mountains for the rich and mad of Europe.

He let himself drift off, still feeling the thrum and rattle of train wheels in his bones. He must have slept quite deeply in the end, for when he awoke he was disorientated. He realised he wasn't at home – he hadn't slept at home since the night before the car crash – but he thought he was in his friend Graham's bedroom; Graham's parents had insisted he stay with them, even though they were a family of five in a small, three-bedroomed terraced house with the bathroom downstairs. They'd been incredibly nice. And although he'd never have told anyone this, a small part of George had enjoyed his time there. He'd certainly slept amazingly well in the nylon sheets on the Z-bed they had to flip open every night next to Graham's bed, and flip shut the following morning because the room was so small. If it hadn't been for Graham, whom he'd known since day one at Reading Grammar when they'd palled-up over both of them having the wrong games' kit, he wasn't sure he'd have made it to his last two exams. They'd had big plans, he and Graham, about going to London for the day, to the King's Road, when the exams were over. George had been saving up his clothes allowance. But the accident had put paid to that, obviously.

George came to his senses when he heard girls' voices and laughter and the sound of water being splashed. He went out onto the balcony and saw the twins and Isobel sitting in a rubber dinghy on the Round Pond. Jack was standing thigh-deep in the water with his hands on the stern of the boat, rocking it violently from side to side, which was what was causing the girls to squeal and beg for more.

George went downstairs and into the kitchen, where he found Thomas helping himself to a large slice of strawberry tart. Mathilde stood at the sink, peeling potatoes.

'Hello, George,' said Thomas. 'Good to see you. Will you have some? My grandmother's tarts are, without question, the best in the region.'

'I would have made two,' said Mathilde, turning round and smiling at Thomas. She put the potatoes in a pan of water and moved the pan to the stove. 'But most of the strawberries weren't good for anything except jam. Leave enough tart for supper. There will be cream as well, then. In fact, I must fetch it.' She went out of the back door.

'I'd love a piece,' said George. 'Thank you. How are you, Thomas?'

Thomas, George worked out, must be twenty-one now – a year older than Jack and three years older than George. He had the physique and the temperament of many mountain guides: he was only of average height and his build was slight, but there was a confidence and vitality in his movements which, George assumed, transmitted itself to those he walked or climbed with; he was energetic, serious, trustworthy. During the winter, Thomas took lodgings in Chamonix and was employed as a salaried ski instructor there. In the summer, he worked for himself, accepting only the mountain guiding work that appealed to him.

'I'm well. But George, I'm very unhappy.'

'Unhappy?'

'Yes. I'm unhappy for you about your parents. It's a bad thing. You must be suffering. I'm so sorry. And I'm also unhappy about my father and the election.'

'Yes. Why is Mathilde so against him standing?' asked George, automatically steering the conversation away from any more talk of his own parents.

'She says, if the people on Papa's list are elected, she'll lose the farm.'

'I don't understand.'

'There's an American company,' said Thomas, 'from Colorado, who want to invest in Hext. Build more ski lifts. Develop the land. Papa thinks it makes sense. Grandmother won't listen to sense. She's very angry. She was so proud of him, George, having qualifications, being a teacher, being the head of the school. I've never seen anyone happier than she the day Papa told her he'd been appointed head. But now . . .' Thomas's voice trailed off.

'Now?' George prompted.

'They don't speak. Or, if they do, they argue. She wants Papa to remove his name from the list. Before the public meeting coming up in July. And she says, if he doesn't—'

'Yes?'

'She can make him. Force him to.'

'Blimey.'

'Yes. And she means it. She's as tough as climbing boots when she chooses to be.'

Mathilde returned with the cream and a jug of milk. She poured the milk into a saucepan and set it to heat.

Behind Mathilde came Jack and the girls. There was chaos as the excited girls greeted George. Isobel flung her arms round him and, squeezing tight, said, 'Sorry, sorry, so so sorry about your mum and dad.' The twins, like their brother Jack earlier, muttered embarrassed condolences and Jack himself clowned, trying loudly to persuade Mathilde to let him have cream, there and then, with his tart. The milk boiled over and Mathilde shooed everyone except Thomas out of the kitchen.

'I don't want to see the rest of you in here again today,' she said.

'Are you staying for supper, Thomas?' asked Isobel.

'I can't,' said Thomas. 'I've an early start tomorrow.'

'Why? Who's going where?'

'A group of Dutch. Just a day trip, near the Mer de Glace. I'm meeting them in Chamonix first thing tomorrow.'

'You'll never make it in time, will you?' Isobel looked puzzled.

'I will. I'm going to walk over the pass. I'd never make it by road. You're right.'

'But it'll be dark,' said Isobel.

'Yes.'

'Won't you get lost?'

Now Thomas looked puzzled.

'I'm never lost in the mountains,' he said. 'Besides, it promises to be a clear night. There won't be any moon to speak of. But the stars will light and guide me.'

After supper, the girls begged for a game of Monopoly, but Jack said it was too late.

'You've paideia tomorrow, remember. You need an early night.'

'Paideia?' said George. 'Surely not?'

Paideia was one of Arete's conventions – quirky, silly, really rather awful, in George's view – passed down from Sir A, who'd tried to bring together all sorts of erudite, or pseudo-erudite, notions at his summer home in the Alps. Arete: what a pretentious name for a holiday home. Excellence in all things, was the gist of it. There was no doubt that Sir A had loved the mountains, and he'd devoted as much time to a thorough study of them, apparently, as to the pure pleasure of being in them. Fair enough. But George could do without the rituals and the garbled philosophy, which, as far as he could see, was basically just a belief in the training of the body alongside the training of the mind.

'Surely, yes,' said Jack. 'Scarper, you lot.' He waved an imperious, dismissive hand at the girls. 'I must initiate George into the Alpine Club. In secret. Sign him in.'

'In blood?' asked Isobel.

'Of course.' He winked at George. 'Nelson's best.'

When the girls had gone upstairs, Jack told George to come with him.

'No rum, actually. Sorry. That was a joke about Nelson's Blood. But we could have some génépi, if you like. Or is it another Martini moment?' Jack pushed open the door to the games room.

'No thanks. What's all this about the Alpine Club and paideia? We were kids then.'

Several open maps were spread out across the ragged green baize of the billiard table. Jack poured himself a small tumbler of génépi from the bottle on the sideboard and went to stand on the far side of the table, facing George.

'Cheers,' he said and swigged the yellow-green liquid down in one. 'I've resurrected the dear old Alpine Club just to keep the girls amused. And paideia,' he added, 'to keep them busy.'

Poor them, thought George. He had experienced both and enjoyed neither. Paideia, in the Valentine world, meant little more than a physical challenge. He recalled being told at the age of eight to jump from a slippery ledge halfway up the waterfall into the dark, deep Ladies' Pond at least twenty feet below. There was no corporal punishment at Arete for failing a challenge, but the shame was enormous, and one was an outcast for days or until another challenge was successfully met. In this instance, George had not failed. He'd jumped. He couldn't remember the jump itself or the descent, but he did remember the shock of the icy water, so great that he didn't notice, as he pulled himself out, that he'd cut himself quite badly on the rocks: both knees were bruised and grazed, and one shin spurted blood. It had hurt like hell, but George bit his lip and didn't cry.

As to the Alpine Club, its rules were legion and arcane, varying from one year to the next depending on the whims of whoever was the president. Sir A had been a member of the real Alpine Club in London, and one year was nearly elected its president. The president of Arete's make-believe Alpine Club wasn't elected, but chosen by drawing lots at the beginning of each summer.

'I'm the president this year,' said Jack. 'We didn't bother tossing a coin or anything. Unilateral decision, you could say.'

'And what's my role?' asked George.

'Sign in,' said Jack. 'There's a red biro somewhere under all that. We'll tell the girls it's blood. And then I'll explain.'

'They're not that stupid,' said George. 'Nor that young any more. Polly and Tess are fourteen, aren't they? And Isobel must be twelve. She's the only one likely to believe.'

'It doesn't matter. Just get on with it,' said Jack. 'There's something else.'

George found the biro and opened the old cloth-bound Alpine Club book that Jack took from the sideboard and passed to him. It was the original logbook started by Sir A more than a century ago. It contained the names and dates of all the visitors to Arete stretching back to 1865, alongside the climbs and excursions they'd done – scrambles or rambles, as they sometimes called them – plus a list and brief explanation of various paideias.

George flipped through the pages. He liked the really old handwriting, always in ink, cursive and with grand flourishes. He paused at the pages for the 1950s, noticing Ma's jagged, still quite childish attempts at italic letters. By the late 50s, this had transformed into the still jagged but firm, neat handwriting George used to see all over the exercise books she marked on Sunday nights. And there was Da's handwriting too, surprisingly small for a man and with the letters not all joined up. 'I'm a man of numbers, not words,' Da would say, exaggerating his slight northern accent when forced, grumbling, to play Scrabble or dress up for charades.

George skipped over the 1960s. He didn't want to see his own primary-school efforts. Nor did he wish to see any more of his parents' handwriting. The effect of seeing it had been visceral – a shock of recognition followed by a sickening, sucking hollowness.

He signed his name and closed the book.

'I think I'll have that drink now,' he said.

'Good,' said Jack. 'Génépi or – ?'

'I'll try the génépi. Just a small one.'

Jack poured a tumbler of génépi and passed it to George. He refilled his own and said, 'Challenge: down it in one.'

George was afraid he'd splutter on the bitter drink, but knew he'd look a fool if he didn't accept Jack's challenge, so he put the glass to his lips. The taste wasn't as bad as he'd expected and he managed to swallow the liquor, if not in one, at least without coughing it all up. Jack filled the tumbler again.

'Now take a look at this.' Jack swept a hand across one of the smaller maps.

'Why? What is it?'

'It's the gold, old boy. Remember the gold?'

'What do you mean?'

'The hunt for gold.'

'The golden ibex?' George frowned at Jack. 'But that's kiddy stuff too.'

'No, no, no. Not the golden ibex. Gold – the hunt for it, here in the valley of Hext.'

George downed his second génépi and looked at the map spread out on the baize. It was a very old pen and ink map, inaccurate, he could tell, in many ways, and not even very detailed for the most part. One section, however, was painstakingly drawn and very pretty, in a greetings-card sort of way: little huts nestled among little trees indicating a forest; tracks were differentiated from paths; rocks, crags and even boulders were outlined and shaded. Next to one of the huts, at the very top, there was an even more detailed section, with a minute bird, its wings spread and tilted in flight, the branch of a tree – just the needles – and a number of tiny animal footprints. What was most intriguing, though, was the line that ran in loops and zigzags from Àrete to a point near the top of the detailed section. At the end of the line, in thick black ink, there was an 'X'.

Jack put his index finger on the 'X'.

'X marks the spot,' he said. 'Of what, if not of gold? That's what I'm going to tell the girls, anyway.'

'Oh, come on, Jack.' The génépi was making George bolder. He poured himself some more. 'This is a joke. We don't even know who the map belongs to. Belonged to, I mean. Who drew it? When?'

'Easy. Our great-great-grandmother, Lady C. I found it in a portfolio of her watercolours. When I was looking for booze last night in the mazot. Mathilde freaked.'

'Because of the booze?'

'She seems to have a bee in her bonnet about everything at the moment.'

'What do you mean?'

'Listen to this. I dumped the map and the crate of Martini in the games room last night. Okay, I had a few slugs, I admit – made a bit of a mess with my fag-ash on the sideboard and the billiard table. But this morning Mathilde was in there ranting and raving in bloody patois as if someone had committed the crime of the century. She tried to take the map.'

'Why?'

'No idea. I said, "Hang on, calm down, Mathilde, it's not yours to take." To which she replied, "That's debatable, young Master Jack – I've rights." She spat on the floor then – a great, oiky gob – and stomped off, muttering and spluttering.'

'Okay. I see what you mean by cantankerous. But Lady C drawing maps, Jack. That's not a big deal. Drawing, painting, isn't that what Victorian women did?' George shrugged. 'And wasn't mapping the land, recording the sights, itemising every anthill, every ant, the craze, back then?'

'Yes, so let's pretend there was a purpose to their pastimes and try to retrace their steps.'

Jack was convinced the map would provide a fantastic paideia and keep the girls occupied for ages. They disagreed. They drank. They stayed up very late. George remembered looking at his watch at one o'clock and emptying the last of the génépi from the bottle into his tumbler. He remembered slurring his words.

'Everybody knows there's no gold around here, Jack. It was a rumour, a hope, a dream. That's all.'

'Sure,' said Jack. 'And that's what the story of the golden ibex was for. But there's no harm in playing along with it.'

George didn't contradict him, and their talk became a blur of green liquor, green baize, needing to pee, weep, wanting to sleep and, eventually, sleeping.

Four

The hunt for gold was a craze in Sir A's time, but the legend is probably as old as the mountains themselves.

I remember first hearing about the golden ibex at the *lavoir*.

September, I remember, because of the leaves I made crack underfoot as I walked with Maman and my sisters down to the village. Cédric's family were on the track in front of us. Cédric kept turning round and sticking his big tongue out at me.

My sisters and I each carried a different-sized bundle of aprons and dresses, trousers, shirts, blouses, skirts and underwear. Papa would follow later with the cart piled high with linen. I was too young to do very much in the way of work, but Maman had me ferrying wet blobs of clothes from one sink to another and scooping soda from a bucket to sprinkle onto them. I had to stand on a milking stool to reach the sink, and as I sprinkled I listened to the two women opposite me talk about the golden ibex. They were disagreeing about the details of the story. One of them said that only the hooves of the animal were golden, and he left a trail of golden snowflakes behind him. The other woman claimed that the ibex's whole body, legs, horns, eyes and tail shone as bright and gold as the sun. Either way, I got the gist: the golden ibex was a magical creature who lived in the mountains above our valley; rarely seen and never caught, he and he alone knew where gold in the mountains was to be found.

I remember looking up from the *lavoir* at the church opposite, whose coloured, patterned windows and gleaming, onion-shaped dome reflected that morning's sun. The light was white and hurt my eyes, so I lowered them to the very different white of the soapy water swirling in the basin. I sprinkled some more soda and imagined it turning to golden flakes of snow.

The second time the golden ibex came to my attention was at school. Some of the boys were taunting Henri le cretin, who'd found a centime in the street and was showing it off. He put the centime on the palm of one hand and jabbed at it repeatedly with the index finger of his other hand.

'Gold,' he insisted. 'Rich me, rich me.'

The boys took the coin from Henri and told him if he wanted to be rich, he'd better find the golden ibex.

After that, I pricked up my ears whenever the golden ibex was mentioned. I probably asked questions too, and it can't have been long before I'd pieced together the bare bones of the story. A Swiss hunter was doing his rounds in our region. He killed an ibex in the mountains, high above Hext. When he came to look at the dead animal, he saw that its hooves were covered in a yellow powder, like gold dust. The hunter followed the animal's tracks, sprinkled with shiny particles. They led him to a place full of gold. The hunter took some of the gold and went back down to Hext. Later, when he tried to return to the place full of gold, he could not find it. All the tracks had disappeared.

The legend raised a lot of questions in our minds.

Even Benoît couldn't answer them, even though Xavier, Benoît's grandfather, lost his way – that's how Benoît put it – in the hunt for gold in the 1860s and '70s. Lost his mind was how most people put it. The kinder villagers said Xavier was obsessed – he believed absolutely that somewhere up there, seams of gold awaited him. Possessed, said the less kind. And some said Xavier was simply greedy and too big for his boots, because he was Sir A's guide, overpaid and underworked.

The facts of the matter were indisputable. Xavier set off alone one day from Arete into the mountains and never returned. No body was ever discovered and there was no sign of an accident, no evidence of landfall, mudslide or avalanche. The mystery gave rise to the murmurings we still heard from time to time about Xavier and mixed in our minds with the ibex.

As young children, Benoît and I believed absolutely in the existence of the golden ibex. Like the women at the *lavoir*, we wondered what he looked like. We also wondered, how come?

Benoît gave me his version in 1908, the summer I had the pox and missed the first haymaking.

It was the end of June, so everyone was up in the fields, cutting and stacking, piling and packing round the clock to beat the weather. I was at home – in, or at least on, the bed. I wasn't infectious any more, but I didn't feel right and I was covered in red crusty spots which got worse with the heat. I was so hot and cross from the itching and being stuck inside our stuffy old farmhouse that I nearly didn't answer the knock on the door. But the door was wide open to let in the air, and I was worried it might be one of those thieving peddlars from Annecy come to try and steal something. I crept halfway down the stairs and sneaked a look from behind the banisters.

Benoît was standing on the threshold. He smiled as I approached, said he was thirsty and might he have some water? I filled Papa's bowl to the brim and gave it to him. When he'd drunk, Benoît said he'd heard I was still poorly, so he'd come (all the way down from le Nid, on the other side of the valley) to cheer me up. He also said it was boring without me, up in the fields. We sat on the bench outside the farmhouse, and Benoît tried to amuse me with anecdotes about the haymaking, but he could tell, I think, that I felt unwell. He said I should go back to bed. I did. Then Benoît sat on the bed and asked if I'd like him to tell me a story. I wasn't going to say no, was I?

In Benoît's version, the ibex wasn't born golden, he became golden. Benoît's ibex was born without any horns, which made him unattractive and useless. He had no friends, so he spent his days wandering alone in the mountains. As a result, he became very strong and expert at finding his way around. He wandered further and further into the wilderness, beyond the highest peaks in the region, but he never once got lost.

One day, the ibex came across a seam of gold in the rock. He put his hoof on the seam and his hoof turned to gold. When the ibex went home later that day, all the other animals saw the golden hoof and were amazed. Suddenly they all wanted to be his friend. So the ibex returned to the seam and put another hoof in it. It too turned to gold. That night, he acquired even more friends. This is good, he thought. Now I will never be alone again. But just to make sure, he returned once more to the rock with the seam of gold. He put a third hoof into the seam and, like before, it turned to gold. He was about to put his fourth hoof in when the sound of other animals startled him. He'd been followed. All his friends wanted to have golden hooves as well. Be my guest, said the ibex. But when the other animals put their hooves into the seam of gold, nothing happened. They taunted the ibex that he had made the story up. But the ibex told them to watch and he put his fourth hoof into the seam. This time, his whole body turned gold and a magnificent pair of golden horns sprang from his head. The other animals were frightened and weren't his friends any more. So the ibex still roamed the mountains alone, but now he was the golden ibex and many stories were made up about him.

I didn't think Benoît had got it quite right, but I liked his explanation and I was very grateful to him for coming to visit me, even though I had the pox. He went on talking, and I fell asleep with his words in my ears, soft, like fluttering flakes of snow.

Five

'George! Georgio? Rise and shine. It's nine o'clock.'

'I feel ill.' George pulled the sheet over his head, but Jack dragged it off.

'Can't take your drink, old boy. That's all,' said Jack.

George struggled into his clothes and followed Jack down to the kitchen.

'Bacon and eggs?' said Jack, reaching for a frying pan. 'I'm a dab hand.'

But the thought of eating made George nauseous.

'You'll regret it,' said Jack, dropping three rashers of bacon into the pan. 'You'll be hungry later. Paideia, remember? Adventure, exciting.'

'I think I'll give paideia a miss,' said George, collapsing onto a kitchen chair and putting his elbows on the table and his head in his hands.

'Oh, Georgy-porgy,' said Jack. 'Don't be a pansy.'

'Sorry,' said George. 'But I simply can't. I'm going back to bed.'

When he next awoke, it was past midday. George felt better but ravenously hungry and desperately thirsty. He went downstairs and found a note on the kitchen table from Jack, confirming he'd be out all day with the girls.

So, thought George, apart from Mathilde, he was alone at Arete. He opened the kitchen door and saw Mathilde busy with a mower in the far corner of the patch of land used as a lawn or for ball games. Man's work, George caught himself, like Da, thinking, but hearing simultaneously Ma's reprimand, 'Chauvinist pigs, the both of you.'

George drank two glasses of water and poured some coffee from the jug sitting warm on top of the oven. He made himself scrambled eggs, ate them with a knob of stale bread and poured a second bowl of coffee, which he carried along the corridor, across the hall and out through the front door.

There were two deckchairs on the terrace, a low table and Sir A's old star-gazing chair. George chose the latter to sit in and put his bowl of coffee down on the table next to it.

The sun was still high and the sky was an electric blue. A few shreds of cloud hung above the higher peaks at the eastern end of the valley and, to the west, the foothills on the way down to Geneva were hazy with heat.

For a wooden chair without a cushion, Sir A's star-gazing chair was remarkably comfortable, and George enjoyed the magnificent view, the peace and quiet, the clean, clear air. He was just putting his empty bowl of coffee down on the table when Mathilde appeared around the corner of the house.

'There you are, George,' she said. 'I was beginning to worry.'

'Hello. Sorry. No, I'm fine.'

The older he got, the harder George found it to talk to Mathilde. Her quaint, idiosyncratic English was better than his schoolboy French. It wasn't really a language thing, though. Mathilde was treated with kindness, fondness even, by all of them. But she was also still treated as the servant she was. She slept in the old servants' quarters. She ate alone in the kitchen. She obeyed orders. And yet her deference was offset, George thought, by a knowing familiarity and her evident intelligence imbued with keen, peasant cunning.

'Are you busy, George?' Mathilde took a step towards him, into the sun, shielding her face with her hand.

'No, not at all,' said George.

'I would like your help.' Mathilde pointed to the roof of the house. 'There are some things I need from the grenier.'

'Of course,' said George. 'Tell me what you want. I'll go now.' He stood up.

'No.' Mathilde shook her head. 'I don't know exactly where they are. I haven't been up there for years and I need to look myself, but my legs won't get me up the ladder very easily any more.'

'Oh.' George was surprised. 'Well, yes. If you're sure?'

'I'm sure,' said Mathilde.

So George went inside with Mathilde, up the stairs and up the ladder behind her to the attic, putting, as she instructed, his hands on her clogs to help her thick, stiff, veiny legs bend, and placing them one by one on the rungs. At the top, Mathilde had no trouble heaving herself over the edge; her arms had lost none of their strength.

'Thank you,' she said, brushing down her apron as George too pulled himself up into the attic space. 'Now. To work. My, the mess! A bloody *anglais* mess.'

She swivelled away from the girly chaos at the window end of the attic where the unmade beds were scattered with skimpy bikinis, damp towels and several odd-shaped, tie-dyed garments. George could see, under one bed, pony books, a new-looking Penguin *Jane Eyre*, *Jackie* magazines, an empty singles' bag from a Harlequin record shop and the purple glint of a scrunched-up wrapper from a bar of Cadbury's Dairy Milk chocolate. Under another bed there was a small stash of illicit candles, matches and a packet of Jack's Disque Bleu cigarettes.

George swivelled too and was surprised at how essentially unchanged the attic was since he'd last slept up there four years ago. Tea chests, trunks, boxes and discarded furniture were packed tightly together, taking up almost half the floor space. Some of the larger items of furniture had white dustsheets draped over them. The dustsheets were still white because the air in the mountains was so clean. 'Goitre? Yes. Asthma – almost never in the Alps. No dust to speak of.' Da said he'd read an article about it.

The only major change George could see was the addition of a hatch in the roof. To help the air circulate, presumably, he thought. But despite the new ventilation it was suffocatingly hot. George folded back his cuffs and undid another button of his shirt.

'*C'est la canicule*,' said Mathilde, stretching *canicule* into four long Savoyard syllables.

George nodded, thinking how well the French word '*canicule*' conveyed the claustrophobia and threat of that summer's heat. The English 'heatwave' made it sound like a much jollier affair.

'Could you move those for me, please?' Mathilde pointed to a bath chair and two large trunks, one on top of the other.

The trunks were heavy and George couldn't push them aside. He had to tip the top one off and use all his weight to shove the other one away, leaving a gap wide enough for Mathilde to pass through.

'Thank you,' she said again.

She knelt down next to a lidless gramophone and began moving two piles of 78 records to one side. Behind the records was a tea chest. Mathilde reached into it and pulled out a grey box file.

'Here we are,' she said, standing up.

'That was quick,' said George. 'Shall I put the records back?'

'No.' Mathilde turned and walked a few steps. 'I'll just sit on this bed here for a moment, if you don't mind. I need to check inside.'

Mathilde sat down on the bed with a grunt. She opened the file which, George could see now, was the same sort of Eastlight type they had at home. His parents' box files – and they had a whole row of them in the living room, in the study-corner, underneath Da's mathematics textbooks – were labelled in Da's handwriting: Household Bills, Tax, Bank and so on, including, at the end of the row, files with each of their names on. Da – Donald, Ma – Peggy, and George – George. George's file also had his date of birth written in small roman numerals under his name. It contained his birth certificate, his baby-clinic book and child-vaccination card, certificates from various prizes he'd won at primary school, all of his school reports, primary and secondary, and a clutch of official letters to do with doctors or school, everything clamped securely together – you had to watch out for your fingers – with a shiny metal spring. Da used to buy the box files in WH Smith, but when he last went to stock up they'd been discontinued. He was cross about that; he said he'd been buying them since he was a student in Manchester in the 1950s and they were an excellent design.

Inside the file on Mathilde's lap were scraps of paper and letters, some loose and some tied together with grubby string or frayed black ribbon. Mathilde untied and unfolded several of the sheets.

'Tss,' she closed the file. 'No. This isn't the right one. I'll try over there now.' She nodded to a corner of the attic where pictures were stacked or lying propped against other objects.

'Why don't you let me do it?' George was worried about getting Mathilde down the ladder later and didn't want her tiring herself out unnecessarily.

'Well. I suppose you could. Thank you, George. All you need to do is move those pictures. Careful, mind. But you'll find, I think, behind them, a mirror and, behind that, another box file like this one. Bring it to me, please.'

George found the file and brought it to Mathilde.

Once again she opened it, and once again she was disappointed. It contained nothing but a few thin and tatty notebooks which she flicked through quickly and dismissed.

'All right,' she said. 'You'll have to move Sir A's astronomy equipment. It's heavy, I warn you.'

George, who'd had a passing interest in astronomy himself and had been given a telescope by his father for his eighth birthday, was indeed amazed at how heavy the odd-shaped padded canvas bags were. He could feel tripods and telescopes through the material, but there were square bags and round bags and even a triangular one, which was particularly heavy.

'There's another trunk here, Mathilde,' said George, dragging the last bag to one side. 'Sort of blue.'

'Open it,' said Mathilde.

Inside the trunk, on top of a pile of folded clothes, was one more grey box file. George lifted it out. 'Anthony Oswald Valentine' was written, italicky, but not in Ma's hand, on the cream and green Eastlight spine. George took it over to Mathilde.

'Only one?' she seemed surprised, but glanced inside and nodded. 'Yes, these are Sir A's diaries. What's left of them, that is. Thank you, George.'

George sat down on the bed next to Mathilde.

'If you don't mind my asking, what exactly is it you're looking for, Mathilde?' he asked.

'A needle in a haystack,' said Mathilde. 'A French needle in an English haystack, to be precise.' She gave a snorty, unamused laugh, then began removing the diaries from the file. She held each one by its cover and shook. A few tattered leaves fell out, which she examined but put back.

'What are you looking for?' said George again. 'Can I help?'

'No,' said Mathilde, returning the diaries to the file, shutting the lid on them and sighing. 'There's nothing here. I was looking for a letter, but it must have gone the way of all things.'

'Oh,' said George. 'I'm sorry.'

'Two wars and more than half a century of half-hearted *anglais* tidying.' Mathilde gestured to the mess in the attic. 'It's not surprising.' She sighed again. 'But the letter would help me decide what to do. That's why I'm looking for it.'

'I'm afraid I don't understand.' What letter, and decide what to do about what, George wondered?

'I already have irrefutable proof,' Mathilde continued. 'But do I use it? That is what I am asking myself.'

'You've really confused me,' George said.

Mathilde frowned.

'Do I use my evidence, if that foolish son of mine persists in his views and in putting himself forward to become mayor? I don't know, George. It's a bigger decision than you realise. The letter I'm looking for would help me decide.'

'How?' George was relieved that this seemed basically to be about Luc and the election – maybe just the bees in Mathilde's bonnet buzzing again.

'It will tell me,' said Mathilde, 'if certain people – two, at least – are tarred with the same brush. Two women. And if they are, that will make my blood boil.'

'You're talking in riddles, Mathilde,' said George.

'Like a *rosbif*?' Mathilde let out another odd, snorty little laugh, picked up the box file and hugged it to her chest. 'All right,' she said, suddenly decisive, like a teacher. 'I will try to be clearer. Imagine a crime is about to be committed, George. By someone you love very much.'

The first thing that popped into George's head was the ludicrous scenario of Da contemplating burgling the house next door to theirs in Reading. It belonged to a grumpy old woman called Mrs Peters.

'Now imagine you have irrefutable evidence of something that would prevent this person committing this crime, but you also have good reasons not to reveal your evidence.'

It was no problem for George to imagine coming across, in one of Da's desk drawers – which he wasn't really supposed to rifle through – a neatly handwritten list itemising equipment, exact timings and precise procedures for the burglary.

'What do you do?' Mathilde continued. 'You consider the matter rationally, yes?'

'Yes, I suppose so,' said George, thinking he'd probably, actually, immediately tell Ma what he'd found, but yes, he could also imagine prevaricating, wondering and worrying.

'But what if you then discover there might be, if you hunt for it, further evidence, suggesting your original evidence represents a pattern of behaviour that you know could make you very, very angry? What do you do then? Do you pursue the hunt for the further evidence?'

'I expect so,' said George although he found it hard to imagine the sort of further evidence Mathilde meant.

Mathilde nodded.

'Yes,' she said. 'And even if it means you might end up being so angry you would be in danger of allowing emotion to get in the way of reason?'

'I think so. I think my curiosity would get the better of me,' said George.

'Exactly. Curiosity is the problem, my problem. And if I do find out that there are two people in the *panier*, not just the one—'

'People in the *panier*?' George interrupted.

'*Dans le panier*. We don't tar with the same brush. We put *dans le même sac*, bag, basket. My blood will boil and I will be so angry that, ignoring logic, my decision will be made, and Luc won't be the only one to suffer. We will all pay a price.'

George thought he had an inkling of the troubled thinking behind Mathilde's search. However, she clearly didn't intend to explain further or name names, other than Luc, so George decided to ask her about her son.

'You must be very proud of Luc, though, Mathilde,' he began. 'Thomas said—'

'Proud?' Mathilde turned to George and her soft grey eyes had become slatey. 'No, George, I'm not proud of Luc. I'm ashamed of him.' She let the box file drop to her lap.

George wished he'd kept silent. But Mathilde went on:

'He ought to know better. The land, *le pays*. *Paysans*, we are peasants, George. Without our land, we are nothing. Luc is willing to sell. Why? He's been blinded by the glint of white gold and—' Mathilde hesitated, 'gilt-edged ambition – greed – has got the better of him. That's why. So . . .'

'So?' George couldn't help prompting her.

Mathilde patted the closed box file and George noticed the old burn mark that puckered her knuckles and part of the back of her hand; it wasn't as dark as he remembered and it was almost hidden by liver spots. He couldn't see, but he knew that it ran round to her palm, where it became a straightish line, darker and ridged, as if she'd been branded.

'So.' Mathilde hesitated again. 'Spit, spat.'

'What does that mean?' Was she going to spit on the floor again? George sincerely hoped not.

'It means I'm tired of the lies, George. It's a phrase I learnt from Miss Margaret Valentine. Your great-aunt. You never knew her. It means I'm angry, or about to be. I'm angry at the mere notion of this further evidence, so heaven help us if I do find the letter. And I'm angry anyway with my . . .' Yet again she hesitated. 'My family. If I want to, I can tell the village something that will make all of us, including Luc, the laughing stock. He will never be on the municipal council, let alone mayor.' Mathilde put the box file down beside her and started to push herself up off the bed.

George stood to give her a hand. He was aware that he hadn't been able to piece together Mathilde's fragmented explanation of things, and he couldn't think what bearing a lost old letter could possibly have on Luc's electoral campaign, but he did feel he comprehended, on some level, the mixture of emotions motivating Mathilde: her anger and passion, which came across as the empty threats of an upset old woman, were balanced by an intelligent, even, George would say, intellectual grappling with some sort of private moral predicament. And George knew what that felt like: the days following his parents' death had been fraught with such predicaments. Seemingly simple decisions became complex ethical dilemmas.

Bodies, what was left of them: bury or burn? *Burn.*

Ashes: scatter or keep, together or separately? *Scatter, together.*

And for the funeral reception: bread and cheese – a mixed platter, or cheddar by itself? Tea, coffee, squash, or something stronger? Cake. Plastic forks and paper plates, disposable serviettes, polystyrene for the drinks. Ma and Da would have hated it. They had both left clear, straightforward wills – in the Eastlight box files – but neither of them had stipulated anything about funeral arrangements. Neither of them had expected to die.

'Shall I put the files back?' George tried to shake the morbid thoughts out of his head.

'If you would. Yes, please.'

Getting Mathilde down the ladder was harder than getting her up it and George, who went down first, had to stop her toppling several times.

'Thank you,' said Mathilde. 'Thank you very much, George.' And with that she hobbledehoyed down the stairs, leaving George at the top not knowing what to make of her.

He climbed up the ladder to put the box files back where they came from, but he decided, despite the stifling heat in the attic, to have a dekko first. He sat down on the bed nearest the window, where Mathilde had been sitting, and sifted quickly through the scraps and letters, all of which were in some way damaged – dirty, torn or scorched. The scraps were Sir A's jottings – books read or to be read, plays seen, observations of his bowel habits, lists of people he needed to write to.

The letters were all to Sir A from his friends, mostly men, mostly alpinists like Sir A himself, detailing their climbs and what fine times they were having – in Grindelwald, Chamonix, Zermatt, Cervinia. There was also an abundance of thank-you notes – Arete was 'paradise', 'a dream', 'heaven on earth', and Sir A's hospitality quite something, it seemed.

Next George opened the box file containing the notebooks. These were filled with facts and figures, descriptions, dates and details about the weather, the moon phases and about the flora and fauna in the vicinity of Arete – all in Sir A's distinctive and controlled but not easy-to-read hand. Fascinating, if you yourself were keen on such matters. George put the notebooks in chronological order as far as possible, but there were gaps, big ones.

It was the same with Sir A's diaries. There were lots of years missing and those that remained all had burnt, or at least singed, leather covers. George chose the volume that looked the least damaged – 1912 – though upon opening it he discovered the pages were scorched and the writing almost indecipherable. 1913 was one of those missing. 1914 had lost half its back cover; inside, the pages were various shades of brown, but most were readable. The entries began in May. George flicked through, not reading, just noticing the vigorous crossings-out and the fluent, confident handwriting. Then he opened the diary properly and read what turned out to be the penultimate entry, 4th August.

I leave for London tomorrow. But tonight I will climb, one more time, to the snow line. There I will lie, with my hand on the Solicitor General –

The Solicitor General? That was a new one on George.

I will lick the earth's covering, lick it like a beast, like some poor desert horse deprived of salt, licking until there's a softening: ice then snow. Afterwards, I will lie with my cheek on the milk-white breast of the mountain, bury my head in the virgin snow and nibble, and lick again, lick until there's a hardening: ice then rock. The explosion of my insatiable land-love.

George was amused by the hyperbolic, erotic terms in which Sir A described his experience of the alpine landscape. In the last entry, it transpired that there had been no climbing to the snow line due to 'bad squits'. Sir A had the collywobbles after a picnic lunch en famille, and spent the last few hours before his departure running to and from the thunderbox.

George turned back through the diary to earlier entries. Conventional, olde-worlde banalities about the beauty of the landscape – its soaring glory, wondrous majesty, heavenly splendour et cetera – were interspersed with these weird, sexy, sensual passages.

References in Sir A's diary to people and events were few and relatively mundane, but July had clearly been chock-a-block with guests. George's own name caught his eye. George Mallory. George used to think he'd been named after the famous mountaineer and had been secretly pleased; Mallory featured highly in Arete lore and there were photos of him on the wall in the hall, next to a small framed family tree, drawn by deranged, elderly Daisy in 1964. What a good-looking chap Mallory was. But when George had asked Ma, she'd laughed and said no, sorry, darling – George was named after Da's bachelor uncle in Penzance.

Mallory only stayed two nights at Arete in 1914, but on both nights, he organised a game of football.

Not fair, Sir A had written a propos of the football match. *Mallory and the beanpole are Carthusians. The beanpole in goal. The latter is such a good-humoured, gallant fellow, however, he moved the goalposts – actually two alpenstocks – another foot, a good foot, further apart. Still my grandsons couldn't get the ball past him: Stephen, Ted and Johnny were quite fagged out by half-time and let the Valentines down badly. Daisy cheered from the sidelines for the wrong team.*

The beanpole? A chap in his forties called Will, George gathered, from flicking back and forth in the diary; a junior colleague of Sir A's, and a regular fixture at the chalet, unlike the 'gregarious greenhorns' who arrived en masse for 'a one-off shorty' in the summer of 1914. The exuberance of these rowdy, boisterous students and schoolboys, Sir A had written, 'baffled the loafers – my cousin Irish Arthur and his posse, although you can't beat Arthur for good company in the evenings.'

George returned to the entries about his namesake. 'Mallory, as always, a delight,' Sir A had written. 'A damned fine alpinist. Reminds me of myself in my younger days. But he's a dreamer.

Always has been.' And George couldn't tell if that was a compliment or a concern.

He put the diaries back in the box file and the box files back where he'd found them. He went down the ladder and, squelch-squelch with the rubber of his desert boots, down the stairs.

Six

'I'm a dreamer,' Daisy said when I'd finished telling her what I knew about the golden ibex. 'I bet I'll dream of the ibex tonight. Now you've put the idea in my head.'

Daisy was a great one for dreams. I didn't have many myself, but I didn't mind listening to Daisy's. They often made me laugh. Her daydreams too.

'If I don't dream about gorgeous Georgeous, that is.'

We were in the kitchen when this conversation took place, two nights before Daisy's fourteenth birthday in 1914. It was very late. I was under orders from Sir A to stay up until midnight and then wake him, plus Ted and George Mallory. They intended to climb one of the peaks on the other side of the valley and needed to summit before mid-morning, when the sun would melt the snow and make the descent treacherous. Mallory was going straight on to Chamonix afterwards by road.

Daisy had said she'd stay up with me to keep me company. Her real motive, though, was George Mallory, who, she said, had multiplied her enthusiasm for mountaineering by a million, and with whom, she said, she was madly in love. She called him Marry-Me-Mallory. Never mind that Mallory was twice her age and due to be married in England in a few weeks' time – Daisy was dizzier than ever when he was around.

'Isn't he the most handsome man you've ever set eyes on?' Daisy said. 'What colour would you say his eyes are?'

'Violet,' I said without hesitation, for Mallory's heavily lashed, oval eyes definitely reminded me of early spring wood violets.

'Yes,' said Daisy, raising her own brown eyes to the ceiling and sighing melodramatically. 'You're right. Eyes like beautiful flowers, but deep and thoughtful too. Firm, clean-cut features, and I don't mean only his face. He's lean. Long, long legs, strong but not over-muscled. I like that. He is, without doubt, the most attractive man in the world. You have to agree.'

'I wouldn't say that,' I said, although it was true that Mallory's eyes, his smooth, fair skin and ready smile sometimes made him seem prettier than a pretty girl and drew people's attention as much as his manly athleticism.

'Well. Who are you dreaming of marrying, then, Miss Hard-to-Please?' Daisy didn't wait for an answer. 'That boy. Benoît. I bet. You're always talking about him.'

Benoît would have moved further up the mountain by now, from le Nid to his family's summer chalet. He'd be helping his mother with the cows and goats. He'd be making the cheeses from dawn to dusk. Benoît didn't complain, and we never spoke about the gas explosion in Geneva five years ago which killed Tall Paul, but the death of his father meant hard, hard work for Benoît. He had very little free time (less than me). If he did have a spare moment, though, I knew he'd be reading one of the books Madame Tissot had lent him for the summer.

'Don't look sad, Mathilde. Is Benoît already taken? If so, *tant pis*. Aunt Piss. There are plenty more fish in the sea. I—' she tossed her glossy brown Valentine curls – 'if Marry-Me-Mallory won't have me, will find me a penniless poet or a fat millionaire.'

After begging me for more details about the golden ibex, which I couldn't supply, Daisy fell asleep, her head on the kitchen table. Ted had to carry her up to her bedroom. She was awake early the next morning, however, and at breakfast she regaled all present with a vivid account of the nightmare she'd had.

'I was riding an ibex,' she insisted. 'Clutching his golden horns. We were being chased.'

Stephen tut-tutted and Johnny laughed, but Daisy continued.

'He spoke to me, the ibex. He said I will be the one to find the gold.'

Daisy may have been a dreamer. She was also a liar, a cheat and a thief. I didn't find this out until later in the summer. But I did find out soon enough that Daisy had a temper (some would have said a streak of madness, even way back then).

Daisy had plans, that first summer I spent at Arete, to celebrate her fourteenth birthday and the end of her pertussis with an excursion, en famille, Daddy *y compris,* to the lac de la Miche.

However, rain came before breakfast on Daisy's big day and showed no sign of letting up. The excursion was cancelled, and none of the Valentines went further afield than the thunderbox, except for Daisy, who, after lunch, waded fully clothed into the Round Pond carrying a small axe from the woodshed. She declared in a very loud voice – and repeatedly – that she would hack holes in both of Sir A's boats if the excursion didn't take place. Her outburst was ignored.

Poor Daisy. Moreover, her party that day, despite the elder-flower cordial, Marmite sandwiches and *anglais* sponge cake, made by Sylvie and me, iced and decorated by Beatrice, was a dismal affair. It took place at teatime in the games room with the doors to the sitting room folded back. Johnny put a record on the gramophone, but no one felt like dancing. Ted suggested charades, but no one could be bothered to fetch the dressing-up clothes. In the end, Daisy and her brothers joined the adults, quiet and grim, grouped around Daddy, at the front of the house. Daddy had brought with him on *le petit train* newspapers and news – all bad – about a war.

'It's only Ireland, for God's sake, isn't it?' said Daisy, coming into the kitchen for a top-up of the juice jug. 'Spoilt my bloody birthday. Daddy's going home at the end of the week because of it. I don't understand what banking's got to do with war, do you?' She dipped her little finger into the pot of pease pudding simmering on the hob, then sucked it clean.

Daisy sulked for the rest of the week, refusing to go on paideia or indeed any of the family outings. All she did was teach me to play 'Chopsticks' on the piano, and then she made me play it over and over again with her until it drove everyone up the wall. Beatrice sent her to her room, but the next we knew she'd exited onto the balcony and was parading up and down in a yellow kimono purloined from the dressing-up box.

'I've a passion for fashion,' she declared, untying the belt of the kimono and flapping the sleeves of it.

After the departure of Daddy, Arete – thank goodness – was inundated with young people (friends of Stephen, Ted and Johnny), which cheered Daisy up no end. And no sooner had they gone than another, and then another group of guests turned up. Will, who'd arrived with Mallory, but stayed for a fortnight, was my and, I think, Sir A's favourite. He and Sir A spent a lot of time discussing books. Will was thin and bendy, tall, polite and friendly. The Valentines called him the beanpole, and he brought Cadbury's Dairy Milk chocolate from England which, he said, beat Kendal Mint Cake hands down at reviving one's spirits on a difficult trek. He gave some to Daisy, who gave some to me. It definitely tasted better than Kendal Mint Cake, and I liked it so much that I ate too much and felt sick.

The beanpole was a chatterbox and spoke a dozen different languages. He read a lot of poetry and once, late at night, on the terrace, after a glass too many of Sir A's malt whisky, recited some, badly. Another time, while I was serving bubble and squeak with a cold meat lunch, he held forth about the golden ibex. There was bound to be a rational explanation for the phenomenon, he said, and he described comparable sightings and legends in Africa, the Himalayas and South America – anywhere remote and poverty-stricken enough. Besides, he concluded, the mind has mountains, does it not, where anything can be found if you look hard enough?

'Talking of which,' he added. 'Margaret. How is she?' My ears pricked up. 'She prefers to remain in London this year, yet again?' he probed.

The vague, unsatisfactory Valentine reply – her work, immensely busy, many commitments – renewed my interest in the matter, and when I heard Sir A say, sotto voce, to Lady C, 'It's been seven years. He asks every summer. I do wish he wouldn't,' I decided to try Daisy again later: why did no one really talk about Margaret and why didn't she come to Arete any more?

'It's annoying,' said Daisy. 'I don't know. I used to pester everyone to tell me. Did she go down with the Titanic, run away with a black man? Is she a lesbian lady author in Bloomsbury or married to a sheep farmer in Australia? But it was all, "Hush, hush" and "Don't worry your pretty little head about it". Some sort of family scandal, obviously. The boys couldn't give a fig. And I stopped thinking about it, after a while.'

*

The house and the huts were completely full when, uninvited – but everyone was delighted – Irish Arthur turned up, along with six young men in their late twenties. Arthur himself must have been fifty at least. They'd walked all the way from what Arthur called his boys' only bolthole on the Italian Riviera and planned to continue on foot as far as Geneva. Arthur was a distant Valentine relative, a gentleman-explorer, according to Daisy, with a great crumbling mansion, dozens of tumble-down farms and acres of peaty bog in Ireland. Arthur said he needed to return to his estate in Ireland as soon as possible, the situation there was so bad. Nevertheless, he and his friends spent five nights at Arete, sleeping in tents, loafing during the day, taking communal baths in the evening. All the guests stayed up late while they were there, listening to Arthur's traveller's tales.

'He's been to China and Tibet,' Daisy told me. 'And he's walked across India with a dog, or was it a bear? I think it was a bear. He dyed his skin brown, using walnut juice, to disguise himself.'

'Why?'

'To look like a local. Unfriendly natives and all that, I expect.'

We uglies had our work cut out, cleaning and cooking and keeping everything pukka as the days sped by. There were dinner parties in the evening with sedate dancing, afterwards, on the terrace, and parties in the daytime requiring elaborate picnics and the drink called Pimm's.

At the beginning of August, Sir A left for London. The bells in all the chapels, in all the hamlets that made up the commune of Hext, had rung up and down the valley to announce that France was going to war. Sir A said that England was bound to follow suit. There was talk of Lady C, the whole family, everyone striking camp, but Lady C said she preferred to stay and Beatrice saw no reason to rush off ('we summer here until the end of September – that's the tradition, that's what the Valentines do'), so in the end, it was just Sir A.

The day before he left, he requested a family scramble. It would take everyone's mind off the conflict with Germany, he said.

Beatrice pointed out that the weather wasn't ideal and said he shouldn't tire himself before the long journey back to England, but Sir A would hear none of it.

'Mathilde will assist me if I need assistance,' he said. 'Won't you, dear girl?'

Sir A had taken quite a shine to me; he liked my tidying in the library, apparently. And he frequently commented on my proficiency in English. 'Don't call her a cretin,' I heard him say to Beatrice when she did. 'The child's gifted linguistically. Could be she's one of these idiots savants we've been reading about recently. She'd make an interesting case study, or experiment, like that cockney we saw in Shaw's *Pygmalion*.'

Daisy explained what cockney meant – lower-class stinky Londoners.

'I wonder, though,' she said. 'It may be one of those rude words. It sounds like pizzle, dibble, little prick, doesn't it?'

That's not what I found when I looked it up. Pygmalion I couldn't find at all, but purloined, proficiency, polysyllabic – I rolled the words around on my tongue. A plethora of words. Pukka.

The family were still seated at the breakfast table. I was standing upright, shoulders back, by the door, confidently rolling *rosbif* words not round but off my my tongue – more toast, ma'am? Perhaps some eggs or jam?

'Honestly, Father,' said Beatrice. 'I don't think that's wise. The servants are needed here, packing and preparing for tomorrow. Yes, Mathilde: the milk jug needs refilling, and I'd like my eggs fried tomorrow – these are hard-boiled to stones. If I've told you once, I've told you a dozen times, two and a half minutes maximum for me.'

'Yes, m'am,' I said, bobbing correctly as she'd taught me I must.

I walked over to the table to pick up the milk jug, but my fingers never reached it because Sir A put his long, smooth hand on my outstretched arm.

'Not today, Mathilde,' he said. 'Today you're one of us, part of the family.'

'Hooray.' Daisy pushed back her chair. 'I'll fetch the milk. I know where it's kept.'

I didn't feel like part of the family, and it wasn't actually much of a scramble. More of a stroll. Sir A and Lady C, however, were very pleased with themselves for making it to their favourite sheltered knoll on one of the spurs of le Luet. As well as having vistas up and down the valley, the knoll afforded a bird's-eye view of Arete. While we set up base – folding chairs for Sir A and Lady C, a large tartan rug for the rest of us – Sir A reminisced about his first visit, with Xavier, to the valley and how, when they came across the piece of land where Arete would be built, Sir A declared – and Xavier could only agree – it was the most beautiful place on earth.

'I defy anyone,' said Sir A, 'not to fall in love with this land.'

Stephen, Ted and Johnny yawned ostentatiously, and Beatrice told them to stop it, this was Grandpa's treat, and if he wanted to spend it down Memory Lane, so be it.

'We were trailblazers in those days,' Sir A continued. 'New word. Good word. Young Coolidge brought it with him from America. He was only fifteen when I met him in Zermatt, late in 1865. He was with that strange, trouser-wearing female relative of his, Meta Brevoort and she was a remarkably strong, competitive, very clever climber.'

'Strange name.' Ted made an effort to show interest.

'Yes.' Sir A nodded. 'Coolidge was a bit odd himself. And they had a dog, Tschingel. But Coolidge is a first-rate historian. Encyclopaedic knowledge. Cambridge are lucky to have him. He's rigorous and more pedantic and pernickety than my good self about language. Yes. We were trailblazers. New peaks, new routes. There seemed no limit to our horizons.'

Daisy announced that she was going to trailblaze for four-leafed clovers and she told me to help her. What with the coffee in my belly, along with the nip of brandy Sir A had given me when we'd first stopped on the knoll, this most absurd of occupations became quite a pleasure and it didn't seem to matter that neither of us found any clover at all, let alone the four-leafed sort.

Lunch was bundles of ham and cheese, prepared by me and packed by the Valentines, along with bread, into their satchels. I carried water, wine and Robinson's lemon barley.

After lunch, Sir A suggested a challenge involving climbing to the next ledge above us on the little Loo. Both Lady C and Beatrice put their feet down.

'I'm all for a challenge,' said Beatrice. 'But we're not equipped for real climbing. I've an idea, though. Let's send the children into the forest to find specimens.'

'Oh, that's too boring for words,' said Daisy.

'Grandpa's got hundreds already,' added Ted.

'Not hundreds,' corrected Sir A. 'But it's true. I've more than I need for now. However, there is something I need. And that's a new alpenstock. Not for climbing, just for walking. So that's your paideia. I'm sending you to find the best wood you can. Then you're to use your penknives to whittle the point and carve an appropriate design for me. The person whose alpenstock I choose wins the challenge.'

Stephen and Ted strolled off together towards the forest. Johnny rushed in the opposite direction, down the rock face. Daisy said she didn't feel like participating in the challenge. Beatrice, however, insisted.

'Can Mathilde come with me then? Help me?'

'I don't see why not. She's not needed here for the time being, is she, Pa?' said Beatrice.

'I've a better idea,' said Sir A. 'Since Mathilde is en famille today, she must take part in the challenge. She must fashion an alpenstock for me too.'

Off I went into the forest. I heard Daisy calling out to me to join her, but Sir A had said we were to work alone, so I ignored her.

It didn't take me long to find a young fir tree and choose the wood for my baton. I returned to where Sir A and Lady C were still sitting on their fold-up chairs in the shelter of the cliff. Sir A was reading. Lady C had her sketchbook out. Beatrice was dozing on the picnic rug.

I climbed a short way up the cliff and found a comfortable position on a rock fashioned like an armchair. I whittled away with my Opinel knife and soon had my alpenstock ready. The wood curved naturally at one end, like a handle, and I carved Sir A's initials there, copying the design he'd had cut into the lintel above the front door, with the A and the V on top of each other, inside a circle (the circle was difficult and mine was a bit wobbly).

The boys returned and sat on the rug with their backs to each other, pulled out their knives and started to hack at their pieces of wood.

Daisy emerged from the forest some distance away. She saw me and beckoned. I pretended not to notice, for Beatrice was awake now and I didn't want to get into trouble for breaking the rules of the paideia. But Daisy crept closer. She put her finger to her lips and beckoned again. Then she clasped her hands to her chest in a beseeching gesture which nearly made me laugh. Rather than have the Valentines turning their heads at the sound of a guffaw, I decided, after all, to join Daisy. I crawled along the ledge and let myself down.

'Look,' said Daisy, holding out a long, straight, stripped branch to me. 'This is good, isn't it?'

'Yes,' I said. 'But you need to shape it.'

'I have,' said Daisy. 'Can't you tell?'

Daisy's attempt was no better than a five-year-old's.

'That won't do,' I said. 'It hasn't got a point, and you haven't carved anything on it.'

'I've tried,' said Daisy. 'Oh. Look at yours. That's beautiful, Mathilde. Where did you learn to do that?'

'Practice,' I said. 'Patience. It's not hard if you have a good knife.'

'Let's swap,' said Daisy. 'Swap alpenstocks.'

'But why?'

'I'll give Grandpa yours, and you give him mine. That way I'm bound to win. Please, Mathilde.' She made the beseeching gesture again. 'I'd love to see my brothers' faces.'

I couldn't have cared less about the challenge or who won it, so I was only too happy to agree to Daisy's plan. I even offered to add to the simple design of letters I'd carved on the wood. I thought a star might appeal to Sir A and suggested it, but Daisy had other ideas.

'Do a flower, Mathilde. A daisy. That would be perfect.'

I got my Opinel out and set to work again. Daisy watched.

'That's a funny little knife,' she said.

'It's only an Opinel.'

'But it's so small. Almost like a toy.'

I looked at the knife in my hand, stroked its blade with my thumb, rubbed the warm wood of the handle.

'Give it here,' said Daisy.

'No.' I closed my hand over the knife.

'Oh go on, Mathilde. Please.' Once more she did the beseeching gesture, but this time it annoyed me.

'No,' I repeated and began whittling again so that she couldn't see the whole knife any more.

'It's only a pathetic little knife,' said Daisy. 'Let me have a go.'

'I can't,' I said.

'Why not?'

Because it was Benoît's knife. Because he'd given it to me from his box of twelve, all different sizes, which Tall Paul, who knew a man, who knew the man who manufactured them, had given to Benoît. Because, when I held it in my hand, I liked to think about Benoît's hand on it too – as if the wood of the handle held a part of Benoît. I was afraid if Daisy held it, that might be lost.

'Because we don't do that,' I said. 'We don't share knives. Like clogs. The wood moulds itself to our shape.'

'Oh, rubbish. Really, Mathilde, you can be a very stubborn, very strange ugly, sometimes. Get on with my daisy then.' She started looking for four-leafed clovers again.

It had been easy carving the flower. I was particularly chuffed with my petals. All I needed to do now was the stalk. I carved a long and graceful line, curving down and round the alpenstock. Then I added one more line, this time straight and not as deep, so that the two lines made, if you wanted them to, a 'D' shape.

Daisy was delighted with the result and in a hurry now to return to base.

The boys' alpenstocks were already lined up on the rug. Daisy laid hers next to them, and I placed Daisy's feeble effort, pretending it was mine, next to that.

Sir A and Beatrice looked at the results.

'Well, the winner's obvious,' said Beatrice.

'Is it? I'm not so sure.' Sir A picked up one staff at a time and examined each closely.

Johnny pointed to the alpenstock I'd fashioned. He nudged Ted.

'Daisy didn't do that herself.'

'No,' agreed Ted.

'Our sister's a cheat,' said Stephen. 'Come on, own up.'

But Daisy shook her head. She was grinning like mad.

'Mathilde then,' said Johnny. 'Spill the beans.'

'Let Grandpa concentrate,' said Daisy. 'I'm going to win. I'm going to win,' she chanted. 'The best of the best.'

Sir A held the alpenstock that Daisy was pretending was hers for a very long time between his hands. He ran his finger over the carving. He even, I saw, noticed the 'D' I'd made. He felt the point. He wrapped his hand around the handle and, stroking the circled initials with his thumb, 'By God, monogrammed,' he muttered. Then he laid it down again on the rug and picked up the alpenstock that was supposed to be mine. He went through the same rigmarole, except that this time he didn't put the alpenstock down. He held it horizontally, flat on the palms of his two hands.

'I declare Mathilde the winner,' he said. 'This is my preferred alpenstock. In fact,' he held up one hand to stop the outbreak of protests from all three boys and, indeed, from Daisy herself. 'I like it so much, I will take it with me to London and it will have pride of place in the umbrella stand in our hall. Come, Mathilde. I need your assistance now to get me down the slope. Charlotte dearest and Beatrice dear, organise the young people to clear up.'

And with that, he set off and I had no choice but to go with him. He was chatty as we walked and told me he'd be lonely rattling around in the big house in Seymour Street, four storeys tall, five if you counted the basement; the university would be deserted, war or no war – it was the long vac; apart from brekker, he'd probably eat at his club.

He didn't need my help until we were fording the stream at the bottom of the gully, where he deliberately dropped the alpenstock into the water and, as we both watched it wash away, said, 'Don't hide your light under a bushel, child.'

Back at Arete, he dismissed me summarily saying he was off to the thunderbox.

I went straight to the kitchen. Sylvie and the uglies wanted to hear about my scramble with the Valentine family, but I told them there wasn't much to say, it was the usual stuff and nonsense. Sylvie set me to work slicing onions, and the rest of the day passed uneventfully, except for the extra work of preparing matters for Sir A's departure the following afternoon.

When I'd put away the supper plates, glasses and silver, I hung my apron, as usual, on a hook by the stove to dry. I did my business in the thunderbox and was about to go to the servants' quarters when I noticed a glow still coming from the kitchen. It looked like the glow of an oil lamp, but I'd been taught always to be on the qui vive for fire, so I thought I ought to go and check. I opened the back door just as the door from the kitchen into the corridor was closing, and I caught a glimpse of yellow kimono. I heard footsteps slipper along the corridor and up the stairs.

I didn't think anything of it at the time, and as I crossed the lawn to the servants' quarters I saw the same glow of oil lamp in Daisy's bedroom. But the next morning, when I came to put my apron on and felt in its pocket for my knife, the knife had gone.

*

Britain declared war on Germany, but August at Arete was quiet. News about the fighting in Europe took a long time to reach us. There were fewer and fewer guests, though, and the boys seemed to argue less. I still spent time with Daisy. We swam together in the Ladies' Pond, both of us in the buff these days, and Daisy still occasionally inveigled me to join her for a duet, a game of Snap or to help her with a jigsaw. However, I was wary and watchful now.

Once, in the bathtub, as we pinked ourselves with hot water and carbolic soap, Daisy fingered her titties.

'Bubbies, diddeys, bosom friends,' she said.

She poked at my private parts, and her own,

'Mount Pleasant, the Altar of Venus. A fluffy little tuzzy-muzzy, with, underneath, a silken sheath and – I'm quoting him – a cuntful of quim,' she said. 'You know who – he likes you – Grandpa, Sir A.'

But I pretended not to understand (and I didn't, really) and ignored her; I rinsed my private parts clean, stepped out of the bathtub, dried and dressed myself quickly.

Eventually, the Valentines became rattled by the letters that arrived, almost daily, from London, urging them to pack up and leave. The journey home, tiresome at best, might become impossible if they waited much longer; there was already talk of having to take a circuitous route, keeping west of Paris.

Daisy cried when the time came to say goodbye.

'Write to me, won't you?' she said.

*

We uglies remained for another week at Arete, closing the place up for the winter. I'd just finished packing away the kitchen utensils when Mallory appeared at the back door. He'd walked over from Chamonix and had no idea the house was empty.

'I promised to come back in time for the garden party,' he said, looking around at the bare kitchen in embarrassment.

It seemed like yesterday that I'd been so mystified by the garden party. Sylvie had explained what it was, but talk of it had ceased when Sir A departed. I'd been looking forward to finding out about scones and crustless cucumber sandwiches.

Marry-Me-Mallory declined my offer of a drink. He said he'd leg it down to the valley in time for the morning train to Geneva, if it was still running. Was it still running, he asked? I didn't know. Why wouldn't it be?

I watched him walk across the turf towards the track down to Hext. He paused at the corner to relight his pipe. The smoke lingered in the still, clear air long after he'd gone.

I walked down the track the next day with Sylvie and the uglies. I'd more or less minded my P's and Q's and was half-expecting Madame Tissot to meet me at Hext-en-Haut, but of course she wasn't there: it wasn't the 30th of September, and the summer hadn't gone according to plan.

Seven

George went out onto the terrace again, but it was baking hot now. He tried sitting in a deckchair, but within minutes he felt the prickle of sweat and then a seeping through the none-too-clean creases of his trousers and shirt. George realised he could probably do with a good wash. He wondered whether the bathroom set-up at Arete had changed since his last visit and decided to go and inspect. He already knew that the loo set-up – a so-called thunderbox in a smelly outhouse – hadn't. And no: the lean-to hut that contained the enormous bathtub with Sir A's famous hot-water tap coming straight through from the kitchen looked the same as he remembered. George tried the tap and water jetted out with amazing force. He put the plug in the plughole and waited for the bath to fill up before going upstairs to fetch his sponge-bag, towel and clean clothes.

'Ready for lunch?' asked Mathilde when George, fresh in a rugby shirt, shorts and Green Flash sneakers, and feeling much better for the wash, entered the kitchen half an hour later.

'Not really,' said George. 'I'm not very hungry yet. Thank you, though.'

Mathilde looked disappointed.

'I could heat up some soup.'

'No. Honestly. Perhaps later,' said George. 'I need to find boots. Do you know if we've got any spares kicking around? I remember seeing loads last time I was here. Outside the back door. You'd been cleaning and waxing them.'

'In the darkroom. I tidied it only last week.'

George wasn't too keen on the darkroom. An Arete version of Sardines had got out of hand in 1966, and George had found himself squashed, locked – by Jack? – in the darkroom along with three of Jack's friends. One of them kept breathing hotly in George's ear, simultaneously putting a hand on George's crotch – even though George kept removing it – and squeezing.

The darkroom hadn't been used for developing photos for ages. Strictly speaking, George wouldn't have called it a room at all. It was a cupboard under the stairs really, albeit a very large one: the staircase at Arete was remarkably, almost ostentatiously wide, quite disproportionate in size and splendour to the more rustic pretensions of the place. Nevertheless, everyone still called the cupboard under the stairs the darkroom.

George propped the door open with a chair and stepped inside. Walking boots, wellies, tennis shoes and plimsolls were lined up under the sloping ceiling made by the wide stairway in two rows. On the shelves opposite them, torches, lamps, tent pegs, tent poles, crampons, harnesses, alpenstocks and coils of rope were arranged in an orderly fashion, and the workbench was covered in neat piles of folded groundsheets, fly-sheets, rolled-up tents, several small knapsacks and a camping gaz. The smell of the place reminded George of his school changing rooms, and he had no desire to linger. He grabbed two pairs of boots and took them out to the hall to try on. One pair was far too small and the other a bit too big, but the latter, George decided, clomping a few times around the hall, would be fine with thicker socks.

He spent the afternoon reading. He chose a Dick Francis from the shelf of dog-eared paperback thrillers in Sir A's old library and took it across the hall to the sitting room. The folding doors that separated the sitting room from the games room had been opened and last night's tumblers cleared from the billiard table.

The games room could have been a gloomy room: its windows looked north and west, and in the evening only a few strips of setting sun reached through the west-facing one, due to the lie of the land. There was a homeliness about it, though, which George liked and which the rest of Arete lacked. The ancient battered piano was in the corner, to the left of the west-facing window. To the right, the art deco sideboard. And opposite, there was the falling-to-pieces but incredibly comfortable brown leather couch, the radiogram, which no longer worked, and a bookcase containing children's books – some Ladybirds and Puffins, Enid Blytons (which Da disapproved of) and Arthur Ransomes (which Ma said were just as bad in their own way), but also older storybooks and novels, a *Guinness Book of Records* from 1970 and a red set of the Children's Britannica, with the *Moth to Oyster* volume missing. The sideboard, upon which stood a fresh, full bottle of génépi, a clean ashtray and an old Bush record player, had drawers that contained dozens of packs of cards, and in the cupboards beneath there were piles of board games alongside little boxes, bags and tins of chessmen, draughts pieces, tiddlywinks, dice, jacks, beads and cowrie shells. They'd used the cowrie shells as currency last time George was there, playing Pontoon, which he'd quite enjoyed, and Racing Demon, which he hadn't.

George lay on the couch and read until Mathilde appeared at the door and asked him if he was hungry yet.

'I'd love some more of that strawberry tart,' said George. 'If there's any left?'

'And a nice cup of tea, perhaps?' Mathilde was smiling.

'That'd be lovely.'

George went back out to the terrace. It was cooler now. The chalet and all of the plateau on which it stood were lit with a lower, calmer, more lemony light. He shuffled Sir A's star-gazing chair round to face the sun. Leaning back in the chair, he shut his eyes and tried not to let his thoughts stray to Ma and Da. Not easy. He'd hoped that by coming to Arete he'd be getting away from them, or rather the not-them-any-more. But no, they kept flitting across his memories. Irritating. Like flies on a film screen from the projector's lens.

George focused instead on Graham, who'd started his summer job at the open-air swimming-pool in Wallingford the day after their last exam, which they'd celebrated by drinking cider and smoking two joints each in the shed at the bottom of George's garden. It had felt good, not needing to be nervous about getting caught by Ma or Da, but strange, too, not needing to keep an eye on the kitchen window where one or the other of them often used to appear to fill the kettle or rinse a cup. The next day, Graham, exhausted, unwashed and hungover, had jumped on his bike, cycled the nine and a half miles down the A4017 to Wallingford, arrived on time, 'worked like a nigger' – the boss's words, not mine, said Graham – and everything turned out fine. Last summer he'd been washer-upper at the back of the ice-cream and drinks kiosk. This year he was at the front, serving, and George knew he had high hopes: 'I will be in a position to scrutinise, if not attract,' he'd said with his customary good humour, 'gaggles of half-naked girls. Totty, all day long. There are worse jobs. And I can swim during my breaks.'

George had been going to the pool for as long as he could remember – by bike, with Graham, from the age of eleven, and before that on the bus, accompanied by Ma, who'd usually, but not always, take a dip, as she put it, too. Ma wore an unflattering navy-blue cozzie and a bubbly, black rubber swimming cap, and as she poked the hair from her forehead into the cap, George always noticed the small raised blemish near her hairline – a run-in with an alpenstock, she said – whose contours he knew from feeling it with his fingertips when he was very, very young. Ma used to let him sit on her lap, suck his thumb and stroke her neck or face or hair with his other hand. He knew she was waiting for him to fall asleep and he usually did in the end, but not before he'd run his fingers over the hard, thickened skin.

George became aware that he was lightly moving his fingers back and forth across the bevelled edge of Sir A's star-gazing chair. He could hear cowbells in the distance, birds and crickets nearby, water in the stream and any number of lazy, buzzing, teasing, humming insects. The lure of sleep was great, but George resisted.

He thought again about the box files in the attic and how they resembled the ones in Da's study-corner. He wasn't looking forward to going through those. Graham's mum had helped George empty the drawers and cupboards in his parents' bedroom. She'd put all the clothes into laundry bags and Graham's dad had taken them away in his car. George was thankful to them for this. He'd found it difficult seeing, let alone touching, the clothes.

Graham's mum said she'd return to the house while George was in France and pack the rest of the things into boxes, but she'd leave Da's study-corner to him, for when he came back in September. It had been agreed that George would spend September in the house before going off to university – he needed three C's for Sussex – and the house was put up for sale.

'But you can stay with us any time. Holidays, weekends. You know that, don't you, George?'

George heard the sincerity in Graham's mum's voice and was grateful. Da had always liked Graham, approved of their friendship, said he'd grown up in a home not dissimilar to Graham's. Sensible, salt-of-the-earth parents, and Graham, like Da, the first in the family to go to university. Now, for George, there was a sad little measure of comfort in knowing Da would have wanted him to accept the extraordinary profusion of help offered by Graham's family.

'Yes. Thank you. I will,' George replied to Graham's mum. 'There's a payphone, apparently, at the end of every corridor in the first-year accommodation blocks at Sussex. I'll ring you. Warn you when I'm coming.'

'No need, George. You're welcome any time, warning or no warning.'

They'd been standing in his parents' bedroom during this conversation, and George kept noticing the grey cuff of Da's pyjamas peeping out from under the pillow and wondering whether he should mention it so that his parents' nightclothes could be added to the laundry bags. He didn't, and later that afternoon, when Graham's mum nipped home to put the tea on, George slid into his parents' bed, which he hadn't done since he was nine years old and ill with mumps. He swaddled himself in the sheet and blankets, made a sort of tent with the pillows and a nest for his head with Ma's white Laura Ashley nightie and Da's stripey pyjamas from Heelas. Only the notion of Graham's mum returning to find him there, blubbing like a baby, made him get up, strip the bed and chuck everything – sheets, blankets and nightclothes – into the bottom of one of the empty cupboards.

George opened his eyes to see a cup of tea and a slice of strawberry tart on the table next to him. There was a dead butterfly floating in the milky tea, one dull blue wing folded across the other so it looked like the sail of a miniature capsized boat. The strawberry tart stood next to a dainty silver fork on a white paper napkin on a china plate that matched the cup and saucer; juice from the strawberries had spread through the pastry and stained the paper napkin, pink and red.

The twins were staring at him. They both began to speak at once. Oh good. You're awake. Snow. We saw snow. Touched it. Walked on it. Loads. Loads and loads. Jack had to give Isobel a piggyback.

It was gibberish to George.

'What they mean,' said Jack, coming up behind them with Isobel on his back, 'is we reached the snow line.'

'Gosh,' said George, not sure how impressed by this he should be.

'Not bad for day one.' Jack stooped to let Isobel slide off. 'A tad tiring for the youngest member of the Alpine Club, but she did herself proud. Only flagged in the last half-hour. Will you join us for day two, cousin George?'

'I will, yes. I even have boots.'

*

Damn, damn, damned boots. George knew within minutes of setting off the next morning that they were going to give him jip. By the time he'd climbed the slope to the east of Arete, which they called Parliament Hill, the heels of both his boots were beginning to rub. He was in agony before the snow line was even in view. And George was unfit. His head throbbed, and on the steppy, rocky bits of the route, his thighs ached. They also rubbed together at the top, by his sticky crotch. At the sight of yet another steep climb ahead of them, George admitted defeat.

'I'm going down,' he told the others, not caring if Jack or the girls sneered.

He limped back to Arete with, he felt, his tail between his legs.

Mathilde made him sit on a chair in the kitchen and put his feet into a bowl of scalding hot salted water.

'It'll help heal the blisters and also toughen your skin,' she said.

The salt stung but, as the water cooled, the effect was soothing, and George kept his feet in the bowl with his trousers rolled up to his knees while he drank the coffee Mathilde put before him. Mathilde was rinsing lettuce at the sink, so she didn't see Thomas slip in through the open back door. Thomas, who was barefoot and wearing knee-breeches and a string vest, put a finger to his lips and winked at George. He crept up behind Mathilde and placed his sinewy arms around her non-existent waist.

'Surprise!' he said as Mathilde turned in amazement, a gummy smile spreading across her face. They hugged, and George felt a stab of envy – not of the hug, exactly, but of how genuine it seemed. George had stopped hugging Ma in public in the second year of primary school and had stopped hugging or kissing her completely by the time he started secondary, and as to Da, he couldn't remember the last time they'd even touched.

'And I'm here to stay. Hip, hip, hooray. As you *anglais* say. No?' Thomas sat down at the kitchen table opposite George.

'But your work?' Mathilde looked concerned.

'A Parisian family with a chalet in St Gervais had me booked for the whole week. But the wife is ill. They had to cancel. They've paid me in full, nevertheless. So I've decided to spend the week here. I won't be idle, I promise.'

When Mathilde went off to make up a bed for Thomas in one of the huts behind Arete, Thomas touched George on the arm and said, 'It's the truth, what I told my grandmother, but there's a bit more to it than that. I'm here to try to persuade her to change her mind about the election.'

'Luc, do you mean?'

'Yes. My father didn't send me here, though. I came by my own . . . on, off my own . . .'

'Off your own bat?'

Thomas laughed.

'Yes. Off my own bat.'

'You agree then?' said George. 'Hext should sell up. You think your father's right?'

'It's not quite as simple as that. But yes, basically. Yes. I think it's going to happen anyway. Sooner or later. I've seen it around Chamonix and many other places in the region: villages turning into ski stations. So I think better to have someone intelligent and educated to oversee it. My father is intelligent and educated and, in addition, not unsympathetic to the peasants who oppose it. He would manage the situation well, I believe. But now tell me. What happened to your poor feet?'

George lifted one foot out of the bowl, aware of his soft pale calf, thick ankle and puffy foot, and how they contrasted with Thomas's lean shins and bony feet.

'Ouf,' said Thomas. 'Painful.'

George looked at the crumpled, almost transparent flaps of skin on his ankle and next to his little toe. 'What happened? Tell me everything,' Ma used to say when George was hurt or upset, followed by, 'I've all the time in the world.' To George, these were some of the most comforting words in the world.

Tears pricked at George's eyes. Pathetic, he thought. I'm just pathetic.

'We'll put white spirit on the wounds as soon as they're less open,' said Thomas. 'It'd hurt too much now. But tomorrow, in the evening, we'll do it then.'

The matter-of-fact words were reassuring. George was dreading Jack's return and the jibes he would inevitably make about George's less than spectacular Alpine Club performance.

However, before Jack returned, an even bigger surprise than Thomas arrived at Arete in the form of eight of Jack's friends. They had high-back knapsacks with sleeping bags and tents strapped to them and enamel mugs and metal billy cans hanging off them. They'd just finished a month's Interrailing, they explained. Jack, they said, had invited them to drop in at Arete any time, so here they were.

Here they were, five strapping young men and three lively young women who, to George's relief, provided Jack with enough distraction to make him, if not actually forget, then at least to care less about George and his blisters.

Thomas spent the evening repairing the warped door frame of the hut where Mathilde slept. Had no one else noticed how dilapidated her hut had become? George was able to slip off to bed early and undetected, while Jack and his friends smoked the pot his friends had brought and replayed *Dark Side of the Moon*, side two, more times than George could be bothered to count.

The next day – and for the next ten days after that – Jack was fully engaged in entertaining his friends. This meant involving them by day – all day – in the hunt for gold. His friends found the pretence hilarious and the girls were in seventh heaven.

'I was hoping,' said Thomas, 'to join Jack – I mean Jack and the girls – on some excursions while I'm here.'

George and Thomas watched from outside the back door as the group departed, and George was ashamed that none of his cousins had thought to invite Thomas along.

'But what about you, George?' Thomas's effortless politesse returned as he and George walked together round to the front of the chalet. 'What are you going to do while your feet heal, and afterwards, while you're here? You are here for several weeks, I believe?'

'I've no idea.' George lowered himself into a deckchair. He gestured to Thomas to sit next to him, but Thomas remained standing. 'I'm here until the end of August, but I don't feel too confident, if I'm honest, running around the mountains with Jack in charge.'

'You lack trust in him?'

'In myself, more than anything. And I was expecting Inez to be here. I was expecting – I don't know what. Jack makes me nervous. Not just nervous. He teases me. He makes me feel like a fat idiot. A feeble fattyarbuckle.'

George looked up at Thomas, who didn't respond immediately. He was frowning slightly.

'You're not fat,' he said. 'But you are weak, I see that. Here's an idea. I am weak in English. I need to improve. If you help me while I'm here, I, in exchange, will help you.'

'I don't quite follow you.'

'Make you strong. Able to keep up with Jack. Perhaps even overtake him.'

'That'll be the day.'

'Trust me. Jack will soon be begging me – I mean you – to join him in his wild herring.'

'Wild goose chase, you mean.'

'See – I have much to learn.'

*

Thomas was as good as his word and fairly put George through his paces over the next few days. George enjoyed Thomas's company so much, however, that he didn't mind the burn in his muscles and the tiredness in his limbs when he lay down at night to sleep. He enjoyed refining Thomas's English, too. Thomas was a quick learner and George wasn't a bad teacher. Must be in the genes.

The time for Thomas to start his next guiding job came, and he confided in George that he'd made no headway with persuading digging-her-heels-in Mathilde to see reason. George decided to tell Thomas about the trip to the attic with Mathilde.

'What sort of proof do you think she meant?' he asked when he'd finished explaining.

Thomas considered carefully what George had told him, but then shrugged.

'I think my grandmother is barking madly up many wrong trees. Digging for dirt where there is none.'

When Thomas had gone, George kept up the good work, doing the exercises Thomas had set him and walking a bit further and a bit higher each day. Thomas had said it was fine to wear the Green Flash sneakers if they were comfortable, but he should buy himself some leather walking boots next time he went down to Hext. George had planned to do this on Saturday, the day Jack's friends were departing, but on Thursday evening a telegram was brought up to Arete.

'Bloody Inez,' said Jack, holding the telegram out towards George.

'What's happened?'

'God knows. Read it yourself.'

George took the telegram. 'Problem. Ring. Fri. 12 on.,' he read, and then a series of numbers.

'What does she mean?'

'She means we're to ring her.'

'So?'

'So that means going down to the village and ringing from the post office. Tomorrow. On the dot of twelve. Damn nuisance.'

'It must be important, though,' said George.

'I doubt it. I'm tempted to ignore it. Pretend we never got the message. We're doing the big Loo tomorrow. Weather's perfect.

Not a breath of wind. And I reckon the streams that normally hamper progress will all have dried up with this weather.'

'I'll pop down to the village if you like,' said George, surprising himself by the confidence in his voice. He realised that his time in the mountains with Thomas had made him feel better in all sorts of ways, not just physically.

'Pop? You? It's not exactly a pop for a feeblosity, is it?'

'You're right,' said George reasonably. 'But I'm a lot stronger than I was. And it'll do me good. Besides, I'm expecting a letter.'

'Fine,' said Jack. 'Take the telegram. The number's on it. And take money.'

*

The walk down to Hext was a piece of cake, though it was unbelievably hot in the valley. The daytime temperatures at Arete were tolerable and the evenings had a delicious cool edge to them. Dew kept the colours bright, flora abundant and the air soft. Down in the village, the sun – a flat white plate glaring from a blue-white sky – had baked the place hard. Apart from the cracked, mottled grey of the road, all was brown rutted earth. Shops and chalets, their window boxes empty or removed, had their shutters closed against the heat. As George passed them, he could feel it reflecting off the wood of the buildings and bouncing up from the road.

He hurried to the post office. He was anxious about making the phone call at the right time. The queue moved slowly. The postmistress was surly. Yes, there was a letter for him. Where was his passport? No, he couldn't make a phone call, it was almost *midi*, he was too late, he should have booked the call earlier. George showed her the telegram and desperately jabbed a finger at the date and at the 12. She relented and pointed to the shabby booth next to the entrance. George went into it and waited until the phone rang. He picked the receiver up.

'*Non, non! Il faut attendre*,' shouted the postmistress.

George dropped the receiver and saw her shake her head crossly. He placed it carefully back. Again he waited. It was sweltering in the booth. There was no ventilation whatsoever. He put the knapsack he'd borrowed from the darkroom down on the floor and the letter from Graham into one of its pockets. Again the telephone rang. He waited.

'*Allez-y. Décrochez. Vite.*'

George lifted the receiver.

'Hello?' he said. 'Hello? Inez?'

The line crackled and there was a sound like wind in the background, but Inez's voice was unmistakeable.

She'd twisted her ankle, damn it. Thought she had. Climbing . . . Damnation. Not twisted. Maybe broken, bugger it. Mummy's damned birthday. Six weeks, possibly, in plaster. Driving impossible. Walking bloody difficult. Not painful. Stuck, damn it. What a bugger.

George asked when she would be able to drive again, but didn't hear the answer. He asked how Daisy was, but Inez went on cursing and repeating, between curses, how stuck she was.

'You'll have to manage without me,' he heard and, just before the line went dead, 'How are you?'

George replaced the receiver carefully and went to the counter to pay, then back out into the sweltering midday sun.

He walked to the square and sat on one of the stone seats built in to the wall surrounding the church. He was very thirsty. Opposite him, the Auberge Dorée was busy. All of the tables outside, shaded by the hotel's awning, had people at them: big families nattering at each other, an old couple reading different sections of *Le Monde*, several groups of three, four or even five men, and a pair of hikers with maps and guidebooks on their table.

Through the open swing doors of the hotel George could see more people inside, men at the bar, men and women on stools and chairs nearby.

George's thirst was beginning to make his throat hurt. He decided to brave it and go and order a drink. There was the fountain in the middle of the village square, and George longed to drink from that, duck his head into its bowl and soak his hair like they had when they were kids. But the fountain was in full view of the people sitting outside the hotel, and he didn't want to draw attention to himself.

He made his way through the tables and into the hotel, where the heat was intensified by the thick, smoky air and a sweaty, aniseedy smell. There seemed to be some sort of meeting going on. One man and two women were shouting at each other. People were talking in groups, fanning themselves with hats and newspapers, waving cigarettes around.

George wished he hadn't ventured in, but it was too late. The barman had seen him. Visitors often overnighted at the Auberge Dorée on their way to or from Arete, even though there were two smarter, more modern hotels near the station. The proprietor of the Auberge Dorée made a point of being polite, obsequious even, to anyone connected with Arete, and, having elicited from George where he was staying, today was no exception.

George was told to take a seat outside in the cool and he would be served there. And when George pointed outside, indicating there was no space, the barman shouted at one of the waiters, who went bustling out of the door. George saw the waiter lean down and say something to a group of three men. The men glanced up, nodded and shuffled their chairs over to the next table, joining two other men. The waiter beckoned to George.

George's table was in a good shady position. The waiter brought the Coca-Cola George ordered, and a tall glass tinkling with ice cubes. George poured the Coke and drank, and despite being uncomfortable about having forced the group of men to move, he felt better. Besides, the men took no notice of him; they were all engrossed in looking at each other's Loto tickets.

From the half sentences, half French, half patois, that George caught, he gathered there'd been a significant win in one of the villages further down the valley, and the men were stating and restating how close to the winning number they'd come with their tickets.

At one o'clock, George ordered another Coca-Cola. Raised voices and intense chatter could still be heard coming from the bar, but the tables outside began to empty. One thirty. George got out his wallet and was just looking around for the waiter when, 'Cigarette?'

A man's voice he didn't recognise, from the table next to him, made him turn. The man, old and brown, with dark sharp eyes, was extending a packet of Gitanes towards him.

'You're English,' he said as George shook his head. 'You smoke only English cigarettes?'

George laughed. 'No. I don't really smoke at all, actually.'

'Ah.' The man pulled out a cigarette, put it to his lips and lit it. He inhaled.

'Costanza,' he said, blowing the smoke out again. 'Alessandro Costanza. Pleased to meet you. People call me Costa.'

'George,' said George.

'What brings you to our valley, George? You're not clothed for climbing.' The old man glanced at the hikers, who were shouldering their knapsacks, tucking maps into their pockets. The woman left a five franc piece and some smaller change on the table. After they'd left, striding off across the square, Costanza stretched across and counted the money.

'They bought four drinks – Coca-Colas like you, George – and they've paid for eight. Fools. But the proprietor will be happy.'

He let the money drop through his fingers onto the table. Costanza's hands, George noticed, despite being old, were remarkably supple; elegant, even. They were long, with slim, strong fingers. The fingernails were worn and rough but very clean, and his knuckles, the backs of his hands and the narrow, bony, delicate wrists poking out of the frayed cuffs of a summer jacket were a wonderful, almost shiny, dark woody brown colour. A royal blue handkerchief was tucked into one of the cuffs.

'I'm staying at Arete,' said George.

'Ah. Family?' asked Costanza.

'Yes.'

'Are you many this year? Is Mathilde among you?'

George wondered what Costa meant by many.

'Yes, Mathilde's there,' he said.

'So you'll know about—' Costa jerked his head in the direction of the bar.

There was still no sign of the hubbub abating.

'I've no idea. I was wondering.'

The waiter came out and Costanza nodded him over.

'Two coffees,' Costa said. 'You'll join me?'

'Thank you,' said George. 'May I have some water too, please.'

The waiter departed, scooping up the hikers' money, smiling to himself, and Costanza said, 'I myself came here to pose questions.'

'But can you at least tell me,' said George, 'what they're doing in there? What are they all so het up about?'

'Het up, I don't know. I think they're doing what you *anglais* call letting off the steam.' Costanza looked very pleased with himself. 'Is that not, as you would say, correct usage?'

Costanza's English was quite stilted and he spoke with a strong accent.

'Yes,' said George. 'But we don't let off steam like that.'

'They are discussing the election. It's no surprise they are animated.'

'But they're so serious, so upset. Some of them sound furious.'

'They believe their way of life is threatened. That's why.'

The waiter brought the coffees, two glass tumblers and a carafe of water.

'What do you think?' Costanza turned to the waiter. 'Which list will win? Who are you going to vote for?'

The waiter said he hadn't decided yet and went back into the noisy interior.

'I do know there's a dispute,' George said, 'between Luc and his mother about it all.'

'Yes. Mathilde.' Costanza paused. He lifted his eyes and looked beyond George. His pupils shrank to blue-black dots in his brown-black eyes as he gazed into the distance. 'Mathilde will not be persuaded. She will not change her mind. She is determined. Stubborn does not begin to describe the woman. No one knows that more than I.' The old man paused again. 'Give her my regards, won't you?'

George nodded and poured himself some water. Small, already half-melted cubes of ice splashed around in the tumbler, and when George brought the glass to his lips, he let them slide into his mouth and sucked on them, waiting for Costanza to continue.

When he didn't, 'What's your view,' George asked, 'about the land, the election? The candidates.' He took another mouthful of water and ice.

'Fuck the bloody lot of them!'

George swallowed the ice cubes in his mouth, nearly choking, while Costa broke into laughter.

'Don't worry. It wasn't your *anglaïs* gentlemen or women who taught me that obscenity. I learnt it from the yanks, in Paris, there are many, many years ago. But I apologise. The truth is, I haven't made up my mind yet. Like the waiter, I sit down on the fence.'

The clock in the village square struck two. George had told Mathilde he'd aim to be back by teatime and he still needed to buy his boots.

'I must go,' he said.

At the bar, he paid for his Coca-Colas and the two coffees. The waiter took his ten-franc note and gave him his change, along with a leaflet announcing a public meeting: Sunday 18 July, 7 p.m., in the *salle des fêtes*. George deduced from the small print that a representative from the American company in Colorado wanting to buy the land would be present.

When he went outside, Costanza had gone. George looked around the square and up the road. There was no sign of him. He left the change the waiter had given him on the table, knowing it was a stupidly generous tip but knowing, also, that it was somehow expected, even though – perhaps even more so because – he was a member of the family who owned Arete.

*

The purchase of a well-fitting pair of boots was straightforward, and George wore them for the climb up to Arete. He stopped for a short rest at the turning off the track at Hext-en-Haut, where Jack's 2CV stood exactly as they'd left it more than two weeks ago, its exhaust dangling down to the ground. It wasn't until then that George opened Graham's letter. The scrawl on the blue airmail envelope, postmarked Reading, 5th of July, had told him it was from his friend before the palaver with the postmistress had made him stuff it into a pocket of his knapsack. The letter was short and not exactly bursting with information, except about the heatwave. 'Hottest day ever yesterday. 96.6. Dad heroically continues not to wash the car, but won't let me put a "Bath with a friend" sticker on it. Mum is contemplating having a go at water-divining!' Graham wittily described a typical day at his swimming pool job. It was, he wrote, 'a breeze, but, I'm sorry to report, no totty yet. There's a very tall Romanian woman who works as a lifeguard, though, who keeps looking across at the kiosk. I think she might fancy me.' In your dreams, thought George, appreciating the Grahamness of the letter, despite its brevity.

Eight

'Will you write to me, Mathilde?' Daisy had said between sobs as she left.

I said I would, and I did, twice, to the address she'd given me of her school in Hampshire, and Daisy replied ('Dear Matilda'), once.

But there was the war.

Benoît was killed.

Then there were the terrible winters of 1919 and 1921, Papa dying, Maman dying, and both of my sisters marrying, neither of them to boys or men I knew – not that there were many marriageable ones among those left in Hext. Women who wanted or needed to marry were having to venture further afield. One of my sisters went all the way to Grenoble, where she met and wed a rich glove maker; they moved to Lyon and I never heard from her again. The other found work down in Cluses, in a factory that made small watch parts. She married the boss and died eight months later in childbirth.

I took over the running of the farm. Madame Tissot asked me to help her with lessons at the school, but I was far too busy. She urged me not to neglect my books and I said I wouldn't, but I already had. Reading was the last thing on my mind when I'd eventually finished all the chores for the day. And I was glad of it, because reading reminded me of Benoît, and thinking about Benoît made me sadder than I can say.

I no longer dawdled in the orchards, in the autumn, beyond Costa's house. I picked the fruit quickly and hurried back along the track to the village. One day, however, I paused, as Benoît and I had paused so many times before, at the spot where the wild roses intertwine with the bramble and nettles just below the windows of Costanza's workshop. I put down the baskets I held in each hand, but kept the third, containing the bilberries, on my head. The windows were open, but there was no music, only the sound of tapping and a quiet sort of scraping. I was about to proceed on my way, half relieved, half disappointed, when a voice called, 'Who is it?'

I jolted, causing the basket of bilberries to fall from my head. Some of the bilberries landed in the basket of pears, but most of them rolled off into the grass and dandelions. The basket itself bounced across the path and ended up on its side in the brambles.

'Who is it?' I heard again as I scrabbled to retrieve the fallen basket, thinking only to get away as quickly as possible. But it was too late. I heard the front door open, footsteps, and there was Costa on the path in front of me.

'I'm sorry,' I said. 'I've been fruit-picking. I'm on my way home.'

'Mathilde,' said Costa, and this time I nearly pissed myself.

'Don't be afraid. I didn't mean to frighten you. There's nothing to be frightened of.'

'But my name,' I blurted out. I really was frightened. 'How do you know my name?'

'Because of Benoît,' said Costanza. 'You and Benoît used to loiter here. Frequently. Didn't you?'

'Yes, but—'

'You thought I didn't know. Did you think that because I didn't ever come out, I didn't know you were here? You whispered. You listened. I too listened.'

'We meant no harm. That's all we did. We listened. We stole nothing. We never came further than here.'

'I know that, Mathilde. What harm could you have done? You were children. How old are you now?'

'Twenty-two, monsieur.'

'And Benoît, I know – and I'm sorry – is among our dead.'

'Yes.'

'One of too many. And one is too many. I'm deeply sorry, Mathilde. To lose such a friend. You must miss him very much.'

Costanza's kind words caused a rush of gratitude mixed with pain: my cheeks heated and tears made my eyes blurry.

'You must come inside,' Costanza said.

'But my bilberries,' I said. 'And I need to go home to my farm. The cows.'

'Come inside. I can help you with the bilberries. Have a drink, refresh yourself. The cows can wait.'

Costanza turned and went back into his workshop. I looked at the splatter of bilberries on the ground and wondered what Benoît would say if he knew what a pickle I was in now. *Courage, mon amie,* probably, which is what he used to say when he wanted me to leap, like him, across a gully or stream or, for pure *joie de vivre,* from rock to rock in the river Ouiffre.

I followed Costanza inside.

It was bright and hot in there and smelt of fresh wood and wood resin, like all woodsheds, but there was another smell too. I sniffed.

'Glue,' said Costanza. 'I've been niggling at this old thing all afternoon, but I can't get it right.'

He picked up a fiddle that had no strings. He held it by the neck and pointed to the curve of its thin belly.

'There's the smallest of cracks, right there,' he said. 'I doubt you can see it.'

I peered at the wood, at the place where he pointed, and shook my head.

'But we can hear.' He tapped, twice, on the belly of the fiddle. 'Do you hear?'

'I hear your taps.'

'Do they sound good to you?'

'They sound like taps, monsieur,' I said.

'Listen.' Costanza picked up another fiddle, this one with strings, which was lying on its side next to a pile of woodshavings. When he tapped on its belly, the sound was different, deeper, fuller. 'Tell me what you hear, Mathilde.'

'This one,' I said, 'sounds like a stone plopping into water. But that one,' I pointed to the damaged, stringless violin, 'is more like stone on stone.'

'Or even grass,' Costanza added. 'Muted. Toneless. Excellent: I guessed you had a good ear. Why else would you have lingered so often by my house?'

Nobody had ever complimented me like that before. My ears were small and the left one had a lobe missing where Papa pulled too hard when, once, aged five, I tried to skive my chores; there was a lot of screaming and shouting, bandages and poultices, but the damage couldn't be repaired.

'Will you ever be able to repair the sound?' I asked.

'Perhaps tomorrow. I'm giving up for today. I've tried. A thousand different ways. But so far, no luck.'

Costanza moved both of the fiddles to the back of the workbench.

'I'll fetch us some water,' he said.

While he was gone, I looked around me. What caught my eye the most were the tools, which were similar to many of the tools I'd seen before in Papa's toolshed, except these were tiny. There was a hammer no bigger than a finger, a saw that would fit in the palm of my hand, and delicate, bone-handled knives that made the shortest of Benoît's Opinels seem long.

'Here we are,' said Costanza, returning with two bowls of water. 'I've no seats, I'm afraid. I work standing up.'

'Thank you,' I said. 'I'm happy to stand. Besides, I can't stay.' I took the water and drank thirstily from the bowl.

'Perhaps you'll visit more often now?' said Costanza.

'I was only picking fruit,' I said, as before, worried he was reminding me again, of having eavesdropped on him when I was a child.

'No, I mean, come to visit. Me. I'd like that.'

I didn't know what to say.

'I'm inviting you to visit, Mathilde. Whenever you like.'

Still I remained silent, unsure how I was meant to respond, unsure how I wanted to respond.

Costanza walked over to a tall, narrow chest of drawers.

'Shall I play for you before you go?' he asked.

'I'd like that.' I nodded, realising I'd used the same expression he'd used when he'd invited me to visit again.

'Good.'

Costanza opened the third drawer down and took out yet another violin and a bow.

'This is my own,' he said, holding both violin and bow up in the air. 'A poor old thing compared to those.' He waved the bow towards the two fiddles on the workbench. 'But I'm fond of it. And it's mine.'

'Who do those belong to?' I asked.

'Two Lyonnaise ladies. Sisters. They play abominably. I heard them when I went to collect the instruments. But their papa is very rich. He bought them each an excellent violin, thinking the excellence of the craftsmanship would make up for their lack of skill. He was wrong. And moreover, the ladies didn't look after their fiddles. They left them lying around. Both got broken. I'm paid to repair them. Now, Mathilde, close your eyes.'

I frowned at him, wondering if, after all, the villagers were correct and Costanza wasn't quite right in the head.

'Like this.' He shut his own eyes.

I stared at the closed lids of his eyes, at the angular cheekbones, at the dark stubble on the jaw.

'You're shy,' he said. 'You're afraid of me. Afraid of what I might see if you shut your eyes. You can trust me, Mathilde, I promise. But if you're shy, turn away. And then shut your eyes.'

I moved to the window and looked out of it. I tried to imagine being Costa looking out of that window and seeing – or at least hearing – the two peasant children, as carefree as crickets, on the path outside: Benoît throwing his cap in the air, both of us munching on apples; what must he have thought of our childish, chirruping conversations, our stories and our secrets?

I kept my eyes open while Costa adjusted the strings of the violin until they sounded correct together. And I kept them open in the long pause that followed. But then he started playing and, after a few notes, I shut my eyes because he was playing one of the very same tunes we'd listened to on the path outside, Benoît and I, and although it didn't take my pain away, it changed it into something more bearable, for a while.

'There,' said Costa. 'You can turn round now.'

But I stayed facing the window for a moment with my eyes closed.

'It's a love song,' said Costanza. 'Do you like it? There are words. But who needs words with music such as this?'

'Yes,' I said simply, turning round, and I could tell, from the way he looked at me so intently with those piercing, near-black eyes of his, that Costa and I understood each other.

'I must go,' I said. 'I'm late already.'

'Yes.' Costa's affirmation echoed my own.

'Thank you again for the water,' I said and hurried out of the door.

I retrieved the empty bilberry basket from the brambles, picked up the basket of apples and the basket of pears, and walked as quickly as I could back to the farm.

The following morning, I rose as usual, at dawn, to milk the cows. When I opened the front door, I nearly tripped. On the doorstep was a large, old wicker basket, and it was filled to the brim with bilberries.

*

Two weeks passed before I found the time to go back and see Costa, and meanwhile I hatched a plan.

Market day. I took some of my best ham and meatiest, tastiest diots down to the village square and spread them out on a cloth. I then produced my bilberry tart. The English have their uses: in 1914, I'd learnt to make pastry the *anglais* way. In 1922, I combined Mrs Beeton's advice with Maman's tried and trusted recipe and, I must say, the result was excellent.

I placed my bilberry tart on the middle of a flat stone and lifted the stone onto the wall by the church. Then I borrowed a knife from slimy-faced Cédric, who was selling chickens next to me, and I sliced the tart into sixteen pieces. Cédric licked his thick lips with his fat, drooling tongue, but I was giving nothing away. I'd sold the whole tart within half an hour.

I'd never made so much money so quickly. The success of my plan almost scared me. But I stuck to my guns and ventured over to the wagon that came every week from Annecy, loaded with rolls of brightly coloured fabric and an abundance of pretty caps, bonnets and lacy shawls. I bought two new caps and a shawl with tassles.

*

Costanza didn't hear me approach, so I went right up to the window and knocked. I didn't want him thinking I was eaves-dropping again.

He looked up from his workbench, smiled, nodded, gestured to the door.

I opened the door and went in.

'I've come to thank you,' I began, holding out his empty wicker basket.

'No, Mathilde. It's I who was thanking you. After you left the other day, I suddenly had an idea for that fine fiddle I was trying to mend. And it worked. Within an hour of your leaving, I'd mended it. As good as new.'

'But—'

'No buts.' He took the basket from me. 'I'm happy you're here. And what a nice shawl you have. Let me just finish this.' He flapped the basket at the workbench, where his own worn old fiddle rested on its side as if he'd been playing it recently. Next to it was the bow and a large, untidy pile of papers – bills, receipts and sheets of squared paper covered in neatly written lists, and rows and columns of numbers and sums, less neat. 'My accounts,' he added. 'Long overdue.'

'You're busy. I'll leave.'

'No. Wait. This won't take long. Please don't leave. Stay right where you are. I've something I'd like to show you.'

Wondering what that could possibly be, I took Costa at his word and remained standing at the door, tweaking at the tassles of my shawl. Lined up next to the door were five black violin cases. They had labels stuck on and tied to them, many, but the newest on each was in Costa's handwriting, the same as that I'd just seen on the workbench: names and addresses. I bent down and read them. All the cases that day were destined for Paris. So some of the rumours were correct – Costa did receive commissions from as far afield as the capital.

'It's no good.' Costa sighed. 'I can't make things tally. Later, maybe. Perhaps you'll bring me luck again, Mathilde. Now. Come with me.'

He picked up the violin and bow and led the way out of the workshop, round to the back of his house and past some sheds to a large barn. It was cool inside and dark, until Costa switched on the electricity. I blinked and let out a gasp, because electricity was still a novelty. We'd had it for less than a year – our valley was one of the first in the whole of France to receive it, and we considered ourselves very fortunate.

The light in Costa's barn seemed to fling itself down like water from the dozen or so overhead bulbs unevenly strung from the rafters.

'Thank God for white coal,' said Costa, pointing at one of

the pools of light where the dust whirled. 'Plenty more of that. And I'll need it if I go ahead with things.'

He looked around the barn and seemed to be seeing more than was there.

'A man,' he said. 'A client – perhaps I should call him a business partner – from Paris gave me an idea. Well, more than an idea. Do you know what an investment is, Mathilde?'

'Yes,' I said, thinking of Cédric's family investing in eight red-crowned, white-feathered, blue-footed Bresse chickens last year.

'This man wants me to convert my barn into a club. For music. He will pay. He says it will be a good investment. I thought at first it was just the whim of a rich Parisian. But he insists he knows more about these things than me, and he's probably right. My objection wasn't to the idea. The idea I like very much. But can you really see people flocking all the way here to this hidden, hanging valley, all the way to Hext, to listen to music?'

'No,' I said.

'No, nor could I,' said Costa. 'Until this man reminded me that all my clients have cars. And this man has many friends. They too have cars. And cars, he said, are the future: city people will drive miles and miles, hours and hours, just for the hell of it, and if, during their driving, they were to come across a place they liked, a club, for example, they would stay put and spend a lot of money. And—' Costa stopped speaking for a moment and, with a flourish, switched the overhead lights off, then on again. 'There's the electrification of the train line. Handy for the Geneva crowd. They could do with a decent music club.'

'Music club.' I said the words slowly and carefully, trying them out.

'In Paris,' said Costa, 'there are many such clubs. Wonderful, magical places. Musicians come together to play in them. People come together to hear the musicians play, but also to dance to the music. They pay to do that.'

I was confused.

'Like a carnival, or festival?'

'Similar. More like going to church, except that there is no God, just music, and instead of a sip of communion wine, gallons of beer, magnums of champagne and rainbow-coloured cocktails from America.'

'A music club.' I repeated the words.

'A jazz club. Costa's jazz club. That's the idea.'

Costa lifted his violin, plucked a few notes, placed his bow on the strings. He played the same simple tune as before, paused again.

'Now.'

Costa replayed the notes, but in such a startlingly different way, I'm not sure I'd have recognised them if he hadn't played the old melody first.

'That's jazz,' he said. 'I think you'd like it – taking music you know, or making some up, if you like, and then adding to it. Changing things. Improvising.'

Costa continued to play the same tune, but employing strange, wild rhythms, making almost jarring sounds, and lengthening and shortening the notes of the refrain in ways that made my innards stir.

'Imagine more instruments,' he said loudly above the music, swaying his body, nodding his head, tapping his foot, but going on playing and playing until I started swaying a little bit too. 'A piano, clarinets, trumpets, trombone. A whole band.'

'Accordion?' I asked, which made Costa laugh and stop playing.

'Yes. Why not? No rules forbid it.'

We went back to the workshop.

'I'll fetch us some cider,' said Costa.

He was out of the room for less than a minute, but I glanced at the figures on the top piece of squared paper on the workbench, and I could see immediately where Costa had gone wrong with his sums. I'd been doing our farm's accounts for as long as I could remember. Since the war, I'd been doing the accounts for Cédric's farm, too, in exchange for wood for the winter. Costa's columns, I could see, were to do with estimates for the club. His Parisian friend's proposed investment was enormous.

I showed Costa his error when he returned with our cider. He was very grateful and let me write the columns out again correctly.

'What do you think, Mathilde? Do you think it could work?'

'No doubt,' I said, convinced as much by his enthusiasm as by the sum of money.

It took time, but Costa's club definitely, eventually, worked – better and more dramatically than either of us could have imagined on that warm, appley, autumn afternoon in 1922.

*

The *rosbifs* returned to Arete in 1924, and my services were requested. The pay was enough to hire help for the farm over the summer, including for the harvests, and to buy a tractor of my own instead of paying to share the one Cédric's family had bought two years ago. I had no reason to say no. Except that Cédric had asked me to marry him. Cédric was already a widower, with elderly parents, brother Henri le cretin to keep an eye on and a big, busy farm to run. His wife had died of the influenza in 1919. I'd helped lay her out, and her dead body was black and blue, purple and pink from beatings. Cédric said that he wasn't too keen on marriage to me because of my ugliness, but there was no doubt it would benefit both our farms. No doubt, I agreed, and I considered his proposal, momentarily imagining unmarriageable me, married and with a family. But I didn't want a black and blue body, and the notion of Cédric's fat tongue in my mouth made me retch. I said no to him.

Arete hadn't changed since we'd left it in 1914. Only the piano needed tuning and the *anglais* garden tidying up. Roses, privet, rhododendrons, holly and perrenials with names like Moonflower, Lady's Mantle and Black-eyed Susan, had been transplanted from England more than fifty years ago when the chalet was constructed. And – against all odds, as Lady C, who did the odd bit of deadheading, liked to say – they'd thrived. With no *anglais* clipping and shaping, they'd grown tall and sprawled, but they still didn't look as if they truly belonged on the land – like a pretty but mismatching patch on a skirt.

Henri le cretin came up to help with the garden for a few days, and I supervised him.

Costa was sent for to tune the piano, but he said the job was beyond him now; too many parts needed replacing.

'I'm only trained in the basics,' he explained to Beatrice. 'I'm sorry.'

Beatrice, whose thick, brown Valentine hair had coarsened and greyed like corrugated iron, was cross and she didn't pay him for his time. He set off down the mountain without staying to eat with us, even though Sylvie asked him to. I was sorry to see him go.

In all other respects, the chalet and its outhouses – laundry room, mazot, thunderbox and the huts used as sleeping quarters by us uglies and the overflow guests – were exactly as we'd left them in 1914. Which is probably why my shock at the change in the Valentine family was so great.

Stephen wasn't there at all.

'Nah-poohed at Ypres,' said Daisy when I asked. 'Shsh, though. We don't mention the war much. And remember not to call Pretty Johnny pretty any more. Just Johnny.'

Last time I'd seen him, Johnny had been a gambolling boy. Now he was a scarred, hulking cripple of a man – a half man, Daisy said, 'with a peg leg. And shrapnel – here.' Daisy put a finger to her head, then between her thighs, at the very top. 'And here. But he's still the life and soul.'

Jolly Johnny: always first to suggest a high jink or jape and last to abandon it. Johnny, in fact, was jollier than ever, except when he wasn't, when he stayed in bed for days on end, refusing to eat or speak, weeping like a girl.

Ted had been a hero in the war.

'And our aunt Margaret was a heroine. She drove ambulances. Saved dozens of lives, apparently. But she's still *persona non grata* chez nous. I only know about her activities via a girlfriend who nursed.'

As for Ted, 'VC for valour. Good old Ted,' said Daisy.

But I saw in Ted, straight away, the despair. I'd seen it since the war dozens of times. In the men who spent the winter not tending to their families and farms, not whittling away the time in their woodsheds making tools and cooking utensils or knick-knacks for the house, but sitting in the smoky rooms of the Auberge Dorée, drinking themselves into oblivion. And in the women – Benoît's mother became one of them – sleeping away the endless dark hours of winter with the shutters closed, the fire left to die out and an empty bottle of wine by the bed.

The Valentines tolerated Ted's bouts of drinking as they tolerated Johnny's moods.

Daisy herself had grown into a fine young filly (Ted's words), 'a stunner' (Johnny's). Even-featured, shiny-haired, slim-limbed and lithe; everything about her was clear and bright. But her face was marred by the expression on it which, if she wasn't smiling, was often confused or anxious, upset and, sometimes, deeply sad. She'd developed her passion for fashion and wore nothing but silk – silk of all sorts and all colours, patterned and printed, two-tone and sequinned, made up into short, boxy, drop-waisted frocks. She smoked before breakfast and ate very little, but things were still fantabulous, 'ilarious, and 'I'm a merry widow' was all she ever said about the fact that she'd married at eighteen – yes, indeed, to a penniless poet, killed in Flanders less than a month after the wedding. She later miscarried the baby in her womb.

Daisy brought me some Cadbury's Dairy Milk chocolate.

'I remembered you liked it,' she said. And, 'The beanpole's probably got some with him in the Himalayas. I'm expecting a postcard soon.'

But there was no more 'we're best friends' or begging me to join her. Not that I'd have agreed to participate in that summer's fad, which involved climbing with skins and skis to the glacier de la Miche. There, I gathered, all sorts of daredevil antics took place in the name of the Valentine Olympics. Ted went to visit the Paris Olympics. He came back chanting, '*Citius, altius, fortius*,' and soon they were all at it, chanting and dancing, cheering each other on, climbing swifter, higher, steeper.

The Chamonix Olympics had been the talk of the valley the previous winter. Cédric went to Chamonix in February, expressly to watch the men's downhill skiing. He invited me to go with him, but I declined. When the snow melted, he invited me to Zizipompom. I declined.

I was still expected to be at Daisy's beck and call, but 'You're no longer fun, Mathilde,' she often complained.

Fun had become what the Valentines sought; the young ones, at least.

Sir A sought no more than a release from earthly pain – that's what he told me. 'My heart hurts and my bones ache – they've had their day,' he'd say. I was sorry to see him slipping away; it was during the summer of 1924 that we became ever so slightly acquainted.

Nine

Someone was sitting in Sir A's star-gazing chair, George saw, when he glanced up at Arete through the thinning trees before rounding the last two bends of the path.

Scarcely tired or aching at all, he went straight to the terrace, where Mathilde was fast asleep. Her hands – knobbly, scarred and rough with crooked fingers, the nails missing on most of them – were folded on top of a book. Her head lolled to one side and she was crumpled in the corner of the star-gazing chair, which made her look smaller than she actually was. If it hadn't been for the rise and fall of her chest, she might have been dead.

George had never seen a dead person. When he thought about Ma and Da dead, he couldn't get beyond an image of their bodies blown to pieces by the impact of the crash. He knew it wasn't accurate; in his head he saw them, not smashing through the car's windscreen, but already hurtling out the other side of it, with individual bits of them, fingers, ears, a foot, and their clothes – Ma's shoes and handbag, Pa's hat, tie, watch – flying through the air. They never landed. The image just repeated itself, like the spray from a fountain, again and again. The idea of their chucked clothes going off with the rubbish men and being strewn in some anonymous dump had felt stomach-churningly appropriate.

George put the leaflet about the public meeting on the table and was about to go when, 'Hello,' Mathilde said as if she'd been wide awake all the time. 'New boots?'

'Yes.' George hid his surprise. 'I bought them this afternoon.'

'Very good. And Inez? What did she have to say?'

George explained how unsatisfactory the phone conversation with Inez had been. Mathilde nodded as if none of this was unexpected.

'It was incredibly hot in the village,' George added. 'I had a drink at the Auberge Dorée. I met someone called Costa there. We chatted. He said to give you his regards.'

'Did he indeed?' Mathilde sat up straight in Sir A's star-gazing chair.

'Who is Costa, Mathilde? He didn't really explain.'

'Costa's a wood merchant,' said Mathilde, her face closing in in that peasanty way it sometimes did. 'Amongst other things.'

George picked up the Colorado company's flyer about the public meeting.

'The barman at the Auberge Dorée gave me this.' He passed the leaflet to Mathilde. 'Costa's still sitting down on the fence, by the way. That's how he put it, that's what he said. Along with quite a few other things.'

'I can imagine.' Mathilde was curt, but George detected the flicker of a smile on her face.

She stood up.

'I've work to do,' she said and went inside.

*

'Do you know anything about Costa?' George asked Jack the next day.

Jack's friends had left early to catch *le petit train* to Geneva. George, Jack and the girls had set off early too, George having requested at breakfast, po-faced, to rejoin the Alpine Club.

'Let's test cousin George's resolve, shall we?' Jack said. 'Nothing too arduous. We'll walk to la Miche and do a few mini-recces from there.'

La Miche, George discovered – after a trek through the mountains to the south of Arete, beyond le petit Luet, along a narrow, winding, rocky path with no views to speak of on either side – was the halfway point between Chamonix and Hext, on the main track between the two. It was a sheltered bowl of land with a green glacial lake in the middle of it – le Lac de la Miche – and a col at either end. A forbidding, schisty rock face ran along one side: les Rochers de la Miche, which rose to a crenellated ridge like a castle, above which towered the grand Luet. The ridge was often topped with snow, even in the summer, and impossible to climb from this side, Jack said, but you could actually get to it fairly easily if you approached from behind, avoiding the glacier; the peak of the grand Luet was reachable from its western flank even by an inexperienced alpinist.

George put his question about Costa to Jack after lunch. The girls had gone off to explore the lower reaches of the rock face. Any hint or glint of gold and you holler, Jack told them.

'Costa who?' Jack lit a Disque Bleu.

'Just an old geezer I met yesterday in the village. Sells wood, apparently. He knows Mathilde. Even older than her, though.'

'Nah, mate. Never 'eard of 'im.' Jack's fake cockney accent wasn't very good. 'Oh. Hang on a mo.' Jack blew two perfect blue-grey smoke rings. 'Actually, now I come to think of it, wasn't that what that weird disco place was called? The one you and I found last time you were here. 1972. I used it for rendezvousing with the barmaid from the Auberge Dorée after you and your ma and da scarpered. Club Costa.'

*

Typical Jack. It had been girls, girls, girls in 1972. And mopeds. Jack was only sixteen in 1972, but to George, at fourteen, he seemed older. His hair, which he'd kept short until that year, curled quite wildly down to his shoulders, and, at least twice a week, George saw him shaving. He claimed to have lost his virginity to a history teacher before his O levels. He said that life without sex wasn't worth living, and since there wasn't any to be had up the mountain just then – some of their girl cousins had brought friends, but they were all too old, too young, too fat, too thin, too brainy or too stupid for Jack – they'd better go down the mountain.

And down the mountain they went, Jack and the older boy cousins. In the village, they hooked up with a group of locals, boys and girls, many of whom had mopeds. They roared up and down the valley, Jack said, often à deux, sometimes even with a third person clinging on, and, in the evenings, phut-phutted around the village square smoking and flirting, hooting and shouting.

George begged to be allowed to go with Jack and the others, but Ma and Da stood firm: no mopeds. Only once did George manage it, on the day Ma and Da accompanied Uncle Josh and his wife to visit the newly built dam. Inez was in charge and either didn't know or didn't care about the no mopeds rule.

The morning went brilliantly – George even got to have a go by himself, on the long, flat road along the valley floor. But then the moped Jack was using conked out, and there was a bit of a fracas between Jack and the boy it belonged to, who thought Jack ought to pay for its repair. In the end, George helped Jack wheel it to the mechanic in the village, who was a relation of the boy and who said it wasn't serious, he could mend it by the evening.

Jack wasn't happy about kicking his heels all afternoon with only George for company. He bought them lunch at the Auberge Dorée, including a beer for George, then he suggested they explore upriver, beyond the village.

'But there's nothing there,' George said. 'It's a dead end, this valley. Da says that's one of the reasons the people who live here are how they are – even more cut off than most alpine villages.'

'There's a track next to the river. You can see it by the bridge. It must go somewhere. It's wide enough, just, for a car, even.'

They walked along the track for ten minutes and came to a chalet, shabby but obviously inhabited. They skirted this, went past some outbuildings and sheds and found themselves in a yard in front of a large, barn-like building. A burnt-out Peugeot, with two rusty Vespas leaning against it, lay in the yard.

The barn's double front doors were semi-open. Above them hung a long, curved piece of metal, once painted blue, with yellow lettering on it, but the sign was skew-whiff, the paint had blistered and peeled, and all you could see of the original lettering were two capital C's. Underneath the sign was a row of empty light sockets.

The place gave George the heeby-jeebies, but Jack was excited.

'What on earth?' he said, already pushing open one of the double doors.

They stepped inside.

It was dark. The first thing George noticed was the chill, and then the smell – old, musty, as if undisturbed for years. When his eyes got used to the dark, he saw tables, chairs, a bar, and a square empty space in the middle of it all.

'Blimey,' said Jack. 'Dance hall, discotheque – what do you think?'

There were glasses and bottles, still half full, on the tables. Some of the bottles had candles in them and wax, in frozen rivulets, down their sides. Beer mats and ashtrays overflowing with cigarette butts lay on the tables, on the jutting-out ends of beams and on the bar, which had stools along one side and, at the far end, a hinged flap that was open. Next to the bar was a small stage with a piano visible at the back of it and, beyond that, a jukebox.

Apart from the dust, which lay like a sprinkling of fine snow on everything, and the eerie stillness of the place – no human sounds, no whirr of an electricity generator, no hum or thump of any plumbing – George found it easy to imagine the barn abuzz with noise and heat, drinking and dancing. Easy, but spooky.

Jack walked over to the jukebox.

'Open the door, George,' he said. 'Let's shed some light on this.'

George pushed open both of the double doors and sunlight coned through the room, showing the rows of optics behind the bar, a big till and strings of fairy lights along the back wall.

While Jack leant over the jukebox, rubbing away the dust and exclaiming at the few song titles he could decipher, George walked across the cone of light to a door on the far side. The door opened into a lobby, off which was a small, windowless room, empty apart from two coats and a jacket hanging on hooks. In the lobby, someone had daubed the letters 'WC' and painted a big black arrow pointing to another, external door.

Back in the main room, Jack discovered a cupboard, full of neatly folded dishcloths and black and white waiter and waitress uniforms. On a shelf behind the bar were bulbs for the outside lights, unused candles and a bundle of account books and stocklists. In a drawer under the till they found a small tin box containing receipts, raffle tickets and a broken stick of rouge.

George stepped up onto the little stage, where a bashed-in accordion stood behind one of the speakers and, next to it, a wooden violin case. The piano was open. George pressed a key and dust clouded up around his finger as the single note reverberated dully. The violin case was empty, but slotted into the lid of it were a pot of resin and a royal blue handkerchief.

*

George recalled the royal blue handkerchief he'd seen poking out of Costa's jacket-cuff and brought himself back to 1976.

'Yes!' he said to Jack. 'I think you're right. But how did you work it out?'

'Barmaid, Georgy. It didn't need working out. Don't you remember? I sent you on up to Arete without me when we'd finished mucking around. I already had a romantic rendezvous organised for that evening. The big-boobed barmaid at the Auberge Dorée. She came with me for a stroll along the river to the old club, and you can guess what happened next. So it didn't need working out. I asked. She told me. Simple. Post-coital chit-chat.'

'Oh. Ah.' George tried to sound laid-back. He did remember Jack fobbing him off with some saga about checking on the moped, which was why Jack wasn't at Arete, later, for the fracas on the terrace with Ma and Inez. 'Did you ever go back there?' George asked. 'To the club, I mean.'

'Not since that summer. It's been demolished, apparently. The barn part, at least. I heard there were plans to build flats, but I don't think that's happened yet.'

Polly, Tess and Isobel returned, downcast and grumpy.

'No luck?' Jack opened his knapsack. 'Explorers need energy. Come on. This'll help.'

'There weren't even any streams,' said Isobel. 'I like it when we do the sieving.'

'Panning,' Jack corrected. 'Never mind. I'll think up some other paideia for you. Lunch first, though.'

After lunch, Jack got the girls to make a shelter, using one of the overhanging rocks at the south col.

'You only really need to block off one side,' he said. 'Look. It's already got three walls, almost. Like a cave. And then you can have fun furnishing it. Why don't you decorate it, even? Twigs, leaves, stones. Whatever you like.'

'We're not babies, Jack,' said Isobel. 'We're too old to play house.'

But the girls went off cheerfully enough. George suspected the shelter might have suggested itself, to the twins, at least, as a good place for a fag.

George was relieved that Jack clearly wasn't too bothered about the hunt for gold. They talked about university, and Jack described how the work wasn't difficult, but fitting it in around your social life could be. George liked the sound of that.

When the girls became bored with their makeshift shelter, Jack made them run round the lake, timing each other, giving each other handicaps, running backwards, hopping, skipping, jumping, crawling. After that, they all played French cricket until it was time to set off down to Arete.

Jack got everyone singing 'Doh, a deer' as they walked, and later, less cynically, 'American Pie', 'Desire' and 'Ch-Ch-Changes'. Then there was a game of 'I love my love', which turned silly very quickly because the twins used it to tease each other about which of Jack's friends they'd had a crush on. Jack changed the game to 'Animal, Vegetable, Mineral'.

'We'll start with Z and work backwards,' he said. 'Youngest first. Isobel.'

But they only got as far as U because Isobel couldn't think of an animal beginning with U.

'Do uglies count? I mean an ugly like Mathilde?'

'Don't be an ass,' said George.

'Why do we call her that, then?'

'I used to think ugly was Mathilde's surname,' Jack said. 'One of those frog things – a *faux ami*. We had a French *assistante* at school called Madame Coffey. And everyone called her Coffee-pot.'

'Me too, I thought it was her surname,' said George, although Ma had put him right fairly early on. Ma had been a French teacher at Reading secondary modern. 'Those poor girls,' she often used to say. 'Such limited horizons. They're not stupid, most of them. But they think they are. And don't look at me like that, Donald. I'm not ranting.' When she ranted, Ma got a rash on her neck and chest which George found slightly embarrassing, because he got a similar one, sometimes, after masturbating.

'The uglies owe their name to Lady C,' said Jack. 'Our great-great-grandmother, *n'est-ce pas*, Georgio?'

'Yes. That's what I was told.'

'She used to choose the ugliest girls in the village to work at Arete,' Jack explained.

Girls, pretty or not, would form a line in the village square or on the station platform, and Lady C, as soon as she arrived, would walk up and down inspecting them. That's what Ma had told George. After a while – not long – the line became self-selecting. Only the uglies presented themselves. And soon Lady C left the choosing to the cook, always an ugly too, of course.

'Why?' asked Isobel. 'Was she being kind? Were they too ugly to get any other work?'

Sweet, thought George, but no.

'No,' he said.

'It was to help Sir A avoid temptation,' Jack said. 'Lady C believed her husband had a roving eye. Isn't that right, old boy?'

'Yep. I think so,' said George. 'But it was always a bit muddled in my head with the redhead business.'

'What redhead business?' Isobel stopped walking. The path had come out onto the flowery meadow behind le Luet; they were less than ten minutes away from Arete.

'There's a surprising number of redheads in Hext,' said Jack, stopping too. 'Some of the villagers think that Sir A, or a crony of his, back in the golden, olden days, impregnated a peasant girl. *Et voilà.*'

The twins giggled.

'But Sir A didn't have red hair, did he? None of us do.' Isobel frowned.

'Correct,' said Jack. 'But when has fact ever stopped rumours?'

'Anyway, did he? Have a roving eye, Sir A, do you think?' George asked. When George had put the same question to Ma, she'd shrugged and said there was only Lady C's word for it, but she supposed so, and, 'Most men do, don't they?'

Jack gave a juicier answer.

'Not at first. But after Xavier disappeared, Sir A used to visit Xavier's widow. That's when Lady C got suspicious and started choosing only the uglies to work for the Valentines.'

'Did Inez tell you that?' George asked.

'Might have been Grandma Daisy,' Jack said, as they fell into single file again on the stony goat track that led through the narrow gap at the foot of le Luet. 'Either way, it doesn't look good for Sir A, does it?'

Ten

Sir A was ill when he arrived at Arete in 1924, and he looked it. Sylvie said there was a problem with his heart, which accounted for the bluish tinge to the skin on his face, especially around his mouth. He hadn't shrunk or become bent with age, but his body had stiffened, terribly; any sort of movement looked agony and he could only walk a few yards at a time. He'd had to be carried up the mountain in a canvas chair slung between two wooden poles.

When the rest of the family had set off for their day's activities and I'd finished the household chores, it was my job, in the mornings, to make sure Sir A had all he required, to fetch and carry for him, serve him his elevenses and attend to his physical needs. After lunch, he went to bed and snoozed until teatime, when fat Josette, a new ugly, took over until cocoa at ten.

Sir A didn't take much notice of me, at first. He spent most of his time by himself, out on the terrace in front of Arete, with the giant view of the valley and sky and mountains all around. He would instruct me to set up his special folding chair in a certain spot, and then he would sit in it, staring at I don't know what. He read less than he used to and he wrote very slowly now because of his stiff fingers.

Beech, birch, elm, walnut, alder and ash mingle freely with the fir and the larch in this rich mysterious mistress of a valley.

I watched him write that single, simple sentence, and it took him half the morning. He always sat at an angle in the chair, with his back in a corner, an arm on the armrest and one leg thrown over the other knee so that if he put his book down, it rested on his thigh. Sometimes he picked up the binoculars from their place on the low table I put next to his chair and, before looking through them, asked me to wipe the lenses with a grey cloth kept in a pocket in their case, and sometimes he requested a cup of coffee, or glass of water, or more tobacco for his pipe. But that was it. All I had to do was be nearby, unless he stood up to set off for a trip to the thunderbox (in which case I followed discreetly, to make sure he didn't fall), or to the darkroom.

'I used to dabble in photography,' he said. 'I've lost my appetite for it since the war.'

The darkroom was not my favourite place. All slopey walls and no proper corners, you had to feel your way blindly across it, watching out for your head. There was an oil lamp on a shelf, on the far side. Once lit, it threw out a feeble light that made everything murky. Sir A no longer developed photographs. He went to the darkroom only to peer at those taken before the war that had never made it into the albums the Valentines lugged back to London. They were pinned to the walls, pegged on lines and stacked on the shelves. My task was to light the oil lamp and find the ones Sir A wished to examine that day. He often requested the sepia prints of himself and Lady C in the previous century, especially those that included Xavier. Occasionally he asked for the only photograph there was of Miss Margaret Valentine, which definitely hadn't been taken, let alone developed at Arete: it was dated 1891; in it, she looked about twenty years old and was standing with a group of other young women. They all wore gowns and had square black hats and were smiling widely. Behind them was a broad white building with stone pillars as tall as pine trees. I remembered Margaret smiling widely like that those six times Tall Paul and Benoît and I brought our best produce (Abondance milk and spicy diot sausages) to Arete and spent the day in her company. Perhaps I could ask Sir A about the mystery of Margaret? But Sir A's frailty, which he did his best to hide, made me prevaricate, and, in the end, I decided I couldn't.

When I'd laid the chosen photographs next to the oil lamp, I would retire to the hall and wait until Sir A was ready to return to the terrace. It could be half an hour or more. I heard him sob, in the darkroom, for the dead and gone, but only in the darkroom – everywhere else, Sir A maintained the stiffest of blue upper lips.

One morning, Sylvie told me I'd to tend to Sir A's feet. They required washing and the nails cutting, she said, and he could no longer reach down to do it himself. I waited until the middle of the morning. Sir A preferred not to be disturbed straight after breakfast. I filled a bowl with warm water, hung a freshly washed towel over my arm, another across the bowl, and put the scissors, clippers and file on top.

'What's all that clobber for?' he asked when he saw me. 'You look like a barber.'

'Your feet, sir,' I said.

'Oh, my feet. Damn it, yes. I'd forgotten. Can't even tie my own shoelaces, would you believe?'

He uncrossed his legs and put down the notebook he'd been writing in.

I knelt on the ground and untied his shoelaces. His shoes – black with tiny holes punched into a pattern on the leather uppers – came off easily. I pulled at one black sock – thin and smooth and soft, unlike any sock I'd touched before – but it wouldn't come off.

'Damn it, girl. Garters. Take the garter off first.'

'The garter?'

Sir A bent forwards slowly and pulled the cuffs of his plus fours up over his knees, revealing the knobbles of his kneecaps, covered in very white skin with a few curly brown hairs flattened on them.

'This is the garter,' he said, pointing to a dark band around the tops of his socks.

I untied both garters, and Sir A's socks slipped off easily then. They were damp, so I hung them on the edge of the table to dry. I moved the bowl of water closer, lifted Sir A's right foot and put it in the water. It was a large white foot and the toes were long and misshapen, with lumps and bumps on them.

'Not a pretty sight, I'm afraid,' said Sir A. 'But you've probably seen worse, haven't you?'

This, I decided, was one of those rhetorical *anglais* questions, so I didn't reply.

'Well, have you or haven't you, alpenstock-girl?' he asked.

'I haven't seen an Englishman's feet close up before,' I said.

'English, French, Japanese. Show me your feet, Mathilde.'

I stood up and shook off my clogs.

'Those seem like fine, strong little peasant feet, to me, made for hard work.'

'Yes, sir,' I said, looking down at my bare feet, which were brown and tiny compared with his. If anything, my feet were on the thin side. They slipped around in my clogs in the summer, more than was comfortable.

'I've got the family feet,' said Sir A. 'Giant Valentine feet. Flat as spatulas. Excellent feet when I was young. Perfect for walking long distances, on snow in particular. Good for nothing now.'

'Barbegazi,' I said without thinking.

'What's that? Speak up, Mathilde. There's nothing worse than a mumbler.'

'I said "Barbegazi", sir. They're dwarfs who live in the mountains. They have long, white icy beards and very, very big feet, which they can use like skis or as snowshoes.'

Sir A roared with laughter and lifted his foot out of the water.

'Barbegazi,' he repeated. 'I like it.'

But then he let his foot drop and said, sadly, 'Useless. Bloody useless. I'll never climb another mountain. Can't bear to look at them, myself. They remind me too much of what I'm missing.'

I washed one foot, dried it on the towel, then the other. Then I set about the clipping and filing. This was easy enough.

I was used to clipping the toenails of our piglets in the winter, when the damp earth in their pen threatened to start a bout of the dreaded foot rot. And I was gratified that Sir A noticed my skill.

'Very good, Mathilde,' he said, when I'd finished. 'Thank you. I appreciate the care you've taken. You can bring me my coffee now.'

I picked a sock up from the table.

'But your feet?'

'Let's leave them to air. Fetch the coffee. And two cups.'

I brought the coffee and two cups, as requested, and poured one out for Sir A.

'And one for yourself. Why else do you think I asked for two cups? I don't have two mouths, do I?'

I smiled.

'That's better,' said Sir A. 'A smile can turn the plainest face into a thing of beauty. Like the sunshine.' He gestured to the sun, too bright to look at, but casting its yellow-white light over most of the valley and all the slopes on the opposite side of it. He pulled his hat down to shade his eyes. 'You should make a point of smiling, Mathilde. Now. Pour that coffee for yourself and tell me more about your barbegazi.'

There wasn't much more to tell. The barbegazi were shy creatures, I said, and rarely sighted by humans. They loved to surf on avalanches with their great big feet, but they were said to give out a low whistling cry, like a marmot, to warn of the danger from above and were always willing to help dig humans out from the snow.

'Where did you learn your English, Mathilde?' Sir A asked. 'Remind me.'

He often forgot what he'd asked, asking the same question again and again, but I didn't mind and I liked the way he said 'Remind me', so I told him for the umpteenth time about Madame Tissot and her school in the village and her reliable book of English idioms from the Charing Cross Road. I didn't say a word about the fact that most of the villagers thought English was a dirty language.

'She's done a good job, your Madame Tissot,' said Sir A when I'd finished. 'And you say you can read and write too? Fascinating. Can you read this?' Sir A held out his open notebook to me.

'Yes, sir,' I said.

'Read, then. Aloud. I wish to hear,' said Sir A.

I read the whole page, but when I'd finished I said, 'I can read it, but I don't understand it, sir. These are not sentences.'

'My dear girl,' said Sir A, 'these are jottings. Notes, that's all. Before you turned up with your barber's tools and your barbegazi tales, I was passing the time listing all the different winged insects and creeping things I could see from here. That you have lizards at this altitude – and higher – always amazes me. I was attempting to describe the trajectories of these beasties and decipher the reason for them. Oh, look at that!'

A fire salamander had stuck its head out from under a nearby stone, and Sir A was as pleased as punch.

'Now, I know what you call that, but I don't know why. Do you?'

'Because of the fire,' I said.

'But there's nothing remotely fiery about the salamander. He looks positively calm, to me – lazy, even, wouldn't you say?'

'Yes, Sir. He is. And he's not a fast mover, either. I could catch him with my hands, if I wanted to.'

'So why the "fire"?'

'He lives in the wood,' I explained, sounding like Madame Tissot explaining the simplest of sums to the simplest of pupils. 'The tree is his home and his food. Cut the tree down. Chop it into logs. Stack it, store it. The salamander is still there. He doesn't know what's happened. But then, one day, bang! Guess what?'

'Go on, go on. This is good. Bang!' Sir A seemed to be enjoying himself mightily now. 'Go on. What happens next?'

'We take the wood from the woodshed, we put it on the fire. The salamander feels the heat. It's pleasant at first. But then it's too hot. He's frightened. He comes scrabbling out of the wood. And there he is, all of a sudden, running for his life – out of the fire, out of the fireplace, rushing across the hearth. The children chase him around the room, but he usually manages to escape under the door or through one of the gaps in the wall, into the cowshed. He doesn't look so calm and lazy then, sir.'

'I can imagine,' said Sir A. 'I would very much like to see that.'

'You won't see it in the summer, sir. It only happens in the winter, when the logs have been stored for some time in the woodshed.'

'Yes. Winter. How different everything must be here then.'

'Yes. No *anglais*, but many fire salamanders,' I said, and Sir A burst out laughing for the second time that day.

After that, I became what Sir A called his right-hand man. I read to him and wrote for him and supplied him with information about our customs in the valley. I taught him some patois and a couple of Savoyard idioms.

'Abracadabra,' he declared when I told him I considered myself *à l'abâda* at Arete, which is what we said when someone was far away from home. 'We've a veritable female philologist in our midst.'

As to the English idioms Madame Tissot had made us learn by rote, I recited many to him, and he taught me many more. He asked me lots of questions about the legends of the region. He liked the white gold legend so much that he laboriously, over the course of four days, wrote the whole thing down. He changed the title to 'Snow Queen'.

There's a woman in the sky, high above the mountains, in Haute-Savoie. She used to be a dancer. Now she is the directrice of winter's crystal ball. The woman, who is nimble, lean and tall, with amber hair and opal skin, wears nothing but a gown of glacial ice, as smooth as milk, and on her agile feet, a pair of buckskin pumps, studded with diamonds, laced with silver. Her eyes are pearls, and when she smiles, there are moonstones in her mouth. She carries a linen sack, as old as man, and frayed, but freshly laundered every year and filled to the top with new white gold, every year the same amount. The directrice unties her sack, lets loose some gold, and when she does, it turns to snow. Off the chosen dancers go, latticed, light, minute as fairy dust – flitting, drifting, pirouetting. The tips of their limbs begin to touch and, undulating like rose petals, like lovers, in soft, seductive folds, they slowly settle. When the sack is empty, the woman darkens like a ptarmigan and descends to earth. The woman finds a sheltered clearing in the forest. She spreads her sack on the springy turf, lies down and, with pine needles for a feather pillow, she goes to sleep.

*

Towards the end of June, news reached Arete of George Mallory's death on Mount Everest. I found out what I could from the out-of-date *anglais* newspapers that arrived with guests and from the flurry of letters Sir A wrote and received on the matter. The Valentines jabbered about little else for a while.

'Did they reach the summit? That's the thing,' said Johnny.

'No question,' said Beatrice, who'd more or less taken over the running of Arete by then and had firm views on everything.

'At least they were roped together when they fell. At least it would have been a painless death.' Ted shuddered.

'The beautiful unscathed bodies of two brave and wonderful men, wrapped in a blanket of pure white snow. What a lovely notion,' sighed Daisy. 'And Irvine only twenty-two.'

The effect of the news on Sir A was to make him restless.

He'd always suffered from mild insomnia. Now he frequently burnt the midnight oil.

'The calf, the goose and the bee, please Mathilde,' he'd say after supper, and I had to go into the library and, in addition to his pipe, prepare paper, pen and sealing wax for him. Henri le cretin was up and down the mountain two or three times a week with letters in the aftermath of Everest.

'I was born too late,' Sir A said one evening as he finished addressing a letter to the beanpole. It was my job to drop hot sealing wax onto the envelope and, while it was still warm, press Sir A's seal – his monogrammed A.O.V. – into the red. 'Weisshorn, Wetterhorn, then the tragedy of the Matterhorn,' he continued. 'I reached my climbing prime at the very moment the golden age of alpinism came to an end. And now, for the conquest of Everest, I'm in my dotage. Born too soon, also, therefore.'

On clear nights, Sir A sat in his special chair on the terrace with his telescopes and notebooks by his side, looking at the stars. I'd occasionally find him still there when I rose before dawn. He'd be wide awake and eager for my company.

'Sit with me for a while, would you mind, dear girl?' he'd say, and we'd sit and stare at the configurations of stars and planets in the sky. Sometimes he'd explain the patterns of light and tell me their English names.

Occasionally he'd pontificate. 'Have I led a good life? That's the thing, Mathilde.' That sort of thing. But, 'Don't let me pontificate,' he'd say. 'Omphaloskepsis. New word, Huxley's, I believe. Bad habit.'

It was a habit that became more frequent as the summer wore on. Sir A meandered between memory and meditation, the present interesting him less and less. He told me about growing up in a place called Surrey and a favourite uncle who took him for rambles on Box Hill and later taught him to climb in the Lake District.

'My uncle was a founding member of the Alpine Club,' Sir

A said one early morning, when dawn was nothing more than a slight lightening between the eastern peaks.

'Yes,' I said, which is what I usually said, simply to let Sir A know I was there and I was listening.

'I was sixteen,' Sir A went on, 'an impressionable age, when the Alpine Club was formed. My uncle enthralled me with his descriptions of its members and their exploits. I recall to this day his account of the ascent of Monte Rosa. The euphoria of reaching the top. The feeling of succeeding. I couldn't wait to become a member myself. But . . .'

Sir A paused. He put a finger to his lips.

'But,' he repeated, looking me in the eye. 'This is a secret. Shhh, Mathilde.'

I nodded solemnly as Madame Tissot used to nod when a child confessed to a minor childish misdeed.

'This falling in love of mine,' Sir A began. 'My falling in love with these mountains, this land. It wasn't only the Alpine Club and my uncle.' He gave a strained laugh.

'I was eleven,' he continued. 'A school friend invited me to join him and his family on a trip to London – a day trip to London, by train. In the morning, we visited the natural history rooms in the British Museum. After lunch, we went to the Egyptian Hall in Piccadilly. And you'll never guess what we saw there, Mathilde.'

'No, sir,' I said and shook my head.

'We saw "Mont Blanc".' Sir A laughed again, then stared towards the grey dawning light.

'You saw Mont Blanc?' I repeated Sir A's words as a question.

Sir A explained that the Egyptian Hall was a place of entertainment, and 'Mont Blanc' was a form of popular entertainment.

'An exhibition, dear girl. Albert Smith's spectacle, theatre, a show. A great humid hall, full of gawdy colours, tawdry jewels, lights and magic tricks. Illusions and cheap thrills.'

Sir A was warming to his subject.

'From the moment we set foot in that hall, I was enchanted. The sights, the sounds, even the smells. Of course I knew it was considered tasteless by many. I'd heard my uncle expostulating about it. Vulgar, he'd said. It would turn Chamonix into Margate-on-sea. But by God it was popular. And by God I enjoyed it. The place was packed, hot. Powdered, perfumed people, shoulder to shoulder, skin to skin. By God it was impressive. There were real chamois, real St Bernard dogs, a replica chalet. Snow. Oh, the snow. So white and blowy, sparkly and pretty. The whole thing was quite extraordinary.' Sir A took several puffs on his pipe as if relishing the memory. I noticed the skin on his hands and fingers, so bloodless and thin, it looked as if it might dissolve, like milk in water. 'And as to the narrative of the climb up Mont Blanc, it was bursting with such drama, daring and courage, I doubt I was the only eleven-year-old boy there whose head was turned. I left the hall giddy with the desire to visit the real alps. And when I did, finally, aged twenty-two, the experience, their beauty, surpassed my expectations.'

There was another pause, which I filled with another 'yes'.

'Unfortunately,' said Sir A, 'the more their beauty revealed itself to me, the more of it I craved. Born from my uncle's stories and the artifice of Albert Smith's entertainment, my desire was insatiable. I've spent as many summers as possible since then here in your mountains, Mathilde, but I've never truly known them. I realised some time ago, I simply don't have the wherewithal.' Sir A stopped talking and looked suddenly so forlorn that I gestured to the sun rising in the east.

'Abracadabra,' I tried, trying to remind him of happier times when he'd use the language of worship to describe my land and its skies, exaggerating their beauty, layering it with images; a common or garden alpine sunrise became the magic finger of dawn, Aurora in all her glory, the abracadabra of life itself.

But this time, Sir A misheard (or pretended to), for he sighed and said, '*A l'abâda*. I've learnt a lot, but, at the end of the day, I'm still less at home here than you, dear girl.'

Nevertheless, the rising of the sun at the start of a new day usually succeeded in cheering him. He'd exclaim – at the quality of the light, the delicate brightening of pinks, the dramatic, changing shadows and the glory of the sunbeams sweeping across the slopes. He'd urge me to 'Look, Mathilde. No poet or painter, scribe or storyteller will capture that.'

I attempted to see the sky through Sir A's eyes, but I'd been taught to read it for signs of what the weather might be up to and I couldn't rid myself of the habit. I described to Sir A what the colours and shapes in the sky meant to me, weatherwise, and he listened intently before saying:

'You remind me of Xavier, my beloved guide. By God, it's been a long time. That's all well and good, Mathilde – useful, interesting, important. But it doesn't preclude an appreciation of nature's beauty.'

He made me help him stand, then walk with him to the edge of the terrace where he leant against me, and we both watched as the sun finished rising.

*

Sir A looked much better by the end of the summer, but he was still ill, and he died in London later that year.

Lady C weakened, but she didn't die for another five years. In the meantime, she returned every summer to Arete, although Beatrice now definitely ruled the roost of the Valentine family. Bossy-boots Beatrice was my least favourite. She had Sir A's strength of character, but not his kindness. Summer after summer I didn't stop missing the thin-skinned, harmless old man interested in fire salamanders, the night sky and me – my language, my land.

Eleven

'None of this land bears any relation to the old picture map.'

Jack indicated a large-scale modern map spread out next to the old picture map on the table on the terrace, where they'd gone to sit after supper. The girls were splashing around in the washroom, shampooing each other's hair. George, satisfied with how the day had gone, felt more relaxed than usual in Jack's company.

'Have you explored everywhere on the map?' he asked Jack.

'Here,' Jack pointed. 'Here. And here. All recced. Nothing. We covered masses of ground while my friends were with us. Leaving only here, where you and I and the girls were today.'

George looked more closely.

'La Miche?'

'Thereabouts. But the two maps don't correlate. The whole thing's hare-brained, probably. There is a coincidence, though.'

'Yes?' said George.

'La Miche just happens to be where Xavier was heading the day he went AWOL.'

'How do you know?'

'It's in the Alpine Club log book,' said Jack smoothly. 'According to Sir A's entries, Xavier was definitely pottering around in that neck of the woods in the days leading up to his disappearance. And on the day itself. The 4th of August 1872. It's all logged correctly. But no details.'

George was aware that the scant facts concerning Xavier's disappearance – fine weather, no body – meant rumours multiplied. Many of them sprang from the belief that there was gold in the mountains near Arete and Xavier was looking for it.

'Totally irrational,' Da had always insisted. When he was young, George had enjoyed the myths of the mountains: dragons, dahus, barbegazi, sacks of snow, a woman in the sky, wolves, bears, gold, the golden ibex. So had his cousins. But they'd grown out of them. For a moment, however, and because he felt more relaxed than usual with Jack, George allowed himself to believe in a world where a hunt for gold wasn't totally irrational.

'Sir A's diaries might have more info,' he heard himself say.

Jack didn't know about the box files in the attic, so George had to explain, which he did clumsily, but Jack cottoned on quickly. Like Thomas, Jack dismissed Mathilde's snooping.

'She's an ugly. They're all a bit demented. And the poor old thing's always enjoyed poking and prying. Under the guise of tidying.' Jack lit a cigarette. 'She might be going senile. But I bet you're right. About Sir A. He's bound to have written something.'

'Shall I get them, the diaries? Now?' George tried to keep what he feared sounded like childish enthusiasm out of his voice.

'Yes, go on. Why not?'

George nipped up to the attic, retrieved the box file with Sir A's diaries in it and was downstairs and out on the terrace again before Jack had finished his cigarette.

The early diaries were in better condition than the later ones, and it took George no time to confirm that the 1872 diary entries did indeed tally with the Alpine Club log book in terms of the whereabouts of Xavier, Sir A and Lady C. They also confirmed that on the fateful 4th of August, Xavier had set off alone to hunt for fossils at the foot of the Rochers de la Miche.

In early July, Sir A and Xavier together had 'discovered a great variety of beautiful specimens' there. George read the relevant diary entries aloud.

The fossils lie in a narrow ravine, scarcely more than a nick on the surface of the mountain forming part of a superb limestone range, called the Rochers or Chaîne de la Miche, which drops approximately two thousand feet, in one sublime precipice after another. From a high spur of the chain, many ages ago, a great flow of rocks, stones and other debris has descended, leaving the most desolate of tracts.

Xavier had made three solo trips in July to the desolate tract near the fossils. The only information the diary added to the records in the logbook was that on each of them there had been a sighting of the golden ibex.

Apropos of the first sighting, Sir A had written: *a golden ibex, or, at least, a beast guaranteed to perpetuate the legend – so beauteous in form and glorious in colouring as to move my guide, usually a most aesthetically unmoveable man, to metaphor.* Sir A was tickled by Xavier's comparison of the ibex's golden coat to Dalmore malt whisky, *which he knows is a favourite of mine, and a wee dram of which he is not averse to himself.*

The second ibex *shone like a wedding ring* and the third *glowed as deeply as the setting sun.*

Sir A's only comment on Xavier's reported sightings was that he himself had frequently, *in my wanderings among the French Alps, come across ibexes with ruddy coats, like Tarine cows,* and, *in Austria, once, an ibex with head and feet the colour of the orange stripes of a tiger.*

'The tiger-ibex sounds a bit rich,' said Jack when George had finished reading.

Jack picked up the picture map and studied it.

'Let's say Xavier had gone nuts and the hunt was for the ibex, not gold,' he speculated, 'then the markings on it might make more sense.' Jack frowned at the map. 'No. Not really. I'm flummoxed for now. Never mind. Show me some of this porn you said Sir A wrote.' He took one of the diaries and thumbed through it.

'It's not porn,' said George. 'It's erotic. Fantasy stuff. But not like dirty mags.' He stopped himself. He didn't want Jack knowing which shelves his eyes always went to in the newsagent.

Jack read in silence.

'I can relate to some of this,' he said, to George's surprise. 'After a day in the mountains, you do feel sexy. It's the physical exertion in that thin, thin air. The pure, bright light, the clear colours, the vastness. You're physically exhausted, but mentally energised. It's a bizarre feeling. Like being stoned, only better. And you want more of it. Oh, look Georgio! Did you read this bit, about the Mackenzie brothers?'

Jack read out Sir A's account of one of the Mackenzie brothers getting into a brawl in the Auberge Dorée. The brother in question had red hair and was accused of having implanted his red-haired seed in a village girl the previous year.

'"Load of old poppycock", Sir A's written,' Jack said. 'The Mackenzies weren't brothers at all. They were a couple. Pederasts, he calls them. Red-headed Glaswegian pederasts.' Jack belly-laughed. 'Is it a queer thing, do you think, Georgy, mountaineering?'

Remembering the episode years ago in the darkroom, George wondered, briefly, whether Jack had an ulterior motive for asking the question. It was a question he'd already asked himself.

'Camaraderie and communal baths, you mean?' he said, but the girls came round the corner just then, all dripping hair and towels, and Jack returned, somewhat ostentatiously, George thought, to comparing the little picture map with the modern map and began issuing instructions left, right and centre about the next day's paideia.

Twelve

For the five years between the deaths of Sir A and Lady C, I skivvied at Arete every June until the end of September. The rumours about the *rosbifs* and the redheads returned in these years. In 1925, there was a record number of births in the valley – fifteen in April alone – and three of those were redheads. I wouldn't have thought twice about this except for the gossip I picked up at the *lavoir*.

I heard the women discussing the new red-headed arrivals before I'd even tethered old Lazybones, who'd been sold on to me by Cédric's family, when Slowcoach eventually died. I unloaded my bundles of linen from the cart and carried them over to an available space.

'Isn't it so, Mathilde?' said the woman next to me.

'What's that?' I asked, but my heart sank. I was rarely invited to give my opinion unless it was assumed I'd agree with the others.

'The redheads. Two in two weeks. It's like before. They've done it again, those *anglais* who pay you so handsomely.'

I held my tongue.

'Why do you protect *les rosbifs*?' asked Angélique Gauthier, who'd married the village blacksmith and was busy helping him turn his sleepy smithy into a lucrative garage. 'They do nothing for you.'

Angélique was considered a great beauty. She had hair that shone like honey and donkey-eyes with heavy lashes. Her skin was as pale and smooth as a mushroom. At school, she'd often mocked my mottled cheeks and tweaked at the strands of hair on my head saying she'd prefer to be dead than look like me.

Marriage had mellowed her. She seemed happy, could be thoughtful, and there was nothing she liked more than a good chinwag.

'They pay me well,' I said, keeping my head lowered to the basin of soapy water and plunging my sheets up and down in it.

'Ah yes.'

There were murmurings of assent all around me.

'That's true.'

'Money from *anglais* hands is as good as any other.'

'And *anglais* cocks?' The woman next to me cackled.

'I expect they're red down there too,' said Angélique. 'Let's ask Mathilde.'

I said nothing.

'See. She's protecting them again.'

'I can't tell you anything,' I said at last, 'because there's nothing to tell. It's plain to me that these red-headed babies are born from red-headed fathers, and their fathers are people of our land as much as you or I. The English at Arete have nothing to do with it. I remember no redheads there last year. Not even a passing visitor. Besides, only we uglies—'

I didn't finish the sentence because Angélique threw back her head and squawked with laughter.

'Oh, Mathilde. You make me laugh. You'll never find a husband if you call yourself that. And you really should do something, you know, about that hair of yours.'

And so the conversation turned to husbands – those who had them complained about them, and those who didn't asked about them, and the red-headed babies were temporarily forgotten.

However, a few days after this, and before the washing week was over, there was a knock on the door and, when I opened it fat Josette was standing there. Even though it was another sunny morning and I'd already stripped off to my blouse and rolled the sleeves up, Josette was wrapped in winter woollens and had a blanket over her shoulders.

'What is it, Josette?' I asked.

'My baby,' she said and pointed to her belly.

'You're having a baby?' This surprised me no end, for not only did Josette look no rounder than usual around the middle, but being so ugly, she was, I'd assumed, as unmarriageable as me.

'I didn't know you'd wed,' I said.

She shook her head, clutched her belly and let out a moan.

'My baby,' she said again when the pain had passed.

Of course I'd realised by then what her predicament was and that it was not the time to be asking about husbands.

'Come,' I said. 'I'll harness the horse.'

Josette shook her head.

'Yes,' I insisted. 'I've seen plenty of animals give birth, and I'm sure I could help you, but it's the job of the *sage-femme* to see to these things. How long have you been having the pains?'

'Three hours. Maybe four.' Josette was bawling now.

'Good. We've plenty of time. Come, though. I'll take you to the *sage-femme*.'

I made Josette climb into the back of the cart, which was already loaded with the day's dirty linen. I pushed the bundles to each side and told her to lie between them.

'That way, you won't be seen as we drive through the village,' I said.

Josette obeyed and off we went. Lazybones snorted crossly as I urged him to hurry down the track. Saliva dripped from his mouth and sweat stood out on his flanks by the time we reached the village, but I could hear Josette in the back moaning again. The moans were louder and came more frequently. I wasn't sure we had as much time as I'd thought. I cracked my whip and we sped, with a jolt, across the village square. The women at the *lavoir* all looked up and, I must say, the looks of amazement on their stupid faces was comic, but I didn't stop. I kept old Lazybones hard at it until we reached the *sage-femme*'s house, which was on the far side of the village, behind the church and near the *curé*'s house.

I left Josette writhing in the back of the cart and knocked on the *sage-femme*'s door. To my relief, she opened the door straight away and wasn't slow to understand the situation. She enlisted my help to manoeuvre Josette down from the cart and into her house, where she led her immediately to a room at the back. I was about to depart, relieved to hand over the matter, but the *sage-femme* called out, 'Fetch water, woman. And the cloths.'

I didn't know where she meant me to find the cloths, but water was easy enough. I'd seen two bucketfuls on the porch outside. I carried them in and through to the room at the back. Josette was in a right old state, and the *sage-femme* was slapping her on the face, telling her to stop writhing around, it wouldn't help, she needed to use all her force to push.

'The cloths,' said the *sage-femme*. 'Outside. Drying.'

I went outside and round to the back of the house. The grass and bushes out there were covered with squares and rectangles of newly washed linen. But when I picked one up, it was still wet. Others were damp. I hurried, collecting only the driest I could find. No time to fold them. I simply flung them over my arm. Nevertheless, I'd been away long enough that by the time I returned, the *sage-femme* was crouched between Josette's open legs. She had her hands on Josette's fat knees.

'Already the head,' I heard, loud and clear, as I entered the room.

A piercing scream from Josette, and the *sage-femme* stepped back, reaching out a hand towards me. I passed her a cloth, and as I did so I saw the head of Josette's baby between her legs. It was bloody and crusty, but there was no doubt at all that the hair on that baby's head was red.

Things happened quickly: in a matter of minutes the rest of the baby was born, its cord was snipped and all bar a triangle of its face wrapped in one of the cloths. Then came the afterbirth, dark and big, which the *sage-femme* placed in a bowl. She saw me glance at it.

'I'll see to that later,' she said.

Everyone knew that the sale of newborn babies' placentas was a profitable sideline for the *sage-femme*. They were in great demand with pig farmers, who believed they added richness and succulence to the meat. No doubt Papa's tasty diots used to owe something to the abundance of placentas in our household from all Maman's dead babies.

Josette was very pale and still bleeding, so there was a lot of mopping and the *sage-femme* sent me for more cloths. This time I didn't worry about whether they were wet or not. The *sage-femme* told me to sit with Josette and keep checking for blood while she went to make a tisane. I sat on the bed and watched as the colour gradually returned to Josette's cheeks. The cloth between her legs was red, but not dripping, so I knew the worst was over. When Josette opened her eyes, I pointed to the bundle of baby on the chest in the corner.

'What is it?' she asked.

I picked the bundle up. Wisps of damp, orangey-red hair poked out of the tight swaddling on its forehead. I passed the bundle to Josette.

'Why don't you have a look?' I said, laying the baby next to her and beginning to unwrap it.

'No, no.' The *sage-femme* returned with a steaming bowl of herby tisane. 'It's a boy. Healthy. Big. He needs to stay warm, though. You,' she said, turning to me, 'can go now.'

I left the *sage-femme*'s house and led Lazybones to the river, where I let him drink and splashed him with water. And then I went home. I couldn't face the women at the *lavoir* that day. I sat for a while on the bench outside the farmhouse. You could see the village from there, with the tow-rope lines of the new ski-lifts fanning out on the slopes behind it; trees from the forest of Zizipompom had been cut down to make room for the lifts, and some of the haybarns had gone. You could see the church and the square, the green and yellow awning of the Auberge Dorée and the blur of movement around the *lavoir*, but my eyes wandered to the church and the small row of houses next to it.

Josette's red-headed baby had made me rethink my vehemence of yesterday about the innocence of *les rosbifs*.

I cast my mind back to the previous summer. But try as I might I recalled not a single redhead.

I waited a month and then I went to see Josette on her family's farm. As I approached their land, I saw Josette, fat as ever, bent over, picking at the potatoes with a hoe. I tapped her on the shoulder.

'Hello,' I said. 'How are you? And *le petit*? What did you name him?'

'He died.' Josette shrugged and returned to picking at the earth with her hoe.

'Oh,' I said. 'I'm sorry. I didn't know.'

'Just as well. I'm unmarried.'

'But the baby's father?'

Josette stopped picking, lifted her head and looked at me.

'Surely you knew? Surely you know?'

'No,' I said, and I felt my heart beat too fast. I was wrong, then. The *rosbifs* had had their wicked way after all.

'Henri,' said Josette. 'Henri le cretin.'

I put my hand to my mouth to stop the guffaw I felt coming. Henri le cretin, skinny, feeble, stupid, mocked, pathetic – more or less the village idiot.

'But—' I started.

'I led him on,' Josette said. 'It was a game at first. A joke, a dare. Me and another ugly. Which of us could do it first with him?'

'But—'

'Henri's capable, if that's what you're wondering. He's stupid. More stupid than me. But he has desires. And feelings. Besides, he was sweet. Gentle. I enjoyed it.' Josette stopped talking, wiped a dirty hand across her eyes.

The image of little Henri's scrawny arse flying up and down on top of fleshy Josette made the laughter keep coming, but for Josette's sake I held it in. Only after I'd bade her farewell and was on my way home did I let the laughter out, but I was laughing also because I was right: for all their faults, the Arete *anglais* were not responsible for the spread of redheads in our valley.

*

My skivvying at Arete helped keep the farm ticking over, just. I didn't always make ends meet, and then I had to go without my fripperies from the market.

Costa liked the colour blue, so quite a few of my fripperies were blue. He said his mother often wore blue.

'It went with her hair, which was very beautiful – the colour of pernambuco wood,' he said. 'Like a violin bow.'

'Reddish brown?' I said.

'Auburn, Titian, Venetian blond: half the women in our village in Italy had reddish brown hair.'

'Just the women?'

'No, but the women were justifiably proud of their beautiful hair, so they found many ways to describe it.'

I steered us clear of any more talk of hair because it wasn't my best point.

Costa offered me a job in his club, which got off the ground in 1926. He'd been to the great Grenoble exhibition in 1925. I read later in the paper that more than a million people went to that exhibition – too many to imagine. Costa said it was a celebration.

'Of what?'

'Progress in general, hydroelectricity in particular. I don't know. It was certainly an education.'

All sorts of engines, water turbines, trains, cars and even aeroplanes were on display there. But that was the least of it, Costa said. He and his investor friend, who drove down especially from Paris, visited Madagascar and Indo-China in the colonial pavilion. They also saw an African village and went to a souk where they watched snake charmers and drank mint tea.

'It confirmed in both our minds,' Costa said, 'that a jazz club in Hext is viable.'

I declined his offer of a job – 'I'm a *paysanne*,' I reminded him. '*Le pays*, the land, that is my métier' – even though Costa also pointed out that it would mean we'd spend more time together. Was he saying he'd like that? Ever since the bilberries, I'd wondered. What with my summers at Arete and Costa's winter trips to Paris, we didn't see each other much at all, but I liked it when we did. I liked Costa's stories about the village in Italy, where his forebears were woodcutters with a knowledge of wood so deep and passed down through so many generations that they became experts in choosing spruce and maple for the violin makers of Cremona.

'Lightness with strength,' said Costa. 'And a good grain orientation, of course. But the magic is in the tone – the character, the feel, the sparkle, the life.'

'Magic?'

'Luthiers love the lore of their craft. Violins, like wine, improve with time,' Costa said. 'The wood they are made from can be decades in the seasoning. Air does the trick, but urine, goats' dung and salt water all have their advocates. Venetian violins were said to be carved from the oars of Venetian galleys.'

Ebony, rosewood, boxwood and willow; ribs, pegs, tailpiece and fingerboard; I learnt to help Costa with some of his repairs. I also learnt how to boil and grind the bones of rabbits together with the hooves of pigs and horses, and mix them with sinew and fatty tissues before adding honey, egg white and chalk to make the solid sheets of glue which looked like chocolate bars and which Costa sold in slabs and squares, cut to size.

In the village, Angélique called Costa my fiancé and asked me when the wedding was. And I liked this too. But Costa had a woman, or women, in Paris. I knew that and I wasn't stupid: all the fripperies in the world wouldn't hide my ugliness.

After his trips to Paris, Costa could talk the hind legs off a donkey when he spoke about the Perroquet Club and the Casino de Paris; pretty girls, and pretty girls who looked like pretty boys; negroes, Americans, Jazz Kings, a street urchin called Grappelli who played the fiddle like an angel, and a racehorse owner called Leon Volterra, who might have been the man with the investment money – Costa was never quite clear about this. Later it was Baker, Bechet, Club Bobino and bananas; Costa went to the *Revue nègre* at the Théâtre des Champs-Elysées and *La Folie du Jour* at the Folies Bergère – after which he made me laugh until my innards hurt with his description of the dancing yellow-gold lady and her banana skirt.

'March, Mathilde. That's when I'll open. As soon as the roads are clear. I've booked the musicians.'

There was a lot of snow that winter of 1925 to '26, and Costa said his riverside chalet was like an igloo because the snow piling up around it reached the snow drooping from the roof. There was too much snow, on some days, for me to get down to the village – the milk went to waste and I worried about money. At the end of February, it snowed unusually heavily for three days consecutively. Apart from tending to the animals and doing the daily outdoor chores, I stayed inside. I tidied and cleaned, repaired my clothes and looked at the books Madame Tissot had given me in the autumn before she moved to Geneva. She taught in a school there now, just for girls, where, she wrote, there were five classrooms – each one bigger by far than our single schoolroom in Hext – with windows through which you could see the lake.

We wrote to each other regularly, and on the third day of snow, in the late afternoon, I began a letter to her. By six o'clock the stock of wood next to the fire was running low; if I was going to finish my letter without freezing to death, I'd have to fetch more.

Outside, it had finally stopped snowing. The air was sharp and the puffy fields and billowing slopes of the valley gleamed blue in the beam of the nearly full moon. There were a few thin, thready clouds and no wind.

I paused by the woodpile and looked across the valley, where the lights in all the farmhouses prickled like stars while the land around them lay as still and calm as a blue summer night sky. But something disturbed my vision. Not on the other side of the valley – on our side, in one of the fields lower down.

A flash of white. At first I thought it must be a fox or a chamois coming out of the forest to look for food. But no. Too big. And it only had two legs. It was moving slowly towards me. It waved. I was standing in the moonlight and I realised, to my horror, it was waving at me. I could only watch as the shape of a man became clearer and clearer. It looked almost like a shadow – and I thought of ghosts and mountain spirits – but as it drew closer, I saw that it was definitely a man, but a man seemingly without a face.

The man stopped waving but went on walking, and then he called out to me. I don't know what he said because he spoke neither patois nor French but a sort of *anglais* I'd never heard before and didn't understand at first. Moreover, the closer he came, the more sure I was that this was a black man.

If the devil wasn't red, he was black, according to many of the people of Hext. Stuff and nonsense, said Madame Tissot. But it took some doing, on my part, to remember the stuff and nonsense as this black-garbed, black-faced man came towards me. I clutched the empty wood basket in front of my belly.

The man was shivering.

'F-freezing,' he stuttered.

This I understood and wasn't surprised by. The silly billy wore no coat, no hat, no boots, just trousers and a long jacket. He was carrying a black, oblong, heavy-looking case. The white I'd seen was the white of his shirt, which was tied at the neck with a white bow. His shoes were shiny black and so was his face, at least in the light of the moon. I led him indoors and saw that his skin was actually more mud than black. Only his hair was truly black – wiry and coarse, like a wild boar's.

It turned out that he spoke 'a smidgeon' of French – a sort of babyish Parisian French – and with his smidgeon of French and my excellent English, and what with my being a clever clogs, I soon put two and two together: the black man was a trombonist on his way to play at Costa's.

'We start rehearsals tomorrow,' he said. 'Opening on Saturday.'

The trains weren't running, so he'd hitched a lift from the road outside Annemasse. The car had come a cropper in the snow further down the valley. The driver decided to stay with his car, but he, Warren, was expected at the club, so he'd walked and walked and, good Lord, he'd walked. He was completely lost.

Could I direct him to Club Costa, he asked? I could have done, but the stringy black man with his smidgeon and his slidey-shiny shoes was in no fit state to follow directions. I said I would take him some of the way there myself.

I tried to make the black man put on Papa's old boots, but he said they were too small. He accepted a blanket and I showed him how to tie it around his head before wrapping it over his shoulders.

I led him along the track, past Cédric's farm, all the way down to the bottom of the valley. It took ages because of the snow, which, although soft, came nearly up to my waist, and the man kept falling over. When we reached the river, I pointed to the track that led to Costanza's. But now the black man seemed nervous.

'Come with me,' he said. 'Show me the way.'

I hesitated. I'd heard the clock in the village square strike ten. I was usually in bed well before then.

'Please,' said the black man, like a frightened little boy. 'I'm from the city. City born and bred. This place is something else.

And what's this Costa guy like? And his club – I was told to expect a roaring success. Didn't realise I was hitching a ride to the Wild West.'

'You only need to follow the path,' I said.

There was less snow on the floor of the valley, the clouds had dispersed and the brightness of the sky would light his way. Not to mention mine – I'd still the wood to fetch in and the fire to relight, never mind about finishing my letter to Madame Tissot.

'The path follows the river. You won't go wrong.'

And as the black man slip-slopped off, lifting his knees high-high like a horse and holding his trombone case horizontally at shoulder level, I added, because I believed it then, 'You can trust Costa.'

Warren ended up trusting Costa so much that he returned to work season after season at the club, sometimes staying the whole year round if business was good.

*

1926, '27, '28 – Club Costa went from strength to strength.

Arete stayed the same – with Beatrice as queen bee – except for Lady C becoming frailer, Ted more often drunk, and Daisy crazier.

Bicycles were all the rage one year, and Johnny organised races down the mountain and a Tour de France, by road, from Hext to Chamonix. Another year it was cocktails: Ted ordered a walnut-wood sideboard from a cabinet maker in Boëge; he paid four men from the village to lug it up to the chalet and install it in the games room – he called it a cocktail bar and spent hours arranging glasses, swizzle sticks and brightly coloured bottles on top of it. I became a dab hand at mixing and shaking, making lemony sidecars, pink Mary Pickfords and fizzy gin rickeys.

Will, Frank, Jolyon, Albert . . . Richard, Roland, Harriet,

Ernest . . . Shelagh, Catharine, Jean, Jane, Peter, Paul . . . Old Uncle Tom Cobley and all. Apart from kind Will the beanpole, whose passion for both climbing and describing the mountains made Sir A's seem tame, the names of Arete's visitors blurred, even to me, during these years.

Summers went by in a frenzied whirl. Paideias became parties; extra porters were employed to carry the worse-for-wear down from picnics, and guides were continually being called upon to rescue Arete's carousing guests, stuck on crags, in ravines, or simply lost in the forest. At the drop of a hat, games room, sitting room, hall and terrace were turned into dance floors. When bad weather kept everyone indoors, the games room was chock-a-block with people playing halma, go-bang and mah-jong, or with cards, gambling. Shots of whisky, brandy, génépi and rum replaced cocktails. Cigars, as well as pipes and cigarettes, were smoked. The room became hot and foetid – salty *rosbif* sweat mixed with a sweet tobacco smell, which reminded me of church. I described the smell later to Costa, and he said it sounded like opium. By the end of the day, everyone always had cabin fever.

*

In 1929, it rained more than usual in June – light rain, but enough to keep Arete in cloud for days at a time and the *anglais* confined to barracks.

Lady C was dying of a cancer in her innards. Against all odds, she'd rallied for the journey from London, but within days of arriving was bedridden and could scarcely eat. Beatrice demanded quiet, if not silence, in the house at all times.

One morning at breakfast, Johnny suggested the young crowd all walk down to Hext.

'We could take *le petit train*. Go whoring in Geneva.'

'I've a better idea,' said Ted. 'Stay put and get drunk.'

'We could get drunk at the Auberge Dorée,' Daisy pointed

out. 'But I'm with Johnny. Jazz in Geneva. Sleep in a hotel. Dance. Black Bottom by the lake. I'm on the lookout for a new hubby. It'll be a lark. I wonder if the Swiss can Lindy hop. Shall I tell them I'm a widow or pretend to be a spinster?'

'If you want jazz and to dance,' I said, serving Daisy her porridge and thinking she looked and behaved, at twenty-nine, more like a schoolgirl than the war-widow she was, 'you need go no further than Hext.'

All eyes were on me, but I didn't care: it seemed like a good idea – Valentines and visitors would be occupied, Costa would be grateful and the house would be quiet for Lady C. I continued calmly to serve the porridge. I told them where the club was and how to find it.

To my relief, they all went off after lunch, sceptical but curious.

'We'll hole up in the Auberge Dorée first,' said Johnny. 'When we're oiled and rearing to go, we'll shimmy along to the barn dance.'

They had a hextraordinary night, said Daisy – and there were regular trips to Club Costa after that. And what a blessing at the time! The weather remained inclement, Lady C required nursing round the clock, and Beatrice made a fuss about how we uglies carried this out.

Daisy even chose to go to Costa's for her birthday that year. In fancy dress. She and 'her girls' – which is what she called her women friends, whether married and matronly or footloose and fancy free – stripped to their underwear and draped sheets around their bodies.

'We're the Oreads,' said Daisy. 'Claea, Daphnis, Echo. And I'm Ida.'

Johnny said they looked more like Roman prostitutes than Greek mountain nymphs. Which made the four grown women snicker.

'Did you enjoy it, Daisy? The sex?' asked unmarried Daphnis.

'No one enjoys it,' interrupted Claea. 'No woman, that is.'

'Lie back and think of Blighty. Count sheep. Make a shopping list. That's my advice,' said Daisy.

*

In the middle of July, Lady C took a turn for the worse and Margaret was sent for. Margaret Valentine – not seen in the valley since 1907. Spit, spat.

The Valentines' guests discreetly left, Beatrice rolled up her sleeves and helped with the dirty work of dying – the shit and the piss and the blood in them both, which left stains on the sheets, despite my soaking and scrubbing – and Sylvie made her best broths, but the steaming bowls, not easy to transport up and down stairs, came back to the kitchen cold and untouched.

Arete smelt of death, and I didn't blame Daisy and Johnny for escaping to Costa's whenever they could. Ted occasionally went with them, but he tended to conk out after lunch.

'With you toot de sweet,' he'd say before disappearing into his room. He scarcely bothered to hide the bulge of bottles under his jacket.

'Warren's really not bad on trombone,' said Johnny. 'And I've seen worse pianists at the Trocadero.'

Daisy liked the dancing.

'And I adore the people. Such an eclectic mix,' she said. 'Shopkeepers from Chamonix, students from Annecy and businessmen from Geneva. Plus a handful of country bumpkins. And the niggers, of course, in the band. So exhilarating. Costa sometimes improvises with them on his violin.'

'How is Costa?' I asked.

'Garrulous,' she said.

As if I didn't know! I pressed for more.

Costa was a most intriguing man: courteous, knowledgeable, tireless, handsome, popular, fun. Daisy's words. But they didn't answer my question.

'And he's an excellent dancer,' she added. 'I'm teaching him to tango.'

'Is he well? Happy?' I asked. I hadn't seen Costa since May, when he was in a worry over the club and its sums again because the Parisian investor was already asking for a return on his investment. I redid Costa's sums and then I melted Gruyère over the previous day's crozets and left-over morels, and Costa helped me carry this cheesey pasta, with bread, across to the club, where the musicians were practising their jazz on the little stage Costa had built.

'Never had such tasty mushies,' said Warren, and the others, busy munching, nodded, which pleased me.

'All Mathilde's work,' said Costa. 'I don't know what I'd do without her.' Which pleased me even more.

'Is Costa well?' Daisy considered the question. 'Yes, I think so. Is he happy? Who knows? Who cares? You do, don't you, Little Broomhead?'

I cared about Costa more than I cared or dared to think about, but I didn't want to say so to Daisy.

*

I was on my knees in the dining room, sweeping shards of glass into a dustpan (Ted had knocked over an empty wine bottle, reaching for a full one), when I heard Beatrice announce that Margaret had been sent for.

'I've written to Edmond and Harold,' she said. 'And Mother's been asking for Margaret. So, somewhat against my better judgement, I've sent a letter to my sister too.'

'That's a turn-up for the books,' said Ted.

'Bloody hell.' Daisy was intrigued. 'I scarcely remember her. Everyone went on about what a good alpinist she was. I remember that. How old was I when she buggered off?'

'Enough of the language, Daisy,' said Beatrice. 'And I don't know. Young.'

Seven. The same age as me. And I, like Daisy, was intrigued, having been there when Lady C and her daughter argued and Margaret departed from Arete in high dudgeon. I realised I must have been one of the last people to see Margaret Valentine before she boarded *le petit train* in 1907 and, to all intents and purposes, vanished into thin air.

*

I was six when the visits began – the summer after a year of school with Madame Tissot.

From Hext to Hext-en-Haut, Madame Tissot carried Papa's diots, wrapped in cloth, in her basket. She would hold my hand if she heard me panting for breath, but if I moaned or stood still, she would ignore me and walk on ahead. I had to rush and stumble to catch up, and then she would say, 'It doesn't pay to complain, Mathilde. The mountains won't change their shape for you.'

At Hext-en-Haut she would hand me the diots, and, after her instructions and goodbyes, I had to make my own way up to the high pastures. There was no danger of getting lost, because there was only one track. Nevertheless I made sure to stop from time to time and look back the way I'd come; it's surprising how the world changes, viewed from a different angle, and in the mountains this is particularly so. Madame Tissot knew many things, but she wasn't from the mountains. We'd been taught, as soon as we could walk, to stop and turn regularly – it helped to imprint the changing shapes of the landscape on our minds, and prevented us from getting lost. I also, out of habit, crossed a few twigs here and there, like we did in the woods above the farm, so as to find our way easily home.

Benoît and his papa, Tall Paul, were waiting for me at the far end of the pasture, having set off much earlier to milk the summering cows.

Tall Paul was away in Geneva most of the time. He worked at the 'usine à gaz de la Coulouvrenière', Benoît told people proudly, spooling the syllables slowly and rhythmically. He only came home for three days each month and – as if that wasn't bad enough, said Benoît's mother – he often, on one of those days, worked for the Valentines. But it was the job in the gas factory that paid for the Abondance cows, which were the envy and pride of the valley and filled up the money-chest in their mazot, Benoît explained; his mother couldn't complain that loudly. The rich creamy milk from their Abondance cows was specifically requested at Arete approximately once a month, and no one in the village turned down such a request; the Valentines paid handsomely.

It was therefore an exceptional thing – a treat, not a chore – for Benoît to rise at four with his papa and climb to the pastures for the early milking. I could tell how excited Benoît was by the way he sped towards me, snatched the diots, grabbed my hand and dragged me across the grass to Tall Paul.

'Here she is, Papa. Let's go.'

Usually, Tall Paul would swing me onto his shoulders for the rest of the way. I didn't mention this to Madame Tissot, let alone that from my privileged perch the mountains definitely seemed to be changing their shape for me at every twist and turn.

'I don't need to be carried, do I, Papa?' Benoît boasted. 'And look – I can manage our lunch, and the milk and diots too.'

'That's because you're a good, strong boy,' Tall Paul would say.

'Like you, Papa.'

'*Oui, mon fils*. Like me.'

*

Margaret must have watched and waited for us, because as soon as we turned the second bend, we'd see her waving from the balcony. Tall Paul would put me down on the ground and draw me back with him a few steps and to the side of the path, where we waited for a minute or two. During this time, Benoît delivered the milk and the diots to the kitchen door. Benoît rejoined me and Tall Paul on the path and we'd set off walking very slowly back the way we'd come. Margaret, smiling widely, always caught up with us in no time. She trod lightly and although she looked about the same age as Maman or Madame Tissot, she was more sprightly.

We'd soon turn off the path, and Tall Paul would lead us, via goat tracks and the marks left by chamois, to some sheltered place – a nook in the rocks, a glade in the forest, a warm grassy nest in the thicket at the base of a cliff. We'd share the lunch Benoît had carried: bread, still fresh, cheese, sweeter than any I'd ever tasted, and sausage somewhat dull – I'd have preferred Papa's nutmeggy diots, but they, like Tall Paul's milk, were the reason for our trip to Arete.

After lunch, Benoît and I would lie on our backs while Tall Paul told tall stories. Benoît and I liked the funny ones about Geneva – the *usine à gaz de la Coulouvrenière*, the lake like an ocean, the fountain like a firework, the trams quite a hazard – but Margaret preferred it when he spoke about himself and his boyhood in the mountains. Tall Paul never used patois (and told Benoît and me not to) in front of Margaret. He talked in Parisian French, good but slow.

Margaret spoke slowly too. Her short French sentences were faultless, but she paused between each word and said everything in the same tone of voice. Ocassionally she used English expressions, some but not all of which she would try to explain.

Later, we'd make our way back to the path, say goodbye to Margaret and walk to the pastures. Benoît and Tall Paul stayed there until it was time for the evening milking, but I, exhausted, went on ahead. At Hext-en-Haut, Madame Tissot was waiting for half-asleep me, and, tenderly now, with her arm around me, she'd accompany me back to the farm. At the threshold she handed over money to Papa; he would count it and chuckle;

sometimes he'd even give me and my sisters a few sous of our own.

The year I was six, I made this trip four times.

The year I was seven, only two.

The second time was in June. It was drizzly and grey in the valley, but from Hext-en-Haut on ('Goodbye, Mathilde. Mind your P's and Q's'), an egg-yolk sun was busy burning off the remaining scraps of cloud, and at Arete all was blue and bright.

The windows were open, and the sound of a piano being tuned drifted across to where I stood waiting with Tall Paul.

'Costa,' said Tall Paul. 'He passed us earlier while we were milking.'

Margaret came round the corner. She was wearing the biggest straw hat I'd ever seen. She said the day was a scorcher and the hat was to protect her pale skin.

'Scorcher.'

'Scorcher.'

Benoît and I passed the word between us as we walked.

Perhaps because of the scorcher and Margaret's pale skin, we didn't stray far from the path that day. Tall Paul found us a peaceful spot in a hollow by a stream, which trickled quietly down through a pile of rocks about the height of a mazot.

When we'd eaten our lunch, Tall Paul told a long story – a local legend about a lost marmot. I shut my eyes; I knew the story inside out, but it was good to hear it again, especially with Paul's special flourishes and unexpected additions. When I opened them, I saw Margaret had shut her eyes, and I watched for a while as little smiles shivered across her mouth and eyelids. I could see from her chest and the air coming out of her nose that she wasn't asleep. Her breathing was quick and fluttery, like her hand, which kept brushing against Paul's.

Afterwards, Benoît begged Tall Paul to retell his adventure with Xavier in the Aosta valley, where they had been chamois-hunting. Tall Paul had just got to the best part (where he and his father stumbled upon some Italians fleeing a bear) when a shriek from above made me look up, and it was suddenly, 'Lady C!' and '*Vite, vite!*' A scrabble and rush to our feet.

'Margaret!' The woman's voice was clear and shockingly loud.

We looked on as Lady C descended the rocks. At the bottom she was calm, but I noticed her cheeks, beneath the second biggest straw hat I'd ever seen, were as pink as bacon.

Spit, spat. Margaret and Lady C exchanged cold, clipped English words which I didn't understand. There was a lot of kerfuffle as Margaret talked to Paul, then Lady C, then Paul again. Benoît and I huddled behind Tall Paul, and when Margaret held out her hand to me, I withdrew even further. But Paul moved, pushed me forwards, and, when I looked up at him, he nodded. So although I didn't take Margaret's hand, I followed her. And we both followed Lady C.

At Arete, we walked round the side of the house and went in at the front door. Margaret indicated that I was to sit on the bench in the hall. She and her mother disappeared into the sitting room.

I sat on that bench for a very long time. My feet didn't touch the floor and my legs began to get pins and needles. I swung them back and forth. All I could hear from the sitting room was Lady C's voice, high-pitched and squeaky, and Margarets's, quieter and lower. Their words were gobbledegook to me, but I was familiar with the rhythms of dispute and recognised when this one was nearing its climax. In my household, a row usually ended with Papa losing his temper and beating Maman until she couldn't have argued with him any more even if she'd wanted to. At Arete, the door to the sitting room was flung open and Margaret came out.

'I must go,' she said, halting, toneless, correct. 'We must depart.'

We didn't depart immediately, though. Margaret went upstairs, leaving the door to the sitting room open. Lady C was far too agitated to notice that I was watching as she paced back and forth, then stopped by the fireplace and took a great wodge of papers out of her pocket. She clutched the mantelpiece with one of her hands and bowed her head. She was still wearing the big straw sun hat and it jiggled up and down as gurgling noises made her whole body shake like a pig being slaughtered.

Margaret came downstairs carrying a small suitcase. She took my hand and led me out of the house.

'Spit, spat,' she said. 'That's that. I'm leaving and I won't be coming back. That's families for you.'

After that, we walked without talking all the way down to Hext and through the village to Madame Tissot's house. Madame Tissot ushered Margaret inside, but, giving me a handful of coins, told me to hurry home. Margaret objected. Madame Tissot insisted. I skedaddled.

I hadn't expected to see Margaret again, but she was at the train station the following morning when I dropped off the milk. She didn't notice me unloading and reloading my cart at the end of the platform.

No more diots were requested at Arete after that, and Benoît said no more Abondance milk was requested either. We both wondered why, but nobody could give us an answer. And when we questioned Tall Paul, he tried to fob us off with a very tall story – cock and bull, I'd call it – about the milk being sour, the diots rancid and Lady C losing her temper with Margaret for receiving the goods without checking.

Two years later, in 1909, there was a gas explosion at the factory at Coulouvrenière and Tall Paul was one of the thirteen dead. Benoît's mother still had the Abondance cows, but she had to rely on them entirely from then on, and she'd only Benoît to help her.

*

Margaret returned to the valley in 1929, but she arrived too late to see her mother die. I wasn't there either when Lady C passed away. I'd been dismissed from my job at Arete by then.

Part Two

Arête

Sir A = Lady E

Edmond

Harold

Beatrice = Bill

Margaret

Stephen

Ted

Daisy

Johnny

Rory

Josh

Peggy = Donald

Inez = Bob

George

Tess

Polly

Jack

Isobel

Family Tree | 1864 ~ 1964 | By Daisy

Thirteen

There's a small, pear-shaped mountain in Haute-Savoie. Behind it lies one of Europe's greenest and most fertile valleys. The hanging valley of Hext is little known and rarely visited, and yet it may be reached in one day from the plain of Geneva. Its attractions are legion and rank among the finest of any Alpine valley I have seen.

I happened upon the valley through luck – chance or fate – but love made me stay and I have been unable to resist returning.

Luck, chance, fate . . . But, thought George, it was actually Xavier who led twenty-two-year-old Anthony Oswald Valentine deep into the valley of Hext and introduced him as Sir A. And what sort of love made Sir A return and purchase the land, employ locals as lackeys, build a sawmill, a lime kiln, erect a *maison de plaisance*?

George read on.

*

Mathilde had requested Wednesday off, Bastille day – '*la fête nationale*, I'd like to watch the parade in the afternoon' – and Jack had offered to drive her down from Hext-en-Haut in the 2CV. He could do with stocking up at the tabac, he said, and the girls would enjoy seeing Thomas in the parade.

George said he'd remain at Arete; he'd letters he needed to write. This was true – he hadn't replied to Graham yet, and he ought to drop a line to Graham's mum and dad, too. But once he'd done that, at a bit of a loose end and regretting his decision not to go with the others, George picked up the box file he hadn't got round to returning. He carried it up to the attic, intending to put it back where it came from, when he decided he might as well have another dip into the diaries while he was at it. He sat on the least untidy bed and started at the very beginning.

There's a small, pear-shaped mountain . . .

The writing was pretty much the same old flowery Victorianese that George had skim-read in the attic and on the terrace with Jack – exaggerated and scattered with lubricious passages. Visitors were listed and, occasionally, a thumbnail sketch of them given – clergymen, barristers, medics, some gentlemen farmers, publishers, writers, artists, 'newspaper types' and a good number of academics from the looks of the letters after their names.

There were glimpses of everyday Valentine family life at Arete:

Charlotte enjoys weekly trips to the market in Hext. She's away all day, but she brings me back Reblochon, fruits of the valley and little earthenware pots of golden honey. She's blooming . . .

Edmond and Harold much amused by damming the stream and floating paper boats on the Round Pond . . .

Yarned all afternoon on the terrace with fat Cadbury, my dearest Charlotte having borrowed Xavier . . .

Billiards in the evening with the Mackenzie brothers. We polished off the finest whisky, while dearest Charlotte taught Xavier to strip the willow . . .

The most interesting entries in the early diaries were those in the immediate aftermath of Xavier's disappearance. Sir A and

Lady C both seemed to have gone a bit potty. Lady C, George gathered, took to wandering alone in the mountains. Hitherto, she was always accompanied, if not by Sir A himself, then by one of his climbing buddies, along with a porter or two, or a guide – often Xavier – to carry her easels and painting equipment.

As to Sir A, he spent a fortune in August 1872 and again, in the summer of '73, paying local men, hunters, guides, farmers – chancers, George suspected – to comb the area, looking for signs as to how and why Xavier had disappeared. Sir A's obsession diminished gradually, but he still referred frequently and with the utmost respect and affection to the irreplaceable 'guide and mentor, friend and educator', who was 'wise beyond words' and 'the embodiment of arete'.

It was clear from the diaries that Sir A was a regular visitor to Xavier's widow. There was nothing, however, to suggest hanky-pank. 'She bears her grief with dignity,' he'd written and, 'She is an exemplary mother to her fatherless son, and Paul himself, I'm happy to say, resembles Xavier more and more, although his mother won't hear of him following in his father's footsteps to become a guide'. Paul trained as a skilled engineer at a small factory in nearby Celliers, and by the mid 1880s was working, at least some of the time, so it seemed, in Geneva.

The only thing resembling hanky-pank was Sir A's purple, semi-pornographic, rather cringeworthy prose, going overboard about the effects on him of 'nature's masonry' – 'huge-crested crags, with shaggy sides', 'noble, manly peaks' – and 'the deep, sea-green beds of softest moss', into which he sank, 'spent', in an erotic haze.

Events in the outside world were usually mentioned only in passing, although Sir A reported at length his reaction to the Matterhorn disaster in 1865, concluding 'it ruined the summer'. He also described the inauguration of Lake Geneva's fountain in 1891 and the opening of the railway line to Hext in 1892, the same year as Beatrice's wedding. She married a 'buttoned-up banker', referred to by Sir A as 'boring Bill', which made George laugh out loud.

Beatrice, George noticed, didn't receive as much diary space as Margaret. The elder daughter, Margaret, had definitely been the favourite. 'Beatrice takes after me,' Sir A had written. 'Her athleticism is hard won. She loves the mountains, but she is not a natural alpinist.' Margaret, on the other hand – a quick learner and, in looks, like her mother – 'has an innate physical grace that will make her an excellent climber, one day, if she chooses.' Sir A later expressed his sadness that Margaret preferred dabbling in politics and 'good works with an odd Swiss woman and her cronies in London' to perfecting her mountaineering skills. But he was proud too:

> *My Margaret has a brain as sharp as any man's. Her degree from London University makes her a trailblazer.*

George read that Margaret, born in 1870, became actively involved, from the late 1880s, with the women in London petitioning for the right to vote, with Misses Buss and Beale, and reforming the education of girls. Beatrice, meanwhile, gave birth to three sons in quick succession: the birth of Johnny in 1898 caused Sir A to write, 'Beatrice is blessed. Margaret, I fear, will never know the delights of a fruitful marriage or motherhood'; and in one of the last diary entries of the summer of 1899, 'My Margaret becomes more spinsterish every year.'

Fourteen

Pretty Johnny died in an awful accident in 1929. The avalanche that killed him came about because of Daisy, partly. Daisy blamed me entirely, and I didn't naysay her.

It happened a week before Lady C died. I'd been up most of the night assisting Beatrice with turning Lady C's skin-and-bone body in a hopeless attempt to relieve her weeping bedsores.

'It's the least we can do,' said Beatrice, sadness and fatigue combining to soften her features for once.

I think she meant it was pretty much all we could do, at this point, and it wasn't very much. I nodded. When I next went down to the kitchen to fetch water for Lady C, I made a pot of Earl Grey tea for Beatrice, exactly how she liked it – on a tray, with matching china and a silver teaspoon.

'Thank you, Mathilde,' she said. 'One can't beat a nice cup of tea. How thoughtful of you.'

She was uncharacteristically talkative, while she sipped her Earl Grey tea, and seemed to enjoy telling me how Lady C – 'Marmee' – had been as keen an alpinist as Sir A 'in her own way', as Beatrice put it.

'It was before my time, really,' she said. 'Before Marmee went incommunicado. But I remember, when I was a very young girl, her teaching Margaret and me how to sew loose threads of wool or cotton into the linings of our skirts and dresses in such a way that we could hoik them easily up to our knees for climbing – a sort of pulley system. Most ingenious.'

As day dawned, the grey light that filtered through the closed curtains of Lady C's bedroom grew brighter. I drew back the curtains and we saw clear skies for the first time in ages.

The lifting of the weather led to Daisy proposing an expedition.

'Not down the mountain, but up, for a change. Over the hills and far away.'

Ted demurred at first. He'd not touched the omelette I'd prepared for breakfast, but was dosing himself with black coffee and sponge fingers. He said he had a headache. Johnny, however, was all for it.

'Why not?' he said. 'Buck up, Ted. A brisk trot up one or two peaks will do you the world of good.'

In the end Ted agreed, but only if porters could be found to carry the provisions, and a servant brought along, also, to dish out lunch and clear away afterwards.

Two boys from the village were working on the garden at Arete at the time. They were told to put down their tools and prepare for a trip into the mountains. And I, relieved for the day of my Lady C duties, was to be the accompanying servant.

Daisy had found the four alpenstocks rejected by Sir A and abandoned by the Valentines before the war. She insisted we take them with us. She gave Stephen's baton to me, handed Ted and Johnny theirs, and kept the one I'd carved for herself.

We walked to the north col of la Miche and had lunch on the spit of land looking down to the lake, with the la Miche rocks on our right. Ted drank too much. As I helped the gardening boys repack the detritus of lunch into the canvas bags, I told them they might need to assist Ted back to Arete. Johnny overheard me.

'Ted's as fit as a fiddle,' he said. 'He'll outstrip us all, once we get a bit higher up. Hop it,' he said to the gardening boys. 'Take the afternoon off. Go back to Arete. Loaf.'

Up we climbed, without the gardening boys, and I soon saw that the good weather, which the morning had seemed to promise, was only temporary. As soon as we'd reached the end of the corridor behind the rochers de la Miche, you could see an ominous line of clouds to the west and I could smell change in the windless air. Nevertheless, I sensed no real danger, not yet.

We reached a small, exposed col, and Johnny said I should wait there.

'Prepare a little tiffin for us, would you, Mathilde? Some refuelling, before we all descend, might not go amiss.'

I glanced at the sky and my skin started to tickle with anxiety. Perhaps it was the day's sun that had caused a change in the quality of the air. Or the combination of this and the new weather front coming in from the west. I felt obliged to say what I knew:

'To go any further or higher would be foolhardy.'

'What are you talking about?' said Ted.

'I think this mountain is in a dangerous mood,' I said.

'Oh, Mathilde.' Johnny put an arm around my shoulder. 'You and your mountain moods. Look at the sky. It could scarcely be clearer. And the snow. Feel it. Packed good and proper.'

I turned to Daisy, certain that she would back me up.

'You,' I said. 'You know what I'm talking about. I've often spoken of the moods of the mountain.'

'No,' said Daisy. 'I've no idea. You peasants believe the silliest things.'

'Hey,' said Johnny. 'No need to be nasty. Mathilde is only showing due caution. Isn't that right, Mathilde?'

'More than caution,' I replied. 'Common peasant sense.'

'Well, while you lot discuss it, I'm going to have a drink,' said Ted, pulling out one of the three hip flasks I knew he had about him, for he'd removed his jacket during lunch and I'd seen the lumps in its pockets. 'Cheers.'

Johnny was chomping at the bit to get going and his excitement had infected Daisy. They were betting with each other on who would make it to the top first. I became more and more concerned. To go any further inebriated, or in the overexcited spirit which had now possessed Johnny and Daisy, would be dangerous.

'It's tempting fate,' I said, seeking an *anglais* expression that I thought would drive my point home. This was a mistake, because it caused Daisy to snort with derision.

'Fate,' she said. 'Whatever next? You'll be telling us soon the devil still resides up there.'

'If he does,' said Ted, 'we'll jolly well kill him, won't we brother?' He offered Johnny the flask, but Johnny shook his head.

'Come on. Let's get going,' he said.

'If you insist on going, I insist on accompanying you,' I said, realising, with surprise, as I said it, that I cared about these foolish *anglais* as if they were children. They behaved like children. Even Sir A. There had been something endearingly, childishly sincere in his lists and his descriptions, in his overblown language and the outpouring of his land-love.

'That's fine by me,' said Johnny. 'What about you two?'

'Fine,' said Ted.

'If she must.' Daisy turned and set off up the snow field in a straight line. 'Beat you to those rocks, boys.'

All went well for the next hour. The peak was reached and the Valentines were very pleased with themselves. Johnny gave me his camera and told me to take a picture of the three of them. Daisy leant nonchalantly on one side of the iron cross. Johnny stood on the other side, put a foot on the vertical post of the cross, and posed as if he were about to climb the cross too. Ted sat on the ground and swigged from one of his hip flasks.

'It looks as if your misgivings were unfounded,' said Johnny as I passed the camera back to him.

'Yes,' I said, and even I wondered if I'd misjudged the mountain's mood.

'Still,' Johnny said. 'Better get on down before the devil gets us, eh?'

'Yes,' I said again.

But when we reached a part of the ridge we'd traversed easily only an hour ago, I saw that the snow had changed. It was as packed as ever, but narrow fissures had appeared in it near the top of the ridge on the south-west side. If we walked along the ridge we might easily set off an avalanche, and although that would have caused no danger to us, the snow would gather at the bottom, fill up the ravine and block our route back. One flank of the slope however was still in shadow, so although the snow had softened there, I could tell that it was less dangerous.

'We must slide,' I said, pointing. 'Down that bit there.'

'Fantastic,' said Ted. 'Shortcut. We can use the alpenstocks. See you at the bottom, you lot.' And he sat, put his alpenstock between his legs, pushed himself off and disappeared for about half a minute in a harmless spray of snow. He emerged with no alpenstock but with only a few more yards to slide. At the bottom, he stood up, waved and raised an imaginary glass in cheers. Then we saw him trudge through the thick snow and round the bluff to the safety of the overhanging rocks on the other side.

'Good,' I said. 'One at a time. And don't follow Ted's track exactly.'

'Ladies first,' said Johnny.

'No,' said Daisy. 'I'm not doing that. Look at the snow.'

It was true that Ted's descent had set off a number of tiny, harmless avalanches, but these, I knew, were relatively superficial. So long as we each took a different route, sufficiently far apart, and hurried quickly round the bluff at the bottom, there would be little danger.

I explained this to Johnny and Daisy. I said I would go last, so that if their descents did cause a more serious dislodgement of the snow, I would be the one to confront it. To encourage them, I told them I'd been in plenty of small avalanches before and I knew exactly what to do. Benoît and I used to set off little avalanches deliberately on the roofs of barns and chalets and in the sloping meadows at the bottom of the valley. We'd learnt how to move with the snow, not resist it, and how to paddle our way quickly to the surface when we came to a standstill. We would never have dreamed of making a game with the real avalanches that thudded down from the mountains, taking everything in their path with them.

Johnny and Daisy argued. Johnny, ever the gentleman, was still trying to persuade Daisy to go first, while Daisy was still saying she wouldn't go at all.

In the end, exasperated, Johnny said, 'Very well. Here I go. Mathilde, make sure Daisy starts her slide in the safest place. Look after her for me.'

These were Johnny's last words.

As he lowered himself over the ridge, Daisy set off along the top of it.

'Stop,' I hissed to her, but it was too late.

'I don't need looking after,' Daisy shouted.

Johnny had gone sliding off.

The shout, or perhaps Daisy's footsteps along the precarious ridge, or both, and my 'stop' (or perhaps it would have happened anyway) caused one of the narrow cracks in the snow to widen and a great slab of it broke away from the ridge. It slid slowly, but not slowly enough, down the mountain. Daisy and I both watched helplessly as the slab of snow made its way towards the track of Johnny's sliding body. They collided about thirty feet above the bottom, and Johnny was lost to view. The build-up of snow from the descending slab was enormous. It filled the ravine and made a hummock on top of it, more than blocking the path we'd taken earlier, but also, I could see, allowing us to use it to steer round and glide to relative safety.

'Now we have no choice,' I said. 'Stay completely still. Until I tell you to go.'

There wasn't any need to tell Daisy to stay still. She stood frozen with shock. It was too dangerous for me to walk the few steps towards her. I could easily have set off another slab avalanche. I lay down in the snow and wriggled my way along the ridge, inch by inch. When I reached Daisy, I knelt and placed a hand on her leg. She didn't budge. Very carefully, I stood up. There was a look so vacant in her eyes that I was afraid I'd never get her safely down. I rubbed Daisy's limbs until they softened enough for me to bend them. I got her into a sitting position. I straightened her legs, placed the alpenstock between them, folded her hands around it and then, ever so carefully, pushed her off, down the slope, with instructions to veer right at the bottom. I waited until I saw her come to a stop, then I prepared for my descent. I had to wait another few minutes because I couldn't go until I knew Daisy was safe round the corner of the bluff, and that didn't happen until Ted appeared and I saw him take her hand and lead her out of sight. I descended, losing my alpenstock en route, and joined them.

Neither of them were in any fit state for talking, Ted because he was as drunk as a skunk now, Daisy because of what she'd seen happen to Johnny.

Getting them both back to Arete without mishap was a job in itself. I knew there was no hope of Johnny being found alive and didn't waste my time thinking about it.

I heard later that the dozen men who went to search retrieved his peg-leg, but only bits and pieces of Johnny's body, strewn around and buried in the snow-filled ravine.

I was called, before supper, to the sitting room. Beatrice stood by the mantelpiece. Daisy lay on the chaise longue.

'Daisy's told me what happened,' said Beatrice. 'You're dismissed. Pack. Leave in the morning, as soon as it's light. I'll send your wages on.'

I looked at Daisy but she kept her lying, thieving, cheating eyes lowered.

'No,' I said. 'I'm owed a lot more than money.' I turned to Beatrice. 'But I want my wages. Now. I won't go until you've paid me.' I spoke in the firm voice I reserved for business transactions. Then, looking Beatrice fair and square in her too-strong-for-my-liking face, I added, 'It's the least you can do.'

I went to my hut and waited. Sure enough, half an hour later, a gardening boy knocked on the door and handed me a pouch of money. I counted the money and had to recount it: there was so much more than there should have been.

I packed my bag, but I didn't leave in the morning because Lady C had started raving, and Sylvie, who'd been up all night with her, begged me to stay, secretly, for just a few hours. Could I do one or two of her chores so that she could sleep? I agreed, and I ended up not leaving Arete until nearly dusk, just after Daisy and Ted, who, despite all the goings-on, were off to Costa's.

'Drown our sorrows, the tooter the sweeter,' Ted muttered.

'I need to let off steam, unwind, make some whoopee. Cheerio,' I heard Daisy shout, but Beatrice was too busy with Lady C to answer.

On the walk down from Arete to Hext, I had plenty of time to think, and I decided to go to Club Costa too. I might want that job there, after all. And I realised I wanted very much to tell Costa what had happened. We'd go to his workshop, and I'd explain everything to him there.

*

Costanza's place was ablaze with light – from the windows and from the sign that read 'Club Costa' above the double doors – and it seemed almost to shake with the noise that came out of it.

The double doors flew open and I stepped into the shadow. I watched a man and a woman exit. The man had his hand on the small of the woman's back. He steered her to one of the parked cars and opened the door for her. He climbed into the driver's seat and leaned over for a kiss. I saw her reach her face up towards his, put a hand behind his neck and pull him down to her.

Through the open double doors, I could scarcely see Warren and the other musicians on the stage at the back because there were so many people in the way – their bodies were incredibly close together and they were dancing the Charleston extraordinarily fast, all zigzaggy knees and criss-crossy hands. Ted was at the bar. No sign of Daisy or Costa.

I decided to walk round to the back entrance. Costa might be in the small room off the corridor there, which they called the green room. It was really for the musicians, Costa said, but he quite often nipped in there himself to tune up, or for a rest when things got too much in the club.

The back door was unlocked, so I stepped into the narrow corridor and opened the door to the green room – empty. I left my bag in the corridor, went out again and walked across to Costa's workshop, but there were no lights on there or in any of the outhouses. I returned to the yard in front of the club. More cars had arrived. They were parked almost bumper to bumper now, and I wondered how they'd ever get out. The double doors were still open and this time I stepped a bit closer to the entrance to get a better look.

Gaps appeared in the crowd as the music temporarily came to a halt. There was Ted, still at the bar. There was the pianist, wiping sweat from his forehead with the back of one hand, and the trumpet player shaking the spittle from his instrument. Warren leant across and said something to the pianist and they both laughed. And there were Costa and Daisy, evidently dancing, or rather, finishing dancing together. Costa stood straight with his arms by his sides, but Daisy still had a hand on Costa's shoulder and was patting his chest with her other hand. Costa, who was smiling, shook his head and tilted it forwards. Daisy went on tiptoes and whispered something in his ear. It looked as if they were about to kiss. It looked as if they were happy – very, I'd say.

A few yards from me, the engine of one of the cars in the yard spluttered into life and the car's headlamps lit up. They shone directly on me. I moved sideways one way, then the other, confused. I ended up standing slap bang in the middle of the entrance to the club, which meant that when Daisy glanced over to the door, she saw me. She frowned, said something to Costa and began to walk towards me.

'What are you doing here?' she said when she reached me. Her eyes glinted in the light like the pipe-smokers' in the games room.

'I came to see Costa,' I said.

'Snap! At least we both have good taste.' She grinned – a bit madly, I thought. 'Don't run off, little Mathilde. Come inside and say hello – to Costa, the band, Warren.'

'No thank you,' I said.

An urge to get away swept through me, but Daisy put a hand on my arm.

'We're lovers, you know,' she said.

I shook her off and scooted round to the back of the building to retrieve my bag. It was where I'd left it, but the door to the green room was now open and the light in there on. As I picked up my bag, I peeked and saw Costa. He had his back to the door and was holding his violin under his chin with the bow poised above it, about to play.

Costa. I almost called out.

Were he and Daisy really lovers? The thought filled me with despair from top to bottom of my squat, ugly body. I shut the back door quietly behind me and walked along the track next to the river in the no-moon, black-tree dark until I came to the bridge over the Ouiffre. For home, I only needed to turn left and follow the track up the slopes, through the woods and across the fields, past Cédric's house, to the farm. I knew it like the back of my hand. The road on the right led to the village. I turned right.

*

I spent the night on a bench at the railway station. The ticket-master, who was employed by the railway company and didn't know me at all, woke me up in the morning and I purchased a ticket from him for the early train to Geneva. I told him I'd never been on a train before, but he didn't seem interested.

I settled myself on a wooden seat, facing forwards, by the window, and put my bag on the seat next to me. The train started with a series of jerks and grinds and I held onto the seat with both hands. The movement became smoother, but it was such a strange sensation, and the world outside the window seemed to move backwards with such rapidity, that all I could do was hold on and stare out until I fell into a jiggled half-sleep. By the time *le petit train* pulled into the Gare des Eaux Vives, I was stiff all over.

As soon as I descended from the train, I checked the pouch was still in my bag. It was, and its weight was reassuring. There were two hotels opposite the station and I decided to approach one of them.

The man at the desk in the hotel foyer wore a uniform with shiny lapels and brass buttons.

'How may I help you?' he said in excellent Parisian French.

'I don't know if you can,' I began.

'Let me try,' he said, looking into my eyes, not letting his own eyes wander, as most strangers' did, to my ugliness.

'I'm looking for someone. I have the address, but I am unfamiliar with the city.'

'Tell me what it is, and I'm sure I can help.'

I told him the address I'd memorised from Madame Tissot's letters.

'Ah,' he said. 'Near Plainpalais. The university quarter. You won't have trouble finding it. It's a fair step, though. You'll need to take two trams.'

No. I shook my head again. I didn't think I could face any more mechanical moving though the world. Besides, there was the problem of currency.

'I prefer to walk,' I said.

'If you're sure?' said the man, looking with concern at my clogs and at my bag on the floor next to them.

'I'm sure,' I said.

'In that case, let me draw you a map.'

He picked up a pen and, on a sheet of paper with Hôtel de la Gare printed at the top, wrote down the the address I'd given him and drew a map of lines and squares.

'Can you make sense of that? Perhaps you can't read maps.'

I took the piece of paper and thanked him.

'I read very well,' I added.

'Well, good. I wasn't suggesting otherwise. But I'm from the country too. The Jura. I've lived in the city for twenty years and I still get lost. Besides, you look very tired.'

The man was so polite and sounded so genuinely worried that when he said I could take a nap, if I liked, in one of the unoccupied hotel rooms – he told me he and the other hotel workers often did – I said yes, please. The sheets on the bed in the room he showed me to (and where I said no thank you to his offer of company) were as white and nearly as crisp as the writing paper in the foyer. I'd have liked to try them out, but I fell asleep fully clothed on top of the bed as soon as I lay down and didn't wake up until late afternoon. Back in the foyer, the same man was still at the desk.

'I expect you're hungry now,' he said, producing a plate from behind him. 'Have these. I swiped them from the tea room. The old ladies don't eat them anyway.'

I took the plate of petits fours and had no trouble popping them, one by one, whole, into my mouth while the man repeated the directions to Madame Tissot's.

'If you get lost, the main thing to remember is, the university's in the old town. On a hill. Keep your back to the lake and your eyes to the skies.'

'Thank you,' I said again, the sweetness of the *friandises* still swilling around in my mouth. 'Goodbye.'

'Good luck,' said the kind man.

I did lose my way, several times, but the man's words about the hill were useful and I knew I must be getting near when the wide streets became narrower, the tall houses older and closer together, and there were familiar cobbles underfoot, not wide, flat paving stones. Some of the buildings had blue plaques on them, with their street name printed in white, so I was sure it was only a matter of reading all of these, if necessary, and sooner or later I would come to Madame Tissot's street.

I found myself going in circles, though, returning again and again to the same small square. It was time to seek help once more. I chose a café that looked cheerful and friendly from the outside. The man behind the bar, however, was neither cheerful nor friendly. He sneered when I spoke and I think he said something rude to another man, because the other man looked me up and down in a most unpleasant way. I took out the piece of paper and laid it on the bar, pointing to the address.

'All right,' said the barman. 'You're not far. Take the alley opposite. Left at the end, then first right and you're there.'

I hurried off to the sound of nasty laughter. I expected their directions to have misled me even more, but in fact I found myself outside number nineteen, rue Garnier, in less than five minutes.

I stood contemplating the tall building in front of me for a moment – it was a pinkish colour, with green-shuttered windows and ornate black metal balconies, some of which had geraniums in flowerpots on them. Then I went up close to the large, green-painted door and was about to knock when, 'Mathilde!' I heard.

I jumped – not out of my skin, but with joy.

Madame Tissot had come up behind me. She was carrying a basket over one arm and had a man's leather satchel slung over her shoulder.

I was so relieved and happy to see her that all I could do was smile, and I didn't care that saliva ran out through the gaps in my teeth. She didn't either; we embraced.

'Mathilde,' she said again. 'What? Why? But no, wait. You must come in first.'

I followed her into a long, narrow hallway with apartments off on either side, and then up flight after flight of stairs. At the very top, Madame Tissot stopped, pulled a key out of her basket and unlocked one of the doors.

We went in and she led me to the front room and told me to wait there.

'I finished work late today,' she said. 'I needed to buy food.' She nodded at the basket still on her arm. 'Let me unpack this first. I won't be long.'

The front room had two low armchairs placed next to a small fireplace, shelves filled with books, a square table, some upright chairs and three windows. I walked over to one of them and looked out. The street was so narrow that you could see into the houses opposite and, where the electric lights were on, the view was as clear as day. There was a whole family in one room, sitting at a table, eating. In another, a man was playing the piano. In yet another, two women sewing.

'Take a seat, Mathilde,' said Madame Tissot, 'and tell me what brings you here.'

I sat on the edge of one of the armchairs, with my bag at my feet, and Madame Tissot settled herself into the other one.

'I was at Arete,' I began. 'I've been dismissed.'

Madame Tissot remained silent. I pulled the pouch of money out of my bag.

'But I have money,' I said. 'I can pay for a hotel.'

'Oh, Mathilde,' said Madame Tissot. 'Are you in trouble? Did you not behave correctly?'

I was her best pupil, her clever clogs. How could she doubt me?

'What about your P's and Q's?'

The P's and Q's were the last straw.

I put my head in my hands and wailed like an injured dog until the tears came and, with them, great heaving gasping sobs.

Madame Tissot let me weep myself out.

'You're exhausted,' she said when the tears stopped flowing and the gulps became hiccups. 'You must sleep. Come. I'll show you your bed.'

The room Madame Tissot showed me to was at the back of the building, overlooking a courtyard. It was small but cheerful, the panelling painted yellow, the ceiling white. There was a rush mat on the floor and a cream-coloured blanket on the bed. A plain upright chair stood next to the bed and, against the opposite wall, a chest of drawers. On it were a hairbrush, hand cream and photographs in frames. I put my bag on the chair and studied them. They were of people and places, classrooms and cities I didn't know, all except one, which appeared identical to the photograph Sir A used to request in the darkroom of Margaret Valentine and the other women. Why would Madame Tissot have a picture of Margaret? Intrigued, I stepped closer to get a better look. It was very similar, but was it the same? I reached out to pick it up, when I heard Madame Tissot in the kitchen next door. However curious, I shouldn't touch my teacher's personal things. I took my bag and crept out of the pretty bedroom. How could I sleep in my teacher's bed? Where would she sleep? What I was doing was definitely not correct.

I tiptoed along the corridor and back into the front room. There, I curled up on the rug in front of the unlit fire and put my head on my bag. I heard Madame Tissot come in. I shut my eyes and pretended to be asleep. She stood over me for some time. She said my name, but I kept my eyes closed and my breathing steady. She sighed, left the room, came back again and placed a warm blanket over me.

My eyes were tight and achey from the crying. They felt better closed, but I stayed awake for a long time, nevertheless, listening to the groups of young people – mostly men but mixed with women's voices too – talking, shouting and laughing in the street below. Students. They'd obviously been drinking, but not too much.

I slept well, and when I woke up the room was daubed with sunshine coming through the gaps between the shutters. Madame Tissot was sitting on one of the upright chairs. She was dressed as if about to go out and held a hat on her lap. I stood, brushed myself down and picked up my bag.

'It's all right, Mathilde. No panic. I've a class at eight, that's all. I've made coffee. In the kitchen. The bathroom is on the landing outside. It's shared with other tenants, but they too will be at work, so you won't be disturbed. I'll be back at lunchtime. Why don't you choose a book to read while I'm gone?'

And with that, she departed.

I went into the kitchen, where Madame Tissot had put three rolls on a napkin next to the coffee pot. I pressed a finger into one of the rolls. It was warm and as soft as Daisy's pink powder puff. Madame Tissot must have been out already once to buy them. I downed them all, for they were sweet and almost as delicious as the petits fours. I drank some coffee, then washed the bowl and dried it with the napkin where the rolls had been.

The bathroom on the landing had a shower, as well as a basin and a toilet, but I didn't spend long in there for there were noises coming from all sides of the building, the noises of people getting up, doors opening and closing, talking, and I was afraid Madame Tissot may have been mistaken about everyone having gone to work.

Back in the front room, I opened the shutters and then, as it grew warmer, the windows too. I spent most of the morning at the window. I could no longer see so clearly into the apartments opposite, but there was plenty going on in the street below to hold my attention: people hurrying as if to catch a train, delivery boys on bicycles, two children playing in a doorway, an old man in rags with a harmonica. Some of the buildings had shops on the ground floor, but I couldn't see what they sold and people seemed to go into them but come out carrying nothing. If I leant out far enough, I could see a small square at one end of the street and, at the other, perhaps it was only my imagination but I thought I could glimpse, between the roofs and orange chimney stacks, the sparkle of the lake.

Clocks all over the city struck the time, and at midday I took a book from the shelf and sat down in one of the armchairs. I only took it because I didn't want to disobey Madame Tissot. Actually, I was trying to think. What was I going to do? What was I going to say to Madame Tissot? The valley, Hext, Arete and the bloody Valentines were over the hills and blessedly far away from the busy city and this calm apartment, where I felt very safe. But I knew I couldn't stay there for ever.

When Madame Tissot returned, she heated some onion soup and put two bowls of it on the small table by one of the windows, and while I spooned the thick broth into my mouth, she talked about her morning. She said she was very happy in her work at the school in Geneva.

It was a big, progressive school, she said. Pioneering. With an art room, a science laboratory, more than a hundred girls and ten teachers, all of whom were her friends as well as her colleagues.

'I'm blessed,' she said. 'To enjoy one's work all one's life, and still, at my age – I'll be sixty soon – is a rarity.'

Many of the girls were clever, she said, but many were lazy. Only the most diligent succeeded in winning a place at the university. Those girls, I could tell, were her favourites.

It wasn't until the table was cleared and the dishes washed that Madame Tissot gestured to the armchairs and said:

'It's Wednesday, so there are no classes this afternoon. I'm all yours, Mathilde. Tell me everything now, please.'

I hesitated.

'There's one secret I can't tell you,' I said, having decided that I'd never tell anyone about the hopes I'd cherished concerning

Alessandro Costanza and how they'd been shattered. 'But it has nothing to do with my dismissal.'

I narrated the events of the last two months at Arete, including the decline of Lady Ç and culminating in the avalanche, as succinctly as possible.

'So Beatrice will lose her mother within days of losing a son. Poor woman,' said Madame Tissot.

I explained about Daisy's lie and the blame for Johnny's death being wrongly placed on me. Madame Tissot nodded thoughtfully.

'There have always been deceptions at Arete,' she said, and her face took on the gravest expression I'd ever seen.

'I don't know what to do,' I said. 'That's why I'm here.'

'Listen, Mathilde. I'm not asking you to reveal your secret. But before I can help you, I need to ask you one question. Just one. If I ask you, you must answer honestly. Can you do that?'

'Yes,' I said, but my belly lurched, for I was certain she was going to ask me about Costa, even though I'd mentioned him as little as possible and only as being the owner of the club, not anything else.

'Tell me then. Does the secret to which you refer – and which troubles you, I can see – does it have anything, anything at all, to do with Margaret?'

'Margaret?'

'Margaret Valentine. Answer me honestly, Mathilde.' Madame Tissot leant forwards in her chair, still with that gravest of looks on her face. She seemed to be searching mine.

'Why, no!' I said, astonished at the question, relieved at how easy it was to answer.

Madame Tissot's face relaxed. She closed her eyes and breathed deeply, but her hands remained clasped very tightly together on her lap.

'Good,' I think she said, but it was almost a whisper. It might have been 'thank God'. Then, in a louder voice, 'Now is not the time for secrets, Mathilde – yours, mine or anyone else's. We must be practical. You must return home.'

'But the gossip. What will I say to people?'

'It will soon pass. Tell them you were dismissed. They don't need to know the ins and outs.'

'But I have money,' I said. 'Perhaps I could stay here. Not here with you. Here in Geneva. Find employment. I saw from the window many people going to work this morning.'

'That's not possible, Mathilde. If you stayed here, people in the valley would wonder. Tongues would wag. Words would fly and make a rumpus. More untruths would be added to the sorry state of affairs at Arete. No. For now, you must return to Hext. But not without a plan. Tell me, how much money do you have?'

I fetched the pouch from my bag and passed it to her.

'That's a lot of money,' she said, peering inside.

'I know.'

Madame Tissot put her hands together and lifted them to her chin, which she rested on their tips. The old gesture, even though it often used to presage the announcement of a difficult task or, for the naughties when they'd been naughty, an unpleasant punishment, was reassuring. I waited. At last, Madame Tissot nodded.

'Yes. I've done the sums,' she said.

'You've counted the money?'

'Don't be an imbecile, Mathilde. How could I have done that? I thought you were my clever clogs.'

I was.

'I am.'

I wanted to be again.

'There's enough money in your pouch, I think, for you to continue, for some time, to hire extra help on the farm and also to put a considerable amount aside, yes?'

'Yes.'

'Put the money aside in a very safe place. You will study, Mathilde. I have books. I will borrow more for you. And I will write to you – direct your studies, set you exercises. This is your opportunity to escape, Mathilde.'

'Escape?' I echoed stupidly.

'Escape the confines of Hext. You will have to work very hard, but I believe you can do it. You will matriculate next summer. And after that, university, here in Geneva, where I can keep an eye on you. You'll be too old to live in the women's halls of residence. You'll have to rent a room. But you could teach to support yourself. That is the plan, Mathilde, for now. That is how I can help you. If you agree to it. Do you agree to it?'

All I could do was nod. Matriculation, university, halls of residence: I didn't know what to make of all that, but I understood Madame Tissot's plan in the short term. I was to go home and resume the studies I'd dropped fifteen years ago. A streak of excitement bolted through me.

'Good,' said Madame Tissot. 'In that case, we've just time to choose your first books and get you to the station in time for the late afternoon train.'

With Madame Tissot leading the way, the walk to the station was quick and unproblematic. I glanced into the lobby of the Hôtel de la Gare as we passed, but it was a different man behind the desk. I said goodbye to Madame Tissot, thanked her once again and climbed onto *le petit train* to Hext.

*

I did my best to follow Madame Tissot's instructions and thereby escape the confines of Hext.

Instead of dismissing the help I'd hired for the summer when I returned from Geneva, I asked two of the men to stay on indefinitely. I buried most of my money under the mazot and cleaned the house from top to bottom. I set myself to study for a minimum of two hours a day. This was hard at first. I was ashamed at how much I'd forgotten. But it became easier, and

I found myself gradually studying for longer without realising how time passed.

The villagers wanted gossip, of course, but the grisly details of poor Johnny's demise were soon superseded by those of Lady C's – she'd died writhing in agony and screeching like a Morzine witch, according to all reports. In her will, she stated that she wished to be buried in the graveyard on the hill between Hext and Hext-en-Haut. Although the *mairie* granted her request, people murmured that it wasn't right, *anglais* Protestant bones in sacred Savoyard soil. And then there were the rumours that Margaret had arrived, had left, was staying at the Auberge Dorée, was, wasn't at the funeral, was the spitting image of Lady C, wore trousers, wore goggles, drove her own car.

With all this going on, the villagers lost interest in my dismissal from Arete.

I didn't stop thinking about Costa, of course, but I stopped mentioning his name. I ignored Angélique and the women in the village who asked me when the wedding was and I vowed to myself I'd never so much as speak to Costa again if I could help it.

Costa came to the farm at the end of August, but I saw him approaching and shut the door in his face.

'Mathilde,' he called quietly, tapping lightly on the wood. 'Please open up. There are things I wish to say. Shall I say them from here?'

I pressed my ear to the door, straining to listen to his long-winded, musical whispers. I heard him say 'Daisy' and 'crazy', 'anglais', 'money' and 'fuck the bloody lot of them', but there was no 'I'm sorry' or 'I apologise', no 'marry me, Mathilde', so I refrained from answering or opening and, in the end, he went away.

Daisy came to see me too. She didn't knock or say my name.

'Oh my God. The stench,' she said, pushing the door wide. 'I'd no idea you lived like this. What a hovel. What a stink!'

'It's only the animals next door,' I said. 'They help keep us warm. And soon there will be the smell of fresh hay.'

'Do you mind if we go outside?' Daisy put a handkerchief to her face.

'But it's raining.'

'I don't care.'

I didn't offer her water or food. I didn't even offer her the side of the bench that was protected by the overhanging roof of the farmhouse. I no longer cared about Daisy's comfort.

'Edmond's inheriting, of course,' she began. 'But he doesn't want the bother. The upkeep and all that. He's asked Mother to take the helm. She's only too happy.'

Daisy's voice trailed off. She began to play with the handkerchief between her two hands. She scrunched it up, flattened it on her knee, then scrunched it up again.

'The thing is,' she went on. 'I might be pregnant.'

I didn't say anything.

'Mother's not going to be too happy about that, is she?'

I remained silent.

'Will you help me?' she asked.

'How?'

'Help me get rid of it. Potions and lotions. A secret brew. Don't you peasants have recipes for everything? Gin, génépi, magic berries. I don't know.'

'I can't do that,' I said. 'And even if I could, I wouldn't.'

Daisy stood up, then, and put a hand in her pocket. She brought out Benoît's Opinel knife.

I instinctively reached for the knife, but Daisy held it away from me, up in the air. There was a scuffle. I got hold of the knife and ran inside with it, but before I could close the door, Daisy was in there with me and she grabbed it again.

'Say you'll help me, Queen Mathilde.' She flicked open the knife and waved the blade above my head.

'No.'

I tried to take hold of Daisy's wrist, but she slid away from me.

'In that case—'

She stood by the fireplace.

'Goodbye, little knife.' She threw it into the fire. 'And goodbye, little ugly. I'm no more preggers than you, by the way. And if I were, it would be a mulatto baby – Warren's. We've been at it like rabbits all summer. Ha ha. Clown Daisy.'

She walked out, leaving the door open.

I immediately got down on my knees and stuck my hand into the fire. The knife had landed at the very back and I could feel the lash of the heat on my skin as I stretched in and pulled it out. I rested on my heels and looked at the knife smouldering on my palm. Its wooden handle was scorched, especially around the neck where the metal ring held the blade in place – you could no longer fold the blade into the handle – but it was still perfectly serviceable and I was over the moon to have it back.

That evening, I took down the little wooden ibex from its dusty, ashy beam. I wiped it clean and placed it on the shelf, in front of my books.

I sat by the fire until well past dark that night, thinking about Daisy's dirty lies and Costa's skulduggery. I didn't believe a word of the at-it-like-rabbits with Warren. And as to Costa's efforts through the front door – feeble! But my anger dissolved into sadness at the thought of no more Costa and I ended up weeping so much I got the hiccups. I drank some water and went to bed without supper. The hiccups stopped, but the weeping went on half the night.

*

Throughout September, especially after I heard that Daisy had returned to England ahead of the rest of the Valentines, and Costa had gone on one of his trips to Paris, I was able to concentrate on reading the books and completing the writing exercises Madame Tissot had set. I made good progress.

However, in our reckonings, Madame Tissot and I had failed to take into account the weather.

*

The rainy summer of 1929 turned into a warm, wet autumn, with torrential downpours at the end of November before any sign of snow. The Ouiffre, swollen and angry, nearly burst its banks. There was a mudslide in the orchards beyond Costa's, then several small landslides on the opposite side of the valley. Cédric said we were safe on our side, because our slopes weren't as steep and there weren't any ski lifts. He, like many, was excited by the new sport of skiing and the wealth it might bring to the valley, but he also believed superstitiously that nature took revenge on our feeble human efforts to cultivate and control her – that the activities of man were balanced, if not outweighed, in the end, by those of nature. It was true the land on the other side of the valley had looked wounded while it was dug up, but that was several years ago; now the three tow-rope ski lifts were like neat little stitches. And Cédric was wrong: the fact that the terrain on our side of the valley hadn't been disturbed didn't prevent one of the biggest landslides in Hext's living memory.

It started in the gully above my farm and took most of the outhouses, the stable and mazot with it before tumbling down through the fields, killing eight cows, two mules and my donkey, then spilling into the meadows by the river – a hideous spread of rocks, stones, earth, mud, trees, roots and other unidentifiable debris.

I was in bed asleep when it happened. The roar woke me up and I saw at once, when I went outside, that something appalling had occurred. Squawking chickens and squealing piglets were running amok among the ruined buildings. But it wasn't until morning that the full extent of the damage to my land became apparent.

There was no question of continuing with my studies. I would need every hour in the day and every ounce of strength in my body to make a go of the farm again. The money I'd buried so hopefully beneath the mazot would have to be dug out again straight away and used for essential repairs.

Two days after the landslide, the temperatures dropped and the first snows came, which meant it was time to bring the hay down from the fields where it had been stored since the summer in the snug haybarns up there. As a child I'd enjoyed this time of year even more than the two summer harvests. It was the only time the farmers put aside their petty disputes and jealousies and joined forces to get each other's hay down as fast as possible. You had to act quickly, before there was too much snow. Otherwise the sledges would tumble and the hay would be lost. Wet hay was useless hay.

It took at least an hour to haul the sledges up the slopes, another two hours to load them, but the descent, if all went well, was a matter of minutes. And how we jostled to ride up front – the cold air, the fresh snow and the speed of the descent made you forget about the hard labour of the previous hours.

At the bottom, all the hay had to be unloaded again and packed away, tight and dry, for the winter. It was up and down, up and down, until well after dark. Sometimes the very last descent wasn't until nearly midnight. But then we would gather in the Auberge Dorée, someone would bring out an accordion or fiddle, and there'd be singing and, often, dancing.

The year of the landslide, after the descent of the hay, I sat next to Cédric in the Auberge Dorée, and when he asked me to dance, I said yes.

Two weeks later, I assisted his family with the slaughter of their pig. My own had been killed in the landslide, but Cédric's family offered to give me some of the meat from theirs if I helped with the gutting. I was up to my elbows in pig's innards when Cédric leant across the stone where he was decanting blood from a bucket into jugs and asked me to marry him.

This time I said yes.

'You must be desperate,' said Angélique at the *lavoir*. 'Cédric's a brute.'

'I can't manage the farm by myself,' I said.

'What if I lent you money?'

Angélique's offer came as a surprise, but I couldn't accept it. Never borrow, never lend, Papa used to say – there's always another solution.

Cédric was my other solution. He wasn't much of a talker, and he liked a gamble, but I knew he was a hard worker. We married – at the *mairie*, no ceremony – he moved his belongings into my house and I began to worry less about the farm. Gruelling work on the farm drew us together during the day, and the arrangement wasn't quite as bad as I'd feared. Cédric hit me less than Papa used to hit Maman. I wondered what Maman would have said if she could have seen her unmarriageable Little Broomhead now and whether she would have been pleased.

If the rumours in the village were correct, Daisy remarried in 1930: a millionaire who may or may not have been fat. The comings and goings, summer after summer, of the Valentine family continued to cause murmurings in Hext, but we never saw the millionaire. People said he was too busy making money to visit the valley. He was the source of crude speculation, however, with Daisy apparently constantly pregnant. Angélique told me there were miscarriages and stillbirths, but, she informed me, a healthy boy (Rory) was born in 1933, another one (Josh) in '34, and Inez came along less than two years later. I did my best to ignore the gossip, but it was hard not to be curious, especially since Daisy didn't come to Arete every summer, and when she didn't, people said she was in an asylum for mad people in England.

Cédric's parents died, leaving Cédric's brother, Henri le cretin, to be taken care of. Cédric suggested we send Henri to the asylum in Chambéry, but when we told him this, Henri's toady eyes filled with tears and I persuaded Cédric he should move in with us.

I learnt how to find tasks for Henri that he could do independently and ways to keep him out of trouble. There wasn't a bad bone in that poor man-boy's body, but he was a burden and a worry and, when he failed to control his sexual urges, a damned nuisance.

Cédric's sexual urges were worse than a nuisance. His damp face, rough mouth and fat tongue were the least of things. I loathed what he did to me in bed. He expected me to tolerate it, however, even when he took me from behind like an animal, becoming angry and thwacky if I complained. I tried silently reciting Madame Tissot's Racine to myself while Cédric pumped away, but his yelps and moans made me forget where I'd got to. I tried to lie back and think of Blighty, as Daisy had advised, but in my case this meant Arete barging into my head, which wasn't what I wanted. Costa barged in too occasionally, and occasionally, I let him. That happened less and less, though, and eventually I learnt simply to put up with it. And then it didn't matter, because in 1936, we had Luc.

Fifteen

'Inez can't resist carnal desire. She's probably shagging one of Daisy's consultants.'

Jack wriggled out from beneath the 2CV, where he'd been reattaching the exhaust pipe with string and wire.

George had never become accustomed to Jack and his sisters calling their mother and father Inez and Bob. Inez and Bob had an open marriage. When their children, Jack and the twins, were young, this was basically an excuse for Bob's infidelities at international conferences, George's ma said. Poor Inez, she said, often used to cry on her shoulder. Later, however, Inez burnt her maternity bras and embarked upon a series of affairs – a voyage of sexual discovery, as Inez insisted on calling it – and middle-aged, running-to-fat Bob, Ma said, had egg on his face.

The reason for Jack's original unperturbed reaction to the information George had given him about Inez's ankle and inability to drive became clearer, and George was shocked.

'You mean – ?'

'Porky pies, probably, the ankle story. Oh, it might be based on something real – a sprain or whatever – but I bet she's not actually hobbling around in plaster.'

'Why didn't you say so sooner?'

'It didn't occur to me, old chap. We're all used to it.'

George decided not to pursue the matter further. Since the excursion to la Miche, he and Jack had been getting along rather well and George didn't want to put an end to that by coming across as a prude. He was flattered when, the day after Bastille Day, Jack asked for a hand fixing the exhaust of the 2CV;

Mathilde wanted another lift on Sunday, Jack said, for the public meeting, and she and the girls had done nothing but complain about the noise from the exhaust in both directions.

While Jack lay on his back with his head and shoulders twisted and hidden under the car's bumper, George sat on the ground nearby and tried to think of intelligent questions to ask about the exhaust pipe or the car's engine, but only came up with a few feeble queries about how fast the car could go and whether the canvas roll-up roof would ever work again.

'No. It needs replacing.'

'Where did you get the car from?' George asked.

'Present,' Jack said. 'From Inez. She bought it off Luc. A reward for getting into East Anglia.'

'Really?' George's ma and da didn't believe in rewards for academic achievement.

'No, not really. Really it was to shut me up. Inez was busy bonking one of Uncle Rory's friends that summer.'

And that's when Jack – wriggling out from under the car, his short shorts bunched up near his crotch at the top of his dirt-smeared, suntanned thighs – said that Inez couldn't resist carnal desire. George got a sudden uncomfortable erection and hurriedly stood up.

'Bodge job,' said Jack.

George thought for one, blush-inducing moment he'd been rustled.

'Oh dear,' he said.

'But it'll do.' Jack rubbed his dusty, greasy hands together. 'Cinderella can go to the ball.'

*

Mathilde went to the public meeting, and George and Jack went with her – Jack as the driver, George because he was intrigued. The girls were under strict orders to behave themselves and be in bed by ten.

The *salle des fêtes* was already fairly full when they arrived at half past six, but they found seats, together, at the back. George saw Costa a few rows in front of them, and Thomas, with his mother and Luc, right at the front.

Windows and doors were open and two fans whirred on the stage at the front of the *salle des fêtes*, but with every person entering, the heat seemed to increase and the amount of air decrease. George sat as still as possible. The heat didn't prevent the villagers from turning round in their seats, standing up, scanning the hall for friends and foe, carrying on conversations across it. Luc stood up, and George saw him notice Mathilde. He made his way along his row of seats and up the aisle to his mother. Mathilde turned as Luc knelt down next to her at eye level.

'I'm glad you're here, Maman,' Luc said.

'I'm only here to find out whether you've withdrawn from the election yet.'

'I don't intend to do that, Maman.'

'It's not too late, *mon fils*. Remove your name from the list, I beg you.'

'No.'

'You will regret it,' said Mathilde.

'That's possible.' Luc stood up. 'It's the risk I take.'

The end of the exchange was brusque. Luc returned to his seat, and at twenty past seven took his place on the stage next to two other men and a smartly dressed woman. The woman introduced herself as the representative of the Colorado company interested in buying the land. She spoke French fluently and clearly, with a recognisably American twang. She started by talking about other ski resorts in the region and how successful they were. She showed colour slides of smiling people on skis, smiling people swinging their skis as they sat on chairlifts and smiling people sitting in restaurants with their skis planted in the snow, in lines, next to them. She reeled off facts and dozens of figures which George couldn't follow, but to which Mathilde, he noticed, was listening intently. Jack yawned.

'Auberge Dorée?' He nudged George.

George shook his head.

Jack left, and his place was immediately taken by an old farmer; George hadn't noticed that in the last half an hour the hall had filled to capacity. It was standing room only at the back. Mathilde and the farmer nodded at each other.

Questions were invited and they came thick and fast. Some of the questions were fielded by the woman, some were taken up by Luc or one of the other men. People expressed their views loudly. The farmer next to George stood up at one point and waved a fist at Luc. Things degenerated into a shouting match and there was a minor skirmish between two women jostling each other at the back of the hall.

The meeting didn't finish until gone eleven, and many of the villagers moved straight from the *salle des fêtes* to the Auberge Dorée to continue the debate there. George and Mathilde went with them to fetch Jack, but he was nowhere to be seen. George stayed by the door while Mathilde made her way through the crowded room to the bar. Behind it, on a high shelf, was a television showing what looked to George like the news, an item about the Montreal Olympics, gymnastics, but you couldn't hear anything above the French jibber-jabber. He saw the landlord lean down to Mathilde, mime a drinking action with his wrist, then gesture with his thumb towards the door.

George and Mathilde found Jack asleep in the 2CV, slumped across the steering wheel, stinking of booze and cigarettes. George wanted to get him back to the Auberge Dorée and pay for a room overnight there, but they couldn't rouse him.

'Let him sleep it off here,' Mathilde said. 'Serve him right. I hope he has a very sore head in the morning.'

She was cross because of the girls, she said – Inez was irresponsible, leaving them with Jack and Jack was irresponsible, leaving them alone. But really, George thought, she was cross because of the public meeting – it had been clear, even to him, and despite the numbers who rallied behind the fist-shaking farmer, that Luc was a very popular man in the village. He had also noticed Mathilde frown and look down when Costa turned, saw them and raised his hand in greeting. And she'd hurried off at the end of the meeting without saying a word to Thomas and his mother, let alone Luc.

'You and I will sleep in our own beds tonight,' she said firmly to George. 'You walk on ahead, George,' she continued. 'You are stronger and healthier now. I will go at my own pace, slowly.'

George had never done the walk up to Arete at night and he was amazed at how matter-of-factly Mathilde proposed it. But there was a shiny half moon and a million stars, so it was scarcely dark, and he did feel stronger and healthier than he had in a long time.

Nevertheless, Mathilde kept up with him as far as Hext-en-Haut. She surprised him by saying just before they got there, 'I miss the telly, don't you?'

'Television? I didn't know you had it. I mean, I didn't know you liked it.'

'Yes. Seeing the one in the bar reminded me. It's the one thing I miss, nowadays, when I'm at Arete. Do you have a colour set at home?'

'Yes,' George said.

'I am looking forward to that. I intend to buy a new colour television this autumn.'

'Have you always had a telly? I mean, how long have you had it for?'

'More than ten years,' Mathilde said proudly. 'I was among the first in the valley. Before that I had radio. Wireless. Immediately after the war. 1946. Again, I was one of the first.' She slowed her pace. 'And the radiogram at Arete – it was mine, you know, until I let the girls have it.'

'The girls?'

'Inez and your ma. That poor radiogram took quite a bashing in its day. Or rather, night. It was in use almost every night when Inez and your ma were young.'

'Ma? She never listens to music.'

'Perhaps listen is not the correct word, George.'

'Listened. Sorry.' George felt the familiar disappointed lurch in his gut as he realised his mistake.

'I didn't mean that.' Mathilde put a hand on George's arm. They had just reached Hext-en-Haut and her hip was visibly hurting. 'I apologise, George. I didn't intend to upset you. I was referring to the fact that your ma may not have listened to the music on the radiogram with concentration. But she danced to it. My, how she danced!'

'No! Surely not? Ma used to dance?'

'Oh yes.'

'I thought Inez was the dancer.'

'She was. But your ma wasn't bad either.'

George left Mathilde resting at Hext-en-Haut, and as he climbed up through the forest he thought about seeing Inez dance – in 1972. He thought about her taut, lean body, bare feet, long brown legs, and the tight, ruched cheesecloth sundress stretched across her breasts as she twirled around with the twins and then, more sedately and, oh God, so sexily, with Jack. George had longed to swap places with Jack. Inez must have seen his look of envy. She'd tried to get him to dance with her. Taken his hands, even, in hers. He remembered the rings on her fingers and how they'd dug into his palms and her long painted fingernails and wondering what those would feel like on his skin. But he'd pulled his own hands back, shaken his head, and Inez had whirled off again, dancing alone this time, one of the yellow straps of her sundress falling from her sunburnt shoulders, her Valentine curls swooshing dark and daring across her bare back.

George had never seen Ma dance.

Sixteen

Luc's birth in 1936 was straightforward: he was small, came early and quick, fish-slippery and all of a gush. By the time Cédric had fetched the *sage-femme*, I'd cut the cord and was already feeding him.

Luc's suck was strong, he slept deeply, blubbed rarely and soon grew into a plump and limber baby we both doted on.

He was born in June and I carried him every day in the winnowing basket up to the fields where the men were haymaking. Cédric would down tools before the others and take Luc in his arms while I unpacked the men's lunches. Cédric gave me extra money for Luc and let me spend it as I wished.

A few days before Luc was born, when my belly was so big I could scarcely sit on the milking stool, I had spied Daisy in the village with a large perambulator. It was market day, and I'd set up shop in the square with our hams and eggs. Daisy had parked the unwieldy, big-wheeled vehicle next to the fountain and was dipping her fingers into the bowl, dabbing her forehead with the water. The sing-song voice of the man who sold second-hand farming tools caught Daisy's attention, and she pushed her way through the throng around him, leaving the perambulator by the fountain. I nipped over and peeped beneath the pretty canopy, which was white and sprigged with pink embroidered flowers. There was little Inez – not that I knew her name then – about six months old, curly and gurgly as she bashed her baby-hands at a line of dancing wooden animals strung from the canopy's hinges.

I went back to my post, but I kept an eye out and when I saw Daisy return to the fountain, I twisted and took a step sideways so that Daisy would see, if she looked, that there was a baby in my belly. But Daisy didn't look. Or if she did, she ignored what she saw. She took the handle of the perambulator and walked right past me.

I bought four white cotton cloths at the market that day. I didn't tell Cédric. However, the first time I put Luc into the winnowing basket with the folded cloth (his pillow), the spread cloth and the two cloths I'd sewn together and called his canopy, Cédric noticed. To my delight, he gave his approval and the extra money began after that; our Luc, in his winnowing basket, looked, I thought, as bonny and blithe as any Valentine child.

I never managed dancing monkeys or giraffes, but I did pop my old wooden ibex into the basket, and when Luc was older it became a favourite plaything.

Our years of hard work, Cédric's and mine, on the farm were beginning to pay off, especially after Cédric inherited his parents' land. I made sure Luc was always the cleanest boy in the village and the best dressed. Seeing us in church, in our Sunday finery, even wealthy Angélique Gauthier, who had three boys, two girls and another infant on the way by then – and was definitely no longer considered a great beauty – might have been jealous.

It was a Sunday in the late summer of 1939 when I next saw Daisy. I'd just come out of church with Cédric and Luc. Rain and wind were whipping round the village square. Wind in our valley was rare. (Sir A said it was one of the features of the place.) No one was ever prepared for it. Shop signs had blown over, a chair from the Auberge Dorée had been upturned and one of the tablecloths had flown into the fountain. I told Cédric to go and buy our Sunday brioches while Luc and I sheltered in the Auberge Dorée.

I took Luc's hand and we walked across the square. The awning to the Auberge Dorée flapped wildly. It was only midday, but the lights were on inside the hotel. As we approached, I saw Daisy at a table in there. She had a little girl on her lap, and three small children sat on a bench beside her. Two men were also at the table. One of them I recognised as a friend of Ted's. The other had his back to the window. Daisy clicked her fingers to make the waiter come over.

Luc tugged at my hand. We were both getting soaked.

'No,' I decided. 'We'll wait for Papa outside. Look. Here, where it's sheltered.'

I pulled Luc under the awning and found the driest spot.

Cédric seemed to take ages. The wind was still blowing like billy-o around the square, and, wherever we stood, water from the flapping awning dripped on us. Luc began to whine. I was hungry for my brioche.

Daisy, warm and dry with her brood in the Auberge Dorée, while my son and I shivered outside, elicited my pity: she was thin and her shoulders drooped. The expression on her face was a sulk turned sour. I could see her sadness. For a moment I wanted to bang on the window, forget my P's and Q's, make the razzle-dazzle English girl who'd called herself my friend smile again. I put my nose right up to the glass, but Luc tugged my hand.

'Here's Papa,' he said.

As I turned round to take the brioches from Cédric, I saw the man who'd had his back to the window stand up. It was Ted, but a thin-legged, fat-bellied Ted, swaying to the bar like a doddery old codger, dead drunk.

*

A few weeks later, Cédric and I, together with Henri, took Luc mushrooming. Luc was only three, but he was a sturdy little thing and eager to learn – the names of the mushrooms, where to look for them, how to distinguish the poisonous ones. He was too young to use a knife, but he enjoyed watching the clean cuts I made with my Opinel through the stems so as not to disturb the delicate mycelia for future crops. Cédric, who had a special mushrooming knife with a brush on the end, let Luc use it to brush the mushrooms carefully clean.

After a damp start, which we hoped would bring the mushrooms out, it turned into a sunny day and the mountain air was autumn-crisp. I'd brought cold lamb, instead of ham, as a treat for lunch, and goats' milk for Luc. We became so busy filling our baskets with late summer girolles and chanterelles that we ended up wandering much further afield than usual and found ourselves, in the middle of the afternoon, up near the high pastures above Hext-en-Haut.

'Sir A said he'd a notion there'd be good early cèpes and bolets in the woods over there.' I indicated the Arete side of the pasture. 'Shall we look?'

'No, we've no time.' Cédric shook his head. 'The animals. Unless Henri and I go down without you and you go on with Luc?'

'What do you think? It's perhaps too much for *le petit*.' I said.

Cédric looked fondly at Luc.

'What do you think, *petit bonhomme*? Will you go mushrooming with Maman or help Papa and Uncle Henri on the farm?'

Luc lifted his arms up to Cédric, making his choice clear. Cédric transferred the mushrooms we'd collected earlier from three into two baskets and gave me the empty one.

'Good hunting,' he said.

But there wasn't a single mushroom to be found yet in the woods on the opposite side of the pasture. I penetrated further and further, not wishing to return home empty-handed, and when I realised I was only two bends away from Arete, I decided to take a look at the place. The *anglais*, I knew, had decamped, en masse, ten days before.

The house was shuttered and locked. I could have picked the lock, using the little knife in the bottom of the empty mushroom basket. Easily. But I didn't. Instead, I walked around the chalet to the front. The table was still on the terrace, but all the chairs had been put away for the winter. I stood, as I'd stood so many times before, looking down on the valley of Hext, and at the alps surrounding it.

New snow already covered their peaks: as white as linen, as shiny as silk, as soft as wool – as easy as *anglais* pie to describe snow thus. By the end of the winter, the same peaks would yellow and furrow with waxy streaks; couloirs of slush would grey with grit and scree; the softening snow would stretch, sag and wrinkle like a woman's belly after birth. Of all the things we and *les anglais* compared our mountains to, only skin made sense to me now, for the land, to me, was these days basically bovine: there wasn't a single peak, dip, contour or curve, not one ridge or knoll, slope, plane, angle or incline for which I couldn't find a counterpart in the body of a common Montbéliarde cow. Pin Bone and Hook Bone, Tail Head and Poll: those are some of the names I'd have given the mountains around here if I'd had my way. Dewlap and Stifle, Hock, Loin and Withers would have done for the bits in between – the lumps and bumps of hills, slopes and long up-and-down meadows. Parliament Hill, my foot, I thought, but, 'It is, indeed, a magnificent sight.' I said the English words out loud, hissing the 's' sounds, exaggerating the consonants, enjoying the beat.

Then I turned and looked back at the house. There was the date of completion, 1864, carved above the door. Below it were Sir A's initials and, above it, the word 'Arete'. I put my basket on the table, pulled the table over to the door and climbed onto it. I took out my knife.

I cut a circumflex into the wood above the first 'e' of Arete. It didn't take long and I didn't bother to do it that neatly. When I'd finished, I looked up to the arête of the petit Luet above the chalet and I gave it a sort of salute. The least the thieving, cheating, lying *rosbifs* could do was spell our language correctly, use our names and the names of our places *comme il faut*, mind their P's and Q's.

*

I taught Luc to read before he went to school and before Cédric went off to fight, which he did less than a month after our mushrooming trip.

'Don't turn the boy into a ninny,' Cédric said, leaning out of the train window.

There was no danger of that. Luc was as tough as any of the village boys and not only taught himself to ski on the slopes opposite our farm, but soon excelled at the sport.

I wasn't sorry to see Cédric go. There was a lot more work on the farm, of course, especially after the Germans requisitioned my horse, but the nights were my own and it was pleasant not to be bossed or bullied. I also found Henri le cretin easier to manage without Cédric around. One of Henri's tasks was to watch over Luc while I worked nearby. I always kept my eyes peeled and my ears pricked in case Henri forgot to watch, wandered off or started any silly business. But he never did. I'd hear him crooning to Luc, soothing him in the nonsense language he spoke, but which Luc adored. Henri threw fir cones for Luc to chase, whittled sticks for him, and brought all manner of objects for him to explore – pebbles from the river, bits of rock from the mountain, a scrap of rubber from a car tyre, the rim of a bicycle wheel, and a lady's stocking. Henri le cretin said he'd found the stocking on the path by the side of the river. He and Luc spent hours filling it with stones and then emptying it again.

I would never have expected to miss Henri le cretin, but I did when he died of pneumonia in the spring of 1945. He'd been chesty all winter, but worsened suddenly, just before Easter, and died quickly and quietly at the end of April.

I picked lily of the valley to put on Henri's grave from the bank near the bridge over the river Ouiffre. I'd just decided I'd collected enough when the sound of wheels and the slow, steady click of a donkey's feet made me turn. It was Costanza.

Before the war, on Friday and Saturday evenings, you'd see cars making their way up the valley to Club Costa, and you didn't see them leave again until late the following morning. The villagers reckoned Costa must be making a packet of money, but I suspected he was still getting his sums wrong and worrying about his investor friend.

The club had closed at the beginning of the war and Costanza went away. He came back and went away again. We never knew whether he was there or not.

I withdrew into the shadow of the bridge. I'd nothing to say to that man.

Costa had other ideas.

'Mathilde!' he called.

He steered the cart onto the track by the river, stepping down from it just as I'd scrambled to the top of the grassy bank.

'Don't turn away from me, Mathilde. Don't hide. Shut your eyes, if you like. But stay, please.'

I stayed, but I turned away and I did shut my eyes. Costa talked about Easter, the weather, his club, my farm, the war, and the sound of his voice was like the delicate perfume drifting up from the lily of the valley in my hot hand, hinting of summer. I tilted my head back and enjoyed the weak spring sunshine on the skin of my face, but as Costa talked on, I yearned more and more for the sunny, companionable, talk-filled, work-filled, music-filled afternoons in his workshop and the barn. And when Costa concluded by saying, 'Perhaps you'll visit again, Mathilde, when the war's over?' Yes, yes, I wanted to cry out and I very nearly did.

'But I'm married now. I've a son,' I said, inadvertently breaking my vow of silence.

'Yes,' Costa said. He climbed back onto the cart, and as the donkey slowly rolled the cart away, he said, over his shoulder, 'At least you're speaking to me now, though.'

*

Cédric came home from the war two months later. When he walked through the door, Luc hid behind me.

'The boy's nine. You've made him a ninny!' roared Cédric.

He was gruff with his son and told him to go outside and do something useful. Me, he took upstairs, and while he nearly fuck-suffocated me, I could hear Luc, outside, dutifully sweeping and swilling the yard.

When I told Cédric that Henri had died, all he said was, 'One less mouth to feed.'

'You were right. He's a brute,' I told Angélique.

She gave me a jar of arnica for my bruises and asked if he ever hit Luc.

'Never,' I told her. 'Only me, and only occasionally. I can tolerate it. Besides, Luc will be stronger than Cédric before long.'

Luc's physical prowess soon became a source of great pride to Cédric. Luc began to win so many skiing competitions that, during the summer, Cédric encouraged him to train for the winter by allowing him to roam freely in the mountains rather than help us on the farm or with the haymaking up in the fields. He said Luc would become a guide and, moreover, one of the new style of winter guides – ski instructors who, he'd been told, earned more in four months in Chamonix during the winter than a waiter earned in a year.

I didn't contradict Cédric, but I defied him. My pride in our son came from the marks he received at school. He was an exemplary pupil, according to all three of the teachers at the new school. Whenever I could, I made Luc listen to the radio with me and sometimes I took one of my old textbooks from the shelf and we sat together reading it.

Madame Tissot and I continued to correspond, and she never mentioned my not matriculating, but I was glad to be able to tell her how quickly and well Luc learnt as if it made up for my staying within the confines of Hext. My letters, like my days and my thoughts, my hopes and my dreams, were full of Luc and little else now.

Luc kept the peace between Cédric and me by continuing to shine both at school and in the skiing competitions. The latter now took him all over the region, which cost a pretty penny, but Cédric paid for Luc's equipment and bus fares without batting an eyelid. Any little lottery wins (Cédric was a big fan) went straight to Luc. Any big losses (and there were quite a few) came out of my housekeeping.

When a log fell on Cédric in 1950, knocking him out and turning his brain to mush, he had to go and live in the asylum for old people and mad people miles away near Chambéry. It was too far to visit and the doctor said he wouldn't recognise us anyway.

After the log, Luc took on little jobs at the Gauthier garage in Hext. This paid for his equipment and bus fares, and made him an enthusiast for all things mechanical, anything on wheels, preferably motorised. He became friendly with one of Angélique's boys at the garage and they spent hours taking apart and putting back together abandoned engines and motors. When the Malabar Princess crashed into Mont Blanc, it was on the radio all day long, and the only thing those boys could talk about was aeroplanes. Luc told me and the Gauthier boy he planned to visit America on an aeroplane one day.

'And before that, I'll buy us a car, Maman,' he said. 'As soon as I can. When I'm eighteen.'

Four years later, when Luc did turn eighteen, we were still a long way from buying the little car he wanted. The farm, without Cédric, failed to prosper as before and I found myself scrimping and saving again simply to make ends meet. Luc passed his *baccalauréat* at the beginning of June, which meant he had a place at the teacher training college in Bonneville starting in September.

'Without a car, I'll have to find lodgings in town,' he said.

With a car, he could live at home. I did what Papa said never to do: I asked Angélique for a loan. There was no other solution. On the 10th of June 1954, Luc bought a grey second-hand 2CV, and we both considered it an excellent investment.

Seventeen

They were sitting at the kitchen table – George, the girls and Mathilde, who was podding peas – the morning after the public meeting when, at half past ten, Jack strolled in, cheerful and contrite, with a box of goodies from the boulangerie.

'Thanks to Luc,' he said.

'*Hein?*' Mathilde jerked her head up and frowned at the box.

'Not these.' Jack lifted the lid of the box. 'Luc fitted a new exhaust for me, first thing. I zoomed up to Hext-en-Haut in record time as a result.'

'How come?' George asked. 'The exhaust, I mean.'

'He just happened to be passing when I woke up, about eight. He was on his way to the boulangerie, he said. He saw "*le petit problème*" – as he politely put it, frowning at my wire and string – and said he could fix it, "*aucun souci*". All I had to do was drive us, clunk clunk, to the boulangerie and on to the garage.'

'Nice of him,' said Isobel, 'especially since you still stink.'

'And it didn't cost a penny. Luc knew the bloke at the garage.'

George noticed that Mathilde had stopped podding while Jack talked.

'Nevertheless,' Jack continued, 'I've decided we're all too knackered for paideia today.' He took a handful of shelled peas from the colander and popped them, one by one, into his mouth. 'Rest day today.'

The girls moaned at first – they didn't need a rest, Jack was a twat, what about the hunt for gold? – but were soon pacified, partly by the pastries and partly by the promise of a bonfire, with bangers and baked potatoes, that evening on the terrace.

'If you're lucky,' said Jack, 'I might move the record player outside and even allow you to choose the records. And it lets Mathilde off the hook for sups.'

'Thank you, Jack,' said Mathilde. 'I need an early night.'

She'd got back to Arete at three a.m., an hour after George. He'd seen the lamp come on in her hut, from the balcony where he'd gone out for some fresh air; he'd been unable to sleep, having dropped onto his bed without bothering to wash, still sweaty from the climb to Arete, and feeling as if he'd brought the heat of the village and the stifling atmosphere of the *salle des fêtes* up to the house with him.

He hadn't enjoyed the climb. The night sky light didn't penetrate the trees in the forest, which seemed closer together and taller in the dark. And on the rocky plateau des Bergères, the landscape was a dull, shadowy, sinister pewter. The image of Inez dancing not only faded but was overlaid with an uncomfortable memory of Inez wearing the same dress, later in the summer, in the rain, during the row.

'You look like a slut,' Ma had said.

'Oh dear.' Inez had raised her eyebrows and top lip in a sarcastic sneer. 'Do I detect a note of disapproval? Or is it sexual frustration? Does Donald perhaps not satisfy my little sister in bed?'

There had been tension between the sisters all summer. The main issue seemed to be Daisy and whether or not to commit her to the clinic in Megève: Ma said yes, Inez said no, Daisy's millionaire ex-husband apparently didn't have an opinion, even though he was putting up the money for it – whatever's best, he said – and Uncle Rory and Uncle Josh kept out of things. But in the final bitter row, in the rain, on the terrace, all sorts of insults were hurled back and forth between Inez and Ma.

The Daisy issue hadn't been resolved when Ma told Pa to pack their suitcases, they were leaving. George remembered the car journey home vividly. It was raining, but warm and muggy. Ma drove the first leg of the way with the driver's window right down, and George, on the sticky back seat, tried to sleep but couldn't because of the rain coming through the window. When he asked Ma to wind it up a bit, she said no, she'd do what the hell she liked, for once, which was most unlike her.

They'd set off in the evening and only got as far as Dôle that day. The hotel they found there was a cheap two-star affair with a bar on the ground floor full of locals watching a late football match on the small, fuzzy television in one corner. The bar didn't close when the game was over, and even though their room was on the top floor, the sound of raucous French laughter and debate drifted up. Still George couldn't sleep, but he pretended to, watching from his bed in the corner as Ma tossed and turned and Da lay on his back, snoring quietly. It was very stuffy in the room. The shutters didn't close properly, and greenish light from a street lamp opposite the hotel streaked the walls and the heavy, dark furniture.

George saw Ma get up. She removed her nightgown and stood, naked, in front of the oval mirror on the dressing table. When she turned sideways and lifted her arms above her head, still looking in the mirror, George closed his eyes. His parents weren't in the habit of going naked. Nor was he. He didn't think he'd ever actually seen Ma's body completely naked. Pa's yes, on the beach, and once or twice on the landing at home when Pa forgot his towel and nipped out of the bathroom to fetch one from the airing cupboard, but a glimpse only. And Ma, no, never. And it had never crossed George's mind either that she might use a mirror, like he did, to survey her body. It didn't feel right to spy. But when he heard the shuffle of feet and rustle of clothes, he opened his eyes. Ma was pulling on her slacks. She picked up her bra and fiddled with the fastenings. One breast shone yellow from the street lamp, the other was in darkness. On top of the bra, her cardigan, then, slipping into her Hush Puppies, she opened the bedroom door and went out.

George waited for her to return, but she didn't. Or rather, he must have fallen asleep before she did, because when he woke up she was in the double bed with the sheet wrapped tightly round her, and Da was standing, fully clothed, next to the bed, holding a glass of water and urging Ma to drink.

'You're hung-over, Peggy, that's all. God knows what possessed you to go down alone to the bar last night. We're not waiting for you to sleep it off. Get up. We paid for breakfast when we took the room. Stale croissants and coffee will help.'

Ma sat up and took a swig from the glass. She said she'd sleep while we had breakfast. Da told George to go to the bathroom along the corridor and get dressed. When George came back to the bedroom, Ma was fast asleep again.

Da and George breakfasted without her, in silence. In fact the rest of the day was pretty silent. Da drove. Ma dozed in the passenger seat. They stayed, that night, in a small but expensive hotel in the middle of Reims. George had a room to himself, but he heard, through the wall, Da telling Ma to pull herself together. It wasn't an argument exactly. Ma and Da never argued. But George heard Da say, 'Bloody Inez. She's always upset you. You mustn't let her.'

'It's not Inez I'm upset about, it's Mother.'

'Your mother's sick, Peggy,' said Da. 'Inez isn't sick. She's jealous.'

Ma laughed, a low, mirthless laugh.

'Inez – jealous? What on earth has Inez to be jealous about?'

'She's jealous of you.'

Ma laughed again, and George didn't hear the quiet conversation that followed, but he remembered those words. And as he reached the gully on the far side of the high pastures, his thoughts circled back to Mathilde telling him that Ma used to dance. Did Ma outdance Inez, perhaps? Did the sisters have a hidden history of rivalry, George wondered? But why had Ma never said so? And why had she never mentioned the dancing?

'I've two left feet,' she used to say, and George believed her, partly because her feet were on the large side, flattish and wide – certainly not his idea of dancing feet – and partly because Da often added, 'Just as well. I'm the same.'

And George was therefore able to blame his own excruciating awkwardness, when it came to school discos, on the family genes.

Why had Ma stopped dancing? Why had she lied, if only by omission? And why, oh why, had she bleeding well gone and died?

Frustration and a sudden fury overcame George. He felt bizarrely energised and he wished he was the sort of bloke who would pummel a tree, howl or yell obscenities into the pure mountain air. He did try a shout, but only a strange yeeow sound came out. The yeeow echoed surprisingly loudly, which gave George a real fright and he positively ran the last quarter of a mile up to Arete, arriving hot and sad, totally unable to fall asleep.

*

Jack leant back in his chair and yawned.

'I think I'll have a nap,' he said. 'What will you do, Georgio?'

'I don't know,' George said.

George had already decided to use the morning, if possible, to have a snoop in the mazot. It was obviously cobblers about the gold, let alone the golden ibex, but George's interest had been spiked by reading Sir A's diaries. Arete's past was part of his own family history, so he'd better hang onto what he could of it, he thought. And Lady C's paintings and maps were part and parcel of that. George had been counting on Jack not getting back until later, so Jack deciding on a snooze was welcome news. George didn't want him being snooty about his activities.

When Jack had gone upstairs, the girls went into the games room to choose records and practise their dance moves for the evening, Mathilde returned to her hut, and George casually walked across to the mazot, up the wooden steps, and let himself in.

*

The mazot had never really featured in George's holidays at Arete. He knew that it had been built at the same time as the house and along the lines of a traditional Hext mazot – raised on stones and wooden stilts, taller and thinner as well as a quarter the size of the traditional box-shaped farms and chalets. It had been built not as a storeroom, though, but for Lady C to use as a painting studio and when she died, Beatrice, who over the years became more and more of a stickler for tradition, didn't change a thing. Unlike the rest of the place, the mazot survived the Second World War and the empty years after it almost undamaged.

'We spent ages cleaning and sorting, storing and chucking, that first summer. 1954,' Ma said. 'Trip after trip up the ladder to the attic. There wasn't a single room in the house that hadn't been ransacked or damaged – and why deface the name of the place I don't know – but the mazot was more or less intact.'

Inez and Ma planned to turn the mazot into a den – 'I wanted to call it a snug,' said Ma, 'but Inez said it would be a rumpus room' – and the sisters had just managed to persuade Beatrice to let them and started moving the pictures and painting equipment up to the attic when 'Mummy arrived and nabbed it'.

Daisy used the mazot in the '50s and '60s as a study. She told everyone she was writing a racy novel in there and tried to get people to call it a writing room. Daisy became significantly crazier, according to Ma, after the war, after the divorce. 'We were a big, rich, desperately unhappy family,' George remembered Ma explaining to him. 'Expensive boarding schools for Rory, Josh, Inez and me. Expensive clinics and private hospitals for our mother. We hardly ever saw her.'

As Daisy's literary aspirations became increasingly unrealistic, the mazot was used less and less, apart from as the dumping ground for booze, condiments and tins of food left over at the end of the summer; the latter used to be a perk of the job for the uglies, Ma said, but Beatrice had put a stop to that.

The mazot had never been out of bounds, and they'd used it for games of hide-and-seek, but nor was it a place George was familiar with. It always had a quiet, peaceful feel to it, though, which he liked. He left the door open and walked across the warm room to the long, wide work surface built along the back wall. Underneath the work surface there was an empty wine rack, two cardboard boxes, also empty, and the enormous plan chest.

George wasn't looking for anything in particular when he opened the drawers of the plan chest. This was where Jack had found the little picture map; George wondered whether Jack had missed anything or whether the context of the map's discovery might shed some light on it.

The drawers of the plan chest were empty, bar one which contained a cut-glass ashtray, some charcoal, a sketchbook and a portfolio. The sketchbook was full of undated line drawings of various views George recognised as being near Arete and several careful close-ups of leaves, ferns, petals, bark. In the portfolio there were watercolour paintings, all a bit namby-pamby in their colours and effects.

The similarity in style between these images and the artwork on the little picture map was unmistakeable; Lady C was clearly, as Jack had said, the artist. However, Jack appeared not to have noticed that the line drawn on the map between the house and the 'X', and indeed the 'X' itself, were in another hand, George was almost certain of it; not Sir A's – George had seen enough of Sir A's handwriting to be sure of this. And not Lady C's – the watercolours were signed and dated, and whereas Lady C's signature was light and spidery, George recalled the 'X' on the map as dark and heavy.

He decided to go back to the house to check.

The girls were still in the games room and they greeted George with a choreographed sequence to the chorus of 'Fernando'.

'Great,' said George.

'We've done a whole Abba routine. A medley. Do you want to see it?' asked Isobel.

'Later,' said George. 'With Jack.'

He had a quick look at the map – yes, the dark heavy cross and the zigzagging, looping line were as he recalled – and left the girls to it.

*

Jack slept through lunch, but later he moved the record player onto the terrace. 'You Sexy Thing' was playing quietly when George, who'd catnapped himself, came out on the balcony, round the side of the chalet and down to the terrace. Jack immediately turned the volume up and did exaggerated bopping, hopping, head-nodding movements to it.

'Boogie-woogie, Georgy-porgy. Come on,' said Jack.

'Later,' said George.

Later, after they'd built a fire and cooked sausages on it, then dampers, which Ma said were an Arete speciality and Da said were a well-known delicacy at scout camp – a salted flour and water paste wrapped around the end of a stick and cooked until crispy over a flame, then filled with Mathilde's home-made strawberry jam; later, when he'd watched the girls perform their Abba medley, plus what the girls thought was a risqué 'Make me smile (Come Up and See Me)', involving beckoning fingers, hitched-up skirts and wiggling hips; later, when it was dark and he'd drunk a couple of beers and had a few puffs on the joint Jack passed him, George boogie woogied by himself to 'Devil Woman' while the others sang the words and clapped. Then he and Jack danced, side by side, to 'Tiger Feet', copying each other's steps – and George thought one of the girls must have turned the volume on the record player up high, but it was the rocks amplifying the bass and making it pop and echo across the valley.

Jack eventually declared that he couldn't bear the girls' choice of music any longer.

'Bedtime for my teenybopper twin sisters,' he said to Polly and Tess. 'And for you, my groovy cuzzy Izzy.'

There was mutiny. Jack relented and was persuaded to bring out his guitar. Polly and Tess lit candles, fetched blankets and cushions and sat in a huddle by the fire. Isobel mucked around with a torch. Jack perched on the bench, a cigarette between his lips, right knee over left, Dylan-style, and George flopped into a deckchair.

Jack had been playing for about half an hour, the fire was beginning to die out, Isobel was nodding off, when George was roused from his lush, semi-comatose state by the arrival of Thomas. He was wearing his full red and blue guide's uniform, which made him look like a dashing young soldier.

'I don't wish to interrupt,' said Thomas. 'I wasn't expecting anyone still to be awake. I'm between clients, that's all. So I'm overnighting here tonight and tomorrow night.'

'You're not interrupting. Please join us,' said George.

Thomas sat down on the ground. Isobel snuggled into him, while the twins snuggled into each other. Jack strummed quietly on his guitar, and, one by one, the girls dropped off to sleep.

Thomas asked how Mathilde was, and talk turned to the election. Thomas explained that it wasn't quite as black and white as being for or against the development of the land.

'Even those of us who are for it have our doubts,' he said. 'You foreigners bring money to the valley, provide jobs, but a way of life is inevitably lost.'

'Who do you mean by you?' said Jack. 'We're not the Colorado company waiting to pounce and buy your land.'

'But our family,' George piped up. 'We – that is, Sir A and Lady C – were the first to buy land in these mountains, weren't we?'

'Exactly,' said Thomas. 'And we, the people of the valley, are your employees. Most of us, either directly or indirectly.'

'It's not quite the same,' said Jack.

George thought it was, more or less, and felt uncomfortable recalling history lessons on the British Empire and colonialism, and earnest conversations with the Marxists in the sixth-form common room about ownership, exploitation, slaves and masters. He changed the subject by asking Thomas if he'd ever been employed by people he really didn't like. Thomas said no, but there were plenty of very eccentric clients, and he told George and Jack about some of them, including one, a Belgian stockbroker, who'd wanted to play a game of Split with Thomas.

'In the snow,' said Thomas.

'No!' said George.

'Did you?' said Jack.

'No,' said Thomas. 'I took off one ski, a ski boot and sock and showed him the scar from the stitches last time I played that game. I didn't know Split was known except by *rosbifs*. It will be an Olympic sport soon, I think?'

Thomas laughed at his own joke, and George and Jack laughed along.

The girls woke up just as the first light of dawn striped the sky between the mountain ridges in the east. They went uncomplainingly to bed. Thomas said he was tired and would turn in too.

George and Jack stayed on the terrace, watching the blocks of shadow shift and narrow between the peaks and along the slopes on the opposite side of the valley; neither of them spoke until the whole valley was suffused in a misty, early morning glow heralding another sunny day.

'Another sunny day,' said George inconsequentially and immediately regretted it, expecting a dig from Jack for the banality of the observation.

Jack, however, replied, 'Yes. When I was in the Auberge Dorée the other night, it was on the telly. I think they were saying the

French government's planning to introduce some sort of weather tax. And Paris is practically at a standstill. More than half the bus drivers are refusing to drive – it's a hundred and forty degrees on board, can you believe it?'

'Blimey.'

'Mmm. By the way, I also gathered, before I got too sozzled, that it's by no means a cert that Luc's lot are going to win the election.'

'How come?'

'There was a bunch of farmers in there – wealthy-looking ones, landowner-types – who weren't even at the meeting. Conservative, territorial, complacent old bastards, actually. Made Mathilde seem positively forward-thinking. They reckoned they had the numbers and the power to put their own list through for the municipal council.'

'Luc's popular, though. I saw it. He's very charming, suave with everyone.'

'Yes,' said Jack. 'A bit too suave, according to some of the arsey barflies at the Auberge Dorée.'

Eighteen

The loan from Angélique weighed so heavily on me that, very soon after the purchase of the 2CV in 1954, I took a part-time job at the Auberge Dorée – even though the pay was a pittance – cleaning the new annex of bedrooms built by the hotel's new landlord.

The old owner had collaborated with the Germans in the war and decided to make himself scarce after the liberation. His niece, fat Josette – who'd never had the nouse to extricate herself from tricky situations – was tarred and feathered after the liberation for an alleged *collaboration horizontale* with a German officer. Angélique Gauthier nearly suffered the same fate, except that it turned out her collaboration was a front for her *maquisard* husband. Costa was in the resistance too, I heard, and Club Costa was sometimes used as a safe house for on-the-run men and women. Angélique told me that Costa often asked how I was. You can't avoid him for ever, she said. But I did a pretty good job of it. And no one, least of all Angélique, knew how hard that was.

The Auberge Dorée's new landlord arrived within months of the war's end. He wasn't from the valley and already owned a hotel in St Cergues, where, he said, the bedrooms each had a sink and a bath. He went further with the Auberge Dorée's annex: the bedrooms each had a separate bathroom – totally private, with sparkling white toilet, bidet, shower and basin. These added up to a lot of cleaning, and it was while I was at work there that I heard the *rosbifs* were due back shortly at Arete. It was big news. They hadn't been seen in the valley since before the war. The villagers speculated that the Valentines had fallen on hard times, Arete was up for sale, Margaret was sweeping the streets of London, Beatrice's boring banker had died leaving scandalous debts, Daisy's millionaire husband had turned out to be a crook and was in prison. The longer the Valentines stayed away, the longer, more colourful and convoluted the stories about them became.

The only facts I had were from the new landlord of the Auberge Dorée, who told me that Beatrice, 'Madame, la propriétaire d'Arete', had written to him saying the family had suffered several sad losses during the war. Since then they had been preoccupied with domestic matters – moving house, changing schools, doctors, servants – but now Madame Beatrice would like to book a room for herself and use his hotel to interview for domestic help at Arete for June to September 1954. She wrote, he said, that they were looking forward to a traditional Valentine summer in the mountains.

Who are the Valentines, the new landlord asked?

I had trouble explaining. Strictly speaking, Beatrice, upon marrying, would have left the Valentine name at the altar. But I, like Beatrice, clung to the name, using it as shorthand for the family and an aide-memoire to times past.

And there she was, less than a week later: Beatrice, sitting at a table in the bar, a pile of suitcases and bags and a cage with a small dog in it beside her. I'd only gone into the bar to fetch the broom that was kept in a cupboard there, but Beatrice spotted me.

'Mathilde,' she said, pulling up her top lip into a horsey smile. 'How good to see you. And looking so well. I do believe I owe you an apology.'

I stood with one hand on my bad hip and the other holding the broom.

'Please,' Beatrice continued. 'Sit down.'

I sat down opposite her, still holding the broom.

She told me first that Ted was dead. I said I was sorry. His liver, she said. I nodded. And Margaret, in the Blitz. Nod. Then she told me Daisy was sick. I said I was sorry. In the head, she said. A nervous condition.

'It's one breakdown after another,' Beatrice went on. 'She can't help it. Daisy can't help it, you know.'

This was as close as Beatrice ever came to an acknowledgement of my wrongful dismissal from Arete.

I was sad about dead Ted, but not surprised. Sorry about dead Margaret, because it meant I'd probably never find out what happened to her now and I did still occasionally wonder.

Sad, sorry and curious about Daisy. It was on the tip of my tongue to ask questions about the nervous condition. I wanted details. Where was Daisy? Who was taking care of her? How did she spend her days? Beatrice, however, moved swiftly on to 'terms and conditions', 'incentives' and 'a bonus, of course', as if I'd already agreed to come and work for her again.

'The family arrive next week,' she said. 'Not Daisy. She's undergoing a new cure at the clinic in Bournemouth. She may join us later in the summer, if the ECT's a success. Meanwhile,' Beatrice gestured towards the luggage, 'I've this mutt of hers to look after. She refuses to board him. Django. That's his name. I suppose it's the least I can do.'

I sat and observed how eighty *anglais* years had bent but not broken Beatrice. Three dead sons and a bonkers daughter, yet the big, stiff-jawed woman could still sit there, cool as an *anglais* cucumber, talking about terms and conditions and a dog in a cage called Django.

I did the calculations. A summer at Arete and I could begin paying off the loan from Angélique; Luc wouldn't need to go short in Bonneville; the winter on the farm would be easier.

'When do you need me to start?' I said.

*

Arete, at the start of the summer of 1954, was a shambles. The Germans had used it during the war, but it looked as if it had been looted and lived in since then, by every Tom, Dick and Harry under the sun.

There was fire damage and water damage as well as the damage inflicted by war-damaged men. Every piece of furniture in the sitting room was upside down and broken. The baize of the billiard table was ripped and stained, the top of the piano scratched and covered in burn marks. On the terrace were the charred remains of the kitchen table, Sir A's desk and reading chair from the library and the stand for his globe. The globe itself and about half of the books from the library must have gone up in smoke. The rest of the books, torn and scorched, were in the darkroom under the stairs along with what was left of the contents of Sir A's desk drawers, two piss-stinking mattresses and a jumble of kitchen, climbing and astronomy equipment.

Sir A's star-gazing chair, miraculously unharmed, was in the mazot which, itself, had escaped vandalism. Some of Lady C's paintings and sketches had even been nailed, quite carefully, to the walls. There was a pile of German books – including a bible with some verses underlined – on the floor next to the star-gazing chair. A photograph and two letters fell out of one of the books when I picked it up. The photograph was of a woman and girl, about seven years old, standing outside a house made entirely of brick.

The books, letters and the photograph went on the bonfire, where Beatrice was poking at the pissy, smoking mattresses. In the end, most of the bedding went on that fire too because we discovered fleas in all the upstairs rooms.

By the time Rory and Josh, each with a wife and baby daughter, plus Inez and Peggy, both in their late teens, arrived, the house was habitable, just.

I liked Daisy's grown-up, or nearly grown-up, children immediately. Rory, studious and podgy, had already been called to the bar. Josh was a painter, a gadabout rake. They were chalk and cheese, but those two young men – with their younger wives and tiny babies – got on like a house on fire. It was as if we had Ted and Johnny back, without the bad bits.

Inez resembled Daisy in looks and, like her mother, she enjoyed the limelight and tended to make shy Peggy seem shyer than she actually was. There was a twinkle in Peggy's eye and a kindness to her manner that reminded me pleasantly of Sir A. It was she who explained to me about Daisy's ECT.

By the time Daisy arrived at the end of July, most of the debris had been dealt with and Arete, in its own inimitable fashion, was more or less up and running again. With the additional thrill, that summer, of a small, clunky electricity generator.

Daisy arrived – with a typewriter, reams of blank paper and a trunkful of empty box files – in a downpour of rain. It rained solidly for the next few days, and I scarcely saw her because she shut herself away in the mazot with Django, much to the disappointment of Inez and Peggy. When we did bump into each other, Daisy looked at me vacantly.

'How d'you do?' she'd murmur. 'Good morning, my dear.' Or, 'Afternoon, dearest.'

Her face was almost unlined, her hair scarcely grey and she'd kept her slim, boyish figure despite the pregnancies, but she'd lost her passion for fashion; she wore dull, shapeless skirts and untucked-in men's shirts, and her movements were slow. Her eyes were blank – unreadable to me – and there were marks on the sides of her head from her ECT treatments.

Because of the rainy weather and because neither Rory nor Josh could mend the old, wind-up gramophone, I sent word to Luc to bring up our electricity-eating radiogram, which he did – in the 2CV as far as Hext-en-Haut, strapped to his back from there on. Inez and Peggy watched him set it up. When he got it going, all three of them fell about laughing at the scratchy, jumping music from the few records that had survived the war.

The sound of music brought Daisy out of the mazot and

down to the games room. Inez and Peggy begged her for money to buy new 45s for the radiogram.

'And where, in this back of beyond, godforsaken corner of the world do you propose to buy them?' Daisy asked.

'I could ask at the club,' Luc whispered – hopefully – to me. 'They might lend some.'

The club was how the young people in the valley referred to Club Costa. Soon after the war, Costa had let and sublet his club, playing in it himself to make ends meet, I suspected, as rumours of his wealth transformed themselves almost overnight into rumours of bankruptcy, debt, bailiffs. Since then, the club had changed hands, closing and reopening – metamorphosing from cabaret to burlesque, blues and back to jazz – more quickly than anyone could keep up with. Each attempt to revive it failed and the louche glamour of Club Costa in the 1920s and 30s was replaced by drab, shabby seediness.

Costa himself looked dreadful whenever I glimpsed him in the village. He had sent me a letter in 1950 saying he was sorry to hear about Cédric, and another in 1951 saying he'd welcome a visit. I replied to neither, although I was tempted to. If nothing else, Costa could do with a few lessons in spelling and punctuation. I could imagine correcting his writing as I'd corrected his sums, and how mutually satisfying this would be.

I didn't like Luc going to the club, and he rarely did.

'No,' I whispered back.

'I know a shop in Geneva.'

'My son knows of a shop in Geneva,' I told Inez, Peggy and Daisy.

'Let's go. Tomorrow,' said Inez. 'Me and Pegs. With Luc.'

'Luc can't go,' I said firmly. 'Not tomorrow, nor the next day, nor any day soon.'

Luc was, nominally at least, in charge of the farm for the summer.

'Me And Pegs, then. By ourselves.'

'Yes. Why not?' said Daisy, vacant and seeming to lose interest.

Bossy old Beatrice had other ideas. She said Inez and Peggy were too young to be trusted alone on such a trip.

'We're both very mature,' said Inez. 'And I'll keep an eye on Pegs.'

'Mummy lets us run around London by ourselves,' added Peggy.

'Well, Mummy shouldn't,' said Beatrice. 'And this is different. Two silly girls on the loose in a foreign city? No. And the train – strangers on it from Lord knows where. No.'

'We'll stay together,' Peggy promised.

'We'll be sensible,' Inez said. She flashed a grin at Luc.

In the end Beatrice capitulated, but only on condition that I accompany the girls on the train; they could then have free rein, by themselves, for the day in the city. I was happy about this. Apart from anything else, it would give me the opportunity to visit Madame Tissot, whom I hadn't seen for more than four years, when I helped her celebrate her eightieth birthday.

She had retired from her post at the girls' school in Geneva before the war, but she worked voluntarily, during the war, for an organisation that helped refugee children. Luc and I visited her after the war every summer, until things went downhill with Cédric's accident; Madame Tissot had been as alert mentally at eighty, the last time I'd seen her in 1950, as I remembered her from my first day at school. She and I continued to correspond, but her letters had become less frequent in the last couple of years. I liked the notion of surprising her with a visit from her old clever clogs.

*

Luc gave us a lift down from Hext-en-Haut to the station.

'I'll pick you up this evening,' he said. 'Save you some of the walk.'

'Yes. Thank you,' said Inez. 'Don't forget,' she added with a small laugh.

As soon as we boarded the train, Peggy began to sneeze. Inez nudged her.

'Not yet,' said Inez.

'Oh.' Peggy held a hanky to her nose. 'I thought—'

'What's the matter?' I asked.

'Nothing,' said Peggy. 'It's only hay fever.' But she blushed and there were beads of sweat on her forehead. 'I think I'll doze until we get there.'

It was a quiet journey. Inez opened her *Casino Royale* and read speedily, licking a finger each time she flicked a page. Peggy kept her eyes shut, but her breathing told me she wasn't asleep. I looked out of the window – there wasn't much to see, the cloud was so low and the train window had droplets of water on the outside and was steamed up on the inside. The mist lifted as we chugged through the outskirts of the city, but the sky stayed heavy with rain and, as we descended at the Gare des Eaux Vives, the heavens opened.

Peggy shivered.

'What's wrong with you?' I frowned at her.

'We haven't got umbrellas,' Peggy said. 'I'm freezing.'

'We'll buy them,' said Inez. 'I've a purseful of Swiss francs and a mind to spend extravagantly today. We'll take a cab to the shopping district. Can we drop you off somewhere, Mathilde? Does your Madame Tissot live en route?'

'I don't know,' I replied. 'I've only ever walked there.'

But when a cab pulled up, it was raining so hard – and I didn't want to arrive at Madame Tissot's dripping like a dishcloth – that we all climbed in and I gave the driver Madame Tissot's address.

'Gosh, I feel sleepy.' Peggy yawned.

We sped through the streets, spurting water on the already wet pedestrians, and stopped in a dirty whoosh of a puddle at the square where I'd asked directions at the bar on my first ever visit to Madame Tissot.

'The streets are too narrow to go any further,' said the driver. He got out and opened the back door of the cab for me.

'Thank you,' I said, gathering my shawl around me and stepping out. I turned to shut the door. '*Le petit train* leaves at four o'clock, remember. Make sure you're at the station in good time.'

'Don't worry,' said Inez. 'We'll be there. Bye-bye. Enjoy your day.'

Peggy was lolling in the far corner of the cab, apparently half asleep. She lifted a feeble hand in farewell.

I stepped back to avoid being splashed as the cab made a full-circle turn and disappeared back the way it had come. Then I hurried through the rain to Madame Tissot's apartment building. The front door and the shutters had been repainted a slightly lighter shade of green, but otherwise it looked precisely the same as I remembered it. Moreover, precisely as Madame Tissot had said in one of her letters, there was now a panel of electric door-bells to the right of the door. I pressed number twelve and waited.

A young man came and stood next to me.

'Excuse me,' he said.

I moved out of his way and he opened the door with a key.

'Have you rung?' he asked me.

'Yes,' I said. 'Number twelve.'

'Madame Tissot? She'll be a while. She finds the stairs difficult. Why don't you come in? Out of the rain.'

'I think it would be more correct to wait,' I said.

'It would save the poor old thing the stairs,' said the man. 'Come on. In. I can see you're not from the city. I'm not going to eat you.'

I followed him into the hall.

'I'm along there at the back. Number three. You want the top floor,' he said and disappeared down the corridor.

I climbed the stairs but didn't meet Madame Tissot on any of the landings. The door to her apartment was ajar. I knocked, waited, wondered what to do, knocked again and then went in.

Madame Tissot was sitting in one of the old armchairs by the fireplace. She didn't get up. The chair was too big for her, and so were her eyes. But her eyes lit up as she greeted me, clucking with pleasure at my unexpected arrival.

'I'm sorry I didn't come down. My feet simply wouldn't take me. Not today.' She looked at her feet and sighed. She wore slippers, thick stockings with darns in them and an old woollen skirt that reached to below her knees, but her shins, I could see, were as thin as a goat's.

'I didn't know you were unwell,' I said. 'You didn't say in your letter. You should have said.'

'I'm not unwell, Mathilde.' Madame Tissot tilted her head and rolled her eyes. 'I'm old. Eighty-five next birthday, to be precise. And you must forgive me, but I'm afraid I don't have the wherewithal to prepare a meal for us. Perhaps you would be so good as to go into the kitchen and make us both a coffee.'

'Of course,' I said, taking off my shawl and hanging it on the hook on the back of the door.

The room was damp and chilly: I was surprised Madame Tissot hadn't lit a fire. Not as surprised as I was by the sight of the kitchen, though. Not only was the crockery all higgledy-piggledy, but the floor was dirty and the little window that looked out onto the courtyard at the back of the building so dusty and grimy you could scarcely see out.

There was almost no coffee in the canister next to the stove. I opened the refrigerator. A jug of sour milk stood on the top shelf. Underneath, some grey rashers of bacon and half a pat of butter. That was all. Plates and cutlery lay unwashed in the sink and, on the hob, a saucepan of thin soup was growing mould around the edges. No wonder Madame Tissot had shrunk.

I went back to the front room.

'Do you have wood?' I asked.

'It's gas, these days, Mathilde,' said Madame Tissot. 'I need to put money in the meter. But the meter's on the ground floor and . . . I have money, but—' She gestured to her slippered feet.

'Where's your money, Madame Tissot? If you'll let me, I will find the meter. I will also, if you have enough money, go and buy us some food for lunch. And fresh coffee.'

'You're very kind, Mathilde. Yes. I keep my money in the kitchen drawer. Take coins for the meter. And some notes.'

Madame Tissot described where the gas meter was and how to put money in, so, after picking up a basket from the kitchen, down the stairs I went and along the corridor. A row of metal boxes with all sorts of dials and slots confronted me. I stared at them, despairing of ever working out which was which, let alone how to put the money in, when a door next to the meters opened and the man whom I'd met earlier came out.

'May I help?' he asked.

I explained what I was doing. Fearful he would think I was a thief, I told him that Madame Tissot was almost unable to move, and managing the stairs was out of the question for her.

'Is she that bad, now? I didn't realise. I'd have offered to help sooner,' he said. 'Here. This one's hers. My oh my, it's completely empty. Put all the coins you have in, but one at a time.'

'Will that make the gas fire work?' I asked when I'd emptied the purse of its coins.

'Yes. And the oven. But not unless you light them,' said the man. 'Are you leaving already? You look as if you are.'

'No. I'm going to buy food for Madame. She has nothing to speak of in her kitchen.'

'Well, in that case, I'll go up and see to the gas. You do your shopping. And when you come back, ring my bell, number three. I'll let you in.'

I asked where I should go for my shopping and he told me not to go to the bakery at the end of the street, but to carry on round the corner. There, he said, I would find one of the best bakeries in Geneva and next to it a grocery, which was so-so. I thanked him and set off. The rain had turned to drizzle and it didn't take me long to find the shops, and even though the prices and the money were strange, and people in both shops gave me strange looks, I managed to pack that basket with bread, ham, milk, butter, cheese, coffee, flour, sugar and eggs. The vegetables in the grocery weren't much to write home about, but I bought potatoes, onions and carrots, and the shopkeeper put some parsley in my basket without my asking.

When I rang the doorbell marked three, the young man, as good as his word, came quickly and let me in.

'Thank you,' I said, placing a foot on the stairs.

'You don't need to thank me,' he replied. 'I don't know who you are, but if you're a friend of Madame Tissot's, you must be a good sort. And she could do with some help. I've lit the fire. Now you go and cook her something warm and nourishing. I've left matches next to the stove. All you have to do is light one and put it to the holes in the gas ring. Don't stand too close though.'

Before doing any cooking, I set about washing up and cleaning the kitchen. Only after that did I broach the gas stove. I followed the man's instructions and a blue flower of flames sprang to life. I put a pan of water on to boil and made a good rich mix of vegetables and ham.

When I took a bowl of it into the front room, Madame Tissot didn't look up. She was asleep. I woke her, though, and made her eat. The effect was immediate. She wasn't her old self. Far from it. But colour came back into her cheeks, and, after two cups of strong coffee as well, into which I spooned plenty of sugar, she said, 'Well, now the shoe's on the other foot, isn't it Mathilde?'

'I don't think so, Madame Tissot,' I said. 'You will always be my teacher.'

'And you will always be my clever clogs.'

The afternoon passed quietly. Madame Tissot asked me to read aloud to her and I did my best, but she chose poetry and I could tell, from the number of times she furrowed her brow, that I was committing many errors, if not of pronunciation, then of stress. I kept an eye on the clock on the mantelpiece, and when it was time to go, I tried to ensure

Madame Tissot understood that I'd left plenty of food in the kitchen, and told her the man from downstairs was going to come up later to make sure she ate it. But she was nodding off again.

'Ah yes. *Le petit train*,' she murmured. 'Where would we all be without it? You mustn't miss it. Where would you be?'

I walked briskly to the station. It had stopped raining, but the air was still damp, the sky grey and the city looked gloomy and dank. I arrived at the station with five minutes to spare and was about to glance into the foyer of the Hôtel de la Gare when Inez came hurrying across the road towards me.

'What's the matter?' I said, going to meet her.

'It's Peggy,' she said. 'She fainted. Outside the record shop. I didn't know what to do. The 45s went spinning right across the road. They wanted to take her to hospital. In the end, though, she came round.'

'Where is she?'

'At the doctor's. A doctor's near the shopping district. I left her there. I didn't know what to do for the best, but the doctor said she must rest and I knew you'd be here.'

'You did the right thing,' I said. 'Now, look. Here's the train. You get on it. Go back and explain to your mother and grandmother what's happened. I'll take care of Peggy.'

Inez gave me several notes from her purse and a card with the doctor's address on it.

'Get a cab,' she said.

The drive to the doctor's, in my second cab of the day, took me along the edge of the lake, and even though my brain was busy with worry, I stared at the rough, grey water, remembering Tall Paul's tales of fishing boats tossed and upturned by a lake as stormy and treacherous as an ocean, and I admired the *jet d'eau*, bending in the wind like the bough of a tree, its spray thrown and scattered like apple blossom.

The doctor's office was on the ground floor of a tall, thin building wedged between two wide banks. Again, a line of bells next to the door, but this time the door opened immediately and a white-uniformed woman asked me my business. I explained, in my best Parisian French, and she led me through to a room at the back. Peggy was lying there on a low truckle bed. She appeared to be asleep.

'The doctor will be with you shortly,' said the uniformed woman and withdrew.

'Peggy?' I said.

Peggy opened her eyes.

'I told Inez I could make it to the station,' she said. 'But the doctor wouldn't hear of it.'

The doctor, when he came, was abrupt but efficient. He had carried out investigations. He could find nothing wrong. It might be a touch of summer flu. Best not to travel today, but with plenty of water and some more sleep, she would probably be fine tomorrow, he said. He asked if I'd like his nurse to telephone a hotel where we could stay for the night.

'I don't think I've enough money,' I said.

'But the young lady? Surely? Or her sister?'

'Inez gave me what she had.' I showed the doctor the remaining coins in my purse.

He shook his head.

'That won't get you very far,' he said.

'Will it pay for another cab?' I asked.

'To anywhere within the city, yes.'

'In that case, perhaps your nurse could find us a cab. I have a friend—'

'A friend you can stay with?'

'Yes. A good friend.'

'Is it clean there? Will the young lady be comfortable?'

I thought about Madame Tissot's apartment, the cobwebs in the corners, the dusty mantelpiece, the bathroom on the landing. But we had no choice.

'Yes,' I said.

Less than half an hour later, after cab number three, I was

ringing doorbell number three again, and again the young man came out. When I explained, he said he would offer us his lodgings but they consisted of just the one room and he was ashamed of its state. He told me to go on ahead and warn Madame Tissot while he helped Peggy up the stairs.

Madame Tissot appeared to have rallied considerably during my absence, due, no doubt, to the good food I'd made her eat and the warmth now emanating from the gas fire. She stood up, thanked the man and told me to take Peggy straight into the bedroom and put her to bed. This I did, not worrying about correctness. Peggy was wide awake but peaceful and said she wasn't hungry.

Madame Tissot and I stayed up all that night. We reminisced. She seemed to enjoy listening to my memories of the little school in Hext and I enjoyed listening to her tell me how she came to be there: about her time as a student, first in Paris, then in London – meeting Margaret Valentine, going to meetings together and training together to teach. That made me sit up. It had been a long time since I'd given much thought to Margaret and the mystery of what happened to her. Learning that she and Madame Tissot had been friends, not just acquaintances, was a shock and all sorts of questions rushed into my head. I tried to interrupt my old teacher. But Madame Tissot seemed to collect herself. She gave me the sternest of frowns and held up one hand, like she used to when she wanted silence in the classroom. She moved on quickly to explaining how the teaching post in Hext became available and how she decided to dedicate her days to broadening the horizons of the children of the valley; she distracted me with anecdotes about her pupils, including me – 'la petite Mathilde' – and my cushion, and Benoît and his black hair 'comme un chapeau'. Towards dawn, Madame Tissot's concentration began to wander. She told me she had something on her conscience, but not what it was.

'I don't know if I did the right thing, Mathilde,' she said.

I said if anyone knew how to mind their P's and Q's, it was

she, but it didn't make her smile. So I simply recited the La Fontaine fables I still knew by heart and she, peacefully, silently, with her eyes closed, mouthed with me, wrinkling her brow if I skipped or tripped on a single word.

Peggy seemed much better when she woke up, and, after coffee and eggs, well enough, I decided, to depart.

We had sufficient money for another cab and sufficient time to catch the early *petit train* to Hext, where I was very glad to see Inez waiting on the platform, and even gladder to see Luc's grey 2CV parked in front of the station. Inez was uncharacteristically pianissimo, and I wondered if she'd caught the summer flu as well. Luc directed Peggy into the front seat, and Inez and me to the back. As I climbed in, I sniffed: there was the distinct smell of sex, but where it was coming from – the car, Inez or both – I couldn't say.

Nineteen

'It was suave Luc,' George reminded Jack as they cleared away the remains of their night on the terrace, 'who saved your bacon that time with the knives, playing Split.'

'True,' said Jack. 'Luc's a pretty decent bloke, I reckon.'

In 1966, when George was eight, Jack ten and Thomas eleven, Jack found a drawer full of knives in the mazot. Daisy let him take them, and he devised the knife-throwing game of Split. This involved flicking knives into the earth – according to various arcane rules – beside, behind or between one's opponent's feet. The thrill of it was that it had to be played barefoot.

When the grown-ups discovered the game, it was banned – even Inez, the least strict of Ma's siblings, agreed – and the knives were confiscated. Jack, however, retrieved the knives and challenged Thomas (who happened to be up at Arete with Luc that afternoon bringing Mathilde her post) to a game of Split. The result was Thomas requiring stitches to one of his toes.

The grown-ups, including Inez, were livid. But Luc insisted it was nothing: Jack shouldn't be punished, it was evidently an accident, boys will be boys, Thomas would learn, so would Jack, honestly it was nothing.

Jack got off scot-free, but George remembered Jack asking Inez, very quietly, the evening after the incident, 'Will he lose his toe?'

'Oh darling, of course not,' she said. 'There's a big slice of skin gone, but you missed the bone.'

George also remembered being woken that night by the sound of Jack, in the bed next to his in the attic, crying quietly.

But George wasn't going to ruin things by telling Jack what he'd remembered. He'd genuinely enjoyed the last twelve hours: the evening boogieing, the night gabbing with Thomas, and this early morning, warming friendship with Jack. He hadn't thought about Ma or Da once. In fact, George was so pleased to feel finally accepted by Jack, he decided to have a shot at postponing going to bed until even later.

'Shall we have a nightcap? I mean, a daycap. A génépi?' George tried to sound casual.

But Jack yawned and looked at his watch.

'It's nearly eight o'clock in the morning, Georgio. I've usually had my brekker by now. I need my beauty sleep, I'm afraid.'

George didn't push it.

They went companionably upstairs together. George waited on the landing while Jack nipped up the ladder to the attic to check on Polly, Tess and Isobel.

'I feel sorry for our little cousin Isobel,' he said as he stepped off the ladder. 'Dragged from pillar to post in the name of Josh's art. Expected to accept his turnover of women, wives and girlfriends. Dumped on relatives at the drop of a hat. Father, mother and stepmother always busy. Reminds me of me. But—' Jack paused and, to George's surprise, reached out and put his hand on George's arm, near the shoulder. 'At least she and I still have our mothers and fathers. That's what I've been thinking. I really am sorry about your ma and da, George. You must be going through hell.' Jack patted George's arm. 'Good night, George.'

'Good night, Jack.' George thought, for a moment, they might be going to shake on it, or – heaven forbid – hug, but they didn't. They went into their separate bedrooms.

George, Jack and the girls slept until mid-afternoon.

*

Thomas spent the whole day sleeping, but he joined them in the evening in the games room. They taught him how to play

Newmarket and Pelmanism, Beggar-My-Neighbour and Cheat, which had the girls in stitches because Thomas was so hopeless at it. They showed him their maps and talked about the hunt for gold. Thomas shared with them the legends he'd grown up with about the golden ibex and the legendary, contradictory conditions required for a sighting of the mythical beast.

'I'm not taking on any clients for the last two weeks in August,' he told them when they all said good night to each other. 'I want to be in Hext for the election. So you'll probably see me then.'

George woke early the following morning. On his way to the kitchen, he glimpsed movement in the games room. He went in and found Thomas standing at the sideboard. One of the drawers was open.

'I'm looking for a pencil,' said Thomas. 'Ah. Here.' He found the grey stub of a child's crayon and shut the drawer.

'What for?' George asked.

'I will illustrate.' Thomas pointed to the little picture map on the billiard table. 'Last night, you and Jack showed me this map.'

'Yes.'

'And the other maps. Jack explained about making the paideia for the girls. And Jack is pretending to believe this little map indicates gold.'

'Yes.'

'I can tell you the map.'

'Tell me the map?'

'I didn't wish to spoil the fun last night. The pretending and the believing. Amusing. But now, look here, George.'

'What is it?'

Thomas took the crayon and deftly, confidently drew a graceful S-shaped curve, from the right- to the left-hand side of the little picture map.

'Do you see now?' said Thomas.

'See what?'

'The river. I've drawn in the Ouiffre. Now, can't you see?' He pushed the map closer to George. 'You and Jack and the girls have been reading the map wrong. That black line running from Arete: it goes down at first, not up. You can see that, I think, now I've sketched in the river. It makes more sense.'

George considered Thomas's words and looked at the crayoned 'S' of the river.

'So one side of the river's a normal map. This side, the Arete side. The other's sort of 3D, more like a picture. Yes, I see.'

'Exactly,' said Thomas. 'The black line starts at Arete and goes down to Hext. Then it crosses the river – look where I've drawn the river – and goes up again, the map being now a picture-map.'

George stared at both parts of the map.

'Down. And up the other side! Good Lord, yes! How did you work it out?'

'I saw it immediately. I saw what was missing as much as what was there, I suppose. That's all. I must go now. But I didn't want to go without giving you this knowledge.'

'Where does the line from Arete end up, though, on the other side of the valley?'

'Nowhere special. Jack will be disappointed. I think it leads only to one of the many haybarns dotted in and around the Zizipompom forest. There's nothing there. No gold, that's for sure.'

*

As soon as Thomas had gone, George studied the little map yet again. He'd experienced a childish stab of disappointment at Thomas's certainty that there was no gold, but this was superseded now by astonishment that so minute an alteration – one stroke of a manky old crayon – could make such a difference. There was no mistaking the path from Arete to Hext-en-Haut, and the track from there on down to the village. He reckoned it was from Hext-en-Haut that the pictorial map of the other side of the valley had been drawn, and he couldn't resist the urge to see for himself. He scribbled a note and left it on the kitchen table, put on his boots and set off down to Hext-en-Haut.

He reached Jack's 2CV and leant against it, shielding his eyes from the morning sun pouring into the valley. The opposite side of the valley was the postcard-pretty side, and Hext-en-Haut, on a bright July morning, one of its best vantage points.

George looked up to a swimming-pool-blue sky, zigzagged by white, uneven peaks. He looked down to the green valley floor, flat as if pressed by a giant iron, with the Ouiffre a single silver thread running through it. He pulled the little picture map out of his pocket, unfolded it and lifted his eyes to take in the sweep of meadows, forested Zizipompom slopes and striated rock faces in between.

When he'd seen enough to decide that Thomas was more than likely right, he refolded the map and put it back in his pocket. He was about to go when he heard, then saw, Luc's Land Rover roaring up the track from Hext.

'George. Darling.' Inez leapt out and gave George a hug. 'How are you, my poor darling? Has Jack been looking after you? I do hope things haven't been too miz.'

George couldn't get a word in edgeways as his giddy aunt kissed him, then hugged him again, whispering sorries and condolences and cheer-you-ups into his ear. The exaggerated theatricality of it all enabled George to relax and even enjoy the embrace.

Inez stepped back and held him at arm's length.

'You look well, though, nephew. Truly.' She nodded approvingly. 'Now. Are you the welcome party? Shame. I was planning a surprise.'

Inez's return was a surprise.

All thoughts of the ibex, the gold, the map were forgotten or pushed to one side for the next few weeks as Inez displaced Jack as the leader of the pack.

Twenty

'Inez and Luc are lovers,' said Daïsy, watching them dance together at the garden party.

The garden party at Arete in August 1954 was fancy dress and a grand affair – 'in honour of Father', said Beatrice, 'and Hillary's Everest last year, which would have tickled Pa pink.'

The new Queen Elizabeth herself couldn't have been bossier than old Beatrice when it came to the menu. Beatrice wanted devilled eggs and angels on horseback, pigs in blankets, avocado canapés and salmon baked in pastry with currants and ginger. 'In honour of the end of rationing,' she said, to which Daisy added, 'The nurses in Bournemouth brought in Battenberg for that, and I pretended it was birthday cake.'

Beatrice got her devilled eggs, and Savoyard sausage rolls made do as pigs in blankets, but I was having none of her fancy, fishy notions, because I would have had no idea where to obtain the ingredients. Fried river trout was as far as it went in Hext. It wasn't easy acquiring all the fruits Beatrice wanted for dessert, either; we had to send to a supplier in Nantes for early Muscadet grapes and to a hotel in Nice for pineapple and pomegranate shipped over from Morocco. The pièce de résistance, however, was a giant, wobbly *anglais* trifle, which I assisted with and everyone agreed was top-notch.

Bunting was hung from the balcony – Union Jacks and Tricolores side by side. All the doors and windows on the ground floor were opened so that the music from the radiogram could be heard on the grass at the back of the house. The *rosbifs* taught the guides how to play British Bulldog and cricket, and Rory said the guides were jolly good sports and bloody fast bowlers but hopeless fielders. After tea there was dancing – formal couplings and stiff shufflings, except for Inez and Peggy, who jitterbugged together flamboyantly.

I'd have said stuff and nonsense to Daisy's assertion if it weren't for the smell in Luc's car and the fight between Inez and Peggy which took place a few days after the garden party.

Luc invited Inez and Peggy to the club. I was having none of that and told him he'd have to uninvite them, but luckily Daisy put her foot down anyway, even though their sensible, serious brother Rory offered to be a chaperone. Not one to be easily defeated, Luc invited Inez and Peggy to climb with him to the glacier de la Miche. No one put their foot down, no one chaperoned them, and Peggy came back with a gash in her forehead the size of a 50-centime piece.

'Just a run-in with an alpenstock, wasn't it, Pegs?' said Inez.

'Yes,' said Peggy.

No, Luc told me later. It was more than that. The sisters fought.

'Over what?' I asked him.

Luc refused to go into details, but I thought it was obvious that Inez and Peggy had fought over him.

I invented reasons, after that, for Luc to be kept busy with the farm until the *anglais* had departed.

*

'Inez and Luc are lovers,' said Daisy in 1955 (again in '56 and '57, and again).

But I was wiser, much wiser by then.

*

In November 1954, I received a letter from Geneva. The handwriting on the envelope wasn't Madame Tissot's, and the letter I pulled out was typed. It was from a Swiss lawyer. It told me

Madame Tissot had died. It said she'd bequeathed me her library and could I please visit the lawyer's office, at my convenience, to make the necessary arrangements?

A few days later I donned my best skirt, buttoned up my new winter coat – it was a cold and frosty morning – and took *le petit train* to Geneva. This would be my first ever trip to Geneva without Madame Tissot's apartment as my destination. The death of my old teacher made me think about all the horizons she'd broadened for me, even within the confines of Hext. Broadening them had sometimes involved harsh lessons, but Madame Tissot had always taught with love. I realised I'd never told her how greatly I valued her guidance and good faith in me, her wisdom and teacherly friendship, and that thought filled me with sorrow. I had a clean handkerchief on me, so I let some of my sorrow overflow until the train slowed as we approached Geneva and it was time to readjust my clothes and wipe my weepy features.

The shock of my life awaited me as I exited the Gare des Eaux Vives: Sylvie! What on earth was Arete's old cook doing in Geneva? But it was definitely streaky-faced Sylvie, with a basket of vegetables over one arm, clearly just been to a market. We greeted each other, and in less than a minute, the shock of my life doubled: Sylvie was married to the man behind the desk in the foyer of the Hôtel de la Gare. She didn't say so, but I wondered if, like me, she'd gone for a lie-down, but unlike me, she didn't say no when the kind man offered to keep her company.

'Come and meet him,' she said. 'We can take tea together.'

I said I would like that, which was true, but could it be later? Of course, said Sylvie. She'd put on weight – all those petits fours, no doubt – but it suited her. She was a different – fulfilled – woman.

At the lawyer's office, Madame Tissot's books were laid out on a table as long as the *lavoir*. The lawyer told me to look through them and take what I wanted. I picked up a couple of old poetry books I recognised. I turned the pages of the falling-to-pieces *Poil de Carotte*, put the matching Corneilles and

Racines together. Out of the corner of my eye, I saw Madame Tissot's beloved La Fontaine.

'I'll have them all,' I said.

The lawyer seemed taken aback.

'But you're a farmer, aren't you? What will you do with so many books?'

'What do you do with all your books, monsieur?' I replied, gesturing to the leather-bound volumes lining the walls of his office. I noticed that some of the titles were in Latin. '*Pro tempore*,' I added. 'I rest my case.'

After that, it was a matter of signing a few papers and I was free to go. The lawyer would arrange for the books to be dispatched to me forthwith.

'All of them,' he reassured me. 'And this too is for you.'

He passed me an envelope.

'Thank you,' I said.

I walked from the lawyer's office to the street where Madame Tissot used to live. I knew that I wouldn't be able to go into her flat, and anyway, the lawyer had told me, the landlord had already stripped it bare, ready for the next tenant. But I wanted to see the green front door one more time. Madame Tissot, born a Catholic, had become a non-believer in London. She'd been cremated; there wasn't a grave, the lawyer had said.

In addition, I had a desire to go and see the man who lived at number three. When I rang on his doorbell, though, a middle-aged woman opened up. She'd lived there for two months, she said, and no, she'd no idea what had become of the previous tenant, she wouldn't know, no, no forwarding address.

I walked to the square and went into the café there. The man serving was too young to have been the same one as a quarter of a century before, but he was identical to look at – he must have been his son – and equally rude and unpleasant. I ordered a coffee and sat at a table by the window. I opened the envelope. Inside was another envelope, this one with my name in Madame Tissot's hand, containing an ancient dried, pressed, five-petal, faded blue myosotis with a hole in the middle where there should have been yellow and which, as I took it out, almost disintegrated between my finger and thumb, it was so powdery and fragile; the envelope also contained a very brief note from Madame Tissot ('Margaret swore me to secrecy, but my conscience dictates otherwise') paperclipped to a birth certificate – mine.

*

The dark had closed in by the time I returned to the Gare des Eaux Vives. Great wet splodges of snow were falling. I was in no frame of mind to take tea with Sylvie and the kind hotelier. In fact, as the train pulled out of the station, with me damp and tired in the corner of a nearly empty carriage, I felt humbled by my encounter with Sylvie: she was the one who'd escaped the confines of Hext, not snooty boots, clever clogs me.

The further up the valley we rumbled, the lighter and drier, but quicker, whirled the snow outside the train window. At Hext, there was already a two-inch covering, so it was shawl over head and creak, crunch up the track slowly towards home.

When I stopped and looked behind me (which, out of habit, I still sometimes did, even on routes I knew like the back of my hand), the valley had transformed from its green, brown, grey, dull, dead, wet, earthy woodiness into the first startling, sparkling layer of winter. Everything in the valley was different – colours, textures, smells and sounds. But underneath the roof of the Gauthier garage, which was already puffing up like a mushroom, Angélique would be preparing the evening meal, perhaps doing the accounts, or at her sewing machine, listening to the radio, the same as ever. And Costa, in his rundown house beyond the village: it would soon resemble an igloo if the snow continued to fall, but inside his igloo, Costa, who still, after more than a quarter of a century of my cold-shouldering, tried to speak to me each time our paths crossed (occasionally I couldn't help smiling at his tenacity, and I wondered if he saw), Costa would be playing his violin, mixing his glues, tweaking at broken instruments with his miniature tools, the same as ever – at least that's what I liked to imagine.

And me, I thought, as I let myself into the farmhouse, glad to be home: I'm the same as ever, aren't I, even though reading my birth certificate, which stated that Miss Margaret Valentine was my mother and Tall Paul was my father, appeared to have changed everything?

*

It snowed and snowed in the valley that winter of 1954 to '55. Day after day, night after night, the snow fell with scarcely a break. There was more snow than we'd had since before the war. Which was just as well, because, as a result of opening that envelope, I felt as if I was walking around in a daze; I was worried people would notice, but everyone was far too busy shoring up against the unexpected snow to remark not-quite-the-same-as-ever me.

Madame Tissot's books arrived at the post office in Hext at the beginning of December, and Luc made two journeys to fetch them in his 2CV, but it was rough going, he said, with fresh snow falling, melting and refreezing all the time. He unloaded the boxes into the farmhouse and made a neat pile of them underneath the shelves I'd recently constructed. I was pleased with these shelves, designed to house the books of Sir A's I'd retrieved during the tidy-up of Arete over the summer. Mrs Beeton, torn and tattered and with a good third of her pages missing, I kept in the kitchen next to a pretty but cracked rose-patterned teapot. It had the word 'Wedgewood' printed on the bottom, which mystified me, despite multiple forays into the several dictionaries I'd salvaged including a very old, useless but beautiful English–Italian *Worlde of Wordes* by a man called Florio.

'You'll have to put up more shelves,' Luc said, nodding at the two rows of battered old English history and poetry, travel, philosophy and reference books. 'I'll give you a hand on Saturday.'

He departed for Bonneville, as usual, early the following morning, but later that day there was more heavy snow, and in the evening a blizzard raged down from the mountains and blew along the valley floor. The roads became impassable. Luc had to stay in Bonneville for weeks on end. *Le petit train* kept running, although to a much reduced schedule (and sometimes, after a fresh snowfall, not at all), but there was no connection to Bonneville in any case.

It would be January before the roads were even halfway clear again.

I had plenty of wood for the fire and plenty of supplies for my animals and myself. Barring emergencies, there was no need to worry about getting down to the village for a month, at least. I was concerned, of course, about Luc, but, what with the dazed feeling, I was only too glad to be sequestered by the snow, isolated, alone at the farm.

I tried, at first, not to think about the birth certificate. I put it away in its envelope, in the drawer where we'd always put things we didn't know what else to do with.

I built three new rows of shelves, unpacked and arranged Madame Tissot's books, then carefully laid the disintegrating flower between the pages of the *Handbook of English Idioms*. After that, I scrubbed, mended, cooked, moved the furniture around, switched on the wireless, listened to the weather forecast, some music, a programme about the fighting in Algeria. But my thoughts kept straying to the envelope. After a few days, I gave up trying to stay busy and took it from the drawer. I pulled out the birth certificate and laid it carefully in the middle of my bleached-clean, rubbed-smooth, square pine table.

Rereading the names on the certificate wasn't the shock I

expected it to be. Already I could see that a coupling of Tall Paul and Margaret made sense. It made sense of those visits with the cheese and the diots to Arete when I was a child; it made sense of Madame Tissot's special interest in me; and it made a sort of sense of what I'd seen and heard between Margaret and Lady C in 1907 while sitting on the bench in Arete's front hall swinging my legs.

Thinking of Benoît as my half-brother wasn't as easy as pie, but I thought I could get used to it and it might even make me happy one day. Except for the fact that Benoît was dead, so I found myself starting to grieve for him all over again – now as a blood brother as well as a friend. Our father, Tall Paul's death, when I was only nine, made me mournful too. I'd have liked and been proud to call that kind, storytelling man Papa. Everyone on the French side of my family was dead I realised, and that realisation gave rise to new feelings of loneliness.

What it was impossible to do in a minute or hour or even a day of circling the table staring at my birth certificate was begin to understand what it meant or could mean to be the daughter of Miss Margaret Valentine and thus a flesh and blood part of the Valentine family. One minute I was sorry for Margaret – what a predicament for anyone to be in. The next minute I was sorrier for myself – a bastard foundling, poor and deformed to boot. Then I became angry with Margaret for abandoning me. And not once, but twice – at birth, then again with her departure in 1907, after which she made no attempt to see me, ever. But finally, I became angrier with the world. It shouldn't have made unmarried women abandon their infants, ugly and deformed or not.

The days passed. The snow fell. I slept badly and continued to circle the table.

Tap-tap. What was that? A knock at my door.

'Who is it?' Costa? Might it be Costa? I tried to keep the hope at bay.

I opened up to Angélique's husband, though scarcely recognisable with crusts of ice in his hair and snow thick and wet everywhere else.

'Angélique sent me to make sure you were well. She said you were missed in the village. I've brought potatoes. May I come in? Dry myself off?'

I gestured him inside. I popped my birth certificate back in the drawer while Angélique's husband took off his racquety snowshoes and hung his dripping coat by the fire. He stayed for more than an hour, drinking coffee and filling me in – frustratingly snippety, man-style – on news. He asked about Luc and said the whole village was proud of Luc's achievements. I made a big, rich, creamy tartiflette with some of the potatoes he'd brought. We ate half of it and I wrapped the other half in paper and cloth for him to take home with him.

'It'll keep you warm on the way,' I said, pressing the bundle on him as he went to open the front door.

After Angélique's husband had left, I didn't get my birth certificate out again. I was no longer in a quandary. This simple, hardworking man of Hext, our village blacksmith-turned-mechanic, had unwittingly given me the answer to my problem: I wouldn't let it mean anything that I was part of the Valentine family.

I'd built a life for myself and Luc here in Hext. There were people here who cared. I couldn't, I couldn't let it mean anything that I was part of the Valentine family. To do so would scupper my life and Luc's. We were respected. Luc was liked. The villagers would be horrified. They'd ostracise us as sure as eggs were eggs.

I did feel secretly chuffed about my blood bond with Sir A. He'd made me feel special and valued and my acquaintance with him, slight as it might have been, was more precious than ever now.

I did feel secretly sorry too that I wouldn't see the look of amazement on Daisy's face. 'Cousins? Cousins, you say?!' In the old days there would have been amusement also. 'Hextraordinary, 'ilarious, fantabulous!'

I did wonder, briefly, whether I had Valentine rights? Might I inherit if I chose to disclose?

And I would ask myself for ever, privately, not why Miss Margaret Valentine abandoned me – she would have thought she had no choice – but how she must have felt on those outings in the mountains with Paul, Benoît and me and whether, in different circumstances, she could have loved me.

But my secret feelings, my peasanty greed and my clever-clogs, calculating curiosity paled into insignificance in the light of my discovery that my life mattered – enough for someone to worry whether I needed potatoes, enough, moreover, for someone to trudge through the snow and bring me them regardless. Enough. I was wanted, which made me feel warm as a tartiflette.

*

I decided to take just two practical steps as a result of the birth certificate, one of which, involving a trip to Arete's grenier, would have to wait until the snow melted next spring. The other was to enquire of Luc, at the earliest opportunity, had there, or had there not been, rumpy-pumpy with the Arete girls?

No rumpy-pumpy, he promised, which was an enormous relief – a bastard baby would have been bad, an illegitimate cretin even worse.

Inez, Luc added, was a mantrap, but not his type. Peggy was sweet and he enjoyed her company, but she was a bit too young for him. Besides, he said, he was walking out with someone. A nurse. A student nurse. He'd met her when he went for his interview in Bonneville. They'd been courting ever since. He'd been using the car to visit her over the summer. It was serious. He'd been going to tell me. He hoped I didn't mind. He'd had an ulterior motive for wanting the car.

I was delighted.

And thus, so much wiser, when Daisy in her decline made false allegations about every Tom, Dick and Harry under the sun, I was able to refute most of them.

Twenty-One

'We were never lovers,' said Inez. 'Oh, I had a pash on him. We all did. Your ma included. But lovers, no. I don't think we even kissed, not tongues.'

George rolled over so that no one would see the effect of Inez's words. It was embarrassing the way his aunt could turn him on. He adjusted his swimming trunks. Jack, luckily, was busy diving to the bottom of the pool, bringing up pebbles, but the girls lay on their towels, in a row, next to Inez, bikini tops off, eyes opening and closing as they, like George, listened to Inez bang on about Arete, Hext, Ma and 'the rock and roll years of our youth'.

They were at the Ladies' Pond. They ended up there almost every day during the first half of August. Inez claimed her ankle had healed more quickly than anyone could have predicted, but Philippe, the physio in Megève, had told her hydrotherapy was the key to prevent it stiffening up. Hence the trips to the Ladies' Pond. Inez told them that, in the 1950s, it was still by invitation only for men there, which Polly, Tess and Isobel found very amusing. The rule but not the name had been dropped completely in the '60s. George, remembering his paideia at the Ladies' Pond in 1966, could recall the light-hearted – and some more vulgar – banter on the matter of gender segregation.

Most days, they picnicked lazily not far from the house and then, sooner or later in the afternoon, made their way to the cool, deep pool at the bottom of the waterfall.

The days with Inez flowed forgettably into one another. Inez's exuberance, which her own children found tiring, was a tonic to George. He enjoyed listening to her and was working round to getting her talking about the row with Ma. In the meantime, he was happy to hear Inez bang on about anything. He knew it was her method of trying to keep his – and her – mind off sad or bad things. Ma used to do it too: 'Listen, George. Let me tell you something really, really interesting . . .' Inez's method was a lot more effective, though.

The heatwave:

'Unbelievable. Oldies dropping dead on the streets of Paris, I gather. One right outside our apartment building the other day, apparently.' Paris was Inez and Bob's current base, although neither of them seemed to spend much time there. 'Ditto in London. It's the same everywhere, I expect,' Inez went gaily on. 'Last time it was this hot, I was twelve. Peggy was ten. We'd just started, in the middle of the summer term, at a new boarding school. Gruesome. The only cool place was the chapel. And your ma, George, believe it or not, slept naked on a pew in there one night.'

'Did she get caught?' asked Isobel.

'Sadly, yes.'

The election:

'Bollocks. It's all bollocks, these tiny French communes. Bribery and corruption. Inbreeding, infighting: that's how it goes.'

Luc:

'I'd vote for him on looks alone. Wouldn't you?' Inez threw back her head and laughed. 'I know what you're thinking, but no, George.' Inez sat up and started rubbing oil into her shoulders.

When she stated categorically that she'd had no romantic or sexual liaison, ever, with Luc, George – now safely on his stomach – asked, 'What about Ma, then?'

'She was young, darling. All three of us were.'

'But the dancing,' George persisted. 'Why did Ma stop? When?'

Inez stopped smoothing Ambre Solaire into her skin.

'1957. She met your father. It was true love. Really, George. Love at first sight. Pegs seemed to grow up overnight. They married early autumn, and you were born in the late spring. Mummy said it was a shotgun wedding, but it wasn't. Pegs would have told me if she'd lost her cherry. *Au contraire*: Peggy said she saved herself for Donald and her wedding night.'

George literally squirmed in embarrassed discomfort. He turned onto his side with his back to Inez to get away from the smell of her and the sight of her glistening, oily, look-at-me body.

'But the two left feet?' George couldn't help asking. 'She always said—'

'Yes. Well. She was in love.' Inez was dismissive. 'Donald had two left feet – so he said – so Peggy, your ma, pretended that she did too; she told him that she couldn't dance, that she never danced, that she wasn't even that keen on music.'

Silly woman. Typical Ma, though. Feigning ignorance when little-boy George retold her the plots of his storybooks. Feigning interest when big-boy George explained at length and in detail how the Ashes worked, or when Da gave her a blow-by-blow account of a never-ending faculty meeting. Feigning stupidity when George and Da tried to teach her to play Risk or Diplomacy, then beating them both hands down. Feigning liveliness when Graham stayed for supper and George could tell she was exhausted, but she made an effort with a home-baked apple crumble instead of their usual pots of pink yoghurt – a new thing from Sainsbury's, which were, Ma said, a godsend to working mothers, but devilishly expensive.

George frowned. He absolutely did not want to blub in front of his cousins and Inez.

*

George's chance to ask Inez about the row with Ma came when he decided to go down to the village to check for post and Inez said she would go with him, stretch her legs as far as the fancy took her.

The fancy took her as far as the high pastures. From there, the view up and down the valley was breathtaking that morning. George and Inez both paused. Mist lay in the bottom of the valley, creating what Ma used to call magic islands of the mountains. Light rippled across the mist, silvering it like wind on water. The sky was fresh turquoise.

'"Whirl up, sea,"' said Inez.

'Whirl up, sea?'

'"Whirl your pointed pines, splash your great pines on our rocks." It's a poem.'

'Oh. Who's it by?'

'I don't know. Mummy used to recite it. Whirl? Splash? No, I think it was "Hurl your green over us. Cover us with your pools of fir."'

'I like it,' said George.

'Yes. Nice, isn't it? Very short. Mummy recited it over and over in the car, though, when I was driving her to Megève. I mean to Megève to be locked up. Two hours solid. Spoilt the poem for me a bit.'

'Why did you and Ma disagree about Granny Daisy and Megève?' said George carefully.

'We didn't,' said Inez, also carefully. 'Not fundamentally. We both wanted the best for her. Our views differed slightly, but – because we're sisters, because we have a shared history, but different perspectives on it, because that's how things are in families – we took drastically opposing positions. That's all.'

'But the insults. And Luc? You both whirled and splashed his name around a lot.'

'Did we? It doesn't ring a bell. The point about Luc is, we both rather made fools of ourselves. Way back, in 1954. Me first. Peggy and I cooked up a whole spree to Geneva and a ludicrous saga of Peggy getting ill just so that I could try to get Luc between my legs.'

George flinched and Inez noticed.

'Sorry, George, but that's how it was. How I was. Shamebags. Luc wasn't in the slightest bit interested in me. When I got off the train, alone, at Hext, there was Luc, obediently waiting for the three of us. I was so confident about my ability to seduce him that I told him immediately about the plan. He was horrified – genuinely worried about Mathilde and Peggy abandoned in Geneva. Told me it was a silly plan. Told me he was practically engaged to a young woman in Bonneville. I can't describe how humiliating the whole thing was. Then, up on the glacier, Peggy threw herself at him.'

'The scar?' said George, pointing to his own forehead.

'No, no.' Inez was vehement. 'Luc wouldn't hurt a fly. I did that. Peggy got the wrong end of the stick, so to speak. Attacked me. So – in my defence – it was self-defence. Luckily, Luc didn't seem to hold any of this against us. He's a good sort.'

George was aware that Inez had moved the conversation away from the row.

'But the row?'

'What row?'

'On the terrace, in the rain. You were dancing in your sundress, Inez, in the rain.'

'You remember the sundress? You're a funny little boy, George. All right. Not so little. Okay. I'll explain.'

Inez sat down on the damp, dewy grass and George sat on a flat stone next to her. He hugged his knees and stared at the thick sea mist in the valley.

'I'm actually surprised you don't recall more,' Inez began. 'The mopeds, for example.'

'Of course I remember the mopeds. Yes.'

'Jack didn't pay the Gauthier boy for some repairs the Gauthier boy did. Luc, who's friends with the Gauthier papa and was willing to do the family a favour, came up to Arete to ask for the money, and the cat came out of the bag about you and the mopeds – you going with Jack and the others.

All hell let loose. Your ma said I shouldn't have let you go, I was irresponsible, a bad mother. I probably said far worse things. Though I do think she mollycoddled you. She did a bit, didn't she?'

'I suppose so. So I was to blame, was I?' George's stomach caved in as he had a sudden involuntary memory of the last time he'd seen Ma and Da. Ma's – oh, so banal – last words to him. But that way of thinking was dangerously self-indulgent. George often had to stop himself wondering if he could have prevented the accident that killed his parents. If he'd gone with them, for example. They might have driven more slowly, more quickly, made different stops. Or, if he'd been there and seen the lorry, he might have grabbed the car's steering wheel – he might have been a hero. George even managed to feel bad for not answering Ma's question about the salad cream, rhetorical or not – those few seconds might have made all the difference.

The last time he'd seen Ma and Da, he'd been standing at the front door looking down the garden path. Da was already in the driver's seat of the Escort, the window down and a bare, hairy white forearm leaning on it, his shirtsleeve rolled up. Ma walked along the garden path and, at the gate, turned.

'Bye,' she called. 'Quiche in the fridge. Make sure you wash the salad. Did you see, I left the salad cream out?'

George pretended not to hear, waved and went inside.

He had neither eaten the quiche, nor washed the salad. The front door bell had rung, just after six, and it had been the policeman and woman. Much later that evening, Graham's dad had gone out and brought fish and chips back with him. George remembered eating them and guiltily, disloyally thinking how much tastier they were than Ma's quiche and salad would have been.

Ma at the garden gate, Da waiting in the Escort, Ma's stupid rhetorical question about the salad cream. Was everything his fault?

'No, no, no – you're missing the point. It was Luc.'

'Luc?'

'Not that he was to blame, either. But your ma hadn't got back to Arete – I think she and Donald had gone to look at the dam or the glacier – when Luc arrived. It was only teatime but I offered him an apéro. We had some rosé. That's probably what set us off down Memory Lane. I got out some of the old records. We did dance a bit, on the terrace. It was just beginning to rain when Peggy turned up. And exploded.'

'In front of Luc?'

'No, but as soon as he'd gone, she let rip. I was a bit tipsy. Peggy started ranting. We both probably said things we shouldn't have. Peggy hated what she called my promiscuity. I pretended to hate her fuddy-duddiness, but (a) actually, I envied how uncomplicated her life seemed compared to mine, and (b) she wasn't really a fuddy-duddy – Peggy could be great fun. Oh God, sorry, that sounds so stupid. Oh dear.' Inez sniffed back what might have been tears. 'The truth is, I miss her terribly, George. Our chats. The shared jokes. Even our rows. God! You've no idea how much I regret these last four years. I shouldn't have plied poor Luc with rosé, should I? I'm sorry, George. I'm so, so sorry. This must all be ghastly for you.'

'That's okay,' said George automatically. But it wasn't. He turned his head away from Inez so she wouldn't see how he'd taken to frowning in order to hide the confusion of feelings that rushed through him when memories of Ma or Da came unbidden. He'd got to the bottom of the banal family row, yet he'd have given anything now to be ignorant again if it meant he could hear again Ma's voice, 'You're too young to understand, darling,' watch her forehead pucker and notice the adult looks exchanged between her and Da. He hadn't realised until now how safe he'd felt in those moments. George stared down the valley towards Geneva, where the dissipating mist had become a pearly shimmer in the morning sun, with the bosom of *la Concierge* now visible above the sea of cloud. He was relieved to hear Inez scramble to her feet.

'I think that's enough of a leg-stretch,' she said.

George stood up too.

'Goodbye, George. Full moon tonight. 10th of August.' Inez glanced at the cloud in the valley. 'Still only August, but autumn's on its way.'

*

A second letter, nice and fat, from Graham was waiting for George at the post office.

'That's five days it's been here. You should have come sooner,' said the postmistress.

Graham's letter, which George opened and read as soon as he'd left the post office, was slightly longer than the first, but the fatness was due mostly to the newspaper clippings Graham had sent about the heatwave. Graham himself wrote about the big West Indies win at Old Trafford, a book he was reading called *Zen and the Art of Motorcycle Maintenance*, Elton John and Kiki Dee driving him nuts, blaring out at the swimming pool all day long, the official opening of Reading's new civic centre ('you can't get more exciting than that'), and how the tall Romanian lifeguard, 'aka Krisztina, aka first-class totty', had invited him – 'aka Don Juan' – to her bedsit 'to watch Comaneci do her thing'. There had been quite a party of Romanians there, but did George think this was the green light?

Probably not, knowing Graham, but George wished his friend the best of luck. He wasn't exactly a Don Juan himself, was he?

*

'George. Good day.'

It was Costa with a large parcel under his arm.

'Hello.'

'Don't think me rude, George, but I will not stay to talk today. The post office is closing shortly.' He indicated the parcel.

'Of course. The postmistress is very strict.'

'Yes. Tell me quickly, though. Any news from Mathilde?'

'News?' George didn't know what Costa meant.

'You gave her my regards?'

'Yes.'

'And?'

'And?' George didn't know what else to say. Costa looked disappointed.

'And, erm, the election – does her position remain the same?'

'Yes.'

'Tell her, please, that I have decided to vote for her son.'

'Okay.'

'Yes. The opposition are showing their true colours: no new medical centre, no kindergarten, no library. There's talk of closing the railway line. And they're playing dirty: they've started a rumour that Luc is sleeping with the Colorado woman.'

'Is he, do you think?' asked George.

'Of course not.' Costa sounded almost offended. 'I've also heard they're offering to fly two council members to America to appreciate an American ski station. But don't mention any of that to Mathilde. Just tell her, please, Costa will vote for Luc's list.'

'All right.'

George said goodbye to Costa and strolled through the village, across the square and around to the back of the church, where an untarmacked road, like the one from Hext to Hext-en-Haut, led up the opposite side of the valley. The lower slopes were sprinkled with chalets and farms. Above them, George came to the forest of Zizipompom, where the trees were widely spaced with tracks and swards of green between them. Some of the tracks had signposts, small ones, to places with pretty names: Chantemerle, les Abeilles, Hermillon, la Rosière. George followed a few of the tracks and, each time, came to a haybarn. The highest one was called le Nid, and from there, when you turned round, you could see, if you looked carefully, Hext-en-Haut and the path to the chalet.

Convinced now that Thomas's reading of the map was correct, George retraced his steps down to the village. He crossed the square, and this time, there being no one sitting outside the Auberge Dorée, he drank lustily from the water fountain before setting off back up to Arete.

Twenty-Two

Spring was late in 1955, but it came at great speed. As soon as the snow had melted, the valley swelled with dense green foliage, bright bulging trees and extravagant ferns. Glowing thicket seemed almost to explode overnight from the cold earth.

There was so much new undergrowth that when I, plus a girl and two men from the village, walked up to Arete just after Pentecost to open the place up and prepare things for the summer, the men had to use their scythes to clear the path between Hext-en-haut and the Plateau des Bergers. As a result, by the time we arrived, it was dusk. The men said there was no point starting work until the following day and they went straight to one of the huts. I showed the girl, who was nervous and dim, to another hut and told her to bed down.

I myself had no intention of bedding down. I unpadlocked Arete's back door, entered the chilly kitchen and lit the stove so that we would have hot water in the morning. Then I took a Tilley lamp from the darkroom, went upstairs and climbed the ladder to the grenier, to comb through the box files Inez and Peggy had stored there the previous summer. I itched to learn what I could about my mother and father and I believed it was my due. I suspected there wouldn't be much about Tall Paul, but Margaret, I reasoned, must have featured in Sir A's diaries and I intended also to search for the photograph of her that Sir A used to request.

Having found the box files (carelessly dumped in a tea chest), I set the Tilley lamp down, took them out and sat on the floor next to them. I opened the one labelled Notebooks and Photos and was overjoyed to come across the photograph of Margaret almost immediately. Other than this, the file contained half a dozen of Sir A's notebooks and a handful of blurry old home-developed prints of the region.

I studied the photograph of Margaret, but I saw no more than I'd seen before, when peering at it in the darkroom in 1924. All the women were identically attired and their faces very small. I did wonder this time though whether the woman in the back row, tilting her head, might be a young Madame Tissot. The photograph's cardboard frame had softened and become tatty, the corners were bent and water stains marked the back of it. Eventually, I returned it to its box file and opened the one labelled Letters, but it was disappointing because the letters were from Sir A's friends, not his family.

I turned last to the file with 'Anthony Oswald Valentine' written on its spine. It contained the scorched, torn, disintegrating remains of Sir A's diaries, which I settled down to read. I found out nothing about Tall Paul that I didn't already know and very little about Margaret. No trace of spit spat. No trace of me, nor indeed of any pregnancy. I learnt that my mother as a child was 'a bookworm', played the piano 'rather well' and was 'a dab hand at diabolo'. She had a sweet tooth, the looks of Lady C and a degree from London university. 'My Margaret has a brain as sharp as any man's,' Sir A had written. My mother was a clever clogs.

When I'd been through everything, I decided to find the safest places I could for the box files. My itch wasn't soothed; there was plenty more family for me to read about one day and I didn't want the files disturbed or removed by anyone else. The places I chose were the tea chest, the cracked mirror and, last but not least, the dressing-up box; I took the clothes out of this, with the intention of folding them to make more space. Some of Daisy's gaudy silk garments from the 1920s had been relegated to it, and there were various items of menswear from the '30s that I'd never seen before. But there, also, was the purple velvet dress, and before I knew it, I was back in 1914 and Daisy was throwing me the dress.

'Here. For you,' I remembered her saying. 'It probably belonged to Mother or my aunt Margaret once.'

'Your aunt, my mother,' I said aloud now.

I pulled the dress over my head, all the while sniffing and stroking the mangy, frayed and flattened velvet. No tiara, but I did find a pair of pointy shoes, far too big, like the ones I'd worn as a luscious memsahib. I hobbled over to the pictures, moved them to reveal the mirror and stood for a long time contemplating my purple-clad image.

Hobbling back across the grenier, I tripped on the Tilley lamp, knocking it over. In my haste to right it, I trod on one of the box files with the heel of my pointy shoe. The file sprang open and skidded across the floorboards, sending notebooks and photographs flying. I quickly took off both shoes and the dress and collected the scattered notebooks and photographs. I put them all back in the box file, except for the photograph of Margaret, because its frame had split open as a result of my clumsiness, revealing layers of paper and thin card, which must have cushioned the photograph previously but had shifted and come apart from each other over the years, and I could see that one of the pieces of paper had handwriting on it.

Gently, I pulled it out. A single glance told me it was a letter from Margaret to Sir A, undamaged and complete. Trembling, I moved the Tilley lamp closer. The handwriting was like Sir A's only smaller, and there were no crossings-out. A crease was still visible in the middle of the white paper from where it had once been folded.

Quill Terrace, 22 Charlwood Road, S.W.
18th July 1907

Dear Pa,

I wonder what Marmee has told you? I beg you not to judge me too harshly. There is no denying my wrongdoing. I have broken rules and knowingly hidden truths.

I do not wish to bring shame on the family. I shall stay away, keep quiet, make a life of my own.

I have new digs in Putney, a stone's throw from the Thames and most convenient for my job at the girls' school up the hill. I shall sit out the summer here, read, study, take walks by the river. The paddle-steamer service from Hammersmith to Greenwich is frequent, with a stop at Putney Bridge. I plan to use it soon to re-visit the Royal Observatory. You took us all there when I was ten. Do you remember? Edmond, Harold and Beatrice were bored, I recall, but I was enthralled.

You rarely speak of love, Pa, the love of one human being for another, yet you wax lyrical about the land in our little corner of Haute Savoie. I believe I share your land-love and understand it. But I'm a woman. I lack your means of exploring the land and your ways of conveying your love for it. Falling in love with a man of the land gave me the wherewithal. He guided me through the land's beauty and enabled me to express my love for it. I wonder whether you can understand that?

You have my address. I urge you to write.

Your loving daughter,

Margaret.

I couldn't imagine Putney or paddle-steamers, let alone the Royal Observatory, but my mother's words about love and the land transported me to those illicit picnics in the mountains and I could hear her low, slow English voice: thoughtful and restrained, but vibrating with emotion ever so slightly, like a tremor in the eye or the lightest flutter of a hand – a yearning.

Mother, I mouthed. I'd always liked that soft *anglais* word. I'd have given anything just then to have been close to her, my clever, proud, brave mother. But the letter made it clear she hadn't been brave enough to tell the truth about me, and who could blame her? I was glad I'd decided not to reveal my Valentine blood – it was a secret between us, our bond. I'd never let the world know who Margaret Valentine really was: Paul's lover, a most passionate woman, my mother. *Ma mère*.

Without more ado and having folded the dressing-up clothes, I stored the box files in the safe places I'd chosen. Then I moved the tea chest and stacked lots of heavy old records in front of it, replaced the pictures in front of the mirror and shifted trunks and some of Sir A's astronomy equipment in order to hide the dressing-up box.

I kept both letter and photograph however and, when I returned home to the farm a few days later, I put them in the drawer with my birth certificate. This didn't feel like stealing, for all sorts of reasons.

*

That summer, whenever I had the opportunity, I crept up to the grenier, took out the box files and indulged myself in looking through them. I always used the same three places to keep the four files safe, but which went where varied. Everyone else appeared to have forgotten about them. Later, my visits dwindled and eventually stopped.

*

That same summer of 1955, Daisy's decline was dramatic. She started farting in public and laughing like a veritable cretin at *n'importe quoi*. You never knew from one day to the next what to expect, let alone from one year to the next.

In the late 1950s and early 1960s, she underwent a number of drug treatments. Her loyal millionaire ex-husband spared no expense, I gathered, and some of the treatments were imported from America. Their effects on Daisy's mind were impossible to gauge, but the effects on her body were visible and terrible. She lost her figure, became bloated all over, then emaciated, then swollen again, but only her belly. Her skin was often spotty or blotchy, raw and sore or, simply, dull. Her soft wavy hair coarsened and greyed, which made her begin to resemble her mother, Beatrice.

Beatrice died in 1962, and Daisy inherited Arete. In my opinion, which I didn't express, Rory, Josh, Inez and Peggy should have committed Daisy then. But they ummed and ahhed, *anglais*-style, while Daisy's decline, alongside Arete's, accelerated.

In 1963, Daisy threw away her pills and launched a thousand numbered paper sailing boats onto the Round Pond (the result of ten days shut away in the mazot folding two reams of paper).

'It's not fair,' she yelled, launching herself after them.

'Mother's a bully,' she said conversationally to Donald in 1966, apropos of nothing, while picking at her fingernails with a carving knife. 'Oh, and by the way, Ted was a queer, did you know that?'

She never mentioned Costa, thank goodness. Costa and I were on nodding terms by then. He got drunk, which was very unlike him, in November '66, the same month Venice was flooded and I received a letter from Chambéry telling me Cédric had died. Costa came knocking on my door again and shouted through it that ours must be the longest courtship in history and please would I put him out of his misery? I told him to go home and sober up and to leave me alone. A few days later, he dropped off a note apologising for his drunken behaviour, saying he'd been upset by the flooding of Venice. I'd seen this on the television news, and we stayed on nodding terms, which I was glad about.

Scrabble was all the rage in 1967. Daisy kept losing, even when her opponents were the grandchildren, who that year had incorporated the game into the paideias of their Alpine Club. But Scrabble, I decided, having watched several rounds, was not the intellectual challenge *les anglais* cracked it up to be.

'I can help you,' I said to Daisy one wet afternoon in the games room when she was losing yet again to the twins, who were only five, and I felt sorry for her. She seemed surprised rather than upset at her inability to form more than the simplest of words from the seven random letters in front of her. I decided to make them less random. 'Let me choose your letters for you.'

'Go on, then,' she said.

After that, Daisy won hands down, and (with me continuing to choose her letters for her) the next two back-to-back games.

Polly and Tess protested: either I had magic powers or I must be cheating.

'I'm cheating,' I told them. 'Turn the letter-tiles upside down as if you're about to start another game.'

The rosewood tiles were identical in size and shape, about three-quarters of an inch square, but the pattern of the woodgrain on each was completely different. There were only a hundred tiles. It was a doddle to memorise some of these. I showed the girls and they started practising straight away, picking out the high-value 'Q' and the 'Z', then the blank, and after that the 'J' and the 'X'.

Daisy, however, was having none of it; she said it was cheating, not cricket, how dare I, I wasn't a good sport, I ought to be ashamed of myself. She told me to go and find a bag for the Scrabble letters.

I sewed a special little pouch with a drawstsring. There was no more spreading out of the pretty rosewood tiles after that (although the twins enjoyed performing their party trick on unsuspecting guests), and Daisy made do with three-lettered, low-scoring words like 'ant'.

'I have the option of "cant", "pant", "punt" and "cunt",' she said. 'But I like the word "ant". Is it a good word, that's the thing.' She sounded bemused.

No. Nobody, not even the grandchildren, wanted to play Scrabble with Daisy any more. She's a loser, said Tess.

*

By 1971, Daisy's wanderings, without warning, without clothes, had become alarmingly frequent. She called them paideias.

Once, in the village, on market day, she wandered, with clothes on (thank goodness), to Costa's. He led her and her dog back to the square and handed them over to Inez and me.

'Thank you,' said Inez.

'Thank you,' I echoed, which made old Costa punch the air with delight.

'She speaks, she speaks, she continues to speak,' he chanted, walking off, swinging his arms.

Daisy was onto her third dog – some sort of hound-cross called Brel, 'as in Jacques' – and he went everywhere with her, but she'd taken to talking to Brel in a made-up language she called macaroni. Inez said it was pig Latin for schoolchildren. Daisy was often late for meals, and, when she did return, often still wandering in her mind. Instead of answering a question, she might recite a poem, or her lines from one of the plays she'd acted in at her local amateur dramatics club. Theatre was good therapy for her, said Inez. Less good was Daisy's tendency to remember scenes from her past and retell them, apparently verbatim, often at inappropriate moments. Daisy called this memory-laning. Inez said it was attention-seeking. Later we learnt that it was all part and parcel of the illness, her madness.

One afternoon, having missed lunch, Daisy flung open the back door to the kitchen, where I'd just finished gutting a chicken and was giving the sink a good old scrub.

'Kippers and cream, for me,' she said. 'Cake and summer pud too, please.'

It was a warm, sunny afternoon, but Daisy was shivering. There was mud on her skirt, and her hair looked as if she'd been through a hedge backwards. Inez was having a siesta upstairs, and everyone else was at the Ladies' Pond, so I decided to try to calm Daisy myself.

'I'll make tea,' I said.

'Thank you,' said Daisy in a sing-song voice, and went on, 'Yoo-Hoo! Ty-Phoo! Non-u. That's me, these pie day, dee, die-uhs.'

'You and your paideias,' I said, pretending to be more relaxed than I was. 'Don't you think it's time you grew out of them?'

I busied myself with the kettle. Daisy's taste for Ty-Phoo tea, with milk 'plus two', was a result of her spells in hospital. The nurses drank nothing else and the word Ty-Phoo meant doctor in Chinese, she said. I liked the red oblong boxes. As well as tea, they sometimes contained cards – pictures of footballers – which the young *rosbif* boys liked to collect.

Daisy ignored my question and plonked herself down on a chair. She put both her hands into the pan of chicken giblets on the kitchen table and squelched the bloody mess through her fingers.

'What's this?' she said. 'It looks like bits of miscarriage.'

I removed the pan of giblets and put a bowl of fresh water in front of her. She rinsed her hands obediently, then, fingers still dripping, sipped the sweet milky tea I gave her.

'Most of them didn't have fully-formed bodies,' she said, 'my dead babies. And the ones that did, the stillborn – I was never allowed to hold them. I never said goodbye.'

I put the biscuit tin on the table and sat down opposite her.

'I was made to say goodbye to my dead grandmother. Ugh.' Daisy sniffed. 'She smelt of violets and toilets. Mother made me kiss her. We sat up with the body all night, Mother, Margaret and I—'

'Margaret?' I couldn't help interrupting.

'Yes. All three of us. Mother was cross because Margaret didn't get there in time for the actual death throes. She arrived a few hours later. We were waiting for the coffin. All night, Sylvie, our cook, kept popping in with trays of tea, but Mother said Sylvie's tea wasn't a patch on Mathilde's.'

'I'm Mathilde, Daisy. It's me. I'm here,' I said.

'Is that so?' Daisy glanced at me before lifting the lid from the biscuit tin and taking a custard cream. 'Well, you know what they say? Ditsy Daisy. That's me.' She pulled the biscuit in two and licked at the filling.

What else did dizzy, ditsy, round-the-twisty Daisy remember about that night? Not much, was the answer. She said she kept dropping off to sleep. However, I asked her point-blank what she remembered about Margaret, and she did recall Margaret saying that she might nip to Geneva after the funeral, and then Margaret and Beatrice talking about Madame Tissot, Geneva, Dover, Paris, boats, trains, babies and Morzine.

'Babies? Morzine?' I prompted, but this elicited a dreadful, laughing sort of wail.

'Do I sound as if I'm in labour?' said Daisy, stopping the wail abruptly. 'Labour is a paideia the boys won't ever experience. An ugly once told me Morzine is where the local witches come from. Is that what they sound like, do you think? Shall we invite them to tea? Shall we see if they like custard creams?' Daisy took two more biscuits from the tin and dropped both into her teacup. She stabbed at them with her teaspoon.

I could see that she was becoming agitated, but I couldn't quell my desire to ask more about Margaret. Did Margaret mention me? That's what I really wanted to know.

'What else do you remember about your aunt Margaret?' I said. 'Tell me, Daisy. Please try to remember more.'

But Daisy was concentrating on piling bourbon biscuits on top of the custard creams in her teacup. She was clenching her jaw and grinding her teeth. I wouldn't get any more sense out of her. The jaw-clenching and teeth-grinding were bad signs. I decided to fetch Inez from upstairs.

By the time Inez came, Daisy was in an awful state, scratching her arms, making them bleed and tugging at her loose hair as if trying to break it off. Inez made Daisy down four pills, but twenty minutes later she was still agitated, muttering 'Fee Fi Fo Fum' as if conjugating a Latin verb.

Inez suggested a bath.

'It might calm her,' she said. 'It does, sometimes, somewhat.'

Daisy agreed, but only if I agreed to bathe with her.

'Can you face it?' Inez asked me.

I nodded, and Inez said she'd walk over to the Ladies' Pond to see if she could find her brothers or Bob in case we needed reinforcements.

We went to the bath house and I helped Daisy remove her shoes, skirt and shirt. I was shocked at how thin, underneath, her body was.

'I can do it myself,' said Daisy, unclipping her suspenders and rolling her stockings down her legs.

She managed her knickers, but her hands were trembling too much to unhook her bra, and she began to cry. I took off the bra and practically lifted her into the bath, which I'd run warm and deep, noticing, as I did so, the dozens of little different-coloured bruises on Daisy's arse from the hypodermic syringe Inez sometimes had to stick in her that summer.

Daisy sat like a child in the water, with her knees pulled up to her chin and her arms clasped around them.

'Aren't you going to get in, Mathilde?' she asked in a small, flat voice. 'Do as you're told?'

It wasn't a command. There was no beseeching gesture, no attempt to cajole or persuade me. I could have ignored her. Inez would never have known. But Daisy in her madness filled me with pity. All I saw was a waste of an old woman, sick, skinny, sad and needy. She could have been anyone. I took off my clothes and climbed in.

Daisy topped up the hot water and the bath became very full. I stayed sitting, but with my knees apart and my hands on the edges of the tub, to stop myself slipping. Daisy turned round and slid down in the bath so that her head was resting on my belly. She put her hands on my knees and rested her arms along my thighs, letting her legs straighten and float.

'Like lesbians,' said Daisy, wriggling her toes. 'Just as well Grandpa installed such a big bath. All those homo climber-boys.'

Daisy yawned and nestled her head more comfortably into

my belly. She asked me to stroke her hair. I did, although keeping my balance in the bathtub wasn't easy. She asked me to tell her a story. I did. I retold the legend of the golden ibex, and she seemed to like that. The trembling stopped. She knew who I was.

'What about the witches? Tell me about the witches of Morzine.'

I explained that the witches of Morzine had actually happened, and less than a century earlier. They weren't really a legend.

'The snow queen, then. The woman with the sack of white gold. I like that one,' Daisy said. But as soon as I began – 'There's a woman in the sky, high above the mountains in Haute-Savoie' – Daisy interrupted:

'She disappeared,' she said, pushing herself to a sitting position. She swivelled on her arse and faced me, clasping her arms around her knees again.

'Who?'

'Margaret.'

'Yes. Do you know why?' I seized the moment. 'Did you ever find out?'

'Not really.' Daisy frowned, then went on, but there was a lilt of madness in the way she spoke almost conspiratorially: 'I think she might have been preggers, you know, Mathilde. But—'

'What makes you say that?' I said.

'Oh. You know. Things I overheard that night.'

'But can you remember anything specific?' Now I'd started probing, I was loath to stop. 'Come on, Daisy. I bet you can. Think.'

'Of course I can.' Daisy grinned (and I couldn't help admiring her neat English teeth, which seemed to have escaped the ravages of the drug treatments and were as clean and white as ever). She wiggled her feet, making ripples of water which unbalanced me and made my body wobble to the surface. I hooked my elbows onto the sides of the tub and decided to let the rest of me float.

'Go on, then,' I said.

Daisy told me, surprisingly matter-of-factly, she was fairly sure Beatrice had not only helped Margaret through her pregnancy but had also assisted her with plans for the birth and the disposal of the baby.

Me. The temptation to tell Daisy who I was and that we were cousins was enormous, but not as big as the desire to hear what else Daisy might be able to recall.

'They talked about Dover,' she said. 'Saying goodbye there. Margaret getting on the ferry. But then it was Geneva, Morzine and Madame Tissot again, and I'm afraid I couldn't keep my eyelids open any longer.'

Daisy stood up, capsizing me and sending the bath water splashing over the sides.

'Gosh, it's cold,' she said.

I climbed out of the bath and brought Daisy a towel. She was starting to shiver again and she wrapped the towel around her midriff like a kilt.

'We're still best friends, you and I,' she said, clenching her teeth to stop them starting to grind. 'Aren't we?'

'Yes, yes,' I tried to soothe her. 'The best of the best.'

'Don't humour me, Mathilde.' Daisy's switches into brief periods of sanity underlined how lost in madness she was most of the time. 'Don't patronise me. You asked me why Margaret disappeared in 1907. See: I even remember the year. I've told you what I think. She gets herself up the duff – a one-night stand, father irrelevant, he's a cad. Sister Beatrice steps in with advice and practical help, but this doesn't stop their mother, Lady C – old-school, shock-horror – from banishing Margaret, Victorian-style, for ever. That adds up.'

I'd dressed myself while Daisy talked, and I started trying to dress Daisy, but it was just as well Inez returned then with her husband and brother. Daisy's shivers became violent. She began flailing so much that Bob and Rory had to manhandle her up to the bedroom and hold her down while Inez prepared the liquid for the hypodermic syringe.

Daisy sank quickly into a deep sleep, oblivious to the shape she'd given my family history. Her memories didn't add up to much, and not at all in the way she thought they did. She'd got the year wrong, for a start. Dover and so on (and on to my birth) would have been 1900, not 1907. Daisy had tracked matters as far as the ferry to France. I could imagine the scene in Morzine: the *sage-femme*; a wet-nurse – Maman; Madame Tissot making arrangements for the transport of the baby girl (me) to Hext; and the rest. What I couldn't imagine was Margaret – bleeding, sore, tired and empty – making the journey back, alone, to England. Let alone the years that followed – those furtive summer picnics – and then her departure in 1907. Lady C may have banished her in the heat of the moment, but my impression was that Margaret left in a rage and may well have chosen to stay away. As if that was that. It so obviously wasn't, and I couldn't help wondering if Daisy, for all her dizziness, had imagined, sensed or knew some of this too.

*

I only saw Daisy once more – at the 1971 damp squib of a garden party a few days later. Heavy rain stopped play. Heavy rain meant everyone standing around in the smelly marquee, paper plates piled high with Wagon Wheels, Smiths crisps and dollops of butterscotch Angel Delight – all of which I tried, and none of which, compared with the Cadbury's Dairy Milk chocolate *les anglais* still occasionally brought with them, was much to write home about.

The only excitement was the tannoy Rory set up. Everyone wanted a go. But Rory insisted on using it first, to give the traditional Arete thank-you speech. He'd not got further than the usual Valentine platitudes – the beauty of the valley, its many attractions, how Sir A fell in love with it – when Daisy snatched the loudspeaker from him.

'The valley's a vagina,' she said, and the tannoy made the words boom. She repeated the sentence and added, 'If the valley's a vagina, then this is its womb—' She indicated Arete. 'Arete.' 'Arete' boomed.

The *rosbifs* were aghast. The guides were confused. Luc, at Josh's behest, slung Daisy over his shoulder and carried her into the house, not kicking and screaming, but waving her legs and calling merrily, 'Hiya, boys. Hey, ladies. See – I'm riding the golden ibex!'

It was only a week later that the soldiers had to take Daisy down to Hext, and she never came back to Arete after that.

Twenty-Three

The golden ibex could only be sighted during a full moon. The golden ibex could never be sighted during a full moon. The golden ibex could only be sighted during a full moon if, in addition, it was a leap year, if there was an 'm' in the month, if the day fell on the Sabbath.

'When's Thomas due back? Can anyone remember?' George asked at supper one night.

'No, but he promised he'd help with the hunt for gold,' said Isobel.

'He didn't,' said Jack. 'He said he'd help put an end to it, which is different.'

'The hunt for gold?' Inez raised her eyebrows. 'Whose idea was that?'

Jack explained briefly. Later, after the girls had gone to bed, he elaborated to Inez about devising a paideia for the girls based on the map and the ancient rumours of gold. George kept quiet about the 'S' Thomas had drawn on the map; he wanted to see Inez's reaction to the picture map first. But Inez wasn't interested in the actual map. She didn't even ask to see it. Instead, she asked Jack where he'd found it, and when he told her, she said:

'Ah, yes. The empty plan chest in the mazot – empty except for those few old drawings and paintings, that is. After I'd dumped Mummy in Megève, I snooped in there. Hoping to find something, I suppose – something to suggest Mummy wasn't totally cracked. But there was nothing, apart from those pictures. No sign of there ever having been anything, either. Way back, in 1954, when Mummy arrived here with her typewriter and box files and said she was going to write a novel in the mazot, we all so desperately wanted to believe her.' Inez's voice trailed off.

'Box files?' said George. 'Those greenish-grey ones?'

'Yes. Why?'

'They're still here. In the attic.'

'Well, they would be, wouldn't they? I put them there,' said Inez. 'Helped, at least. It was an odd time. We were all hands-on that summer of '54, cleaning the old place up.'

Inez pushed back her chair, stretched, took one of Jack's Disques Bleues, didn't light it.

'The mazot wasn't too bad,' she continued. 'But we decided to move all the old pictures and painting stuff up to the attic anyway. Peggy and I had great plans for the mazot, you see. We'd nearly finished doing that when Mummy arrived. Mathilde set us to work, then, dealing with all the junk in the darkroom under the stairs, and we used some of Mummy's files for storage.'

'You transferred all the junk into the box files?' said George.

'Not all of it. We got rid of the real rubbish. The broken china. Loads of books. An old flower-press. Knick-knacks. And we were organised. Notebooks in one box file, diaries in another, et cetera. I even labelled the files.

'Did you read any of the stuff?' asked George.

'Of course we did. There were some bawdy bits in Sir A's diaries. We were looking forward to reading more. He'd reduced the landscape to tits, slits, clits and cunts. It was side-splittingly funny. Don't look so shocked, George. And we adored his favourite word for bush – fuzzy-muzzy, was it? But we'd just got everything up to the attic when Mathilde called up from the terrace that Luc had arrived with the radiogram.'

'The enormous broken old thing in the games room?' said Jack.

'The very one. We spied him from the little window up there in the attic. He had the radiogram on his back. We watched him lower it onto the terrace. He was naked from the waist up. Strong torso. Brown snakey arms. It was raining. He was sweating. And, oh dear, there we were – Pegs and I peeping out. Can you imagine? It's a very small window. At this poor young man. "This is Luc," Mathilde shouted loudly and proudly. "My son." Whoever would have thought an ugly could produce such a dish? But Peggy and I didn't care where he came from. We couldn't believe our luck. I chucked all the box files into the nearest tea chest and we skedaddled down that ladder and down those stairs as fast as our rock-and-roll legs would carry us.'

*

The election, which took place five days later, on the Sunday, was inconclusive; neither of the two main lists won an absolute majority.

'There'll be another round of voting next Sunday,' said Thomas, who'd accompanied Mathilde back up from Hext where she'd gone, early, to vote, and waited, late, for the result. 'A simple majority wins next time.'

Mathilde was taciturn.

'I'm busy,' she said after breakfast on Monday and went straight to her hut.

'What does she do in there all day?' asked Inez.

'Nothing,' said Thomas. 'She says she's thinking, she's got a difficult decision to make. She's fixated on the election. We're really worried about her. My mother and father talk about little else. I've promised them I'll keep an eye on her until it's all over.'

George was worried too. When he'd passed Costa's message on to Mathilde, she hadn't spoken, but she'd narrowed her eyes and spat on the ground.

'Is that what you think of Costa?' George had asked.

'I don't waste my time thinking of him,' she'd replied.

The light was on late every night in Mathilde's hut, George noticed, and sometimes he saw Thomas leaving the hut in the early hours.

'She's still digging her heels in, then?' George asked Thomas.

Thomas assented. He looked tired, but he didn't complain, and George didn't press for details because he didn't want to spoil the amazing time they were having with Thomas that week.

'No ibex, no gold,' Thomas had said firmly before their first outing with him. 'Sorry, Isobel. I believe in neither, but I promise to show you better than either. Many stories are born in our mountains, partly and very simply because many illusions occur in them. Follow me. I will make disappear, for all of you, *le monde extérieur*.'

Like a magician, slipping into his role as an impeccably trained guide, Thomas led everyone, including Inez, into the mountains behind Arete and, with no map, followed animal tracks and took routes none of them knew about in order to demonstrate countless quirks of perspective, conundrums of the light, tricks of the time of day.

They climbed to the glacier near the lac de la Miche. It had receded, Thomas said, because of last year's – and now this year's – unusually warm weather. They walked along its ridge, where the snow, which should have been inches thick, even in the summer, was thin and patchy – except in the shadowed gullies where it had slopped on top of hard-packed ice in wet and heavy, ugly grey blobs. They abseiled down rocks, sat by the lake and watched, as the sun set, how the south col turned orange, then blood red.

'Look,' said Thomas, 'at the little corridor to the west of the col. If an ibex walked through there now, he would be golden, as sure as eggs are eggs.'

By the end of the week, there wasn't much, George felt, he didn't know about alpine weather phenomena, including will-o'-the-wisps and sun dogs – both oddly named; Brocken spectres – spooky; and what he and Ma used to call fairy dust, but was actually just tiny frozen particles of moisture drifting, rainbow-coloured, in the cold, sunny air.

Ibex, chamois, stag, deer, roebuck: all left different tracks and different shits, many of which George learnt to recognise. Stoat, snow hare and ptarmigan: they didn't actually see any of these, but Thomas drew their footprints in the snow and described how their coats changed colour from ruddy browns and greys to a winter camouflage of white. Whistling marmots were nothing new, but whistling with them, or to them, as Thomas did, made George aware how close to nature Thomas remained, despite all his know-how. George realised, on a much deeper level than before, what an extraordinary privilege it was to be guided by him. He himself was immeasurably stronger than he'd been at the beginning of the summer, and Jack, athletic and agile, had grown up with the land around Arete as his summer playground, but not even Jack moved among the alps with the same ease, dignity and grace as Thomas.

'You look like some sort of snowbird,' said Isobel, having watched Thomas take a flying leap from a narrow precipice to a tiny buttress of rock.

'I'm not a fan of birds,' said Thomas. 'They make me think, always, of carrion.'

Nevertheless, he knew the names of all the birds they observed, pointing out buzzards by the dozen, yellow-billed choughs and even an eagle owl, which Thomas called *le grand duc* – a large-headed, round-bodied, aloof, mysterious thing with the biggest wingspan George had ever seen. It gave a haunting, nasal, barking call as it glided east, away from the evening sun, its wings seemingly tipped – another illusion – with gold.

*

Later that evening, when the girls were in bed and Thomas was again with Mathilde in her hut, Inez suggested Scrabble, and because there was a very slight chill in the air, they played it indoors at the kitchen table. They'd almost finished the game,

George was winning, Jack was losing, but all three of them were close, when Inez used her valuable 'X' on a triple-letter score, making the word 'sexy' and overtaking both Jack and George, effectively ending the game.

'So what does make them so sexy, these mountain guides and ski instructors?' Inez said, folding the Scrabble board and tipping the letters from it into the worn old hand-sewn pouch Jack held open for her. 'Tell me.'

'Thomas, you mean?' said Jack 'You think he's sexy?'

George couldn't believe that Jack and his mother were discussing such a matter so openly.

'Maybe sexy's not the right word.' Inez frowned. 'But attractive sounds too feeble. They do attract, though, don't they? And not only us weak and feeble women.'

'Maybe it's really primitive,' said Jack. 'Cavemen stuff. Their strength and knowledge. Our utter reliance on them. If the world were a kingdom of alps, blokes like Thomas would be the overlords.'

'Conduits,' said George, surprising himself. 'They don't just protect us, they lead us. You could say,' he added shyly, 'they educate us.'

'You're getting carried away now.' Inez laughed. 'You're making them sound like gods. It's probably just the uniform. Not many women can resist a man in uniform, can they? And it's those bums of theirs – sculpted. Small but hard and contoured.'

'Like the land,' said Jack.

George snickered and tried to cover it up by coughing.

'I don't think it's the uniform,' Jack went on. 'Because it's not only the guides, is it? Luc has it too, whatever it is, doesn't he? Come on, Inez, Mater, you've admitted you and your girlfriends all fancied him something rotten.'

'Sir A tries to describe it in his diaries, I think,' George offered. 'It all boiled down to arete for him, though. I think he called Xavier the embodiment of arete.'

'And Xavier's wife was the embodiment of charity.' Inez laughed at her own joke. 'She opened her legs for Sir A plenty of times after Xavier disappeared, by all accounts.'

'No, I don't think so.' George was still horribly self-conscious, but he was enjoying the conversation now he could contribute properly. 'I've read Sir A's diary entries for those years and they honestly don't suggest anything untoward happened.'

'Lady C seemed to think it did, but maybe she was just a super-jealous, possessive, paranoid woman,' said Jack.

'Yes. And the rumours in the valley could well have been just that,' Inez added. 'Rumours. We know how the villagers loved – still do love – making up stories about us. *Les anglais*, the English, *les rosbifs* – you still hear them mutter that, like an incantation, under their breath occasionally.'

'Xavier had a son.' George recalled the mention of Paul in the diaries and the fact that Paul was not going to be allowed to follow in Xavier's footsteps to become a guide. 'He wasn't a guide, was he?'

'Tall Paul?' said Inez. 'No. You're right. He wasn't. I think he was an engineer. He worked away from the valley a lot of the time. But I suspect he was up there with the best of them when it came to arete. He taught my grandmother, Beatrice, and her sister, Margaret, when they were still girls – so this must have been the late 1880s – to mountaineer properly. "Like men," I remember her saying proudly. They used to wear trousers underneath their great, long, heavy skirts. But they would remove the skirts as soon as they were out of sight and hide them under a rock.'

'That sounds pretty straightforwardly sexy to me,' said Jack.

'It probably was sexy, but feeling free – for the first time in your life, or for a few hours in your life – is probably pretty damn sexy too.'

Inez sounded sharper than George was used to, and it reminded him of Ma and her sometimes sharp, chauvinist-pig comments. 'You and your women's lib,' Da would mumble when she ranted. But 'I stand corrected', he'd say and raise an eyebrow quizzically at George.

'I think I'll turn in.' George said his goodnights quickly.

Ma and Da had been on his mind more than usual because A level results were due the next day, Thursday 19th August. George lay in bed and visualised the school office and piles of unopened envelopes on the secretary's desk. If it hadn't been for the accident, he and Graham would have gone into school together to pick up their results. As it was, George thought grumpily – and immediately guiltily – he would have to wait for the envelope he'd addressed to himself, Poste Restante, Hext.

*

On Sunday 22nd August, at the second round of the municipal election, the list with Luc's name on it won by a narrow margin, and a new council was formed.

'It only remains for the council to vote for a leader – the mayor – now,' said Thomas. 'The outcome, I think, is a foregone conclusion.'

'When will they do that?' asked George, who'd only eight more days before his stay at Arete came to an end.

'It has to be within a week. They're saying market day, Thursday. In the evening.'

Mathilde, grim-faced, withdrew to her hut and stayed there. Thomas knocked regularly on the door with bread and soup, coffee and tartines. She took the tray from him, Thomas said, but she didn't utter a word.

*

On Monday, Thomas roped them together and led them halfway up the little Loo. They ate lunch on a ledge overlooking Arete. Jack flicked a small shard of rock over the side of the ledge and suggested a paideia.

'Let's see if any of us can hit the roof of the house with a stone.'

'Don't be silly,' said George in alarm. 'We could slip. It's far too dangerous.'

To George's relief, Thomas agreed, which miffed Jack.

'Mind you,' Inez said, 'my grandmother, Beatrice, the one I was telling you about, she used to scale these rocks, alone, apparently, well into middle age with not a harness or rope in sight.'

'Climbing has changed,' said Thomas. 'Partly because the climbers have changed. There are more of you, but you have less expertise.'

That probably miffed Jack too.

On Tuesday, they went to the Ladies' Pond. Inez brought out a Polaroid camera and the girls amused themselves taking photos of each other posing like film stars in and around the water. Jack devised swimming competitions, which Thomas kept winning. Jack pretended not to care, but George could tell that he did.

In the late afternoon, they looped the long way back to Arete via the Chamonix fork and Hext-en-Haut.

'Here, I think,' said Thomas, pausing by Jack's 2CV and looking across the valley, 'is where your little map becomes a picture.'

'What are you talking about?' said Jack.

'Did you not show them how I added the Ouiffre to your little picture map?' Thomas asked George. 'Putting an end to the hunt for gold?'

'No,' said George. 'I didn't.' George didn't think of himself as a secretive chap by nature, but he realised that he'd become a bit of a snooper in the last couple of months, and was fairly notching up the number of things he'd chosen to keep to himself. He had intended to tell the others about the map, but what with Inez's arrival and the expeditions led by Thomas, he hadn't got round to it.

Jack's nose was well and truly out of joint now – with George for withholding evidence, as he put it, and with Thomas for not having run his teeny-weeny, tinsy-winsy theory past him, Jack, first.

On Wednesday, they went to the lac de la Miche with the intention of building a raft, but the water level had gone down so much since their last visit, it would have been pointless. Instead, they mucked around in the lower nooks and crannies of the rocks there, sharing Inez's Polaroid camera again, daring each other to jump across cracks and ravines. After lunch, Jack began to show off, climbing higher and faster than George could keep up with, suggesting impossible paideias to the girls, debating with Thomas, sometimes quite aggressively, about the best route to follow.

'Here! Thomas! Take my photo!' Jack, kneeling on a dangerous-looking overhang, chucked the camera – too hard – down to Thomas below. The camera flew past Thomas's head and bounced along the craggy rock face before disappearing down a gully.

Jack was repentant; they all joined forces and spent the rest of the morning and most of the afternoon searching in vain for the camera.

Late in the afternoon on Wednesday, they climbed behind the Rochers de la Miche to the summit of the grand Luet. Mont Blanc was visible from there, and the chains of mountains on either side stretching in a white and blue-green shimmer as far as the eye could see.

'A pig's ear,' said Thomas, nodding at Mont Blanc. 'That's what my grandmother says it looks like.'

'The snow on it's all smooth and shiny,' said Isobel.

Silk purse, thought George automatically.

'Yes, soapy,' said Thomas. 'From the top layer melting and refreezing all through the summer. Soapy snow is bad snow. Unstable.'

Thomas remained standing with his knee bent and his foot on the highest point of the ridge. He was silhouetted against the sky. One hand was placed lightly on the coil of rope he always carried, slung diagonally from shoulder to waist. The other hand rested on his bent knee. Leather boots, woollen socks, cotton twill breeches, thick knitted jumper, sunglasses and his guide's cap defined him as a man – and a very fine young man too – yet, George thought, Thomas still seemed almost a part of the landscape. The rest of them, George included – milling around, glancing in all directions, gawping at the views, exclaiming at the chasm below them – did not.

Thomas was no longer looking at Mont Blanc, but along and down the precipitous, unclimbable side of the ridge towards the lac de la Miche.

'There's a split in the rock face. Do you see?' He pointed. 'We missed it earlier when we were searching the rocks only from the lake-side. We will return to search there tomorrow for your camera, Inez, yes?'

*

A telegram from Megève was waiting for Inez when they got back to Arete. It asked her to ring Daisy's consultant urgently.

Jack winked at George, but George didn't think it was a winking matter.

'Too late for tonight. I'll go down first thing,' said Inez.

'I'll go with you,' said George. 'My A level envelope might have arrived.'

George slept slightly later than usual the next morning, however, and found Inez had left without him.

After breakfast, Thomas, Jack and the girls set off for la Miche. George cheerioed them, then prepared for his own departure. He should tidy up a bit. Without Mathilde scurrying round, the place was a tip. He decided at least to bring all the dirty bowls, glasses and ashtrays into the kitchen from the terrace and the games room. The little picture map was buried under two half-full wine glasses and a sticky beer mug on the billiard table. It was stained and had lost a corner. He laid it on the kitchen table. As he laced up his walking boots, George wondered whether to knock on the door of Mathilde's hut. He assumed she'd be going down to the village for the result of the mayoral vote, so perhaps he should ask her if she wanted to walk with him now, or wait for Thomas, later.

However, as he came out onto the terrace, he glanced up and saw Mathilde at the open attic window.

'What are you doing, Mathilde? How on earth did you get up there?'

Mathilde didn't answer immediately. George stared. Her little head, framed by the window with its shutters under the wide, upside-down 'V' of the wooden eaves, made her look, for a moment, like a cuckoo in a cuckoo clock.

'Needs must,' Mathilde said, enunciating the words clearly and firmly. 'I need to make my decision this morning. About Luc. I thought I'd look again, up here, for the missing letter. Then, with or without it, I will decide.'

George decided not to argue with her; she might really be going senile, as Jack had said.

'Fine, but how will you get down? I can't stay to help you. I'm sorry. Not today. I need to get to the post office.'

'I will wait for Thomas. Please don't worry, George.'

That seemed fair enough. Thomas had said they wouldn't be more than a couple of hours. So, with only a flicker of anxiety, George set off.

He was tramping across the high pastures, noticing how dry the earth had become since June and how sparse the grass – he'd heard Thomas say some farmers were considering bringing their cows down the mountain early, before the usual festive, whole-village descent at the end of September – when he met Costa.

'I'm on my way to talk to Mathilde,' said Costa without preamble.

'What? You're going all the way up to Arete?' George couldn't help sounding surprised. Costa looked quite spry, but he must be a good deal older than Mathilde.

'You think I am too much on my last legs?' Costa sounded amused. 'You underestimate the health-giving effects of our mountain air, I think, George.'

'But Mathilde will be coming down to the village later. Why not wait?'

'Luc will be mayor later.' Costa spoke seriously, suddenly. 'Although I helped vote him onto the council, I am aware that he has chosen the future over the past, and I understand what that will mean to Mathilde. It is the right choice, I believe, but it will leave Mathilde behind. I think she will feel very alone. We were close once, Mathilde and I. I wish to show her she is not alone. She does not need to be alone.'

'I'd be surprised if she thanks you for it,' George said, thinking about the recent spitting incident.

'Yes, I doubt she will. She probably won't talk to me at all. But I'm used to that, so what have I to lose? I've made up my mind to try.' With that, Costa nodded goodbye and continued along the track to Arete.

*

In Hext, the market had spilled into the roads around the square. It was the last summer market before *la rentrée* and it was busier than usual. George practically had to barge his way through to the post office, where he joined a long queue. The talk in the queue was all to do with the resignation of Chirac and would it affect how the council voted for their leader, the mayor? And Chirac aside, would the new municipal council fund repairs to the church, flip-up cinema seats in the *salle des fêtes*, litter bins outside the train station? No one seemed in any doubt that by seven o'clock that evening, Luc would be mayor.

The postmistress demanded to see George's passport, then handed him two letters.

'Both arrived this morning. You're lucky,' she said.

'Thank you,' said George.

'Not so lucky, Madame – your aunt – earlier.'

'Oh?'

'No.' The postmistress beckoned George closer. 'Bad news. A death. I don't listen to telephone conversations, but Madame was very upset. A family matter, I think. Perhaps you know something?'

'No.'

'Madame asked me where she could rent a car. Nowhere in Hext, I told her. But she was extremely insistent. You could try the Gauthier garage, I said in the end.'

'Thank you,' said George again.

He hurried to the Gauthier garage, where the mechanic confirmed that they'd lent Madame Inez a car to drive to Megève, where Madame Daisy, *la propriétaire* d'Arete, had, sadly, deceased.

George moved unthinkingly back to the village square, which was still thronged with people. He saw Luc and his supporters outside the Auberge Dorée. George's A level results were in his hand, but he didn't open the envelope until he'd walked away from Hext, not realising he'd automatically set off up the road to Hext-en-Haut until he stopped by the cemetery.

Maths, English and French – an A and two Bs. George opened the letter from Graham – three A's. But the main news from Graham, apart from the heatwave, was Krisztina: the music she liked, the clothes she wore, the things that made her laugh – 'You could say we're an item.' Big Ben still hadn't got going again. George didn't know it had stopped. 'See you in a couple of French weeks.' In fact, George was due back in Reading in five days' time.

He looked at the envelopes in his hand: Graham's cheerful scrawl and his own writing, small, like Da's, italicky, like Ma's. Da would have been pleased with the A. Ma would have tried to hide her disappointment with the Bs. She might have made a roast supper. Da would have rustled up some plonk, and they'd have toasted him, 'To you, George. Cheers. To the future.'

'George! George!'

George looked up to see the twins hurtling down the road towards him. He almost instinctively started running towards them.

'What is it?' he yelled.

'Accident! Jack! And Thomas!'

The girls were so out of breath when they reached George that it took a moment to get any sense out of them. Jack had jumped, missed his footing, slipped. Thomas had climbed down to help him.

'Then they both just kept sliding away.'

The girls shook and stuttered.

'Stopping and starting, but sliding further and further away all the time.'

'Until we couldn't see them any more. Just hear them. Thomas moaning. Jack was shouting that he was okay, but kept telling us to hurry and get help for Thomas—'

'Where's Isobel?' George interrupted, a horrific thought crossing his mind.

'We told her to go back to Arete and get you or Mathilde. We've run all the way down from la Miche, via the Chamonix col, not via Arete. We thought it'd be quicker.'

'It is. Much,' said George. 'You did the right thing. Now, can you describe exactly where Jack and Thomas are?'

'It's where Thomas pointed to yesterday. That gash in the rock he saw.'

'All right,' George said. 'You go on down to the village. Make sure someone alerts the rescue services. See if Luc is still at the Auberge Dorée. He'll know what to do. If he's not there, tell the landlord, anyone, it doesn't matter, just make sure you get help. Lickety-split. Off you go.'

*

George hurried up to Hext-en-Haut and on and up, steadying his steps, as Thomas had taught him, to the rhythm of his breathing, onwards and upwards, through the forest. He'd just come out onto the rocky Plateau des Bergers when he heard someone behind him. He turned round to see Luc tearing up the track.

'George. I'm not going to stop. I'll be there before the rescue services. Please hurry, though. I might need your help.'

He jogged off. He wasn't as elegant as his son, but Luc made running at high altitude, after a climb of nearly a thousand feet, look a cinch.

George continued up and along the path as quickly as he could. When he reached la Miche, he saw Luc and Mathilde already at the site of the accident. Luc directed George to stand opposite him, next to Mathilde, on the other side of a narrow crevasse.

'Jack's all right, I think.' Luc said. 'Lower Mathilde's rope to him, George, and he should be able to climb it. Thomas is injured. He's much further down than Jack.'

George immediately lifted the heavy coil of rope over his head and began to unwind it.

'This side,' said Luc, 'here, where I am, is less dangerous. I've been down once, already, to see to Thomas. I will descend again now you are here.'

He levered himself over the edge of the crevasse.

George knelt down.

'Jack?' he called. 'Can you hear me?'

'Here, old boy.' Jack's voice was weak, muffled and distant. 'I'm freezing.'

'We're going to drop a rope down, Jack,' said George. 'Ready?'

Mathilde knelt next to George and looked over the edge.

'Take your boots and socks off, Jack,' she said.

The rope stayed slack for ages, and they could hear Jack fumbling about and groaning. Eventually, though, it tautened and Jack began to haul himself slowly up.

'My arm,' they heard him mutter. 'I can't use one arm.'

Mathilde remained kneeling, urging Jack to feel the rock face with the skin of his bare feet.

'Feel it as if it's another body,' she said. 'Man, woman, child, beast, bird, fish. Any jut will do. Use your feet. It will take the weight off your arm.'

George found himself counting slowly, in twos, under his breath, while Mathilde continued with her words of encouragement. He'd just reached fifty, when a head of brown curly hair, streaked with blood, appeared.

They hauled Jack over the edge, and Mathilde wrapped a blanket round his shoulders.

'Blasted Valentine flappers,' said Jack, looking at his bare feet. 'But thank you, Mathilde. It helped.'

No one spoke after that. Mathilde made a sling for Jack's arm with her shawl and tried to get him to sip water from a flask she'd brought. There was no sign of Luc, but they could hear below them a deep, muted crooning, like a mother soothing an upset child. 'Like his Uncle Henri used to,' George heard Mathilde murmur.

*

A noise above them made George look up, expecting to see a helicopter. But the noise, which seconds earlier had been a vague fluttering, became suddenly much louder – rushing and thundery. Snow was rolling in small, powdery waves down the ridge towards them.

The ridge was an almost vertical drop at the top, and avalanches tumbled from it like waterfalls, but then they hit the jagged rocks below which split, spread and sped them up.

A wave of churning snow hit George.

He floated. He waited. There should have been an impact. A car windscreen. But he, Ma and Da – all three, painlessly, in tiny broken pieces – were already floating on the other side of the glass, suspended in the air above the A303. George wanted to stay there like that, with them, for ever.

'Bloody hell, Ma!' he called out. 'Da! Don't go.'

His words disappeared into the white silence.

When he opened his eyes, George saw that the mini-avalanche had deposited him next to Mathilde on the grass at the bottom of the chain of rocks. Jack was lying face down, a few feet away.

At last. The helicopter. George hadn't heard it come or seen it land, but there it was at the far end of the lake. Two figures were moving around it, carrying a stretcher.

*

As the helicopter rose above the rochers de la Miche, it tilted, and George saw, very briefly, through the window, a line of bare, black rock along the top of the ridge where the soapy snow had slid and lathered into dozens of small avalanches that, in joining forces, had become lethal.

*

George and Mathilde were discharged from the hospital in Sallanches the next day, Friday. George had some nasty cuts and was bruised in the oddest of places, and they said he'd been very mildly concussed. Mathilde, astonishingly, was as right as rain, and they only kept her in overnight because of her age.

Luc picked them both up from the hospital in the Land Rover. Inez, he said, was in a hotel in Sallanches and had told him George would be welcome there too.

'What about the girls? Where's Isobel? The twins?' asked George in alarm.

'Safe and sound with Inez, at the hotel. Apparently Costa brought Isobel down to Hext and looked after her and the other two, until my wife was able to drive them here. There's nothing to worry about. I can take you to the hotel or you can return to Arete'

'I'd better get back to Arete,' said George. 'I've no clothes or anything with me, and besides, I'm due to set off back to England in a couple of days. I'll need to pack.'

'That's fine,' said Luc. 'You can always change your mind. I or my wife will be glad to give you a lift. And here's the telephone number of the hotel.' He handed George a printed card.

While he drove to Hext, Luc told George and Mathilde what he'd managed to piece together from Jack about the accident.

They'd been mucking about by the crevasse when Jack tried to jump across it. He slipped and fell. Thomas climbed down to help him and fell further. The crevasse, Luc said, was new.

'New?'

'Not actually new. Newly revealed. The opening, which is very narrow anyway, must have had a plaque of old ice covering it until recently. Until this summer, probably. When the ice melted, it will have dislodged the rocks underneath.'

'How far down does it go?' asked George.

'A long way.' Luc sounded tense. 'Jack was lucky.'

Jack had a broken arm, a dislocated shoulder and, from the mini-avalanche which had sent him, George and Mathilde flying, a fractured femur. He was in traction and, according to Luc, giving the nurses hell, which George took to be a good sign.

Thomas, in falling, had hit his head and lost consciousness. He'd come round last night, but one of his legs was totally mangled – knee smashed, shin broken, skin and muscle so ripped on his foot that several bones were poking right out, apparently. There was talk of amputation. They were going to operate later that day to try to save what they could. Thomas also, Luc said, had some frostbite.

George found the latter hard to imagine. The weather was as hot and sunny as ever – he was glad to be sitting by the window in the Land Rover – and the valley and the village of Hext were the same as ever, except that, as they approached Hext-en-Haut,

George saw three helicopters in the sky to the south. They looked like hovering birds of prey waiting to plunge for carrion.

'What are they doing, still there?' he said.

Luc parked the Land Rover next to the 2CV and switched off the engine.

'There was a second avalanche,' he said. 'After all of us were safe. Much bigger. The first one missed the crevasse by inches, but not the second one.'

'But I don't understand. We were all safe by then. You just said so.'

'There was a body, George. Even further down than Thomas. Thomas landed on a ledge where the crevasse opened out. But below that it narrowed again. There was ice, rocks, old compacted snow. But while I waited with Thomas I saw through a gap, between the debris. There was a body.'

George kept his hand on the Land Rover's door handle and looked again at the helicopters circling in the sky.

'He, it . . . the body,' Luc went on, 'was at least another twenty feet away. Down. They won't be able to get it out. Not now. Snow from the avalanche will have filled up the crevasse. And most of the snow will have solidified – as hard as concrete. They had to try, though.'

'Could it be Xavier?' George asked. 'After all these years? Sir A's guide. Is that possible, do you think?'

Luc turned in the driver's seat, put his forearm on the steering wheel and answered solemnly.

'In all honesty, George, I don't know if that's possible. It could have been anyone. The route is frequented by hikers from Chamonix, tourists, day trippers even, nowadays. Could Xavier's body have lain there for more than a hundred years so preserved? I don't know. However—' Luc paused and reached for something underneath the seat. 'Near the ledge where Thomas was lying, I found this.' He passed George a short piece of frayed rope.

'It's an old hemp hawser-laid rope,' Luc said. 'The sort they used in the last century.'

George held the rope and looked at it.

'Do you see the thin red strand running the length of it?' Luc asked.

'Yes.'

'Ha!' exclaimed Mathilde, who'd been quiet for most of the journey. 'The bloody Alpine Club!'

'Yes,' Luc explained to George. 'The red strand is the Alpine Club hallmark – a guarantee, in those days, of quality in a rope.'

'So it must have belonged to Sir A,' said George. 'It must surely have been Xavier down there?'

'Not necessarily,' Luc said. 'And we'll never know now. Keep the rope, though, why don't you? Will you be all right walking up to Arete alone? I'm driving my mother home to the farm now, but I could return—'

'No. I'll be all right,' said George, aware that Luc was keen to get back to the hospital as soon as possible.

As he climbed out of the Land Rover and was about to shut the door, he heard Mathilde ask Luc, 'What colour was it, the body? I've always wondered about the colour of frozen skin.'

And Luc's reply:

'What a question, Maman. I don't know. Butterscotch? Caramel? There was an odd lustre to it, like gold.'

*

At Arete, George cleared up the kitchen, put the little picture map back where it came from, swept the whole of the ground floor and tidied away the books and games, boots and walking gear. But then he mooched. With no one else there and nothing to distract him, the place teemed with memories. Ma and Da were everywhere. It was as if the flies on the projector lens had become the film itself. George didn't recall reading about this as a stage of grief in the leaflet he'd been given: Ma and Da seemed real, alive; he could have talked to them, touched them if he'd wanted to. There was Ma, in the kitchen, breaking the knob-end off a baguette – 'best bit,' she always claimed. There she was on the terrace, writing postcards – 'such a bore'. And there was Da, also on the terrace, but it was night-time; he and George were taking it in turns to look at the stars and planets through the telescope George had been given for his eighth birthday. There were a few clouds and only a pale quarter-moon, but enough light to see the outline of the mountains opposite, like the staggered, panicked trace of a heartbeat. 'I'm a mathematician, not a poet,' Da had said. 'An atheist, a rational man, but it does make me wonder sometimes, George, this place, this tucked-away part of the world that most people have never heard of. The hanging valley of Hext – such a strange isosceles triangle of land, nominally French, but infused with Swiss prettiness and Italian passion – it stirs one so inexplicably, doesn't it?'

George was due to catch *le petit train* to Geneva on Monday at midday, but he didn't start packing until Sunday evening due to all his solitary mooching, which, late on Sunday afternoon, turned into weeping and wailing. He'd been sitting in Sir A's stargazing chair on the terrace, trying to finish the Dick Francis he'd started at the beginning of the summer, when a breeze ruffled the pages. He looked up and saw, to the north of la Concierge, pale mauve clouds like jellyfish, moving slowly eastwards. Could it be raining in Geneva? He gazed at the small mountain, guarding the valley and around whose womanly contours he'd be chugging in less than twenty-four hours. Suddenly, George didn't want to leave. At Arete he felt connected: to place, people, family, himself. He was worried about Jack and desperately hoped they'd stay in touch – he'd come to enjoy his cousin's company very much. Thank goodness Mathilde hadn't been injured, but he was terrified that Thomas would lose a limb, or worse. And he was overwhelmed at the thought of how alone in the world he himself would be from now on. George lifted his knees to his chest, hugged them and rocked back and forth in Sir A's stargazing chair, allowing grief to wash through him as he heard himself emit long, primitive sounds, watery and heaving.

George sobbed until the sun sank behind la Concierge and the slight wind began to make him shiver. Ma had been wrong; no one had all the time in the world. Exhausted, he dragged himself upstairs to pack. He pulled his suitcase out from under the bed. As soon as he opened it, he saw at the bottom the photo he'd meant to give to Inez. Bugger.

George set off from Arete early on Monday morning, just as it had started to rain. He bumped his suitcase down the mountain and lugged it to the train station, where he asked the ticketmaster to keep an eye on it for him. He kept the knapsack he'd taken from the darkroom.

George hotfooted it to the post office and was first through the door when it opened at nine o'clock. He rang Luc first. Luc's wife answered: Luc had already left for Sallanches, Thomas's operation had been a success, no amputation, a long convalescence; yes, she'd give Thomas George's regards; she was on the night-shift at the hospital later, so she'd drop in to see Jack too, yes, of course. George was speechless with relief for a moment, but found the words to thank her. He asked her to thank Luc, and she said she would.

Next, George rang the number Luc had given him of the hotel in Sallanches where Inez was staying with the girls. After they'd all said their hellos, and the oh-my-Gods and how-are-yous were over and Inez had briefly filled George in about Daisy's death – 'It was a quiet death, in the end, they said' – George explained to Inez about the photo and apologised for forgetting to give it to her.

'It's a lovely thought, darling. Fab of you. The thing is, from your description we've already got that pic, I think. So really – don't worry about it.'

They said their goodbyes and George paid and walked quickly out of the post office. He slung his jacket and knapsack over his shoulder and headed along the road to the bridge across the Ouiffre and up the track, which he'd never followed before, but which he knew led to Mathilde's farm. As he climbed, he noticed how the air, as well as being heavy with damp, had a whiff of woodsmoke already. Alpine summers were short. George thought about all the logs that would soon need to be cut to replenish all the woodpiles in the valley, ready for the winter months ahead.

The door to the farmhouse was open, so George knocked and entered.

The room he found himself in was smaller and darker than he'd envisaged. He could see that Mathilde had all mod cons: washing machine, fridge and a white stove with overhead grill stood in a row at the far end of the room, and, on a glass-topped, chrome-legged stand next to the fireplace, there was a large old-fashioned telly. And yet the decor was dull. Even the flowery plastic tablecloth which covered the small table in the kitchen-corner was a swirl of murky green and brown, and the wall of books opposite the fireplace was almost invisible owing to the lack of light over there and most of the books being old hard-backs with faded spines. A good smell, however, came from the stove and George could see a pan on the electric hob and hear it simmering.

He walked towards the narrow staircase beyond the telly, intending to coo-ee upstairs, but his attention was caught by the photos on the mantelpiece. They were in chrome frames and were of Luc winning skiing contests, the trophy held high above his head, still on his skis, still holding his ski poles, but holding them triumphantly, almost horizontal, almost like wings; Luc graduating as a teacher; Luc's wedding; Luc with a tiny – two-year-old? – Thomas between his legs, Thomas on what looked like home-made wooden skis; Thomas winning skiing contests; Thomas on a school trip standing next to the Eiffel Tower; Thomas in his guide's uniform.

George hadn't heard any sounds from upstairs. He gave a shout, but there was no answer. He was heading back towards the front door when something caught his eye on the bookshelves – a flash, as a flash of sunshine appeared and disappeared between a momentary, slight thinning in the clouds. It was a carriage clock. George looked more closely. The glass was missing and the tip of the big hand had broken off. It was one of quite a few items arranged decoratively in front of the books. There were pebbles and twigs, a piece of bark, a pine cone, the tiny, dried honeycomb-head of some plant, a miniature metal Eiffel Tower, a miniature wooden animal, which looked like an ibex except it scarcely had horns and, most surprising of all, a very old tube ticket, Gower Street to Edgware Road.

The ticket was propped against a book called *A Handbook of English Idioms* on a shelf consisting mostly of French classics and school textbooks. George was startled to see, on the one above, Macaulay's *History of England*, Hume, Locke, John Stuart Mill and a weighty tome called *The Nemesis of Faith* by James Froude sitting alongside several volumes of poetry, which he didn't have time to look at because he heard footsteps, and when he turned round an old woman was standing at the door. She was clutching a handful of green beans.

'I'm sorry,' said George to the woman he didn't recognise. 'I'm looking for Mathilde. Is this not where she lives?'

'It is where she lives. I'm Angélique. Twice a day I come to make sure Mathilde is well. I brought her a stew.' The woman indicated the stove. 'I was fetching some haricots.' She indicated the beans in her hand. 'And I will help her clean and tidy in the morning. Luc told my son about the accident. My God.'

'Where is she now?'

'At the haybarn. Sortilège. She said she wanted to enjoy the fresh air. I told her she sounded like an English tourist, the air is fresh everywhere here, but go ahead, I said. Climb up there, I said, get wet, tire yourself out. Then come back down – I'll have a good rich stew ready for you.'

'How far away is it, the haybarn?' asked George. 'Is it easy to find?'

'That depends,' said Angélique. 'By the track, easy but a long time – fifty minutes. Straight up, through the woods, not so easy, no real track, but much quicker – half an hour. L'Espérance, Torchebise, Chez Quiquet, La Tataz . . . Sortilège is after that. She didn't take the key – we have to lock up, these days – so you'll see her outside, probably.'

Half an hour later, having found a sort of path marked by crossed twigs, George was taking off his knapsack and sitting down next to Mathilde on the warm bench in the recessed area of her weather-beaten haybarn. The woody recess smelt damp and also, it seemed to George, of pee. There was graffiti on one of the walls, a paint-sprayed blur. The wall closest to the bench was bleached smooth and almost silver from the sun. It was covered in scribbled names and messages, signs and doodles; initials were gouged out; there was a flower, a phallus, a face with specs and a moustache.

'I've come to say goodbye, Mathilde,' George said.

'Thank you, George. You've a long journey ahead. Geneva to Paris, to Calais, to Victoria station, London. Via Dover. I've frequently tried to imagine it. And the house in Seymour Place. Four storeys tall. Five if you count the basement.'

'That was years ago, Mathilde. I've never lived in London. Seymour Place was where Sir A lived.'

'I know, George, I know. I'm memory-laning. Will there be someone to meet you when you reach Victoria station, or will you have to catch a little train home, like here, to Hext?'

George smiled, wondering what Mathilde would make of British Rail, let alone the London Underground.

'I think my friend Graham and his dad will pick me up from Victoria in their car.'

The prospect of returning to England with no family to speak of, to an empty house, and then packing up again for university was daunting, but George didn't feel as panicked and unable to imagine the future as he had at the beginning of the summer.

'Graham's my best friend,' he explained to Mathilde.

He saw himself in the front seat of Graham's dad's Vauxhall, Graham jabbering away in the back about everything George had missed as his dad negotiated the streets of west London: taking a left into the Cromwell Road, grumbling at all the red traffic lights, then eventually accelerating along the elevated dual carriageway beyond the Chiswick flyover, where it turned into the M4 and Reading wasn't signposted, but Staines, Slough and the West were. Home in half an hour.

'Home, James, and don't spare the horses,' Ma or George often used to say at this point and all three of them, Ma, Da and George, found it funny every time.

'Yes, you've a long journey ahead of you,' Mathilde repeated and put her small, gnarled, scarred hand on George's arm. 'But you are not alone. You have friends. And you have family. Remember that.'

They talked about the change in the weather and Mathilde said she thought thunderstorms were on their way. The air, she said, was heavy and charged.

They talked about the accident. Mathilde described how Isobel had arrived at Arete, 'Like a bat out of hell. She was quite hysterical. Lucky Costa was there. I set off immediately to la Miche, leaving him to calm her and take her down to the village.'

They talked about Daisy. Mathilde knew that Daisy was dead, but none of the detail.

'How did she kill herself?' she asked.

'Actually, in the end, she didn't. She died peacefully, they said. She had a cough. She'd had it for ages. She was a smoker, so no one took much notice. It got suddenly worse and when they did X-rays, they found she was riddled with cancer, must have been for some time, apparently.'

'Poor Daisy. Upstaged even in death,' said Mathilde. 'She so longed for the limelight, even – especially perhaps – as a girl.'

As to the election, Mathilde knew more than George, who hadn't given it much thought in the last few days, and Luc hadn't mentioned it.

'Luc jokes that Thomas didn't need to go to such lengths to please his grandmother and stop his papa becoming mayor. The mayor cannot be elected in absentia,' Mathilde explained. 'Luc will be on the municipal council, but he will not lead it.'

'And the land, your farm?'

'With no outright majority, there will be argy-bargy for a long time. That is my prediction. And Angélique tells me the Colorado people are thinking of backing out. They've found somewhere better, they say, where they can build from scratch, like Flaine.'

George leant down and began opening his knapsack.

'I met Angélique,' George said. 'At your farm.'

'Angélique. We call her *la Kinkerne* these days. Old hurdy-gurdy. She's a good-hearted woman, but she does like to gossip. I didn't speak to Costa for more than forty years. And now I've Angélique asking me again already if I've set a date for the wedding! What's the rush? I said to her. *Y'a pas le feu au lac*.'

Forty years, thought George? She was exaggerating, surely? But he didn't want to spoil her story, so all he said was, 'You and your idioms, Mathilde. Talking of which, I couldn't help noticing the English books on your shelves—'

'You think I'm a thief?' Mathilde interrupted.

'No, of course not,' said George. 'I just wondered how come?'

'Many were a legacy from my teacher. The rest were among the things Inez and Peggy threw away from the darkroom when they cleared it out in 1954. The objects on my shelves too. I took a broken clock. I also took a flower press, but I think one of the other uglies must have stolen it from under my bed in the hut.'

'But the books,' George persisted.

'I haven't read them, if that's what you're wondering.' Mathilde sighed. 'I've peeped. I've tried, but I don't think I even get the gist any more. I'm not too bothered about being a clever clogs these days, though. I keep the books merely as aides-memoires. Sir A spent so much time with his books. And he had bookmarks, odd ones, which I liked. I was hoping to find some of them in the books I took. The only one I found was the train ticket, but it made me decide to start my own collection of *objets* with no purpose except whimsy, nostalgia or beauty. Angélique says I've become quite the *rosbif* in my old age.

George handed Mathilde the framed photograph.

'I thought you might like to have this too,' he said, and explained about leaving the photo in his suitcase all summer and forgetting to give it to Inez.

After looking carefully at the photograph, Mathilde passed it back.

'Thank you, but I already have it,' she said. 'Your father sent it to me with a Christmas card and some chocolate.'

'My father?'

'He took the photograph using a timer. It was the year of the timer. He was very pleased with it. Look.' Mathilde pointed to Da in the photo. 'That's why he's standing a little behind you and your mother. He had to run from the camera, quick-quick, to be in the picture. See how Daisy and the others are laughing. It made me laugh too. He was not a naturally athletic man, your father.'

'But where are you? You're not in the photo.'

'I'm there.' Mathilde touched the photo. 'You just can't see me. I'm in the grenier. Looking down from the little window. I was tidying the *anglais* mess up there.'

Twenty-Four

I was in the grenier the day that Luc nearly became mayor and Jack and Thomas nearly lost their lives. I'd hauled myself up there to search one last time for the missing letter. I was convinced it had to be there if I only looked hard enough. I went through all the box files again, to no avail, and had just started poking around somewhat haphazardly when I heard the unmistakeable voice of Alessandro Costanza. I looked out of the window and there he was on the terrace, wiping his dripping brow with a royal blue handkerchief.

Once he'd grasped that I couldn't (as opposed to simply wouldn't) come down, Costa climbed the ladder to the grenier. Or tried to, but Costa's legs, although they were probably bendier than mine, were tired out, and his arms weren't that strong. I heard him struggling, leant over to see, and because he looked so old and vulnerable, as if he might tumble, I felt obliged to offer a hand. This gesture must have surprised him. He tilted backwards and let go of the ladder. I reached further, grabbed his shoulder. Too late: I felt myself being tugged across the rough grenier floorboards, the top rung of the ladder dug into my belly, Costa jerked, we both fell, and the next thing I knew, he and I were in an undignified tangle on the landing. Costa scrabbled to disentangle himself but ended up on his back, stuck like an upside-down beetle, waving his skinny old legs. Laughter and dribble escaped my lips, a fart escaped my arse, and soon both of us were laughing like billy-o – it was as if we were six years old, not seventy-six and eighty-six respectively. I was clutching my saggy belly where it hurt from the ladder-rung, but also from the laughing. Costa kept trying to stand up, but the gales of laughter coming out of him were giving him the shakes and he couldn't even get to his knees.

Which is how we ended up helping each other down Arete's great staircase – ever so slowly, him on his arse, one step at a time, me crawling backwards, arse in the air, also one step at a time. We limped together along the corridor to the kitchen and slumped with groans and sighs of relief at the table. What a pair of doddery old codgers we'd become.

The little picture map was on the table along with a stack of dirty crockery and several half-drunk glasses of wine. Costa picked up two of them, passed me one and clinked his glass against mine.

After Costa had presented his thoughts to me about Luc and the election, after he'd apologised a million times – '*mi dispiace*' – in a mixture of French and Italian for 'the terrible misunderstandings' in 1929 ('*perdonami amore mio*'), and after he'd described the years since then as, for him, not only luckless, but loveless and lonely (he'd been so down on his uppers in the post-war years, he said, that he'd sold the club for two sous and it never got off the ground again, and, shortly before it closed for good, the owner having scarpered leaving a mountain of debts, Costa had been reduced to begging for work there and was occasionally employed, paid peanuts as a quaint comedy-act, an amusing, decrepit, country-bumpkin fiddler, but, Costa said, he didn't mind because playing the fiddle reminded him of me, and he made sure, he said, always to play some of the simple old love songs of the mountains, which the villagers were beginning to forget and would be lost before long, if we weren't careful), after all of that – and my word, he was garrulous! – I decided to try trusting him again. Which is why I found myself answering truthfully when he asked me what I was going to do if Luc was elected mayor.

'I don't know,' I said, 'but there's still time to prevent that happening. I need to decide what to do.' And I told him, then, about my parentage. The smile, which had wrinkled Costa's face and made his eyes small and shiny, vanished.

'Are you certain of this?' he asked. 'You say you are the daughter of Tall Paul and Margaret Valentine, but do you have proof?'

I told him about Madame Tissot and the Swiss lawyer and offered to show him my birth certificate, but Costa shook his head.

'I believe you.'

'So you see,' I said, 'I have the means to stop Luc becoming mayor. He is not the son of the land the villagers think he is. With *rosbif* blood in him, he will never be trusted. But I too have been sitting on the fence.'

Costa looked more and more unhappy.

'This information is difficult for me,' he said.

A terrible thought crossed my mind: Costa was going to turn against me because of my Valentine blood, exactly as I'd feared the people of the valley would. But Costa took a deep breath.

'Mathilde,' he said. 'I must share with you the story of a few hours in my life which meant little to me at the time, which I believed were of no consequence, and to which I have given no subsequent thought.'

A different, terrible thought crossed my mind: Costa was about to tell me something about Daisy and dancing – and maybe a baby – that I knew I wouldn't want to hear.

But as if he'd guessed what I was thinking, Costa reached firmly across the table for my hand and I let him take it. He held my damaged hand between both of his – his brown, woody hands, like aged bark now – the whole time he talked. He talked and talked, and, my word, he talked!

*

In 1907, Costa went to Arete to tune the Valentines' piano. When he'd finished, there was no one to pay him so he ate lunch in the kitchen with the uglies, and when they went to their hut afterwards, he returned to the games room to wait. He lay down on the big, comfortable leather couch in there and nodded off.

He was woken by the sound of raised voices, women's, coming from the sitting room on the other side of the folding doors. He deduced that the women were Margaret and Lady C, but his English was negligible back then, and he understood very little of the argument. He heard a door banging and Margaret going upstairs, coming downstairs, a quick kerfuffle in the hall, then her leaving through the front door.

Costa waited what he considered a polite amount of time before going into the corridor, along to the hall, knocking on the open door of the sitting room, entering, and presenting himself to Lady C with the intention of requesting payment. He'd heard her pacing up and down, but he hadn't realised what a frenzy she was in. There were letters and envelopes everywhere – in Lady C's hands, on the floor, the mantelpiece and all over the chaise longue.

'Pick them up. Burn them. Get rid of them,' Lady C commanded before Costa had a chance to open his mouth.

She had him scurrying around the room trying to pick up all the pieces of paper like a dog chasing flies, he said. He was on his knees by the door, one letter in his hand, when Sir A appeared.

Sir A made Costa give him the letter in his hand, but indicated with words (only some of which Costa understood) and gestures (which were very clear) that he should continue with his task.

Lady C sank onto the chaise longue. Costa finished collecting the letters. He took them to the kitchen and put them in the stove. When he returned to the sitting room, Lady C was still on the chaise longue. She was talking, but with her eyes cast down. Sir A had his back to the door.

Costa waited for Lady C to finish talking before finally being able to request his payment and go home.

*

'It was dark by then, which gives you an idea of how long she talked for,' said Costa. 'She spoke too quickly and my English was too basic for me to understand the detail, but you'd have had to be a complete cretin not to get the gist of it, which was that Lady C and Xavier had been lovers, and Margaret was their love child.'

I jerked my hand away from Costa's. That made Xavier my grandfather, not Sir Anthony Oswald Valentine. And that meant Paul and Margaret, my father and mother, were brother and sister, half. Heavens above!

Costa took back my hand and held on tight.

'Who else knows this?' I asked.

'No one. It didn't cross my mind to tell anyone. The Valentines paid me – a good fee – to tune their piano. That was all. Their lives were of no interest to me. Children are born out of wedlock and created from secret liaisons all the time. It's one of the oldest stories in the world. Why would I care? Besides, I had no one to tell. I have never really been accepted here. My own parents were mistrusted and maltreated because they came from the other side of the mountain and because, in our home, we spoke Italian. There was the fire, the war, another war, and loss after loss, not to mention my money worries. As I said, I as good as forgot what I'd witnessed at Arete. It would have been different if I'd known that you were Paul and Margaret's daughter. I'd have said something in that case, naturally.'

'To me?'

'Yes! To you, Mathilde. Who else?' Costa squeezed my hand. 'Have you not made the connection? Xavier and his wife had a son – Paul. Xavier and Lady C had a daughter, Margaret, but Margaret was brought up by Lady C as a Valentine, as if she were Sir A's. Your parents, therefore, Mathilde, were half-brother and -sister. And we all know the dangers of inbreeding.' Costa paused. 'I'm assuming Lady C banished Margaret because of this.'

I didn't query Costa's assumption, even though I liked to think that anger and pride kept Margaret away from her family, as much as any banishment.

'You mean,' I said, 'banishment because Lady C discovered she'd acquired, thanks to Margaret, an illegitimate, inbred, deformed granddaughter? Because of the shame of that?'

'Yes,' said Costa quietly.

Yes, I thought, and although Costa had witnessed Lady C confess to Sir A about her affair with Xavier and Margaret's paternity, we'd no evidence she ever mentioned me to Sir A. She probably spun him a story of a 1907 pregnancy to account for the banishment of her daughter. His not-daughter. There was no record of Sir A's shock at this revelation, nor of his reaction to Margaret's departure. I knew Margaret hadn't gone from his thoughts though, because of how often he asked, years later, in the darkroom, for that photograph of her holding the scroll of paper. It was hard to believe he complied uncomplainingly with making her *persona non grata*. Was he entirely under Lady C's thumb in the matter? Or might he have kicked up a fuss? I liked to think the latter, but no one would ever know.

'You were lucky, Mathilde.' Costa squeezed my hand again, putting an end to my speculations. 'It's a miracle the effects of such inbreeding were limited to your body. You've a mind more beautiful than most. And you were fortunate again with Luc.'

Costa had confirmed what I'd surmised about the kiss and the cross: Lady C and Xavier were lovers; she, like Margaret, had taken a married man from our land and made him hers; mother and daughter were tarred with the same brush. I hadn't guessed that she'd also grown his seed, mixed herself with him in the form of a child. I slid my hand from Costa's and this time he didn't stop me. I picked up the little picture map and pointed to the cross at the top of it.

'This,' I said, 'is a love map.'

In my beautiful mind's eye, I could see my grandmother, Lady C, practically skipping down the track to Hext: there she is in the market square hastily buying strawberries, raspberries, Reblochon, pots of rich Savoyard honey; now she's hurrying even more, winding her way up through the forest of Zizipompom on the other side of the valley – Chantemerle, les Abeilles, Hermillon, la Rosière – rushing, panting, all the way up to le Nid where Xavier, her lover, my grandfather, awaits her.

'It's a love map of the land,' I said, putting the map down again before continuing, 'I saw a letter once. With a cross like that at the bottom. It's the *anglais* sign for *bisou* – a kiss.' I paused.

'So, a love letter?' Costa prompted.

I'd intended to tell Costa the whole sorry saga of the letter – how I'd more or less buried the memory of it for sixty odd years, then come across the little picture map six weeks ago, and spit, spat: landslide or avalanche – not bees in my bonnet, but hornets in my hat.

I expected the anger I'd described to George at the beginning of the summer in the hot, stuffy attic to resurface and overwhelm me, but I had other things on my mind now – Costa, for one, and the thorough muddle of blood and love in the valley for another. The spit, spat was lessening, like gusting snow that slows and thickens, quietens and settles, as the storm abates.

I still felt like announcing to every English Tom, Dick and Harry under the sun, 'Your men take our land. Your women take our men. I am a product of that.' But I knew, now, it wasn't as simple as that.

A part of me still wanted to scream, 'Only we uglies went to work for Sir A, but it was she, Lady C, who invented the lie of the roving eye and thereby the name by which we became known – my identity.' But I wasn't ugly to Costa, was I?

A part of me longed to declare, 'How dare that insipid *anglais* skilamalink trap Xavier between her legs? Dirty, conniving dolly-mop in her ghosty white dress. How dare she! Xavier – Paul's papa, my papie, and the very best guide in the valley! Rumours of redheads and roving eyes – stuff and fucking nonsense.' But I don't think Costa would have cared.

Costa was right. It was one of the oldest stories in the world, and it could have ended or begun in any one of a number of old-hat *anglais* ways. Lady C hadn't kept a journal that I knew of. If she had, it might have read:

It began the summer I was pregnant with Harold. Edmond had just taken his first steps. Anthony went on ahead of me that year. I was weak and unwell with the morning sickness. I followed at the end of June, with Edmond, the Mackenzies and their soi-disant nephew. It was an easy journey. Glorious weather. Anthony and Xavier both came down to meet us at Hext.

Before the climb to Arete, Anthony took me to the Auberge Dorée to rest for a few hours. I slept deeply, and when I awoke and went downstairs, he and the rest of our group had departed, leaving only Xavier to accompany me to Arete. That's when it began.

And a part of me would never forgive Lady C for making a cuckold of dear old Sir A and letting him take the blame for the murmurings in Hext about the goings-on at Arete. Letting him think, as Daisy did, that Margaret was pregnant in 1907. A fling with a rascal. A family scandal. Hush-hush. But explaining all that to Costa would have taken a month of Sundays, so all I said was:

'I think it was a love letter, but it's lost, gone the way of all things. It doesn't matter.'

And I couldn't continue Lady C's story anyway, because, like all the Valentine women (except, I realised, lucky old, ugly, clever clogs me), she'd only the faintest of voices, and, unlike the writing men, had left only the faintest of pen-and-ink tracks. I glanced, one last time, at the pretty detail of the map – the frayed trace of a neat, light print; brush marks made by laden branches; the feather-etched pressure of a bird's wing.

Costa's face wrinkled with a smile so wide that his eyes nearly disappeared and I could see in his mouth that he had even fewer teeth than me. He took my hand again and began to stroke it.

'Let's forget the bloody lot of them, Mathilde. Cans of worms and knots – or nests – of vipers,' he said. 'Families. It's normal.'

I didn't think 'normal' was quite the right word to describe the slight hump on my back, my slightly crossed eyes and my more than slightly hooked nose. But I liked being stroked, so I kept my mouth shut. And I kept my mouth shut, at first, when Costa leant across the dirty crockery and the little love map on the kitchen table and kissed me on the lips.

It was shortly after this that Isobel practically fell through the kitchen door, gasping for breath, quite hysterical. As soon as we'd understood, there was no time to lose. Lickety-split. Down the mountain for Costa and Isobel. Up it for me, with ropes, first aid and emergency rations.

*

I didn't see Costa again until I was back from the hospital in Sallanches. Luc dropped me at the farm and drove straight off again to be with Thomas. Costa visited in the evening.

A couple of days later, George came all the way up to Sortilège to say goodbye, kind boy. He'd changed from the flabby Georgy-porgy driven drunkenly by Jack from Hext to Hext-en-Haut back in June. He was a strong and handsome young man now, with even, dare I say it, a set to his jaw that reminded me of Thomas. George had done a good job, all summer, of hiding his feelings about his ma and da dying – he was quite a typical *rosbif* in that respect – but I could see in his soft, grey eyes that he'd taken a battering inside as potentially shattering as any avalanche or landslide; I hoped that the summer, with its stories and memories, had at least shown him a red strand of time in the broken rope of history, his family history.

After George had left to catch *le petit train* to Geneva, I sat pontificating (bad habit) at Sortilège until it was time to go home to my farm and enjoy Angélique's stew. Costa was joining us for lunch. Costa and I had agreed on silence concerning my connection with the Valentine family. We'd also agreed we would marry in the spring. Costa wanted to keep that a secret too, but I intended to tell Angélique; I knew she wouldn't stop asking. Besides, she'd be bound to have some sound advice.

It was raining quite hard by the time I reached the farm, and by the time we'd eaten the stew and each had two slices of bilberry tart, fairly bucketing down. Costa took his leave before the storm hit. I lit a fire, not because it was cold, but to offset the gloom. The smell of mountain pine filled the room.

'Autumn soon,' said Angélique after we'd chewed the cud about the avalanche, *les anglais*, my hips, her womb, and it was time for her to go. 'Do you remember how Cédric used to get us to place bets as soon as we went back to school in September on when the first snow would fall?'

'Of course I remember,' I said, helping her on with her pakamac.

It was raining so hard when I opened the farmhouse door that we said our farewells quickly, with raindrops popping on the plastic of her mac.

Of course I remembered.

'I'll see you tomorrow, Mathilde,' Angélique called before vanishing into the curtain of water. 'And perhaps we'll try another pie recipe from that Mrs Beeton book of yours.'

'Weather permitting,' I called back, but I don't think she heard.

When the first snow fell (of course I remembered), Madame Tissot would tell us to down tools. She'd send Henri to fetch wood, then she'd stoke the fire, draw up her chair to it and make us sit on the floor around her.

Deep in the valley of Hext, the snow fell and fell . . .

We took it in turns to tell stories in rich, robust patois or thickly accented sing-song Savoyard – peasanty children's voices, some of them halting and stumbling, one or two fluent yet flat, but many of them honed, nuanced, exuberant. Benoît's stories were definitely the best, his 'Golden Ibex' becoming, over time, the best of the best.

And as the snow fell and fell, deep in the valley of Hext, the outside world slowly but surely, as if by magic, disappeared, and so, for a while – abracadabra – did I.

Did we ever run out of stories? No (because we could always jazz them up or start again from the beginning), but we soon grew bored of the snow. For months on end it kept us shut up, cut off, cold and poor.

'When will it melt? When will it melt?' I'd whisper to old Slowcoach as I drove through the dark of winter to the station with our milk, the snow underfoot rasping and swishing.

By March we were impatient for the spring, and by Easter already clamouring, 'When will they be here? When will they come? *Les anglais*, the English, *les rosbifs*.'

'When the snow melts, when the snow melts,' I'd whisper, after Easter, to old Slowcoach.

Late May, early June. Summer. Summer among the Alps. I couldn't wait.

Author's Note

The Valentine House grew, over a long period of time, out of my fascination with the French Alps. Between 1999 and 2005, I lived and worked in Samoëns, Haute Savoie. While I was there, I came across a chalet in the mountains, built in 1858 by Sir Alfred Wills, a British judge and mountaineer (1828 – 1912). The character of Anthony Valentine was inspired by Sir Alfred Wills and the novel draws on Wills' writings, particularly *The Eagle's Nest – A Summer Home Among the Alps*, which is his account of discovering and exploring the region. But while some features of character and landscape and some details about the chalet have their source in real people or places, *The Valentine House* is a work of fiction – an imagined place, with made-up people, doing fantastic things.

Acknowledgements

I should like to thank the following people: Véronique Baxter, Jo Beckensall, Christine Bonhomme, Lucy D. Brett, Jo Broadhurst, Charlie Campion, Jen Campion, Franck Chapeley, Amy Coquaz, Sylvia Crawley, Frances Donnelly, François Fostier, Jo Forbes Turko, Corinne Garnier, Pat Gillilan, Sahil Gufar, Jocasta Hamilton, Cordelia Henderson Moggach, Carrie Hodgkins, Ann Kenrick, Phil Latham, Philip Longstaffe-Smith, Elissa Marder, Jean-Michel Morland, Jean-Christophe Renand, Jon Riley, Lenya Samanis, Stephen Seabridge, Diane Thornalley, Francine Toon, Juliet Van Oss, Carole Welch.

I should also like to acknowledge the help of the late Tony Moggach while I was researching this novel and his encouragement while I was writing it; *The Valentine House* is dedicated to our daughter.

I gratefully acknowledge a grant from the Society of Authors' Authors' Foundation, which enabled me to complete the novel. It has also been supported, using public funding, by Arts Council England.

EMMA HENDERSON

Grace Williams Says It Loud

Shortlisted for the Orange Prize

On her first day at the Briar Mental Institute, Grace meets Daniel. He sees a different Grace: someone to share secrets and canoodle with, someone to fight for. Debonair Daniel, who can type with his feet, fills Grace's head with tales from Paris and the world beyond. This is Grace's story: her life, its betrayals and triumphs, the disappointment and loss, the taste of freedom; roses, music and tiny scraps of paper. Most of all, it is about the love of a lifetime.

'The conceit is ingenious, and it works . . . exuberant and vivid . . . Grace's story is a life, like and unlike any other'
Tessa Hadley, *Guardian*

'Far more inspiring than a hundred feel-good tomes . . . stands comparison with the linguistic, and emotional, resourcefulness of Emma Donoghue's *Room*'
Boyd Tonkin, Books of the Year, *Independent*

'Mesmerising . . . [Daniel] takes Grace on an incredible journey through love, loss, bittersweet triumph and disaster'
Susan Swarbrick, *Sunday Herald*

'There is tenderness, joy, romance and heartbreak . . . energetic, passionate and not easily forgotten'
Lucy Atkins, *Sunday Times*

'Clever . . . unusual . . . astonishing'
Alyson Rudd, *The Times*

SCEPTRE